W9-DBD-198

SOMETHING MORE

Jackie Khalilieh

tundra

Tundra Books, an imprint of Tundra Book Group, a division of Penguin Random
House of Canada Limited

Library and Archives Canada Cataloguing in Publication

Title: Something more / Jackie Khalilieh.
Names: Khalilieh, Jackie, author.
Identifiers: Canadiana (print) 20220271690 | Canadiana (ebook) 20220271801 |
ISBN 9781774882139 (hardcover) | ISBN 9781774882146 (EPUB)
Classification: LCC PS8621.H3375 S66 2023 | DDC jC813/.6—dc23

Published simultaneously in the United States of America by Tundra Books of
Northern New York, an imprint of Tundra Book Group, a division of Penguin
Random House of Canada Limited

Library of Congress Control Number: 2022941142

Edited by Lynne Missen
Designed by Jennifer Griffiths
The text was set in Arno Pro.

Printed in Canada

www.penguinrandomhouse.ca

1 2 3 4 5   27 26 25 24 23

Penguin
Random House
tundra | TUNDRA BOOKS

To Rob, who has loved and accepted every version of me.

Elsie and Emma—your unconditional love gave me the strength to be my most authentic self and go after my dreams.

To my autistic readers:

We learn early on to mask, to transform into what we think people want us to be—without even realizing what we're doing—often putting ourselves at risk of burnout. Writing this story healed me in so many ways, and I hope, even if it's just in bits and pieces, you will see parts of yourself reflected in Jessie. As far back as I can remember, I felt different from everyone else, but I didn't understand why. My diagnosis was both a relief and a validation. Please remember you are worthy of friendship, love, success, acceptance, and a happy ending.

"We're all pretty bizarre.
Some of us are just better at hiding it, that's all."
THE BREAKFAST CLUB

one

Two parts crème, one part powder, mix and apply with spatula. Or was it the other way around: two parts powder, one part crème? I reach for the folded-up instruction manual on the cluttered bathroom counter and squint at the tiny green font. No, I got it right. *Warning: do not use in vaginal area.* Well . . . yeah. Who'd want to bleach that?

Okay, this should take care of my upper-lip 'stache—now what to do about this eyebrow situation? There are no tweezers in Annie's drawer and nothing more than a hairbrush in mine. I zero in on a pink razor next to the crusty bar of soap. Screw it. I remove the protective plastic shield and bring the razor up to the space in between my thick, black eyebrows. Just one pass should do it. Here goes nothing.

Tiny little hairs fall to the bridge of my nose. I lay my hands, palms down, on the counter and lean into the mirror to assess my first, half-assed attempt. Hmm. Not exactly subtle. Kind of looks like someone took a rusty hacksaw to my brows. How does everyone else do it? Maybe if I had a mother who didn't treat me like I was perpetually eight, I could ask her. And Annie would kill me if she knew I was in here, rifling through her plethora of beauty products. I need tweezers, and someone who knows what the hell they're doing.

Car engines roar outside the window. I peek through the blinds to see Ramsey out front with his friends. His wavy brown hair hangs over his face as he passes around a joint. Sometimes I can't tell if my older brother's very brave or very foolish. With Dad due home any minute, I'm going with very foolish. And likely high. I crank open the window to air out the bleach below my nose, and the heavy beats coming from Ramsey's car stereo cause the panes of the bathroom window to vibrate.

What is that itch above my lip? The bleach! I turn on the faucet and grab a handful of toilet paper to wipe it off. Cold water helps soothe the burn, but it's temporary. With my eyes half open, I face the mirror. Well, the bleach did its job; the hair is no longer black. But my skin is as red as Mars, and, unfortunately, way more visible from Earth.

"Jessie! Annie! Dinner is ready. Wash your hands and come to the table. Yalla! Daddy will be home in two minutes," Mom calls from downstairs.

I pull some strands of hair from my ponytail in hopes they'll help mask my botched attempt at a makeover. With one last look in the mirror, I shrug at my pathetic reflection and head to the kitchen.

Mom places a casserole dish on the table and removes her oven mitts. The front door opens, then closes.

"I'm home," Ramsey mumbles before disappearing into the basement.

"Jessie, get some drinks," Mom says in Arabic. She whizzes around the kitchen getting everything ready for dinner. I stall in front of the open refrigerator, pulling a few more strands out of my ponytail. Annie comes in a minute later and plops herself down on a chair. I barely make it to the table before the pop cans spill out of my arms. They roll around in front of Annie, who's too busy scrolling through her phone to notice or help.

The door to the garage slams shut. Dad pops his head into the kitchen to say he's going to take a quick shower. Mom sighs and brings the casserole dish back to the oven to keep warm. "He said he's hungry and to have dinner ready. I make it ready, and now he's taking a shower." She mutters something under her breath in Arabic before instructing me to get Ramsey.

Once again, Annie escapes having to do any menial tasks. Everyone walks on eggshells around my sister, who suffers from a severe case of middle-child syndrome.

I open the door to the basement and make my way down the carpeted steps. Mom and Dad had the basement finished a few years ago—at Ramsey's request. He wanted to move his bedroom down here for more privacy. It's a walkout basement, which means his dopey friends can come and go at all hours. There's also a large sitting area with a big-screen TV. It's like his own, rent-free bachelor pad. And it always smells like dude.

"Hey," I say, shaking my brother's shoulder. He's facedown on the couch, already passed out. "Hey!" I repeat.

"Go away."

"It's dinner."

He groans and tries to shoo me off but I persist. I can't return upstairs without him. Family dinners mean too much to my parents, and Ramsey has been missing more and more of them lately. He opens an eye to see me still standing above him. "When did you get so tall?" His words come out slow and stretched.

"I've always been tall."

"Not too tall for the tickle monster!" Ramsey reaches out and tickles the back of my knees. I slap his hand away and he giggles as he sits up.

"Ramsey, I'm fifteen. Khalas with the tickle monster." Even though I act annoyed at being treated like a little kid, it doesn't really bother me, at least coming from my brother. Growing up, we bonded over our shared enemy—and sister—Annie Kassis. We'd team up and find different ways to torture her, like switching out her glass of water for vinegar. He's still a great partner in crime, but in the last few years Ramsey has prioritized friendships over family.

"What kind of mood are Mom and Dad in?" Ramsey asks, rubbing his eyes open.

I plop down next to him. "I don't know. Mom's been in the kitchen all day, cooking and on the phone. Dad headed straight for the shower when he got home."

He turns to look at me, then jerks his head back. "Whoa! What happened to your face?"

"Is it obvious?" I ask, running a finger over my raw skin.

"Kinda." Ramsey holds back a smile. "Don't worry. I'm sure they'll be too busy lecturing me to notice what you did. Why *did* you do that?"

I scratch at my neck and study the black-and-white floor tiles. "High school starts next week, and I just thought if I fixed a few things I'd blend in enough to be left alone."

"You'll never blend in, Jessie. That's what makes you your own brand of cool. And is that what you really want? To be left alone?"

"No. But I'd rather that than be made fun of for being the weird girl with a mustache and unibrow. Have you seen eyebrows these days? People take them very seriously."

Ramsey shifts to face me. "Think of Holy Trinity as a fresh start. Put all that elementary BS behind you and open yourself up to new experiences." He pauses, trying to force me into eye contact. "But that means you'll have to let your guard down. Maybe let some people in and give them a chance to get to know the real you."

"Easy for you to say. You never had a problem making friends. You have athleticism on your side. And charm." Not to mention, Ramsey's normal.

"We all have our challenges. Oh!" He snaps his fingers in the air, then studies them for a second before bringing his eyes back to me. "Went downtown today. Stopped by that store. You know, the one that sells records and vintage stuff? Picked something up for you." He reaches for a large manila envelope on the floor and passes it to me.

I smile widely and tear it open to find a stack of magazines from the nineties.

"You like them?" he asks, running a hand over his prickly stubble. "I picked up a mix of music and teen magazines. I didn't know what you'd like best."

"I *love* them," I say, staring at the loud, vibrant covers. "Thank you."

"Ramsey. Jessie. Yalla! Dinnertime," Mom shouts from above just as I'm about to flip through my new treasures.

"Tell the wardens I'll be up in a minute." We rise from the couch and Ramsey leans in. "How do my eyes look?"

"Pupils seem to be returning to their normal size." I nod.

"Perfect." He looks away, then turns back. "And Jessie, don't worry so much. Everything is going to be okay."

I force a smile and make my way upstairs with my magazines, repositioning the locks of hair. In this household people either notice everything, or nothing. My father is a workaholic. We only see him between the hours of six and ten at night and on select weekends. Mom stays home and holds down the fort, but she's so busy cooking elaborate Palestinian meals, keeping things tidy, and talking to her family back in Palestine that she sometimes misses things. Like my autism.

I guess on some level I always knew I was different. I thought growing up in a predominantly white area was what made me stand out, but Annie and Ramsey never seemed to have trouble fitting in. My parents made excuses for me—"she's shy," "she's taller than everyone else," "her head is in the clouds"—and I guess no one cared enough to push. Until Mrs. Bauer. She was my seventh- and eighth-grade teacher. She raised some red flags when I was in her class the first time, but my parents waved them off. Last year, she tried again, and finally wore them down.

She told my parents I "struggle to maintain meaningful friendships" and highlighted how she'd tried to "set me up" with girls she thought would make good friends by repeatedly grouping us together for projects. Instead, I withdrew even more. First of all, group projects are the worst. Second, it was a lost cause. By seventh grade, I'd been in school with most of these people for over eight years. It would have been impossible for them to change their ideas of who they thought I was. In their eyes, I was the loner who lacked a filter and said things that weren't always nice. (I'm working on it.) I'd also developed a reputation as a crybaby. Regulating my emotions in the early years of school was difficult. It felt like no one understood me, or even saw me. But I guess it's harder to ignore someone when they're having a full-on tantrum.

I didn't start doing well in school until fifth grade, and that's only because I finally figured out what teachers expected of me. That's when I took on the role of diligent student. But it's not easy. I get lost in my head, often zoning out, and as a result I end up having to work twice as hard. Even now, people assume I'm rude or ignoring them when I don't make eye contact, or when I respond in what they call a "deadpan" kind of way. I don't get people. I try, I really do, but it doesn't help when they say one thing and do something else.

So I took some tests. Three, two-hour-long sessions, over the course of a month, in a stuffy heritage home turned psychology assessment center in downtown Toronto. They ran the full gamut: psychological, behavioral, and educational. I was given ridiculously simple puzzles to solve, and surveys with odd questions like, "When you look in the mirror, do you hate what you see?" I had to choose from "always," "sometimes," and "never." Who *never* hates what they see when they look in the mirror?

"Some of the most brilliant people are autistic," my family doctor said when he revealed the results to me and Mom a few weeks ago—on my fifteenth birthday, of all days. "People on the spectrum are passionate and are often the ones who . . . save the world."

While my whole life came crashing down around me, my mother's biggest concern was whether or not I'd be able to have children.

"Annie, put your phone down," Mom says, returning the casserole dish to the table. I sit and place my magazines on the empty chair to my left. Dad and Ramsey enter the kitchen, bending their heads under the arch of the doorway. Dad takes his seat at one end of the table, "the head," while Ramsey sits at the other. Dad's thick black hair is slicked back and his face is freshly shaved. Irish Spring wafts from his skin, and his bright, white polo fits snuggly over his large belly.

"Mansef again?" Annie asks, narrowing her eyes at the lamb cooked in a sauce of fermented dried yogurt and served on a bed of rice.

"What would you rather have? Garbage Canadian food like hamburgers and hotdogs?" Dad says.

"There is food that exists on the spectrum between 'garbage' and 'Arabic,'" Ramsey replies, with a wink in my direction.

Mom smiles at my father before serving him a heaping portion. We pass her our plates, and she fills them up, saving an extra marrow bone for me.

"So, Ramsey, what did you do today?" Dad asks. "Obviously you didn't get a haircut or shave. You're starting to look like those dirty, long-haired boys Jessie hangs posters of in her room."

Ramsey smirks. He's the one who introduced me to the "dirty, long-haired boys." He dated a girl in high school who only listened to nineties music, and in a bid to impress her, it's all he listened to. Until she dumped him for another guy. At the time, I was going through a phase where I basically worshipped my six-years-older brother and liked whatever he liked. But my love for everything nineties has since taken on a life of its own. Music, movies, fashion, and heartthrobs from that decade have become an obsession—one of my longer-lasting ones. I rarely listen to anything but early- to mid-nineties alternative rock. Nirvana. Radiohead. Counting Crows. The more depressing the better.

"I tried. I went to the barber shop but Niall didn't have any appointments," Ramsey says with a mouth full of rice.

Mom furrows her overplucked brows at my brother. "You can't just walk in. You have to call ahead."

"Jessie, are you all ready for high school next week?" Dad asks. "Annie, you're going to show your sister around, right? Jessie told me she's worried she'll get lost." Serves me right for confiding in my father. He has the biggest mouth of all of us.

"She'll figure it out. *I had to.*" Annie rolls her eyes while she continues to move food around her plate. She's still bitter at Ramsey for refusing to drive her to school when he got a car senior year, leaving her to take the bus instead. Clearly, the number-one rule for being part of the middle-child club is to never forget anything anyone has ever done or said in your family. Ever!

"No," Dad responds sternly. "She is your responsibility. You will help her on the first day. Understand?"

"Fine." Annie drops her fork and crosses her arms over her chest. Her perfect 32C chest. Unlike my own, practically negative A cups. Annie lucked out genetically and didn't inherit our father's build. She's your typical, run-of-the-mill girl. The kind who blends in effortlessly. When people aren't raving over her straight and shiny black hair, they're feeding her compliments about her #nofilter olive complexion.

We haven't told Ramsey and Annie about my diagnosis yet. I don't want them to know, and since I'm pretty sure Mom and Dad are in denial about it, they didn't fight me when I made the request to keep it between us.

"What about you, Ramsey?" Dad asks.

Ramsey sighs. "Here we go."

"We let you take last year off, and all you did was dick around. It's not enough that you quit university less than one year in, wasting thousands of dollars. Now you goof off all day and night, with no direction. No goals."

"Nick." Mom cocks her head to me. "Language."

Ramsey slams his hands on the table before I can give my mother an eyeroll. "I have goals."

Dad puts his fork down, almost a little too calmly, and clears his throat. "I would love to hear these goals you speak of."

"I'm figuring things out."

"Ramsey, habibi, why don't you just work with Daddy for now?" Mom's tone is so gentle and soft, her accent barely registers.

"Because if I work with Dad, it'll start off as part-time and then the next thing you know he'll be grooming me to take over the business. And I don't know if that's what I want."

"Why? My business isn't good enough for you? Being a machinist isn't cool?"

"I didn't say that."

I make eye contact with Annie across the table, searching for some solidarity in this uncomfortable moment. Instead, she zeroes in on my eyebrows before her gaze lands on my upper lip. I quickly bring my face down toward my plate.

"You can't keep wasting your life, doing nothing. I expect you to have a plan for this year. Or else."

"Or else what?" Annie asks Dad, reveling in the tension. Ramsey gets away with so much—way more than she and I could ever dream of—and it's all because "he's a boy."

"Or else Ramsey will have to find a way to pay for the things he wants, without our help." Dad picks his fork back up and continues eating.

"Fine," Ramsey says.

Two "fine"s in one dinner. One more and we might break a record.

The table is silent except for the hum of the TV left on in the family room. We finish our meals, while Dad works on a second helping. Mom comes around to collect our plates and pauses when she gets to me.

"What's wrong with your face?" she asks, practically shrieking.

I sink into my seat, wishing I could disappear.

Mom puts the stack of plates down and continues to inspect me. She stops again at my eyebrows. "Jessie. What have you done?"

"Did you use my bleach without asking?" Annie chimes in.

Heat creeps into my cheeks. At least now the rest of my face probably matches my mustache rash. "I wanted to fix a few things before school starts."

"You put chemicals on your skin without asking Mommy?" Dad's stern tone matches his disappointed face. My heart starts to race and my lungs battle to keep up. I bolt up from my chair, feeling the rush of tears fighting to escape.

"What did you want me to do? Start ninth grade just as ugly as I was all through elementary school? So I could spend the next four years without any friends again?" My long, lanky arms wave around the table like one of those tall, inflatable tube men in front of used car dealerships. "Mom wants to keep treating me like a baby, and Dad's busy burying his head in the sand, pretending."

"Pretending what?" Ramsey asks.

"Pretending I'm normal. But I've never been normal."

Annie stifles a laugh. "News flash."

"Annie's right," I say, plastering on a fake smile. "Turns out she's been right about me all along. We may as well tell them." I glance at my parents, then immediately pull my eyes away. "All those times Mom and Dad brought me downtown to 'order my uniform' and then 'try on my uniform' and 'get alterations on my uniform,' we were actually visiting a psychologist who was running tests."

"What kind of tests?" Ramsey asks, his eyes clear and glossy now.

"I'm not the way I am just because I reached five feet nine by the age of twelve. There were other tall girls in my class. And I'm not an outcast because I'm an Arab. You and Annie have friends, always have. It's not the braces I had from fifth to eighth grade, my selective mutism in kindergarten, my outbursts at school. It's none of those things and all of those things. I'm a freak with a brain that doesn't work like everyone else's," I say, glaring at Annie.

She looks back at me in bewilderment. "What're you talking about?"

What *am* I talking about? This was supposed to be my secret. My burden to carry. My plague. With my siblings' confused eyes on me and Mom and Dad seemingly seconds away from crying, I do everything to keep the words from coming up. I swallow, trying to choke them down. Ramsey tilts his head, looking at me like I'm the last toy on the shelf at the store, collecting dust. It's what I feel like. My lips open and, in a quiet, childlike voice, I say the words out loud for the first time.

"I'm autistic."

TWO

The next morning, I'm at my desk using the magazines Ramsey bought me to make collages for my school notebooks.

"Can I come in?" Annie asks from behind my bedroom door.

"Sure."

My sister walks in, still dressed in pajamas. She tosses a folded-up piece of paper on my desk. I unfold Annie's paper to find a drawing with labels and arrows.

"What's this?" I ask, looking up at her.

"It's a map of the school. You said you were worried you'd get lost, so I drew the layout for you."

"Oh. Thanks."

She sits on the edge of my bed. "Mom told me you have an appointment with the psychologist today. Is this the same one who ran the tests?"

"Yeah." Annie looks at me as if she's expecting more words to come out of my mouth. "She wants to go over the results and give me some tips to help me cope with my 'changing world.'"

Annie nods. After my outburst at dinner last night, I ran upstairs and basically cried myself to sleep. Ramsey tried to calm me down but I refused to see or speak to anyone.

"You really messed up your brows." She laughs. "At least your rash is healing."

"I used a razor."

"Oh my god, Jessie. You're not supposed to style your eyebrows with a Lady BIC."

"I couldn't find tweezers."

Annie sighs. "Wait here." She gets up and leaves my room, only to return a minute later with tweezers and a tiny brush. "Roll your chair to me," she says, perched on the edge of my bed. "This is going to hurt. Suck it up or I'll stop."

I do as she says. Annie studies my handiwork and uses the tiny brush to comb my brows. She brings the tweezers to my face and says I'm going to need "professional help" to shape the arches. My eyes well up with tears and I have to fight off multiple sneezes as Annie yanks each hair out, one at a time, but I remain as still as possible. I want this, and it isn't often my sister performs an act of kindness.

"There," she says, leaning back. "Done."

I roll my chair to the mirror and smile. "That's so much better."

"Do us both a favor and save the razors for your legs." Annie rises from my bed and walks out of my room.

I can't stop staring at my improved reflection. Maybe if I learn how to tame my frizzy hair and wear a little makeup, I could look halfway decent.

"Jessie, yalla," Mom calls from the foyer. It's time for us to head out to my appointment with Dr. Cassidy. Mom isn't comfortable driving on highways so Dad took the day off to play chauffeur. We rarely ever leave the safety of our suburban bubble. My parents hate going to the city, complaining it's too loud and crowded. And I'm the one who supposedly has sensory issues.

I spend the entire drive in the back seat with my headphones on, listening to the Cranberries playlist I curated. Some of their love songs are so wistfully romantic, I can't help but close my eyes and daydream up my own swoony scenarios. I imagine I'm in a school hallway, alone, with a River Phoenix look-alike. The River clone spots me from across the hall. He's older, probably in tenth grade, and he runs a hand through his shaggy blond hair as he walks toward me. He smiles a sexy, crooked smile, then asks me my name. In my fantasies I'm cool. I never stumble or say the wrong things. He laughs at all my hilarious jokes and tells me I'm different from other girls. And then he brings his lips to mine and—

My eyes blink open after a series of repetitive taps to my knee. I turn off the music.

"We're here," Mom says, nodding to my seat belt. "Leave your headphones. You don't need them."

We walk out of the car and wait to cross the busy street. The late-August sun beams down and I can't wait to get inside the air-conditioned building. I'm a terrible Arab. I hate the sun and summers and being hot. Shorts aren't an option, at least for me. I can't stand the feel of my thighs rubbing together when I walk.

Once inside, Mom repeatedly tucks strands of hair behind my ears. I paint a brave smile on my face for her benefit. Mom's always been the most beautiful, petite woman in every room. With her dyed auburn hair and even proportions, she's never struggled to fit in or make small talk with others. I'm probably such a big disappointment.

I overheard her and Dad talking about my situation last night. Sometimes they forget I understand Arabic and that we share a bedroom wall—something I've had to learn the hard way. Headphones for the win again.

Dr. Cassidy comes down the stairs, smiling. "Nick, Rose, Jessie, nice to see you all again," she says. The adults speak to one another while I sneak away to the water cooler, downing three icy-cold cups of water. "Jessie, I'm ready for you."

I throw my paper cup into the trash and follow Dr. Cassidy up the stairs to her office, leaving my parents behind in the waiting room. I sit on the black leather couch across from her office chair. She carries over a file and some books before she plops down next to me.

"How are you feeling today, Jessie?"

I bite down on my lip and study the red-and-yellow pattern of her blouse. "I'm okay."

"I know Dr. Greenspan delivered your diagnosis a few weeks ago. He gave you some reading material and told you a little about Autism Spectrum Disorder." I nod along, forcing myself to sustain eye contact. Maybe if I do a good enough job, she'll end the session by concluding I'm no longer autistic and tell me this was all a terrible mistake.

Dr. Cassidy goes on to repeat everything Dr. Greenspan said. She even tries to spin it as something positive, like he did. She says I'm "high-functioning" and that I have a "mild" case of autism, but I read they're not supposed to use those terms anymore. I fight the urge to correct her. I'm sure she's just saying those things to make me feel better. Like my autism isn't that severe. But she doesn't know. She'd never understand what it's really like to live inside my head. She doesn't have to worry about everything she says being misunderstood. I do. I even worry about the things I don't say.

"Any questions?" she asks.

"Will people be able to tell I'm autistic by looking at me?"

A smile grows on Dr. Cassidy's face. "No. Autism has nothing to do with how you look."

"Okay. So, like, what's the point of today, then?"

Dr. Cassidy stifles a laugh. I have a tendency to make people laugh—whether I try to or not. "You're beginning a new chapter in your life, and it might seem daunting to do so with this diagnosis."

I try to follow along, but the flickering of the fluorescent lights above us makes me almost as dizzy as the strong floral scent of her perfume. "Although autistic girls might blend in on the outside, you process information differently. And with you starting high school, I think it's important we address a few things."

"Like what?" I ask, feeling my brow furrow.

Dr. Cassidy leans back and pauses. "Your emotional maturity. And how it might not match how you present yourself on the outside. I can see you're very well-spoken, and whether you realize it or not, the way you speak, your vocabulary, it comes from studying other people. Maybe your siblings, or even actors on TV. It's this innate thing autistics do. You mimic how others talk, act, behave, and it helps you blend in. But . . ."

"But what?" I sit up straight, growing slightly defensive.

"But this version of you on the outside doesn't always match what's going on inside. Autistic girls can be more naive, and have difficulty recognizing simple social cues. You might also find yourself waffling between oversharing or not opening up at all."

"So you're saying I'm more immature than my peers?" That's doubtful.

"Emotional maturity isn't something you can see or define, really. It's instinctive, for neurotypicals. For you, well, it's something that takes time to develop." She shifts in her seat and focuses her eyes on me. "Knowing what your triggers are may help you prepare for certain situations and give you a sense of control. I'd like to discuss some coping mechanisms." She places my file and the books on the table next to us. It's cluttered with bins of ancient toys. "Do you want to tell me some of your worries about starting high school?"

My left leg starts to shake and the thump of my beating heart echoes in my ears. I pick up one of the plastic dinosaurs and run my finger through its teeth. "I don't want anyone to know. About the autism."

"Okay," she says with a slow nod. "Is there a reason why?"

"I just don't want to give people an excuse to treat me any more differently than they already do."

"Knowing about your diagnosis could make people more understanding."

"Yeah, but then it's just fake, and I don't see how that's any better."

"What are your goals for this next year?"

"Goals?" I lean back on the couch and stare up at the speckled ceiling tiles. There's a water stain on the one above my head shaped like Mr. Peanut. Cane and all. "Does 'survive' count?"

Dr. Cassidy laughs again.

I shift around on the couch before turning to face her. "I guess . . . I've always daydreamed about being on stage. Maybe singing. Or in the school play. It might sound weird, but performing in front of people doesn't really scare me."

"Well, when you're in front of a crowd, you don't have to make eye contact." She smiles. "The school play is a great goal. It is, however, a big one. Have you ever written in a journal?"

I toss Dino back in the bin with the rest of his friends. "No. Why?"

"I think it would be a good idea if you had a place to put down your thoughts and feelings. And your goals—as they come to you. Big or small. Autistic girls can tend to be a little starry-eyed and grow frustrated when real life doesn't measure up to their fantasies. But perhaps putting things on paper can help manifest your dreams into reality, or at least ground them a little."

"Ground them?"

Dr. Cassidy shuffles in her seat. "What's something you're especially interested in?"

I'm guessing "cute boys" is not the kind of answer she's looking for, so I go with something else. "The early to mid-nineties. Movies. Actors. Fashion. Mostly music, though."

"And let me guess, you fully immerse yourself in all things nineties, correct?"

"Well, not *all*. There are a lot of bad movies and terrible music from that era."

She grins.

"What?" I ask.

"See how you didn't just agree with my statement? Most people would have, to be polite, but you had to correct me. You're very literal, and I find it endearing."

She shimmies herself closer to me. Would she find it endearing if I mentioned her perfume is giving me a headache?

"When autistic people find something they're interested in, it's like a silo. A tall, narrow structure you fill up with information about that one interest. You can't see outside it. You just want to swim in the details of the grains."

I'm not sure what kind of shrink talk this lady is spewing at me, but I nod along, mostly because I'm hungry and want this appointment to be over and done with. But I can't say I hate the idea of writing in a journal. Or setting goals.

"You know what?" She gets off the couch and opens her desk drawer. She pulls out a brand-new journal, covered in gold polka dots. "Here," she says, passing it to me. "Consider it a gift. Like your autism."

"My autism is a gift?"

"In some ways, yes. Autistic girls are less prone to peer pressure. They often have amazing imaginations. You're very witty, and you do really well in school. Certain things come naturally to you. Your report cards go on and on about your artistic abilities and your writing. And when you find 'your people,' it won't feel like so much work. Eventually you'll learn how to respond to social cues, even if it doesn't feel like a natural response."

"That's masking, right? I watched a video on YouTube of an autistic girl talking about it. She made it sound like masking was bad."

Dr. Cassidy sits on her desk chair and leans in. "It's complicated. On some level, we all mask. Do you think adults really like talking about the weather?" She smiles. "Autistic females are particularly good at masking because they've spent their whole lives studying human beings. And as a result, you can sometimes see through people more easily."

"But it makes me feel like such a fake. And it's exhausting trying to figure out the right things to say and when to nod."

"You're right, it's hard. You feel like you're always on, and it can lead to burnout." She appears to be studying my face for a response. I stare back at her blankly. "That's why it's good to have some strategies to help you cope. Use this journal to keep track of your goals. And mix it up: big goals, which might take longer, and smaller ones you can check off sooner and achieve a feeling of accomplishment."

"Can I borrow your pen?" I ask.

She passes me the pen in her hand and I open the journal to the first page. I write down the date and a title: *Goals*.

Goal #1: Convince Mom to buy me a real bra!!!

"Thanks. I think this might work." I force a smile and nod. I'm getting better at this masking thing every day.

After Dad buys us lunch—chicken shawarma sandwiches to go—he drives to the mall. When Dad was inside the restaurant ordering our food, I asked Mom to take me shopping for a new bra. Just as I'd expected, she argued that my training bra was enough. She even went so far as to wave her hands over my chest to remind me I had nothing to hold up. But I eventually wore her down. Maybe another one of my special gifts.

Dad decides to wait for us in the mall parking lot. Thank god for small favors. I somehow convince Mom to go to the trendier underwear store, the kind that has mannequins dressed in thongs and garter belts by the entry.

A blond, buxom salesgirl in her early twenties walks over. I can't take my eyes off them. Mom has breasts. Annie has boobs. This girl has tits. At least that's what Ramsey and his friends would call them. They're so round and full.

"Can I help you?" she asks, looking up at me. Everyone looks up at me.

"I need a bra. Something to make me look like you."

She laughs while Mom raises a discerning brow my way. "Oh, sweetie, these are more trouble than they're worth." Right. I'd probably get nothing done if I looked like her. I'd just stare at my hotness in the mirror all day and smile smugly.

"Mom," she says, "I'm going to take your daughter to the back to get measured, and then I'll pick out some nice bras for her. Have a seat and relax."

The salesgirl takes my wrist and guides me to the back of the store. Her skin is so soft, and she smells like vanilla. It helps distract me from the loud music and array of colorful undergarments. I can't believe my mother agreed to buy me bras from this den of lace and sex.

"How old are you?" she asks.

"I just turned fifteen, on August 7."

"Oh, that's a great age. It's when I had my first kiss." She has this dreamy look in her eyes, and for a second, I feel a pang of nostalgia for a moment that hasn't even happened to me yet. "I'm Sydney."

"I'm Jessie Kassis."

"Oh, first and last name. How formal." Sydney smiles. "Jessie, I'm just going to put this measuring tape under your bustline and then around your breasts. Is that okay?"

I nod and stare up at the ceiling while Sydney gets to second base (I think?) with me.

"You're so lucky you're tall," she says. "Clothes look better on bodies like yours."

I look down at my long, lanky limbs, then across at her sexy curves. "Nothing ever fits me the way I expect it to."

She grins. "It will. Just wait. Your body is working out its kinks. A year from now, you won't even recognize yourself."

"In that case, maybe you could find me a bra I could grow into? You know, make it look like I'm bigger than I am?"

She smiles again. "I'll get you a couple of 34As and some 34Bs to try on."

I'd normally be intimidated by someone so perfect-looking, but Sydney's somehow making this whole experience not as terrible as I thought it would be. I don't easily connect with people, but every now and then I meet someone who treats me like an equal, and it gives me hope that somewhere out there a best friend exists.

She returns a few minutes later and passes the bras she chose through the curtain. She offers to come in and help. I refuse, for obvious reasons. Unfortunately, the 34As fit perfectly, but one of the bras Sydney chose has padding and gives me the illusion of, dare I say it, tits.

Goal #1: CHECK!

Maybe Dr. Cassidy was on to something with this whole journal thing.

THRee

With my polka-dot journal in hand, I walk out the front door and sit on the wooden bench on our porch. It's the night before my whole life is about to change and I figure it would be a good idea to come up with more goals.

Within the last week I've acquired two eyebrows, camouflaged my mustache, and upgraded to real bras. Everyone says looks don't matter, but it's not true. People treat you differently when you're attractive. It's just the way it is.

Maybe if people can get past the things that make me different on the outside, then they might try to get to know the real me. And maybe I'll let them. Which brings me to my next goal.

Goal #2: Make friends!!!

I guess if I want to meet new people, there are certain things I need to keep to myself, like my autism. Not that I had planned on announcing it to the entire school, but I also wouldn't be surprised if it came out of my mouth in the middle of a meltdown. I've been pretty good at keeping my emotions in check—aside from that outburst at dinner. I spent most of eighth grade stoic and devoid of emotion, at least during the school day. Then I'd come home and drown in all the tears I'd held in.

Goal #3: Do not let anyone see me cry at school!!!

Goal #4: Don't tell anyone about my autism!!!

It's not that I've *never* had friends. It's just all my past friendships seemed to end out of nowhere. Sometimes they'd find someone new to hang out with. Other times my "friends" would still come over or invite me to their homes, but then pretend we were nothing more than classmates at school. Maybe it's me. Maybe I come on too strong. I'm probably a stage-five clinger. People can sniff out desperation. I can spot it in others, but it's harder to see in myself.

This year I will learn to edit my thoughts and words. If there's something I want to say, I'll just save it for my journal. I'll play the role of cute, funny, shy friend. Let them be the star of the show. I've gotten used to playing the supporting character.

I've been awake on and off since quarter to four. My brain keeps playing tricks on me, like, if I fall asleep now, I'll have to get up in three hours . . . but then more time passes and three hours turns into two and a half, then two, and then it's like, what's the point? I'm not even tired anymore. I rip the blanket off and place both feet on the floor before stretching my arms.

It's still dark out, leaving me to fumble around in search of the light switch. Under normal circumstances, I would never wake up before the sun rises. But the first day of high school is not normal circumstances.

Downstairs, Dad's heavy footsteps echo.

"Jessie? It's five thirty. Why are you awake already?" Dad asks as I enter the kitchen, his voice still hoarse with sleep. His thick hair sticks up in different directions, and his sideburns show the first signs of gray.

"I can't sleep. It's too hot," I lie.

"Well," he says with a smile, "since you're awake, you can

make me some coffee. You know I love how you do it best." My secret is I add an extra teaspoon of sugar, but I don't tell Dad. Or Mom. Dad opens the sliding door off the kitchen and steps onto our second-story deck.

The sun begins to peek through our multiple windows as I fill the dented metal coffeepot with cold water. I place it on the stove to boil, and condensation disappears as flames engulf the pot.

"Come sit with me when you're done," Dad says from the deck, his face hidden behind today's paper. He's probably the only man under sixty who still reads an actual newspaper. "And bring some peanuts with you."

Dad and I have gotten into the habit of feeding the blue jays every day. Our backyard looks out onto a ravine that's adjacent to a busy street. When we moved here ten years ago, our subdivision was surrounded by farmland. Now it seems a new building goes up every week.

I finish making Dad's coffee and join him outside. He grabs a handful of peanuts from the bowl on the coffee tray and tosses them onto the deck. We sit in silence as birds stealthily make their move from the railing to the deck floor before inhaling entire peanuts and taking off. Imagine being able to escape your problems just by flying away.

"Be strong today," Dad says as he finishes his first coffee. His large hand swallows up the small espresso cup. The tips of his fingers are misshapen and stained from years of working on machines. "Don't let anyone push you around. This thing is just a bump in the road. You'll learn how to deal with it and be just like everyone else."

I nod and dig my fingernails into the sides of the plastic lawn chair. "This thing," he says, like it's a cold or a zit that will go away with time.

After Dad has his second cup, I see him off to work and find myself surrounded by absolute silence. I shower, then blow-dry my hair. When I step out of the bathroom, Annie's in the hallway with her arms crossed over her chest.

"It's about time." She walks past me and slams the door.

Mom beams as I come down the stairs dressed like a kid from the school uniform catalogue in my blue pleated kilt and white button-down dress shirt. She insisted I wear the kilt—not the gray slacks—on the first day, and I agreed, but only so I could show off my new lace-up Doc Martens. We're supposed to wear matching navy sweaters, but Annie says the school doesn't really enforce it until temperatures cool down. I still packed mine in my backpack, just in case.

Mom makes me and Annie pose for pictures, insisting we'll thank her for them some day. We beg her not to post them on Facebook with an overly gushy caption, written in all caps.

Once our photo session is over, Mom fiddles with my kilt by the front door, making sure it's lined up properly. "Annie, remember to stay with Jessie until she finds her first class."

"You do realize I have to find my class too, right? And besides, I made Jessie a map."

"Forget the map. You're her big sister," Mom says with a dismissive wave of her hand.

"Fine," Annie relents. "But she'll learn faster if she does things on her own. Ramsey never helped me."

"That's different. *Ramsey's a boy*," Mom responds.

Annie exhales sharply, then picks up my backpack and stuffs it into my arms. "Let's go."

I kiss Mom goodbye and try to catch up with Annie, who is already halfway to the bus stop.

Annie's a senior this year, which means she has an established social circle and knows Holy Trinity like the back of her hand. Why is she making such a big deal about having to help me? Doesn't she remember what it's like to start a new school, with no friends? As Annie rolls her kilt to make it shorter and unfastens the first couple of buttons of her shirt, it becomes clear: Annie can't possibly understand how I feel. She's never been in my shoes and, lucky for her, she never will be.

The drive to school, including all the pickups, takes about twenty minutes. We pull up to the front of the two-story, redbrick building a whole half hour before the bell. Annie leads me past the foyer and into the atrium. The atrium alone could fit the entire first floor of my elementary school. The skylights above give the building a feeling of limitless space and light. With its two grand staircases and real live trees, this place looks more like a mall than an actual learning institution. On one side is the dreaded cafeteria, and the library is on the other, just as Annie's map illustrates.

"Go over there." Annie pushes me toward the horde of ninth-graders crowded together, trying to read from the same piece of paper on the wall. "That list will tell you where your first class is. All you need to do is find your name."

I gently maneuver through the group using my height to my advantage. *Jessie Kassis, Room 212.* Annie is gone when I come out of the crowd. She seems determined to make me go through this alone. According to my map, room 212 is on the west side of the second floor. I walk up the west stairs and make my way to the first class.

When I arrive, there's a group of students waiting in front of the closed door, all in pristine uniforms and carrying over-stuffed backpacks. The older students continue to socialize in the hall, shouting each other's names and greeting one another with aggressive high fives and hugs.

The bell rings and a tall, shaggy-haired male with a five-o'clock shadow walks toward us. His tie is crooked, his shirt wrinkled. A few girls straighten their posture as he unlocks the door. This guy can't be more than a few years older than Ramsey.

"Good morning, everyone. Come on in and choose a spot."

The tables are set up to seat four. I pick a seat near the back of the room, facing the whiteboard. Two of the spots in the group fill up quickly.

"Welcome to ninth-grade Visual Arts. I'm your teacher, Mr. Trapp. Since this is your first-period class, it's also your home-room. Take a minute to settle in and we'll get acquainted after announcements and the national anthem."

The room is silent, except for the rumbles of empty stomachs. Glad to hear I'm not the only one who skipped breakfast today.

After a bilingual rendition of "O Canada," we recite the Lord's Prayer. I squeeze in an extra prayer asking God to find me someone to have lunch with. I didn't leave the Guy much time, but I figure He owes me one, on account of the autism.

Most Palestinians are Muslim but a very small percentage of us are Christian. My family is Greek Orthodox. So not only am I a minority, I'm a minority within a minority. Anyway, since the beliefs between Greek Orthodox and Roman Catholics are pretty much the same, we've always attended Catholic schools. For the most part it's fine, except, since I wasn't baptized in the Roman Catholic church, during school Mass I have to sit out communion.

We take our seats and Mr. Trapp goes through the class list. When he's done, a boy with big, curly hair strolls in. While Mr. Trapp speaks to him, the girl seated next to me breaks the ice.

"I'm Chelsie," she says, as if talking to strangers isn't the most awkward thing in the world. "I just got braces last month. Bad timing, right?" She has a slight lisp, but with her heart-shaped face and honey-colored hair, the braces barely register.

The other girl at our table, Catherine, seems a lot more reserved. She caught my eye in the hallway, not only because of her flaming red hair, but because she's almost as tall as I am and has a Nirvana patch on her backpack.

The guy with the dark, curly hair tosses his bag on the floor and sits across from me. He nods to us. "Griffin," he says with a kind smile. "My schedule got messed up. I'm supposed to be in tenth-grade Drama, but they stuck me here."

"You're welcome," I blurt. *There is something seriously wrong with me.*

Before I can bury my face in my lap, he grins and says, "Thank you."

"Okay, class, I'm glad you've had a chance to get to know one another, but it's time to bring your attention back to my ugly face." A few girls giggle at Mr. Trapp. It's so cute when good-looking people make self-deprecating jokes. "We have some housekeeping to take care of. I'll start by handing out your individual schedules and agendas. This term consists of four classes, which end in January with exams. Your agenda includes the school code of conduct. Read it, learn it, follow it. I will also hand out the locks for your lockers, which are located down the hall. Once that's done, we will go over the course syllabus."

Mr. Trapp passes out our schedules. My shoulders relax as he places mine in front of me.

"How bad is it?" Chelsie asks.

"I have Science next, followed by Phys Ed and Religion." Aside from Science, the rest of my semester seems pretty easy.

While everyone else at the table engages in small talk, I try to figure out the combination to my lock. Chelsie and Catherine are clicking really well, and I feel myself slowly being pushed out of the equation. I want to bring up having lunch together without coming off as desperate, but the fear of rejection stops me. So much for God giving me that extra push.

The rest of the period passes quickly, leaving no time to set up our lockers. When the bell rings, I grab my belongings and make my way to second period. I ditch Annie's map, using common sense instead.

The halls fill up with students rushing off in every direction. I remain focused on the task at hand: finding my next class. 222, 224, 226. Found it! With time to spare, I examine my seating options. The desks are arranged in pairs, lined up in rows. I grab a seat up front. Whoever ends up sitting next to me better pull their weight during experiments. I fiddle with my lock again, but I can't get the damn thing to open.

"Ah, you know that's supposed to go *on* your locker, right?" a voice from above says.

"Ah, you know, I don't remember asking—" I look up at the same moment my jaw drops. *Holy Mary, Mother of God, pray for us sinners* . . . because I hope to sin all over school and then some with this guy! He's perfect. His eyes are crystal blue. His straight brown hair falls just above his broad shoulders. His tall and lean frame towers over me, and I can't look away. Is this love at first sight? Does love at first sight have to be mutual for it to exist? *Stop!* I'm getting ahead of myself; this guy has only said one sentence to me. Over a minute ago. Why am I sitting here asking myself questions and not responding to his? It's starting to get weird now. *Say something, Jessie!*

"I don't remember my password."

"Password?"

"Code?" I try again.

"Do you mean combination?" He smiles and, no word of a lie, it's both crooked *and* sexy.

"Yes! Combination."

"There should be a sticker on the back." He grabs the lock and his fingers graze my hand. HIS FINGERS GRAZE MY HAND.

He flips it over and chuckles. "It's 25-58-34." His laugh is spellbinding. He works the lock and manages to open it on the first try. "The trick is to start at zero and move clockwise. You'll get the hang of it." He passes it back to me and runs a hand through his hair. He remains standing by my desk like a statue sculpted by an Italian Renaissance artist.

I want to thank him, or at least say something, but my throat is closing on me. I'm breathless in the presence of his gorgeous face, large hands, enchanting smile, and his body. *God, that body.* Michelangelo's *David* has nothing on him.

"What's your name?" he asks, taking the seat to the right of mine. Am I dreaming? This must be another one of my fantasies.

"Jessie Kassis," I say, just above a whisper.

He laughs. "I'm Levi . . . Walsh. Can I ask you something, Jessie Kassis?"

I want to shout *yes.* Instead, I exercise restraint and nod. But hearing my name roll off his lips makes my stomach flutter. His name is like something out of an adventure novel. The bell rings and the rest of the students trickle in.

"Are you smart? Your inability to figure out locks aside," he teases, "are you a good student?"

"I'm pretty smart. Why?" I ask, never more curious to hear someone's answer.

Levi leans in. Even though he smells like my brother does after passing around a joint with his goofy friends, I'm captivated.

"Well, this is the second time I'm taking this class. I figure if I sit next to a smart kid, near the front, I might actually pass."

"You're in tenth grade?" It all makes sense now. He rolls his shoulders, then nods. *Rein it in, Jessie.* "Yeah, sure, I can try to help you."

"Awesome. You're indebted to me anyway, 'cause I taught you how to use your lock. And seeing how I've memorized your combination, I have leverage." He laughs, then playfully punches my shoulder.

The teacher clears her throat. She's an older woman who is both tall and robust. She introduces herself, and her thick German accent is only slightly less distracting than her failed attempt at Kris Jenner's haircut.

Levi taps his fingers while staring at the ceiling. His school supplies consist of a beat-up binder and the tiny chewed-up pencil in his mouth. *Oh, to be that pencil.*

Ms. Muller goes through the course syllabus at a snail's pace, pausing after each line. "It seems I've forgotten a few things," she says, scratching her head. "I need you to add extra notes to the handout."

"Hey, Jessie, can I borrow a pen?" Levi whispers.

I nod, willing myself to stop shaking as I pass him one of my many blue pens.

"Thanks." He winks. I turn away to copy the notes from the whiteboard but feel his gaze fixed on me. "You're left-handed? That's cool."

I shrug. "It makes everything I write smudgy." Did I just say *smudgy*? Is that even a word? Levi doesn't respond. Of course he doesn't. Why do I have to be so inept at making conversation?

"Okay, class, now that you have the full outline, it's time to sign out a textbook. If you lose this book it costs fifty dollars to replace, right, Levi?" Ms. Muller narrows her eyes in our direction.

"I swear it's in my room somewhere." Levi throws Ms. Muller another smile and she backs off.

Levi's room. I wonder what it's like. I bet it's messy. Clothes that smell like him strewn all over the place. What I wouldn't give to have one of his dirty sweatshirts to sleep in. Oh god, it's happening again. I barely know this guy and already I'm falling hard. Haven't I learned anything from past obsessions on out-of-my-league boys? But this . . . this is different somehow. This feels real.

The bell rings and everyone races to sign out their book, except me. Lunch is next, and I'm in no rush to get down to the cafeteria. I work slowly and methodically, organizing my belongings as if I'm being graded on packing skills. Levi has already taken off. Someone like him probably lives for lunch. He definitely has a ton of friends, possibly even a girlfriend. The thought of another girl makes me sick to my stomach. I sign out the book and head to my locker to kill more time.

When I arrive, Catherine, the redhead with the Nirvana patch on her backpack, is there and appears to be waiting for me.

"Hey, Jessie, what're you doing for lunch?" She runs a hand through her wavy, long hair and adjusts her uniform.

"Nothing," I answer honestly, placing the lock on my assigned locker.

"Want to grab lunch together?" The words roll off her tongue as she walks over. Words I willed myself to speak during first period. But this girl? She just strolled right up to me and asked, as if the threat of rejection didn't even occur to her.

"Yeah," I say, trying to play it cool. "So, you're into Nirvana?"

"Who?"

I point to her backpack. "The patch on your bag."

"Oh, that," she says, shaking her head. "I just thought it looked cool. So, here's the thing," she says as we walk toward the stairs. "I met some girls in Phys Ed and they invited me to have lunch with them. But I didn't want to show up alone like a loser, you know? So I appreciate this."

"Well, you know what they say . . . two losers cancel each other out." I laugh, but Catherine looks at me like I'm still sporting a unibrow. I shrug off my terrible joke and readjust my mask. "It's not a problem."

FOUR

Catherine and I arrive at the atrium and stand before the entrance of the cafeteria, a large wasteland with no windows. Even with all the lights on, it feels like twilight. There's a long line by the kitchen, which is surprising since Annie warned me the food was subpar. The cafeteria is apparently also where school plays and most assemblies take place. On the stage, the curtains are drawn, with a large sign warning students to keep off.

It's almost primal in here. As Catherine and I make our way across the room, I feel like a bug coming out of the crack of a sidewalk, trying my best to avoid getting stomped on.

"Catherine!" screams a girl with a voice so loud it bounces off the walls. Catherine skips into her arms and they hug. Didn't these people just meet each other?

"Odelia, Melissa, this is Jessie." Catherine gestures in my direction. "We have Art together. I invited her to have lunch with us. She was like a lost little puppy up at her locker."

"Aww, she does look like a little puppy. You are so cute. I love you already." Odelia squeals and pulls me in for a hug.

My tense body rejects the embrace at first, but I eventually cave. Her hug is genuine and warm, and in a strange way, I already feel connected to her. Odelia's confidence matches her statuesque physique and broad shoulders. She's a quirky kind of pretty, with shoulder-length black hair, thick bangs, and high cheekbones. Her teeth are a little crooked and her skin isn't perfectly clear, but she carries herself with the poise of a dozen stallions.

"So, what's for lunch?" Odelia asks as we all sit down.

"Not sure," I say, taking inventory of their lunches. "What's good here?"

"The pizza's not bad. Just make sure you grab a bunch of napkins to soak up the grease." Melissa takes a gigantic bite of her slice, then laughs. She shares it with Odelia, who hasn't yet opened her wrinkled brown paper bag lunch.

"Catherine, do you want to come with me to get some food?" I ask.

"No thanks. I'm not hungry," she says, examining her fingernails. "Also, I'd prefer if you called me Cat."

Melissa raises her brows in response to Cat's icy tone before standing. "I'll go with you."

"Thanks for coming, Melissa," I say as we head to the kitchen together, breaking the awkward silence. I'm still reeling a bit from the sting of Cat's rejection. Why would she ask me to lunch if she was just going to brush me off? "Lining up for food alone is one of those things that feels embarrassing for no reason."

She laughs. "I get it. And call me Mel. *I prefer it*," she says with a wink. "I have an older sister who gave me the full rundown so, in turn, I will impart my wisdom to you. I know this place looks innocent enough, but this vast space operates under a set of strict rules. Seniors and juniors sit near the entrance. The center is reserved for tenth-graders. And all the way in the back are us lowly niners."

We share our schedules and discover we have Religion together. Mel tells me to save her a seat if I get there first, which makes it seem like she wants to be my friend as much as I want to be hers. She's about the same height as me but has huge boobs. I guess, compared to mine, everyone's are huge. Her long, strawberry-blond hair has the perfect amount of beachy waves, not a frizzy strand in sight.

"So, what're you into? Sports? Art? Music? Drugs?" Mel asks in a deadpan voice. I'm pretty sure she's joking about the last one.

I pick up a tray and follow the line ahead. "Definitely not sports. Or drugs," I add.

"Same."

"I was thinking of maybe joining the drama club."

"You can't."

"Why not?" I nod to the pepperoni pizza and the lunch lady passes me a slice on a paper plate.

Mel grabs a stack of napkins. "You have to be enrolled in Drama. And you can only be enrolled in Drama once you're in tenth grade."

"That sucks." I pay for my lunch and walk with Mel back to the table. Ninth-graders aren't allowed to be in plays? There's got to be a way around such an ageist, unfair rule.

Goal #5: Convince the Drama teacher to let me in drama club. (And to perform on stage!)

After nearly missing the bus, thanks to finding a sea of identical yellow buses at the back of the school, I take a seat behind the driver and pray Annie didn't notice. We're the final stop, and I wait until Annie gets off before standing. My sister forges ahead, while I drag my feet all the way home. I'm greeted at the door by Mom, who has her hands on her hips. I brace myself for a lecture while daydreaming about ripping my itchy uniform off. Starting tomorrow, the kilt will be shoved into the corner of my closet, never to be worn again, and replaced with Option B: gray slacks.

"Annie told me you almost missed the bus."

Good lord, they're acting as if I hopped on the stage and mooned the entire school. My eyes dart over to Annie as she comes out of the kitchen, licking chocolate pudding off her spoon.

"That'll teach you not to goof off with your weird friends," Annie says before walking up the stairs.

"That's not why—"

"You made friends?" Mom asks. Her frown blossoms into a smile. "Do they come from good families?"

I shrug. Does Mom think I screened their families before deciding whether or not we should split fries?

After dinner, I head to my room to relax in bed. My eyes are closed and all I see is Levi. *Levi Walsh.* I want to know as much about him as possible. A search for Levi online yields disappointing results. He's signed up for all the socials but there's no activity. Not even a profile picture! I thought I was the only weirdo who didn't use social media. I have accounts with fake names, but they exist only so I can observe other people living their lives. With how heavily my parents regulate my internet usage, it doesn't seem worth it to have my own accounts. Besides, who would even follow me?

When I got my laptop in sixth grade, my parents had their tech-savvy friend put just about every kind of blocker on it. I guess they were afraid I'd go berserk downloading porn or something. I'm currently in negotiations with them to get a phone. Annie didn't get one until she was sixteen, and god forbid I should receive one before she did.

Oh my god! I know! *Annie's yearbook!* There's got to be a picture of Levi in there. Sounds like an easy enough task, except she's really weird about letting me touch her stuff. But my desire to see Levi's ninth-grade photo is stronger than my fear of Annie. I leap off my bed and knock on her door.

"What?" she asks, somehow already knowing it's me.

I cautiously open Annie's door and find her sitting in bed with her laptop.

"Can I see last year's yearbook?"

Annie smirks. "Why? You want to stalk the boys you have a crush on?"

"No!" *I hate that she knows me so well.* "My friend Melissa has an older sister in twelfth grade. I want to see what she looks like."

"Yeah, right." Annie rolls her eyes. "You have one minute, and it doesn't leave my room."

She points to a stack of books on her desk. I hunt down the yearbook and flip through it as quickly as I can, starting with surnames beginning with W. I come across a Lucy Walsh, who's in the same grade as Annie. This must be Levi's sister—they have identical smiles. With the clock ticking, I skip right to the ninth-grade section and locate Levi's picture. I bite hard on the insides of my cheeks to hide my grin from Annie. He was an adorable ninth-grader, but in less than a year he's grown up to be hot AF. Well done, puberty.

Annie rips the yearbook out of my hands. "Are we done here?"

I fight the urge to snap back and I just return to my room instead. With my door closed, I kneel down and grab my journal from its hiding spot behind my desk.

Goal #6: GET LEVI WALSH TO BE MY FIRST KISS!!!!!

The next morning, Cat and I head to homeroom, where I spend my time counting down the minutes until Science. I haven't stopped thinking about Levi since yesterday's magical meet-cute. My heart races at the mere thought of sitting next to him. How am I ever going to learn anything with his hot bod inches away from mine?

A shadow falls over my desk. "Jessie, did you hear me?" Mr. Trapp asks.

"No. What did you say?"

Cat and Chelsie snicker.

Mr. Trapp closes his eyes and exhales. "Did you bring money for the art supplies?"

"I did."

"And do you have it with you?" he asks with an exasperated sigh.

I reach into my backpack and pass Mr. Trapp the cash in exchange for my fully stocked art kit and sketchbook.

As Mr. Trapp walks to the front of the class, Griffin leans in and whispers, "He must not be a morning person." I shrug slightly, trying to hide my smile.

Mr. Trapp assigns our first project: a portrait of another student in pencil. When it's time to choose partners, Cat and Chelsie pair up instantly.

"I guess that means you're stuck drawing this mug," Griffin says, his confident tone not quite matching his words.

We remain seated across from one another at the table while Cat and Chelsie move to some empty chairs by the windows to work. For the next few days, a guy, *an older guy*, will be staring at me, analyzing my features. Even though I took care of my eyebrows and upper-lip situation, I still can't help but feel some sort of way about this.

A corner of his mouth quirks up. "You go first."

I nod, then remind myself to release my shoulders from my neck. This whole exercise is way too intimate to do with someone you've only just met. Once all my supplies are in place, I scan Griffin's features.

Griffin's got this out of control, curly, dark brown hair. Sitting across from him now, his green eyes shine like emeralds. He has the perfect number of freckles scattered across his face, which stand out against his porcelain skin. His flawless smile is at odds with a nose that looks like it's been broken a time or two. He's cute, in a non-intimidating kind of way. If only he'd quit chewing on his lips.

How can I ask Griffin to stop twisting his mouth without making him self-conscious? This is so awkward. I don't want to talk to a guy I barely know about his *mouth*. Unless those lips happen to belong to Levi Walsh. His looked so soft and inviting, the perfect shade of pink. *I wonder what they'd feel like against mine.*

"May I?" Mr. Trapp asks, once again hovering over my desk. He takes my drawing and holds it up. "Class, turn your attention to Jessie. She's doing a great job of capturing the essence of her partner's face. Jessie started by outlining Griffin's features lightly and has drawn everything to scale. Excellent work."

Cat glances at me from across the room. I smile and shrug, knowing full well my cheeks are beet red from the attention. She doesn't reciprocate and turns away. I make a mental note to give her work a compliment the next time I see it.

"We're nearing the end of the period. Clean up your area and pack it in." When everyone groans, Mr. Trapp continues. "Don't worry. We'll keep working on this for the next week or so."

Griffin helps me tidy up and tells me he's playing hockey tonight. When I make a funny face, he tilts his head. "What? Not a hockey fan?"

"I don't discriminate against hockey. I hate all sports."

Griffin laughs. "Fair enough."

Not sure why I'm so surprised Griffin's an athlete. With his big shoulders and thighs, he definitely looks the part. He just doesn't seem to be as much of a bonehead as the hockey players I've known in the past—Ramsey included.

"If I come to school tomorrow with another broken nose, you'll have to make some adjustments to your drawing." We both laugh, him more than me, and say our goodbyes.

Cat sidles up as Griffin leaves. "Did he ask about me?"

"Who?"

"Griffin. Did he bring me up when you guys were working together? I'm so jealous you're partners with him," she whines. Why does it feel like Cat would rather work with anyone but me?

"Wait, you like Griffin?" I ask, trying to keep up.

"He's pretty cute. I wouldn't mind hooking up with him, you know?" Since I have zero hooking-up experience, I take Cat's question as a rhetorical one and decide not to answer.

"We didn't really talk much."

"Can you suss him out for me tomorrow?"

"Suss him out?"

"Yeah. Like, bring me up and see what he says. You know."

No, I don't know, but I agree anyway.

Cat eats up so much time blabbing about Griffin, I have to race to make it to second period.

When I arrive, the door is locked and a crowd has formed out front. I do a quick scan until I spot Levi. He's leaning against a wall, his head tilted up, eyes closed. God, he's even hotter than

I remembered. The bell comes and goes, with no sign of Ms. Muller.

Levi heads in my direction and I prepare to say hi but he walks past me, then stops to talk to someone else. A girl who isn't even in our class.

A few minutes later, Ms. Muller charges down the hall, muttering something about a rotten egg salad sandwich as she fumbles with her keys.

We all file into the classroom like marching ants, except for Levi, who strolls in casually once he's finished talking to the girl with lavender-colored hair—definitely not natural. I take my seat and anxiously wait for him. He slides in next to me, and I suck in my cheeks to stop the huge smile that is fighting hard to escape.

"Hey . . . you!" he says.

"Did you forget my name?"

"No." His playful expression gives him away. "It starts with a J, I remember that."

I raise one eyebrow. "You should probably learn my name, or else your Science grade will start with a D."

"Ouch." He smiles broadly, and I try (but fail) to stay mad. "I promise, after you tell me your name again, I'll never forget it."

"It's Jess—"

"Jessie Kassis! Now I remember," he proudly exclaims. "First and last name."

I'm caught somewhere between an eyeroll and a Cheshire cat grin. I settle for a smirk.

After Ms. Muller's lesson, she assigns reading from the textbook and adds a worksheet. Levi leans in and whispers, "Do you know how to answer these questions?" His hair brushes my cheek, and the warmth of his breath makes my pulse race.

There's a cluster of freckles under his earlobe that I want to touch. I point to the textbook instead. "Here's the answer to the first one."

He scrunches up his face, giving his nose little wrinkles. "Are you sure?" He points to another paragraph.

I follow his finger over to the text. His hands are huge. Almost twice as big as mine. I want to hold them. Must fight the urge.

"Jessie?"

"Sorry." I clear my throat. "The question asks us to *describe* the proper techniques of handling and disposing lab materials. What you're pointing to is how to *identify* appropriate lab equipment. See the difference?" When I look up from the text, Levi's gaze is focused on me.

"Yeah." A small, sweet smile appears on his face. "This is why I need you. I get so thrown off by the wording." He glances at the clock. "Can we meet in the library after school to finish?"

"Yes! But no, I can't. I take the bus."

"Can I call you, then?" Levi asks.

Well, this is embarrassing. "I don't have a phone."

"Your family doesn't have a landline?"

"We do."

"Then give me that number," he says with another smile.

He's persistent, I'll give him that. I write my number on a piece of paper, spelling my name in capital letters and under-lining it three times.

He laughs. "You're funny."

"I know."

Somehow my daydreams are manifesting into reality. Life is actually happening. And I owe it all to Dr. Cassidy and my polka-dot journal.

After class, I head downstairs to meet the girls for lunch.

There are tables set up in the atrium for club sign-ups. Social Committee—nope. Badminton—really? Student Council— sounds thrilling. Liturgical Choir—well, it is a Catholic high school. HTDCo—Holy Trinity Drama Company. That's the one! But I need backup.

In line with Mel to buy fries, I ask her to come check out the tables with me after we finish lunch. She agrees. There's something so comforting about being around Mel that I end up telling her about Levi—even though I'd planned to keep my feelings for him secret. She seems excited for me, which I wasn't expecting. I've never told another person about someone I liked before. Mel asks me to point him out the next time he's in our path. I, in turn, ask her not to tell the others about him yet. She doesn't question it, just smiles and nods.

When we return to the table, Odelia eyes me up. "Cat tells me you stole her crush in Art."

"You can't steal something from someone if it wasn't theirs to begin with," I say as I take my seat. A long silence settles over the table. I said something wrong. My heart races as the girls exchange glances. I clear my throat and try to backtrack. "It's just . . . Cat had already partnered with Chelsie so I had no other choice. Anyway, I told Cat I'd look into it for her."

"Okay, O," Mel says, turning her attention to Odelia while simultaneously rescuing me. "I know you're dying to tell us. Who are *you* crushing on?"

A Joker-sized grin forms on her face. "Um, practically every guy in eleventh and twelfth grade. I'm not picky." We all giggle while Odelia keeps a straight face. "Let's just say it's been a while."

"You've done it?" I blurt. Mel's and Cat's eyes grow to twice their size. I can't tell if it's because of what Odelia said or my response to what she said.

"Technically. Maybe. Well, I'm not really sure if it counts," Odelia answers, rubbing the back of her neck.

Odelia's so . . . nice. I never would have guessed she'd already done that. Of course, nice girls have sex, too. Everyone has sex. Except me. I can't even get a guy to kiss me.

Up until last year, I didn't know the specifics of sex. I "stumbled upon" a certain kind of website while using Ramsey's laptop (okay, I may have searched) and was shocked to learn the nitty-gritty (okay, it was disturbing). My parents have never bothered to have "the talk" with me. The only thing they've ever said regarding doing the deed is *not* to do it until I'm married. If memory serves, I didn't learn about sex in school, either. I must have been absent that day or something, because everyone else seems to know more than I do.

"Mel, we'd better go check out the clubs before lunch is over," I say, shifting gears.

"You've barely touched your fries," Odelia says.

"You have them. I'm not hungry." I stand and throw my backpack over my shoulder.

"Let's all go look. I want to see what I'm missing out on." Odelia rises and takes my fries with her. "As the designated babysitter to my four siblings, I'm not allowed to sign up for anything that happens after school."

This wasn't the plan. It was just supposed to be me and Mel. I grit my teeth as we all walk to the atrium. Sneaking away from the pack, I hover around the drama club table.

Mel sneaks up next to me. "Are you going to ask if you can join?"

"What's the point? They'll just say no."

Mel locks her arm with mine and practically drags me to the table.

An older girl looks up at us. "Hi. Are you interested in joining Holy Trinity Drama Company?"

"Yes. But we're in ninth grade," Mel says.

"Oh." Her lips form a pout. "Sorry. There's a prerequisite. You need to be signed up for Drama and you can't do that until next year."

"What if we still want to be involved?" I ask, finding my voice. "Is there something else we can do? Like, behind the scenes?"

"Yeah. There's HTTCo: Holy Trinity Technical Company. They're in charge of lighting and sound. Things like that. If you join tech club, you also have to help during assemblies and Mass."

"That doesn't sound bad." Mel nods.

"Where can we sign up for that?" I ask.

"Here." The girl passes me a clipboard.

Mel and I sign up just as Odelia and Cat approach. Odelia yanks the clipboard out of my hands.

"You guys are gonna be AV geeks?"

"Yes." Mel snorts, and they all laugh.

"We're trying to weasel our way into drama club," I say, taking back the clipboard.

"Oh." Odelia nods. "So you're actually an aspiring drama nerd?"

"Yes." I wish I could laugh it off like Mel, but for some reason I feel a little defensive.

Odelia boops my nose with her finger. "I love it."

While the girls stand in the middle of the atrium sharing what's left of my fries, I focus in on my name, printed on the sign-up sheet. It might not be the drama club, but it's one step closer.

"Jessie?"

I look up to see Griffin. "Hi."

"Hi." He peers over my shoulder. "I see you signed up to be a techie."

"Yeah." I want to tell him how I'd rather be in the drama club, but I hold back. I barely know the guy. No need to overshare.

"I guess we'll be seeing more of each other, then." He reaches for the pen on the table and scribbles his name on the drama club clipboard. "Hope you don't get sick of my face."

"Probably not." I shrug. "Not because I like your face. But because I'll most likely be backstage," I say, hearing my ridiculous words instantly play back in my head. I wish I had a mute button.

Griffin laughs, and for some reason, it makes me smile.

Five

Phys Ed was almost as terrible as I expected it to be. I found a corner of the locker room to change into my uniform as quickly as possible. Then my deceptively kind-looking Phys Ed teacher, with her sculpted arms and blond pixie cut, tortured us through circuits to test our endurance. She compared my lung capacity to that of a fifty-year-old smoker and encouraged me to jog in the mornings before school. Yeah. That's not going to happen.

I somehow manage to drag my tired and sore body home after getting off the bus. As I'm about to step onto my driveway, a girl with long, brown hair darts out of our backyard, forgetting to close the gate behind her. She doesn't seem to see me as she makes her way to a parked car a couple of houses up. Another one of "Ramsey's girls." Mom's in the garage emptying the recycling bin and we lock eyes. She pauses, then asks me to close the backyard gate before coming in.

We all know about "Ramsey's girls," but no one ever talks about them. Sure, he's twenty-one and it's not that big a deal, at least in other households. But if it were Annie inviting boys over and asking them to sneak out—well, forget about it. That would never happen. Annie can't even bring up the topic of having a boyfriend before she's in university without Mom shrieking and delivering her signature line: "What would people think?"

After dinner, I retreat to my room to get started on my Science homework. I bring one of the house phones with me so I can pick up right away if it rings. The last thing I need is Mom answering the first time a boy calls me. Something I wouldn't have to worry about if I had my own phone! I have a laptop. What's the difference?

Goal #7: Convince the wardens to get me a cellphone!!!

Goal #8: Get them to chill the F out about boys and everything else!!!

By the time I finish my homework it's after seven o'clock, and still no call from Levi. I open my laptop and type "Instagram" into the address bar. In Religion today, Mel said I should set up a legit Instagram account so we can have a group chat outside of school. This having no phone thing is starting to interfere with my social *and* romantic life! As I'm figuring out a username— JessieKassis, or something more clever?—Dad's voice booms from below. I open the bedroom door a crack to listen.

"A chef? You want to be a chef?"

"What's wrong with that?" Ramsey asks.

"Do you think me and your mom immigrated to Canada just so you could be a cook in a restaurant? I worked two jobs. Took out loans to start my business. In less than five years, I paid back all those loans and bought this house. And yet my son refuses it. He spits in the eye of me and my business. All so he can make people french fries."

"If you would just listen to me," Ramsey pleads.

"Tell us your plan," Mom says, clearly struggling to keep her voice devoid of emotion.

"Well, first of all, I have to apply to this college to enroll in their Culinary Arts program."

"Culinary Arts." Dad scoffs.

"Wait. You'll like this part. I did some research and I can pursue a double major."

"What does this mean, double major?" Mom asks.

"It means I can study to be a chef *and* a machinist. It'll mean double the course load and apprenticeships, but I figure if I don't like culinary school, then I can focus on becoming a machinist—like Dad."

"Why don't we do that and just forget about this chef garbage?" Dad asks.

"Because I really want to do this. Can't you let me try?"

"When does it start?" Dad asks, ignoring Ramsey's heartfelt plea.

"January."

"And what will you do between now and then?" Mom inquires.

"I'll work with Dad."

"Let me think about it," Dad says, cutting the conversation short. "Let me think" is code for "You win, but I'm not letting you think that."

The phone rings. I kick my bedroom door shut and leap to my desk. "Hello?"

"Hi . . . Jessie? It's Levi." The temperature in my body skyrockets as my heart runs a marathon. "Sorry I'm calling so late. I played basketball after school and passed out when I got home. Then my mom made me do the dishes after dinner." Levi rambles on and I picture him in an apron with bright yellow rubber gloves, standing at the kitchen sink. *He's so adorable.* "Do you have a few minutes to help me with the rest of the homework?"

"Homework? Oh. Right. Let me grab my binder." I toss the phone on my bed, then jump up and down a few times, concealing a squeal. After taking a deep breath, I pick up the phone again and sit at my desk. "Where'd you leave off?"

"Question two," he says and, oh my god, I love his voice.

"Okay, so question two wants us to show how to select appropriate materials for experiments. For example, you'd use a magnifying glass to examine something small. The full answer is on page 25."

"Got it. And for the last question, what does it mean by 'emergency response procedures'?"

"We need to come up with two possible incidents and explain what we would do if they were to occur by referencing the chart on page 27. Like, if there's a fire, Muller wants us to locate where the extinguisher can be found." There's a long pause once I'm done giving my spiel. Great, I've bored the father of my future children to death.

"You must really think I'm dense, eh?" Levi asks.

"Not really." I stand and pace around the room with a smile plastered on my face. "Everyone has their strengths. You're good with people, whereas I find human beings both simple and confusing."

Levi laughs. "I would love to be able to read this stuff and understand it the way you do. To me it's just confusing."

"Well, the grass is always greener," I say, sounding like a grandpa in suspenders.

"How old are you?"

"I turned fifteen on August 7."

"My birthday's in August too. I just turned sixteen."

"When?"

"When what?" Levi asks.

"When is your birthday?" I can't help myself. I need to collect as much data about Levi Walsh as possible.

He laughs again, but this time I didn't mean to be funny. "August 20. Now that you know, I'll be expecting a gift next year."

Next year. Is Levi visualizing a future that includes me?

"Hello? Who's on the phone? I need to use it," Mom says with urgency. When it comes to Mom and the phone, it's always urgent.

"Mom, I'm talking to someone from school." I stomp my foot hoping she feels the thunderous roar above her.

"Okay, well, yalla." My mother's thick Arabic accent is not exactly the romantic soundtrack I had envisioned for my first phone call with Levi.

"Sorry about that," I say, once my mother gets off.

"No problem. I have to walk my dog anyway."

"You have a dog? I love dogs. My mom won't let us get one 'cause she's afraid of them. Childhood trauma. But I've always wanted one." *Shut up, Jessie.*

"Yeah." He laughs. "His name's Jasper. He's my best friend."

Lucky dog.

"Thanks for helping me, Jess. See you tomorrow."

Jess. We've now entered nickname territory.

After ending the call, I sit at my desk again and open my journal. It's time I came up with a list of reasons why I need a cellphone. I leave out the obvious ones like privacy, being able to text my friends, and practicing how to take cute selfies for Levi. The list for my parents looks like this: it will be helpful in case of emergencies, they'll have twenty-four-hour access to me, and the pièce de résistance—Mom won't have to compete with me for the phone.

⌒

The next morning, I make a pit stop at the kitchen prior to meeting the girls in the cafeteria. It was Odelia's idea to gather before homeroom to . . . I don't know, discuss important issues like global warming? After purchasing my peace offering, I make my way to where the girls are seated. "I present to each of you a freshly baked chocolate chip cookie, as a symbol of my regret for not being able to chat last night."

I'm met with blank stares from all three of them. So much for rehearsing that line, over and over, on the bus. I sit down, even though I'm not sure they want me here. In this moment, I don't want to be here either, but I'm trying.

"It's okay." Mel accepts my cookie and apology. "But we missed you."

"Are you going to explain your absence?" Odelia asks.

I place the other two cookies on the table, avoiding eye contact.

"And is this going to be a regular thing?" Cat questions. "'Cause we can't exactly play catch-up every morning."

Play catch-up on what? This is only the third day of school. Besides, I've already apologized. With baked goods! What more can I do?

I take a deep breath and let it out slowly, stopping myself from releasing the onslaught of defensive words.

I wanted this.

I wanted a group of friends. And I need to play by their rules if I expect them to keep me around.

"I had a lot of Science homework last night, and by the time I was done, my parents wanted me to chill with them. I'm technically not allowed to be on my laptop after ten."

Odelia places her arm around my shoulders. "I get it. My parents can be pretty strict too."

"So are mine," Cat says. "I just find a way around it."

"It's still the first week of school. Let's not corrupt Jessie just yet," Odelia replies, pulling me in closer.

"*Yet*," Cat repeats with a lift of one perfectly arched brow.

As Odelia and Cat exchange confusing glances, an idea

comes to me. "We should try getting together outside of school. Maybe this weekend?"

Everyone's eyes sparkle at my suggestion. Mel even offers up her house for Saturday. Perhaps more time together will help me open up. And get them off my back.

On the way to homeroom, Cat reminds me of my promise to "suss out" Griffin. I have zero clue how to go about doing this, but it's clear she expects me to follow through.

In Art class, Griffin suggests we go out to the hallway to work on our portrait project, and I agree, thinking this will make broaching the subject of Cat easier.

"Is this okay?" Griffin strikes a goofy pose in his chair that makes me snort. He ends up laughing so loud that Mr. Trapp comes out to the hallway to shush him.

"So, what kind of music are you into?" he asks once Mr. Trapp has gone back inside.

I feel my face light up at his question. "Nineties alternative. Radiohead, Nirvana, Smashing Pumpkins, The Cranberries. It's all about the mood and lyrics for me. There was more depth to music back then."

"The classics. Right on." Griffin nods. "I'm thinking about starting a band with one of my younger brothers and another friend."

"Hold up," I say, sitting up straight. "You play hockey, you're into drama, and you're a musician? Also, *one* of your younger brothers? How many do you have? And how old are they?"

Griffin smiles. "I'm one of four brothers—I'm sixteen, the others are thirteen, ten, and six. And I'm not a musician. I sing." He leans in. "Acting is my real passion, though. Which is why I was hoping to be enrolled in Drama first period instead of Visual Arts. But I missed the cutoff and now I'm on the waiting list."

"At least they're letting you in the drama club."

"True. Wait, do you want to be in the drama club?"

"It doesn't matter. I'm not allowed," I say, sounding like a whiny child.

"Huh." He nods slowly.

"Huh, what?" I ask.

"Nothing. I just didn't take you for a theater kid."

"Well, I'd like to be given the chance," I say. "But school rules."

"Meh. Rules were meant to be broken." There's a pause in the conversation as I get my supplies ready. "You say you're a lyric junkie; do you ever write songs?"

"Oh god, no." I laugh. "I'm more of a sing-in-the-shower type person." Griffin's cheeks turn bright red. Great. Now he's picturing me naked. That explains the underwhelmed expression on his face. "Cat," I blurt. "What do you think of her?"

"Who?"

"Catherine Hannigan. The redhead who sits at our table."

"Oh." My swift change in subject seems to have thrown Griffin. He keeps clearing his throat and swallowing. "She seems nice, I guess. Why?"

"She's also into music. Bands mostly. Singers especially." He presses his lips together, avoiding eye contact, and yet I keep going. "Maybe if you told her about your plan to start a band, she'd be able to bounce some ideas around with you."

"I have a girlfriend," he announces.

"Oh," I say, pulling at my sleeves. "Sorry."

"It's fine." He shakes his head. "She moved away at the end of last year. Lives in Colorado now. So I wouldn't expect you to know . . . not that you would have noticed, since you're clearly doing the legwork for someone else."

"Is it that obvious?"

"Yeah." He laughs. "You're a good friend. Just tell her I'm not interested. 'Cause of my girlfriend."

"Okay," I say, before returning to my portrait.

"So, would it be okay if I started sketching you now?" he asks. "Are you feeling comfortable enough for that?"

I glance up from my drawing to see a pair of kind green eyes staring back at me. "Yeah. I am," I say, meaning it.

He smiles, and I have to lower my head to hide my own.

When class is over, Cat corners me at my locker. "What did you find out?" she asks, grinning from ear to ear, her confidence palpable.

"Sorry," I say, looking her straight in the ear. "He has a girl-friend."

Her mouth falls open slightly. "Yeah, I know. I found that out from stalking him online. What else did he say about me?"

"What do you mean, 'Yeah, I know'? If you knew, then why did you practically force me to interrogate him?"

"She lives in the States. How serious can they be?"

"He's not interested. Like, at all," I say. She's making me late for Science, and I've been dying to see Levi since our phone call last night. Stakes have been raised!

Cat crosses her arms. "Gee, Jess. Learn some tact." Her lips pout, and I suddenly feel awful for being so blunt.

"I'm sorry. I just . . . I can't be late for class again. Griffin's shy," I say, backtracking. "And it's complicated . . . 'cause of the girl-friend." Cat nods, her expression softening. "I have to get going. See you at lunch?"

"Sure."

My stomach drops as soon as I walk into Science. The lavender-haired girl is sitting on top of my desk, talking to Levi. He's so engrossed in the conversation that he doesn't notice me come in. Unsure of what to do, I sit in an empty spot near the back. The girl doesn't leave the room until after the bell.

Ms. Muller starts today's lesson and Levi opens his binder, eyes focused up front. So much for "needing me." *Find someone else to help you with your homework. I'm done. I'm over him. I'm over everything.* Today sucks. First, the girls rag on me for missing out on their oh-so-important chats. Then Cat forces me to harass Griffin and grills me after class. Now I'm stuck at the back of the room and not where I want to be, sitting next to Levi.

I hate everyone.

As soon as the dismissal bell rings, I rush out the door. My eyes start to burn, fighting to hold back tears. *Goal #3: Do not let anyone see me cry at school!!!* I push through the crowd and race to my locker.

"Jessie! Hey, Jessie! Wait up!" Levi calls from behind. "Where were you today?" he asks once he's caught up to me at my locker. "I didn't see you in class."

"I was in the back row," I answer.

He frowns slightly, looking kind of pathetic but still cute. "I thought we were Science partners."

"Well, someone was on my desk when I came in," I say, hugging my textbook to my chest.

Levi runs a hand through his hair. "Oh, right. It's just . . . I like working with you. You're smart and really easy to talk to." The corners of his lips turn up. "Is this one yours?" he asks, nodding to my locker.

I brave eye contact and swallow. "Yeah."

Levi reaches past me and spins my combination. "Told you I memorized your combination. Or was it a code?" He grins as he takes my textbook and places it inside.

I let out a small sigh. "It's just been a long week." I close my locker and face Levi, his blue eyes piercing through mine.

"I hear you. Hey, at least we don't have any homework tonight so I won't have to bother you."

"I don't mind being bothered." I bite my lip immediately, wishing I could take back my overtly flirtatious words.

But Levi smiles. "Good to know. So, we're cool?"

"Yeah, we're cool."

He playfully punches my shoulder before taking off.

"Who was that?" Cat asks, sneaking up next to me.

I'm startled but will myself to remain cool. "Levi. He's just some guy from Science class."

"He's cute," she says. "You're gonna have to introduce me to him next time."

"Right. Next time. But first, food." I press my fingernails into my palms as we head downstairs.

Six

Friday night and I've officially survived the first week of high school. It's not even dark out and I'm already in pajamas, lying in bed. I've never been this tired before. It's more than physical exhaustion—my brain feels like it ran a marathon. It's been in overdrive, taking in all the new sights, sounds, and people. I've been so hyper-aware of my autism that I've been working overtime to try and hide it, which means holding eye contact longer, returning polite smiles, and pretending to listen when people drone on and on.

Then there's Levi.

My relationship with him was so promising at first, but when class was over today he didn't say goodbye or mention calling me this weekend for help. Talk about mixed messages. This is definitely the most complicated relationship I've ever had with a guy—not to mention the *only* relationship I've ever had with a guy. I've toyed with the idea of talking to the girls about him, but I'm just not ready to open up to them yet.

I'm beginning to have second thoughts. What if these girls aren't "my people"?

Odelia is fun and outgoing, but she can be kind of extra—even for me. I've spent my whole life sticking out like a sore thumb, and coming into high school, I just wanted to blend in. Odelia makes it hard to do that.

Mel is really sweet and the easiest to talk to. It's clear she and Odelia have a strong bond. Mel's laid-back personality seems to balance Odelia's desire for chaos. I'm just not sure how I fit in.

The biggest question mark in our group is the person who introduced me to everyone. Something about Cat makes me uneasy. We're only one week in and I'm already noticing some major red flags.

On the other hand, maybe Cat deserves the benefit of the doubt. It's still really early in the year.

Why am I like this? I wanted a group of friends so badly, and now that I have it, I'm standing on my crooked pedestal, criticizing them. The problem here is me. I've spent so much time alone that I'm not sure I know how to be a good friend. I can't expect these girls to be perfect. They're not fictional characters in a nineties sitcom. I should feel lucky they even want to be friends with me.

I sit up in bed and reach for my journal. It's time to check in with my goals. So far, I've accomplished four out of eight. Four and a half if you count signing up for the tech crew. It's, like, one step below drama club. Or better yet, it's drama club adjacent. I think I might be able to convince the wardens to get me a phone by Christmas. And as for kissing Levi, well, that one's still a work in progress.

Levi's not the first boy I've ever had a crush on—not even the fiftieth. I have a history of falling fast and hard—but never this fast, and definitely never this hard. There's something different about him. For one, he actually knows my name and has spoken to me, on multiple occasions. He needs me, he said so, and I kind of like having him depend on my brain. I'll work on having him depend on other parts of me later.

Life would be so much easier if I stopped liking white boys.

I think I need some sub-goals to help me achieve the greater goal of getting Levi to kiss me. Aside from that one time he followed me to my locker, we've only interacted within the walls of our classroom. If I could just get him to see me outside that environment, then maybe he'd look at me differently. I should also try to ask him questions and get to know him. People love talking about themselves. It's how I make it through most conversations. I ask questions and pretend to care about the answers. Except with Levi. He's a silo I want to sink into and swim in the details of his grains.

As for my new friendships, I need to make a game-time decision about whether or not I really want to keep hanging around them. I only get one first year of high school. One chance to lay the groundwork for the rest of my time at Holy Trinity. And I don't want to screw it up. Going to Mel's tomorrow should give me a clearer idea of who these girls are and whether or not I want to keep trying.

Nothing beats waking up to the sound of raindrops hitting the window, especially when you don't have to rush out the door before eight o'clock to catch a bus. I turn on my side to face the night table and put my headphones on, letting the shuffle on my MP3 player decide which nineties love song will serve as a backdrop to this morning's fantasy. Okay, so sometimes I listen to songs that don't fall neatly into the alternative rock category.

I close my eyes and instantly Levi appears. We're at school and he walks toward me, a smile on his face and his hand extended. I place my hand in his and we walk together down the crowded hall. He's oblivious to all the onlookers. All he can see is me. We arrive in front of my classroom door and he leans in for a kiss before we're separated by the bell.

That's how all my fantasies end, with a kiss. I'm not really sure what comes next. I know first base is a kiss and a home run is . . . well, sex. The other two bases are a bit ambiguous. Even when I search online, the responses are mixed. It's a moot point anyway. No need to buy sprinklers when you don't have a front lawn.

Annie bursts through my bedroom door just as Levi's lips are about to meet mine. I remove my headphones and sit up.

"Mom said if you want breakfast you have to come down now. Aren't you going somewhere today?" Her eyes zero in on me, then at the posters hanging on my wall.

"Yes, but not until twelve thirty. And it's only," I pause to check the time on my MP3 player, "eleven." God! If I ever barged into Annie's room unannounced, she'd kill me.

"You're not the only one with plans today and I don't want to be late, so get up. We're leaving in forty-five minutes." Annie turns on her heel and slams the door.

After a quick breakfast, I shower and return to my room to get dressed. This is the first time the girls will see me out of uniform. I take this as an opportunity to experiment with my evolving personal style. In the end, I decide on my favorite light-blue jeans and a vintage, black Nirvana T-shirt. They both fit a little differently than they used to. I guess this means my body is also evolving.

Once Mom drops Annie off at her friend Marisa's house, I move up to the front seat. Mel and Odelia live one town away from us, which amounts to about a fifteen-minute drive. But Mom makes it sound like we're headed to the edge of the earth.

"What? You couldn't meet any girls that live closer?" she asks while her hands grip the steering wheel.

"It's not that far. There's no Catholic high school in their town."

"Remember, I'm picking you up at four! We have a party at the church hall tonight," Mom says.

"If I had a phone, you wouldn't have to worry about me losing track of time, and even if I did, you could call and I'd promise to always answer."

Mom shoots me a sideways glare. "I'll think about it."

Well, that's better than a no.

We pull into Mel's driveway. Mom puts the car in park and spouts the same lecture she gives every time she drops me off somewhere. *"Don't leave the house." "Don't be too loud." "Say please and thank you." "If they offer you food, don't make a funny face, eat it." "Call us if anything is wrong."*

I walk up to Mel's house and ring her bell. She opens the door and grins widely.

"Do me a favor and wave to my mom," I say. "She won't drive away until she can see for herself that you're not a serial killer, or even worse, a boy."

Mel chuckles before waving vigorously. As Mom begins to reverse out of the driveway, Mel pulls me inside and closes the door. She leads me to her basement. Odelia is already down there, sitting on one of the worn couches, her large brown eyes focused on the TV screen.

"Earth to Odelia. Jessie is here." Mel leans in and whispers, "O's parents don't let her watch much TV."

"Oh, sorry." Odelia laughs to herself as she pries her eyes off the screen.

"What're you watching?" I ask.

"One of those fishing shows." Mel and I stare at her with our mouths open. "What? One of the fishermen was hot."

"You're real hard up, aren't you?" Mel teases.

Odelia stretches out her long legs over the armrest. Her T-shirt bunches up at the side, exposing most of her stomach, and she doesn't even bother to yank it down.

"Where's Cat?" I ask before sitting on the opposite couch.

"She messaged and canceled last minute. Her parents apparently had other plans, which is kind of odd since yesterday she said she'd be here," Odelia replies.

"She did say her parents could be strict," I remind them. "And her dad is, like, on city council or something, so they always have events they have to go to."

Odelia frowns. "No one's stricter than my old-school Italian parents, and *I'm* here."

"To be fair, your parents already know me," Mel replies.

"All the more reason they shouldn't have let me come," Odelia jokes. Mel throws a pillow at her, which sparks a small fight between the two of them.

"Whatever the reason, she should have been upfront with us. I've caught that girl in so many lies this week," Mel reveals as she sits next to me.

Odelia and I look at one another and then back at Mel, waiting for her to continue.

"She's always going on about guys constantly gawking at her, but I've never noticed it myself."

"I mean, have you seen how short her kilt is, though? Even I can't stop from checking out her ass," Odelia says.

"Speaking of guys, she's been so insistent about me setting her up with Griffin, as if I'm some sort of matchmaker. Then when I tell her he has a girlfriend, she continues to push me for more information. I don't even know Griffin!" I say, feeling frustrated all over again.

Odelia nods. "She can be a little bossy."

"Maybe she's not as confident as she acts," I try, making an effort to defend her. After all, she's the reason I'm even here today.

"Do you think there's a chance Griffin likes Cat? Girlfriend or not?" Mel asks, leaning in.

"He flat-out told me he's not interested."

Odelia sits up straight in her seat. "That's not what Cat said."

"Well, that might be my fault. I told her he was shy. She just looked so sad, I didn't know what else to say."

"Jess, she told me you said Griffin is into her, but he has to figure out things with his girlfriend first."

Hmm. Another half-truth from Cat. I try to underplay it. "Maybe she misunderstood me. And she's not here to speak for herself."

"Okay, then let's talk about you," Odelia interjects. "You haven't really told us much about your first week. Tell us, Jess . . . who makes *your* tail wag?"

I glance over at Mel to gauge her reaction to Odelia's question, but she keeps a poker face.

"There's one guy in my Science class I kind of like," I say.

"I knew it! Who is he?" Odelia asks, her eyes wide with excitement.

"Promise to keep this between us?"

They nod. I take in a deep breath and hold it awhile before releasing it. I tell Odelia about Levi, then go on to describe his striking good looks and every single interaction we've had so far.

Odelia picks up her phone. "I have to see what this guy looks like."

"He doesn't really do social media. He is in last year's yearbook, though," I say, holding in a smile.

Mel goes upstairs and returns with her older sister's yearbook. We spend the next couple of hours dissecting the photos of all our potential love interests, both online and in the yearbook. Mel points out a few senior guys she thinks are cute, and I lose track of all the guys Odelia shows us, but it's safe to say her taste is wide and varied. Then we pose for pictures together, experimenting with goofy filters before Mel and Odelia post them.

I was wrong about Mel and Odelia. They're exactly the kind of girls I want to be friends with. They seem to see through Cat's actions and sketchy behavior, too. For once, it's not my brain seeing things differently.

Cat just sucks.

Seven

"Ladies!" Odelia bounces down the hall Monday morning, beaming. She stops and spins the combination to her locker. Odelia is like a genie who's been let out of her bottle. When I first met her, I had no idea she was an exceptional student and enrolled in gifted courses. Teachers love her, and everyone seems to know who she is.

"Cat, you missed out on a fun time Saturday," Mel says.

"I saw the pics," Cat replies, adjusting her kilt length. "My father was guest of honor at an important event downtown."

"Well, excuse us," Odelia says while checking her teeth in the locker mirror. "Speaking of important events, we're going on a mission this morning to find Jessie's crush."

"Let's be really clear about this. I'm just going to show him to you, like, from afar," I say, trying to be as explicit as possible about our plans. I wonder if it bears repeating . . . again.

"Is it anyone I know?" Cat asks.

Mel whispers, "His name is Levi."

"That guy from your Science class?"

"Yes," I answer, glancing around to see if anyone heard her.

Cat's expression hardens. "The one I told you was cute?"

"You asked me who he was after he left *my* locker," I say.

"Right, and then I told you I thought he was cute."

I have to dig my fingernails into the straps of my backpack to stop myself from clawing at her face. "Well, I thought he was cute when I met him first. And besides, I thought you were waiting for Griffin to 'figure things out' with his girlfriend." Okay, that last bit was petty, but she just makes me so angry.

"Whatever." Cat folds her arms over her chest. "I'm going to class. Have fun on your little adventure."

And to think I tried to stick up for her this weekend.

Odelia closes her locker, then links her arm with mine. Mel does the same with my other arm. "Let's go find Jessie's boy," Odelia says.

I bite down on my lip, fighting the urge to correct her until I no longer can. "It's 'Jessie's Girl.'"

"I know." Odelia laughs. "You're not the only one here who knows retro music."

"Right. Sorry."

"You don't need to apologize, Jessie," Mel says. "Odelia's just messing around."

"Yeah. I know. I'm just excited to show you Levi," I lie.

"Well, come on then," Odelia says as the three of us make our way down the hall.

⌐

When I arrive at Visual Arts, Cat is already seated at the table next to Griffin, working on her portrait of Chelsie. She doesn't acknowledge me when I sit down. Griffin has a book propped on the table, blocking my view of his work. He wants it to be a surprise. I've rehearsed a few different responses for when he does finally show it to me. I'd hate to hurt his feelings in case it sucks. He was really impressed with mine when I showed him the finished product on Friday.

Griffin lifts his head and tells me he's almost done.

Cat leans over. "You didn't make her nose big enough. There's a bump right here."

Why is she pointing out imaginary flaws? There is no bump on my nose. I would know if there were.

Mr. Trapp walks over to our table and looks at Griffin's drawing. "I disagree. Griffin captured Jessie's nose perfectly," he says with a kind smile.

"I think so too. Be right back. Need to sharpen my pencil." Griffin gets up, and I angle my head to sneak a peek at his drawing. He catches me in the act, narrowing his eyes in a playful kind of way. He covers his portrait with a book and walks to the other side of the room.

"Mr. Trapp, can I speak to Jessie, please?"

I jerk my head back to see Levi in the classroom doorway. LEVI WALSH IS STANDING IN THE DOORWAY OF MY CLASSROOM! ASKING FOR ME!

"Make it quick," Mr. Trapp says.

I feel Cat's eyes burn into my back as I walk toward Levi.

"Jess, I need a favor." Levi pulls me into the hallway. "I spaced on the Science homework and I was hoping you'd let me take a look at yours before class."

I should have known all he wanted was my homework. But as Levi's blue eyes peer into mine, I can't bring myself to say no.

"It's in my locker."

"Mind if I help myself to it? I'll bring it with me to class."

I nod, since the rest of my body doesn't seem to be working.

Levi places his hands on my arms and gives them a squeeze. "You're the best."

The physical contact alone was worth it. Sub-goal met: *Have Levi see me in a different environment.* He somehow knew where to find me. He sought *me* out. When I go home, I'm going to add fifty check marks to my journal. I'm going to cover an entire page with check marks.

I turn to walk back to class. Cat stands in the doorway while everyone else finishes up their portraits.

"You shouldn't let him copy your homework," she says with her nose in the air.

Every muscle inside my body tenses at her words. "He's checking his answers."

"You're going to get hurt. He knows you like him and he's using it to his advantage. I know how to read guys," Cat continues. The way she says "I know how to read guys" causes a chill to pass through me. Does that mean she can tell I don't know how to read guys? Because of my autism? I thought I was doing a good job of hiding it. Her words rattle me, and tears begin to well up behind my eyes. I want to scream at her, tell her to stop being so mean, and tell her she could never understand, but I take a deep breath instead. *Goal #3: Do not let anyone see me cry at school!!!*

"We're Science partners. We've been working together since the first day of school. We help each other."

At this point I'm not sure who I want to convince more, me or Cat.

"If you say so," Cat says before strutting back to her seat.

When I return to the table, Griffin says he's ready to show me his work. He lifts it slowly. "Do you like it?"

My eyes quickly scan the portrait in front of me. It's good. Really good. "Wow, Griffin. That's . . . generous."

Griffin shakes his head. Maybe I should have used one of my rehearsed lines. "What do you mean?"

"It's amazing. You're so talented, and it looks like me, but with a filter added or something." He frowns. Once again I've said the wrong thing. "I mean it in a good way. I wish I looked like that."

Griffin glances at his portrait, then back at me. "Jessie, this is what you look like. I didn't try to make you look better. I drew what I saw."

This is what Griffin sees sitting across from him? I always figured when people looked at me they'd zero in on my flaws the way I do. Thick, frizzy hair. Eyes that are set too close together. A nose that turns up a bit too much because I spent years sniffing a blanket to fall asleep. But the girl in the portrait is pretty. She has big eyes and a sweet smile. Round cheeks and tiny ears. I'm seeing myself the way Griffin sees me, the way others possibly see me, and it's kind of illuminating. "Sorry. What I should have said was . . . you're welcome."

He laughs. "Thank you."

As class nears the end, we all hand in our completed work.

When I get to my locker, Cat is already there, but we ignore one another. I don't have time to deal with her drama. I need to get my binder back from Levi.

I find him sitting with his legs stretched out on the floor outside of Science. I stand in front and clear my throat to get his attention as he quickly copies down the answers.

"And done." He slaps both our binders shut and springs to his feet.

I take another step before whispering, "You didn't copy my answers word for word, did you?"

"Yes?"

I lean in even closer. "If Ms. Muller collects our homework, she'll know one of us copied."

"Don't worry. She usually just walks around to see if you completed it. Trust me. Now, are you going to let me pass by or are you going to frisk me first?" He smirks.

I practically jump out of his way and try to hide the blush I feel taking over my cheeks.

Levi turns back to look at me. "Well, are you coming in?"

I nod and follow him into the room.

"Have a seat, lovebirds," Ms. Muller teases. The class giggles in response while I sink into the chair. Levi decides to keep the laughs going and puts his arm around my shoulders. I sit frozen like a statue.

"Okay class, settle down," Ms. Muller says in her thick accent. "Take out your homework. I'm coming around to see if it's done."

Levi leans his face toward my ear and his breath tickles my neck. "Told you," he says, before removing his arm.

And once again, I've completely overreacted. I struggle opening my binder. Levi takes over, helping me locate the right page. His fingers brush mine and it causes me to jump in my seat.

"You alright?" he asks.

I bolt out of my chair. "I have to pee."

The class laughs as I hightail it out of Science.

In the bathroom, I splash cold water on my face and undo the first button on my shirt. As I'm about to leave, someone lets out a heavy sob from behind one of the stall doors. A backpack with a Nirvana patch rests on the floor.

"Cat? Is that you? It's Jessie Kassis."

Cat opens the beige metal door and avoids making eye contact. Mascara has run down her pale face, leaving black streaks. "You don't have to say your first and last name. I know who you are."

"Sorry. It's just habit," I say, tucking my hands in my sleeves. "I went to elementary school with another Jessie. So . . . what's wrong?"

She walks over to the mirror and tries to make herself

presentable. "You guys made me feel really left out about not being able to go to Mel's. Then Griffin blew me off in class today." She pauses before turning to face me. "And despite what you may think, I was just trying to protect you with Levi."

My autism works in mysterious ways. On the one hand, I can't read people, at least in the moment, but on the other, I see right through them. And I think, for Cat, this is as close to an apology as I'll ever get. I straighten my mask and say something I don't really mean. "We missed you this weekend."

"Yeah, well, I really wanted to be there but my dad's events always come first."

"If you had told us the truth we would have understood. You don't have to pretend around us," I say, the irony not lost on me, a person who is currently pretending very hard to care.

Cat smiles and I try to mirror her. This friendship thing is hard work.

When I return to class, everyone is busy copying notes from the whiteboard.

Levi grins as I take my seat. "Did you pee?"

I shove him with my shoulder and he laughs.

"You missed two pages. You can borrow my notes after class. See?" he says, looking me straight in the eyes. "You need me, too."

If he only knew how much.

After school, Mel and I head to the cafeteria for the first HTTCo meeting. Annie rolled her eyes when she learned I'd signed up to be a techie. She's just jealous, because she doesn't have a creative or technical bone in her body. My parents, on the other hand, were excited when I told them about tech club. As long as it takes place in the school with adult supervision, they encourage any activity that forces me to interact with others.

Mel and I pull up a couple of chairs at a table near the stage and wait for things to get started. The drama club and liturgical choir are also here to discuss their performances for the first school Mass. Mass at school is basically a church service but in the same place we eat soggy fries and greasy pizza.

Griffin is seated on the edge of the stage and waves when he sees me. I shoot him a quick wave then look away.

"Making friends with older boys, I see." Mel nudges my elbow with hers.

"No. We just have Art together."

"He's kinda cute."

"Who's kinda cute?" Cat pulls up the chair across from us.

"What're you doing here?" I ask.

"Well, since you weren't very helpful on the Griffin front, I decided to sign up for tech club. So, who's kinda cute?"

"That guy," Mel says, nodding to Griffin.

"That's Griffin. Don't get any ideas." Cat narrows her eyes at Mel, and even though I'm pretty sure it's supposed to be playful, it reads as "back off" to me.

We spend the next hour going over Friday's Mass. The liturgical choir is busy choreographing moves to a song they plan to perform on a large scaffold on stage. Meanwhile, the drama club has been rehearsing tableaux, which somehow have to do with stories from the New Testament. Sometimes going to a Catholic school is weird.

As for me, the new members of the technical company have to shadow older ones and learn how to properly coil wires and tape floor mics to the stage floor. It's not what I want to be doing. I'd rather be goofing around with the drama kids. They seem to be having a lot more fun.

"We need one more disciple of Jesus for this final tableau," I overhear the Drama teacher, Mrs. Elliott, say.

"Jessie can do it," Griffin responds.

I drop the wire I've been poorly wrapping and whip my head in his direction. He smiles innocently.

Mrs. Elliott presses her finger up against her lips. "Jessie. You're in ninth grade?"

"Yes," I reply.

Mrs. Elliott looks around, probably searching to see if there's anyone older or better who can fill in. "Can I borrow her?" she asks Mr. Wolfe, the teacher in charge of tech club.

"Fine by me," he says.

"Do you have all-black clothes you can wear Friday?" Mrs. Elliott asks, hands on her hips.

"Yes!"

"Okay." She waves me over and I climb up the stage steps and stand next to Griffin.

"Step one of infiltrating the drama club complete," Griffin whispers, while keeping his head forward.

"But—"

"Don't worry," he interrupts. "I got you, Jessie K." He winks before playfully pressing his shoulder up against mine.

Two sub-goals met in one day? Not too shabby, Jessie K.

eiGHT

As days and weeks go by, small moments become memories, and eventually, everything seems to blur together. Then one day you wake up and suddenly all this time has passed, but you're still in the same place.

At least if you're me.

I thought by now things would be different. Some things are: the leaves on the trees have changed color, and there's frost on the grass in the early morning. But my romantic life has hit a big, gigantic wall.

We're all seated at our usual table at the back of the cafeteria before the morning bell. Odelia has her eyes on some older girls who are hanging up posters. She rises from her chair and rips one off the wall. The girl who just finished hanging it up turns around and glares, but Odelia ignores her.

"*Fall Dance: Friday October 14.* That's next Friday! We have to go!" Odelia says with a smile so wide, two dimples I've never noticed before appear in her cheeks. "We'll go together. No dates."

"Speak for yourself," Cat replies. "I've got Noah."

Noah Foster. Cat's eleventh-grade boyfriend. They've been together a couple of weeks. She met him in tech club, and they've been joined at the lips ever since. *Griffin who?* If I had a cellphone and could text, this is where I'd insert an eye-roll.

"Well, I prefer the company of my friends and the flexibility to hang out with whoever I want," Odelia says, while making her eyebrows wiggle. Mel and Cat listen as Odelia lists off the names of the boys she hopes will be at the dance—it's a long list—while I stare off into the distance, thinking about Levi. I'm not sure if he's a go-to-a-school-dance kind of guy. He's barely a go-to-school kind of guy. The bell rings, and Odelia stuffs the poster inside Mel's backpack.

In Art, Mr. Trapp yawns as he clicks through different slides about the principles of design. His yawn is infectious, and soon most of the class tries to muffle the sounds of their boredom. My mind drifts back to the dance. I know it's a long shot, but if Levi happens to be there and I happen to look amazing, maybe he'll finally be able to see me as more than just the ninth-grader he bums answers off of.

I've started to experiment with different looks when I'm in my room at night. Mom let me get my eyebrows threaded at the mall a couple of weeks ago and they now have arches. After my appointment she made me promise never to touch them myself again. She overplucked in her youth and deeply regrets her skinny, shapeless brows. Her words. Not mine. But in Arabic.

Thanks to today's stimulating art lesson, there's no cleanup to do after class and I manage to get to Science a few minutes early. Ms. Muller asks to speak to me as I walk through the door.

"Jessie, can you deliver this envelope to Mr. Powers in the senior building?"

"Oh." I hesitate. "I've never been there before."

Levi bolts out of his chair. "I'll go with her."

Ms. Muller purses her lips before eventually agreeing. I drop off my belongings and head out with Levi, envelope in hand.

"You've really never been to the old building, eh? It used

to be the main school before they built this one," Levi says. He walks so fast, his long hair sways in the breeze.

"I've never had a reason to. It's mostly senior and gifted classes, right?" I say, trying to keep pace with him. Damn fifty-year-old lungs.

"Right. It's also where they hold detention after school." Levi smirks, and I can't help but laugh.

We walk inside the senior building and it reeks of wet winter boots. Levi leads the way, but I stop in my tracks when we pass the large student lounge. I've heard Annie and her friend Marisa talk about how they chill in there during spare periods. There's an unwritten rule that only twelfth-graders are allowed in the lounge, which is fine 'cause I bet it smells like wet winter boots in there, too. Thanks to the room's large windows I spot Annie immediately from the hallway. She's seated on a couch next to a boy who has his arm around her. *Does Annie have a boyfriend? A Black boyfriend?* I always thought she'd end up with an Arab guy, to make our parents happy.

"What's wrong?" Levi traces his steps back to where I've stalled.

"Nothing." I shake my head. "Just saw my sister."

"Which one is she?" I point her out and he turns to me, tilting his head. "You guys don't look alike."

"Yeah, I know." I've heard that my whole life.

"You're cuter," he says, matter-of-factly.

And just like that, the clouds part and a choir of angels sings a roaring rendition of "Oh Happy Day." Levi Walsh just said I was cute! Technically speaking, he said I was *cuter* than Annie!

"What are you doing here?" And just as quickly as it appeared, the choir of angels retreats behind the gray storm cloud that is my older sister and her perma-scowl.

I wave the envelope in Annie's face. "We're delivering something."

"Then go do it and get lost." She turns around and storms back to the lounge.

God, she ruins everything.

Levi cocks his head to mine as we walk away. "What crawled up her butt?"

"Not sure, but whatever it is has been lodged up there since the day I was born."

Once we finish making our delivery, Mr. Powers asks us to go to the Science storage closet to return a few things for him. Apparently, the Science teachers at Holy Trinity see me and Levi as their personal assistants today. But I don't mind.

"How do you know where this room is?" I ask Levi as he leads me down a narrow hallway.

"Because sometimes when you get detention, teachers make you do things like organize the shelves in the storage closet."

"So . . . did you, like, spend your entire ninth-grade year serving detention?"

Levi blushes. "You're funny."

"I know," we say in sync before laughing.

Once we're done, we return to find our Science classroom vacant.

"Where is everyone?" Levi asks.

"The gym!" I say, suddenly remembering. "There's that assembly for ninth- and tenth-graders."

"Right. The drinking and driving one." Levi's eyes light up. "Let's ditch it. If anyone asks where we were, we tell them we got there late and sat in the back."

I scrunch up my face, trying to decide what to do. I mean, I know what I *should* do, but how can I pass up an opportunity to be alone with Levi? It might lead to accomplishing *Goal #6: GET LEVI WALSH TO BE MY FIRST KISS!!!!!* Dr. Cassidy did say it's important to set goals. And meet them.

"Do you drink?" Levi asks.

"No."

"Do you drive?"

I shake my head.

"Is drinking and driving wrong?"

"It is," I reply, nodding slowly and holding back a grin.

"I think we're done here, then."

He does have a point, but to be honest, I'd agree to just about anything while looking into his eyes. "Okay," I say. A satisfied smile appears on Levi's face and we exit the classroom. As we're headed toward the stairs, we hear the clicking of heels fast approaching. Levi pulls me into the janitor's closet and closes the door.

He places his right hand over my lips just as I'm about to speak. His left hand cradles the back of my head. He's standing so close; warmth radiates off his body, while the smell of bubblegum-scented soap in plastic jugs overpowers the tiny room. I can't think straight, being alone and in the dark with Levi. This would be the perfect place to have our first kiss. As it stands, this is by far the most romantic *and* sexual experience I've ever had.

Levi removes his hands and apologizes. He cracks open the door. "The coast is clear."

I follow him outside, past where the potheads hang out and down the wooden stairs that lead to the pond.

We sit on the bottom step and catch our breath.

"Now what?" I ask.

Levi shrugs, then searches through his pockets.

I turn back to look at the school. "We need to return to class at the same time as everyone else."

He places a joint in his mouth. "Do you always overthink everything?"

"Yes," I answer.

He shakes his head and smiles. We sit in silence while I watch him smoke, mesmerized by his mouth. I tuck my hands under my thighs to stop fidgeting. Levi offers me a hit, and even though I'm tempted to put my lips around something his have touched, I turn him down. He twists his body to face mine and looks at me, cockeyed.

"Where are you from? Like, your parents."

Great, this question. At least he didn't ask "What are you?" I don't know why being asked this makes me nervous. I guess I'm afraid people will judge me or think I'm different, which they do anyway. But it bothers me more when they think I'm different just because my skin tone is a little darker and my last name is harder to pronounce. People are afraid of what they don't understand, and they don't understand me.

"My parents are from Palestine. It's got a sad and pretty heavy history. When their parents were born, it was its own state. Now Palestinians live under military occupation in what is recognized by the rest of the world as Israel."

"It's a land dispute, right?" Levi asks, surprising me.

"Yes, but it's become much more than that. The media helps perpetuate the false and, quite frankly, dangerous narrative that all Palestinians are suicide bombers and terrorists. We're not. What the media doesn't talk about enough is the extreme power imbalance. One that leaves Palestinians feeling suffocated. That's what my cousin Rainy tells me, anyway," I say, looking away. "She's the activist in our family."

"That sucks. I'm sorry." Our eyes meet again and he offers me a sympathetic smile. "So, do you have a lot of family there?"

"Oh yeah. Most I've never met. Tons of cousins. And they all seem to have names that start with *J*: Jabra, Jamal, Jehad, Jafar. Okay, maybe not that last one."

Levi laughs.

"Anyway, my parents emigrated in the late nineties, so I was born here. They keep talking about taking us back there, but my dad's a workaholic. And apparently it's a bit of a logistical nightmare just to get there, because my parents aren't permitted to fly into Tel Aviv."

"That's messed up."

"It is."

"My buddy Eli is from Lebanon. He goes there every summer. He's taught me a few choice Arabic phrases."

A smile breaks through my nerves. "I'm sure he has."

"You know what I love? That creamy dip. What's it called?"

"Hummus?"

"No, not hummus. Everyone knows that one. It's got kind of a funny name."

"Oh, baba ghanoush?"

"Yes!" He snaps his fingers then points at me. "That tastes amazing with a warm pita."

"When did you ever try that?"

"Hey, I'm a worldly individual." Levi laughs. "Actually, my dad likes to take us out to eat at weird restaurants. Sorry, I didn't mean *weird*. I don't think you're weird. Actually, I haven't quite figured you out yet."

"What's to figure out?" I ask, even though I know it's a loaded question.

He takes a long drag of his joint. "You're just different from anyone I've ever known."

"Good. I don't want to be like everyone else." I remove my hands from under my legs and tuck them into my sleeves. The wind creates ripples in the pond and leaves blow all around us.

"What do you want to be?" he asks, calling my bluff.

If I'd had my way, Levi and I would have been kissing by now. I definitely wasn't expecting things to go in this direction. All these questions—pretty deep ones—have caught me off guard. I wasn't prepared for any of this. Discussing who and what I am was never part of any of the rehearsed, made-up conversations I had with him. Before I can stop myself, the truth comes barreling out of my lips.

"I'm autistic."

Levi sits up straight and squints at me. "No way."

"I just found out this summer. It's no big deal," I say, trying to downplay it. "It just means my brain works differently and I don't see the world the same way others do."

Levi nods. He's examining me now, as if he's trying to figure out how to respond. "I like that. My teachers say my brain works differently too—like a derailed train."

We laugh, and he stubs out his joint on the step behind us.

The early October breeze blows stray hairs over my face. I undo the elastic of my loose ponytail and run a hand through my hair, brushing it with my fingers. I need to do something with my hands. I can't believe I just admitted my biggest secret to the boy I'm in love with.

"Leave it down," he says as I'm about to tie it up again. I bring my hands to my lap, and Levi's eyes widen as more wisps of hair drift across my face.

As we sit, eyes locked together, the wall I use to keep people at bay falls around me.

Levi's still here.

He didn't run away.

Voices trail out of an open window on the second floor and Levi breaks contact. "The assembly is over."

We stand and walk back to school. I struggle once again to keep pace with his fast feet. We blend in with the large crowd and return to class with no one the wiser. The bell rings almost immediately, and Levi rushes off to lunch without saying goodbye.

―

"Wait, let me get this straight," Odelia says. "You're telling me that you, Jessie Kassis, my little, angelic puppy, skipped class and hung out with Levi by the pond today?" She slams her hands down on the cafeteria table. "Are you freakin' kidding me?"

"To be fair, we only skipped the assembly." I shove a handful of fries into my mouth to hide my smile.

"You're lucky you didn't get caught," Cat says. Interesting. She doesn't seem to worry about getting caught when Noah's tongue is shoved down her throat in the middle of the cafeteria.

"It sounds so romantic," Mel gushes.

Cat excuses herself to go meet Noah and Mel slides over. "How did you and Levi leave things?"

"We didn't," I say. "We went back to class, and that was it."

"I think he likes you," Odelia says before taking a gigantic bite of her apple.

I shake my head. "He had plenty of opportunities to say or do something about it and he didn't."

"It's because he's trying to reconcile his feelings for you."

Mel turns to me and I shrug in response. Sometimes Odelia sounds like a forty-year-old therapist.

"It means he likes you, but there's something stopping him from acknowledging his feelings." Odelia nods along to her words. "Maybe it's 'cause you're younger. Or that you don't really fit in with his friends. Whatever it is, he definitely likes you."

I want so badly to believe Odelia, but it doesn't make sense. Besides, they still don't know the truth about me.

"Give it time," Odelia says. "Don't rush it. This is the fun part."

I thought the fun part was the kissing, and the hand-holding, the phone calls, and the morning hugs. How is not knowing how the other person feels fun? Odelia may enjoy the chase, but it makes me feel like I'm losing my grip on Levi, and everything else in my life.

Nine

"Is Noah meeting you tonight?" Odelia asks Cat.

"Yep," Cat answers with a proud smirk.

The four of us are gathered at our cafeteria table for lunch. The dance is all Odelia has been able to talk about since seeing the poster for it last week. I'm afraid to tell her I've had second thoughts about going. It means so much to her to have us all there.

An older girl walks by with a stack of papers and places a few down on our table. Odelia picks them up immediately. "What is it?" I ask.

"It's for tonight. If you want to make any special song requests for the dance."

Ooh. Song requests. Odelia passes out the papers and I grab a pen from my bag and get to work curating a list.

"Who wants to bet none of Jessie's choices will be from this century?" Odelia jokes.

"You would be correct," I say, scribbling down my favorite songs, by genre. There's a section for dedications, but I leave it blank.

"Jessie, did you find out if Levi's going to be there?" Mel asks before taking a bite of her pizza.

I shrug. "He was away until Wednesday, and by that point

I was so busy catching him up on the work he missed that we didn't have a chance to talk about anything else." It's been exactly a week since our pond hangout. He acts like it never even happened. I probably scared him off with my big mouth. Wouldn't be the first time.

Odelia runs her hand over my back. "Tonight's gonna be fun whether Levi shows up or not. I promise."

I force a smile before glancing at the clock. "I need to get my gym clothes. I'll drop these off in the box for you guys," I say, collecting everyone's requests.

I want to be as excited for tonight as the others are, but the dance only serves to highlight how painfully single I am. Maybe I should just accept that I'll be alone for the rest of my life. If only Mom would let me bring my headphones to school. Then I could tune everything and everyone out. I'm getting tired of always having to be on. Always trying to be the version of myself people expect. What am I doing all of this for?

After dropping off our song requests, I make my way up the stairs and head to my locker. A familiar figure stands in the distance.

"Hey." Levi smiles and walks toward me with both hands in his pockets. "I hate to ask you for help again, but Muller has been riding me about handing in my homework before the weekend. Can you spare a few minutes to help me fill out the scientific method for Monday's experiment? I tried to do it without you, but I'm lost."

"Sure," I answer, a bit deflated.

We sit side by side on the cold floor and lean against the lockers. Our outstretched legs touch. *Breathe.*

Levi opens his binder and splits it between our laps. I read over his responses. He wasn't kidding about being lost. "Levi, this hypothesis has nothing at all to do with Monday's experiment."

He rakes his fingers through his hair and nods. "Yeah. I couldn't remember what the experiment was but I tried to fill in the blanks anyway. Turns out you can't BS your way through the scientific method."

"No. You can't." I grab a pencil from my backpack and erase his nonsensical responses. After I spend a few minutes going over the experiment we were assigned, Levi comes up with a really solid hypothesis, and I'm only slightly surprised. He's a lot smarter than he gives himself credit for.

"You lefties look so funny when you write," he says with a mischievous grin as I jot down his responses.

"Would you like to do the rest of this on your own?" I ask, glaring at him sideways.

"Sorry." He laughs. "It's cute."

Butterflies dance in my stomach, but I need to try and keep it together. We continue to work our way through the assignment, but Levi cannot stay focused. It's no wonder he needs me.

"Maybe if Muller has another rotten egg salad sandwich before class on Monday we won't have to do this useless experiment. I mean, how important is hydrogen peroxide in our daily lives anyway?"

"It's actually an earth-friendly alternative to chlorine bleach, and there's a lot of . . . never mind," I say, looking down at his binder.

"No, tell me," he says, smiling. "I like it when you show off your big brain."

"It's fine," I say, shaking it off. "We're running out of time."

"Then I'll take a rain check on those facts." He grabs the pencil from my hand and scribbles down the rest of the answers.

"Okay, that takes us to 'Step 4: Test your hypothesis,' which we'll do on Monday," I say.

"Perfect." Levi looks at his paper, then back at me. "You know, this whole scientific method thing could easily be adapted into a dating method."

"You're going to tell me whether I ask or not, aren't you?"

He turns to face me. "Step 1: Choose a person to go after. Step 2: Do your background research: *Are they single? What are they into?* Step 3: Hypothesize whether or not they'll go out with you. Step 4: Test your hypothesis by asking them out."

"Don't forget Step 5, *for girls only*: Overanalyze your first date and draw a conclusion. Step 6: Share all the details with your friends," I say, playing along.

"If we're going to classify the dating method by gender, then males can skip right to the conclusion. A successful date only means one thing for us," he says with a smirk.

I laugh along with Levi, even though I'm not exactly sure what he's referring to. *A kiss? More than a kiss?* We get up and dust ourselves off. I can't help but notice that we're standing in front of a poster for tonight's dance. A rush of bravery comes over me and I point to it.

"Are you going to this thing tonight?" I tuck strands of hair that have come loose behind my ear and fiddle with my sleeves while waiting for him to respond.

"We might stop by," Levi answers as he packs his bag.

"We?"

"Just a couple of friends. You?"

My shoulders drop at his response. For a second there I thought "we" meant another girl. Levi puts his backpack on and runs his hands through his hair. I'm dead. He's so perfect. *Just kiss me already.*

The bell rings and the halls begin to fill up with students on their way to third period.

"I think so." I practically shout my answer over everyone.

"Cool. Maybe I'll see you there. I've got to get this to Muller. Thanks again!" Levi says before he disappears into the crowd.

And the stakes for tonight just got higher.

⟶

After what feels like an eternity of grooming, I stand in front of the full-length mirror in my parents' bathroom to view the results of my labor. I'm dressed in light-blue jeans and a fitted olive-green shirt. My long black hair is blow-dried so straight it shines. I put on some pink lip gloss and even manage to get mascara on my eyelashes without smearing it everywhere. A smile cracks through my nerves. I throw on a green flannel shirt and button it up before opening the door to leave.

"Ramsey," I shout, startled.

"My God, you and Annie have been monopolizing both showers for over an hour. Is this what I have to look forward to now that I have two teenage sisters?" he grumbles.

"Sorry. I lost track of time."

"No worries. It only takes me ten minutes to go from stud to Arabian prince."

"Okay, Aladdin."

Ramsey laughs, then frowns. "You look so grown-up. What happened?"

"It's the clothes and hair," I say with a dismissive wave, fighting off the blush I feel creeping in.

"Well, don't go turning into an Annie clone on me now," he pleads.

"Never." I smile.

Mom and Dad drop me off before driving Annie to her party. They spend most of the ride lecturing Annie about trying for her license again, even going so far as to hint that they'd buy her a car. So Annie gets a phone and a car, and I get nothing. Well, that's not true. I get autism. Lucky me.

"We'll be back to pick you up at ten thirty. If you're late, Daddy will come inside to find you," Mom says as I open the car door.

I can't tell if she's teasing, but I wouldn't put it past either of them. My parents remain out front until I enter the building. I turn and wave goodbye, catching a glimpse of my reflection in the glass door. It takes a second to realize the girl staring back is me.

Inside, the foyer is decorated with streamers and an odd mix of fall decorations. The adjacent hallway lights are turned off. It's weird being at school when it's dark, like I'm in an episode of *Stranger Things* or something.

"Jessie." Odelia's voice echoes from across the entrance. Cat and Mel follow close behind. Mel and Odelia are both in cropped T-shirts and tight jeans. Maybe I *should* undo a few buttons.

Odelia wraps me in a hug. She smells like my Amo Sami on Christmas Eve—my uncle likes to have a drink or two (or three) on special occasions. Once she pries herself off me, she throws an arm around Cat and begins laughing maniacally at seemingly nothing.

"Has Odelia been drinking?" I whisper to Mel.

Mel raises her shoulders. "She got into my dad's liquor cabinet and swiped a couple of his tiny bottles of whiskey when I wasn't paying attention. Don't worry, I'll keep an eye on her."

"Can I sponge five bucks off one of you?" Odelia asks. She removes her arm from Cat, yanking her hair in the process.

"Odelia!" Cat whines as she smooths out her red tresses.

I lend Odelia the cash since my parents always give me extra. After we pay admission, Odelia links her arm with mine and the four of us walk to the atrium together.

There's something in the air tonight. It reminds me of the first time Annie and I rode our bikes over to the steep hill at the end of our neighborhood. Back when Annie would occasionally spend time with me. It took forever before I got up the nerve to lift my hands and release the handlebar. I careened down the suburban mountain, wind blowing through my hair and Annie's laughter in the background. I knew there was a chance I'd fall and get hurt, but the ride was so freeing and invigorating—it was totally worth the risk.

The cafeteria has been transformed into a giant dance hall, complete with a disco ball, and all the sticky tables have been moved out. Even with colorful lights bouncing off the walls, it's still dark.

A bald DJ dressed in black and wearing sunglasses nods along to the music on stage. Pop songs with bouncy beats fill the air, but the dance floor remains bare. A few teachers are here acting as chaperones. They have yet to spot the couple going at it in the corner.

"There's Noah. I'll be right back," Cat shouts over the speakers. She races off in her too-short dress and throws her arms around him. Cat's love life has developed in this completely normal and healthy way, and I can't help but feel a little jealous about it. It seems so easy for her. She liked a boy, he liked her back, and now they're together.

Mel shakes her head. "I swear Cat's only with him so she can point the damn safety pin on her kilt up, announcing her relationship status." We both roll our eyes at the tired school tradition.

"Come on, let's dance," Odelia says with an exaggerated pout. She grabs my arm, but I plant my feet firmly on the ground.

"There is no way I'm dancing. Not to *this* music and not with the dance floor empty."

"Fine!" Odelia places her hands on her hips. "But the second the DJ plays a song you like, I'm coming for you."

I nod, agreeing to anything as long as Odelia leaves. She takes a sip of whiskey from one of the bottles she stole and pulls Mel onto the dance floor with her.

Alone, I walk the perimeter of the cafeteria, until I can figure out what else to do.

I like to think people's opinions of me don't matter, but as I watch Odelia dance like a baby giraffe, it's clear she's the one who doesn't care what others think, drunk or not.

Since I can't walk in circles all night, I find a spot that will give me a good view of both the now mostly filled up dance floor and the main entrance. I lean against the cinder block wall next to the closed kitchen, taking in the view before me. *So, this is what it's like to go to a high school dance.* One friend is swapping spit with her pimple-faced boyfriend while the other two make fools of themselves on the dance floor. Maybe I'm being overly cynical. It's not anyone's job to babysit me. But if I had known I'd spend the entire evening debating whether or not to unbutton my flannel shirt to reveal a top that feels two sizes too small and trying to blend into the background, I would have stayed home. I just feel like I'm supposed to be having more fun than this.

"This next song is dedicated to a girl named Jessie," the DJ shouts into the microphone. "Jessie, Odelia is coming for you!"

Oh my god! I could kill her. I *will* kill her. Odelia makes her way off the dance floor and, before I know it, she's pulled me into a mob of my sweaty peers. To make matters worse, she requested the song "Jessie's Girl." I want to run away and hide, but when

I look around, everyone is dancing and smiling. Not one eyeball is on me.

That's it. From here on out, I vow to snap out of this bad mood and let myself have fun like everyone else. Starting with shaking off all the tension I've been holding up by my ears and allowing the music to take control of my body. Every time the chorus comes on, we all sing along. Some of us (me) know the words to this song better than others. This is exactly what I envisioned tonight would be like. Well, almost exactly.

The dance floor fills up, and Odelia continues to sneak in the last few sips of whiskey. Sweat beads begin to form around my forehead and neck. The crowd smells like BO mixed with aftershave, but I'm having a time. I'm no longer obsessed about whether or not Levi will show up. I don't need him here.

As the night progresses, so does Odelia's drunkenness. Her antics are beginning to annoy the others. She repeatedly trips and smashes up against people, never bothering to apologize. At one point, she falls into a group of girls and they go down like bowling pins.

"We should try to sober her up. I'll go buy some water," I say to Mel.

On my way back from the concession stand, I stop dead in my tracks. He's here. *Levi's here.* All sounds echo around me and everyone is blurry, except for him. Levi stands on the sidelines in jeans and a white hooded sweatshirt, his long hair tucked behind his ears. Everything slows to a crawl. I imagined this moment so many times and in so many different ways, and now that it's here, I don't know what to do.

I somehow manage to pull it together and make my way back to Mel and Odelia. I grab Mel's arm and bring my mouth to her ear. "He's here." My heart feels ready to pound out of my chest.

Mel smiles, even though she's clearly distracted by Odelia, who's attempting to start a mosh pit of sorts. Mel grabs the bottle of water and ushers me out.

"Go find Levi. I'll take care of O."

I nod at Mel before returning to my original spot against the wall. Levi should be able to see me from where he's standing. I run my hands through my hair and try to smooth it out, then undo the first few buttons of my flannel top.

Just as I'm ready to use my feminine wiles . . . or something like that . . . to lure Levi in with a look from across the room, a disturbance erupts out in the atrium.

A man with a dark beard flails around, yelling, "Where is she? Where is my daughter?" over and over. Some of the teachers try to calm him down, but he brushes them off. He eventually follows Mrs. Elliott into the cafeteria, and they're both headed my way.

"Jessie, this is Odelia's father. Do you know where she is?" Mrs. Elliott asks calmly.

I hesitate. I can't rat Odelia out, but there's no way her dad is leaving without her. She's made references in the past about how . . . *irrational* he is, but I assumed it was just Odelia being dramatic. I should have believed her. Right now, I need to do what I can to minimize the damage.

I pull Mrs. Elliott aside and plead with her. "I'll find Odelia, but can you please bring her dad to the foyer?"

I glance past her shoulder, and Mr. Rossi's dark eyes pierce through mine. Mrs. Elliott nods, her lips pressed together. She escorts Odelia's dad out of the cafeteria with promises that Odelia is on her way. I make a beeline to the dance floor.

"We've got to go, *right now*," I say, trying to pull Mel and Odelia away from the crowd.

"No way!" Odelia shouts, pushing me.

Time is of the essence. I grab Odelia by the shoulders and stare into her eyes. "Your father is here."

My words sober her up. Fast. Odelia paces back and forth, covering her face with her hands.

"He's waiting for you in the foyer."

Odelia continues to stumble around in circles, dropping f-bombs and other curse words I don't even let myself say in my head.

"It's okay, O. I'll go with you and take the blame," Mel offers. "Here, chew on this piece of gum and try to act sober."

Mel gives me the two empty bottles of alcohol and I tuck them into my back pocket. We stand on either side of Odelia and attempt to keep her from tripping on her own feet as we make our way off the dance floor. I continue to walk with them to the foyer, but then Mel stops me.

"I think it's better if we go alone," she says.

Sometimes the history between Mel and Odelia acts as a wedge between us. I stand back and watch as they approach Odelia's father. He grabs her arm, pulling Odelia toward the front doors. Mel hangs her head and follows them out.

The clock in the atrium reads a little past nine. Over an hour to go. To make matters worse, the DJ has started to play slow songs. The dance floor has thinned out a bit, and I spot Cat. Her body is draped over Noah's as they sway to the romantic music. After discreetly tossing the bottles, I walk over to my spot by the kitchen and lean my head against the wall, eyes closed in defeat.

"So, you did come."

My eyes blink open to find Levi standing across from me. He's kind of invading my personal space, but I like it.

"Yes, well, you know, someone has to keep this wall up,"

I manage to say. It's hard to hear anything outside the sound of my beating heart.

A corner of his mouth turns up. "Mind if I join you? It's a lot of work for one person to do alone."

Before Levi gives me a chance to answer, he's already settled in to my left. He's standing so close; our shoulders graze any time we move in the slightest. As love songs play in the background, there's nothing I want more than for him to grab my hand and hold it in his.

Levi leans his face toward mine, his lips almost touching my ear. "Where are your friends?"

"One is on the dance floor and the other two were just escorted out by an angry parent," I say, trying to keep it together.

Levi raises his eyebrows and laughs. "So what you're saying is . . . you got ditched?"

"Basically," I answer. "Where are your friends?"

"Around." Levi arches his neck and rolls it. Why do I find everything he does so damn attractive?

The lights dim further and "Linger" by The Cranberries comes on. *My number-one request.* And Levi's standing right next to me. I couldn't have orchestrated this moment any better. It must be a sign. Goal #6 might actually happen tonight, as long as I don't screw it up.

Levi nods along with the tempo of the song. "I like this."

"I requested it," I blurt out. Maybe he'll take the hint and ask me to dance. I've never slow-danced before. I wouldn't even know how.

"It's an older song, right?"

"Yeah, but that's all I really listen to. Music from the nineties. Not all of it, though. Not the terrible dance stuff. Mostly alternative." I feel myself starting to ramble as my heart outraces my remaining functional brain cells.

He smiles. "Makes sense, since you're kind of alternative yourself." He turns and presses his hand against the wall over my head. His eyes are so blue they even glimmer in the dark. Levi looks me up and down and an unfamiliar sensation pulses through my body. He's never looked at me this way before. It's different and electrifying.

Levi shakes his head. "I don't know what it is about you."

Normally I'd turn away or make a joke, but my eyes remain fixed on Levi, waiting for him to do or say something else, something more.

"Why is it I always find myself near you?" he asks.

Words don't come to me. Instead I turn to face him. It's just me and Levi. Nothing else matters.

The song continues to play and the haunting lyrics possess me. I take another step, closing the gap between us. He brings up his left hand to remove a strand of hair partially covering my face. He follows it down slowly to where it ends, right below my chest. His hand skims my stomach and it sends shock waves through my entire body.

"I like when you wear your hair down," he says, his eyes continuing to take me in. "You look good tonight."

Is that an invitation? It must be. But what if it's not? *But what if it is?* I look straight ahead, my eyes landing on a faded red circle on his sweatshirt. "You have a stain," I say, pointing to it.

He chuckles softly. "Ketchup."

"You know," I say, swallowing and leaning in, "hydrogen peroxide works as a good stain remover. Just don't leave it on any longer than three minutes."

"Why only three minutes?" he asks, tilting his head down. He smells like Tide and some flowery shampoo he must have borrowed from his sister.

"'Cause it can bleach the fabric."

"Good to know." He smiles, then bites his lip. "Was that my rain check?"

I lift my eyes to meet his. "Maybe."

"Maybe I don't want it to be over so quick." Levi's face tilts lower and his lips begin to open as they make their way to mine.

"Yo, Levi. Let's bolt," someone calls out from behind him.

You've got to be kidding me.

Levi takes a step back, and then so do I.

"I guess I'm leaving now," he says.

I want to tell him not to go, to stay here with me, but the words don't come out.

Levi walks backward and points to the stain on his shirt. "Hydrogen peroxide. Who knew?" He winks before turning to leave.

My legs start to give out once the adrenaline and the shock of the moment have worn off. I lean against the wall to steady myself and take a deep breath. What just happened?

With the girls and Levi gone, there's really nothing keeping me here. I search for Cat and ask her for a ride home, knowing she's getting picked up soon.

Cat and Noah kiss goodbye, over and over, in the foyer while I stand there, alone. They don't pull away long enough for me to explain what happened with Odelia. Not that Cat has bothered to notice her absence, or Mel's. God, just moments ago I was seconds away from kissing Levi. Now I get to be the lookout for Cat's mom. That's me, the always dependable autistic friend with virgin lips.

"I'm back," I yell before heading to my bedroom and closing the door behind me. I plop down in my desk chair and roll it over to the mirror. I study my lips. My still un-kissed lips. I was so close. I could have checked Goal #6 off the list tonight. If only Levi's friend hadn't interrupted us. Couldn't he tell we were in the middle of something?

Levi said I looked good tonight. Not cute, *good*. Thinking about his words now leaves me breathless. The way he stared into my eyes. His fingers in my hair. I'm all tingly and jittery and I don't know what to do with this nervous energy. I take one last look in the mirror before changing out of my clothes and washing my face.

As I'm about to crawl into bed, Mom calls from the foyer and asks me to come down.

"Why are you home so early?" she asks.

"Decided to catch a ride with Catherine. If I had a phone, I could have called you."

"Oh, that's good," she says, once again ignoring my hint. "Listen, Ramsey was supposed to pick Annie up from her party but he's downtown. Can you go with Daddy to get her? I don't want him driving alone at night. He's been up since five."

"But I'm in my sweats," I say, pulling on my hoodie.

"No one will see you."

I sigh. "Fine."

"Good. He's waiting for you in the car," Mom says while smoothing out my hair.

Why did she even bother asking? To pretend I have a modicum of control in my life?

"How was the school party?" Dad asks as I climb into the front seat.

"Kind of boring," I lie before turning up the radio. Dad lowers the volume as he reverses out of the driveway. I spend the entire ride thinking about Levi and what happened. And maybe also imagining what kissing him would have felt like.

It's still pretty early when we arrive at Annie's party. Dad puts the sedan into park and nods to the house. "Go get your sister."

"What? No."

"What do you mean no?"

"I'm not dressed," I say. Not to mention, Annie will be mortified if I knock on that door.

"You need to wear an evening gown to ring a doorbell?"

I want to suggest calling her instead, but Dad's heavy eyes and impatient tone leave me no choice. And after what I witnessed tonight between Odelia and her father, I realize it's in my best interests to obey Dad's wishes.

I make my way up the gravel pathway to the dimly lit home. Music blares out of the house. From what I can see through the front windows, no one is on the main floor. I press the round doorbell. No answer. I turn back to Dad and he gestures for me to knock. I pound on the door until my knuckles start to ache. Someone finally opens it.

I jolt back, surprised. Levi's older sister, Lucy, stands across from me with a red Solo cup in hand.

"I know you." She smirks and points her finger at me. "You're my little brother's friend."

"Do you mean Levi?" I ask. My cheeks feel flushed and my hands clammy. I place them in the front pocket of my sweatshirt. Just saying his name out loud makes me giddy.

Lucy nods and smiles.

"Yeah, we have Science together."

"Is that all?" She winks, then stumbles to the couch. Some of her drink spills in the process. "He's not here. This isn't our house."

"No . . . yeah . . . I know. I'm here to pick up my sister, Annie Kassis."

"She's downstairs. Go ahead, Jessie. We don't bite." Lucy lies across the couch, cup still in hand.

I open the door to the basement and glance back at Lucy, who appears to be seconds away from passing out. *How did she know my name?*

My feet make their way down the steps slowly, in hopes that Annie will intercept me. She doesn't. It's dark, and music blasts from two separate speakers propped up on some bookshelves. The couches are filled with seniors with vaguely familiar faces. Annie's friend Marisa notices me immediately.

"Jessie? What are you doing here?" She stashes her cup behind a picture frame with a photo of a family of four and their big, white dog.

"I'm here for Annie. Dad's out in the car," I say.

"I'll go get her," Marisa replies. Before I can take a step to follow, she places her hand in front of me. "Stay here."

"Hurry," I shout. I cross my arms and attempt to cover my chest, suddenly very aware that I'm not wearing a bra.

Marisa knocks on a door and Annie's secret boyfriend answers, easing it open a crack. I crank my neck to try and sneak a peek. I catch a glimpse of Annie sitting on a bed, but I turn my attention to a bowl of chips as Marisa returns.

"Annie will be right up," she says, before ushering me back toward the staircase.

Ah crap. Dad is at the top of the stairs, about to make his descent. I race up the rest of the way and place my hand on his round stomach to stop him.

"She's on her way," I say.

Dad stands with his arms crossed and breathes heavily as we

wait for Annie by the front door. Lucy is still sprawled across the couch, snoring, her drink spilled on the floor below her.

Annie joins us a few minutes later. "What are you guys doing here? It's not even eleven."

"I'm not a taxi driver. When I come, it's time to leave." Dad raises his voice and his accent grows thicker. "What took so long?"

"Annie has the runs," I blurt. "She was pooping."

Annie opens her mouth, probably to yell at me, but then it all seems to click. She places a hand over her stomach and lets out a soft moan.

"Oh." Dad uncrosses his arms and steers Annie to the door. "Ask Mommy to give you the pink medicine when you get home. It works like magic. Now let's go."

Annie and I look at one another as we follow Dad out the door. We don't say anything, but the muscles in Annie's face relax as she breathes out what appears to be a huge sigh of relief.

Uncharacteristically, she lets me ride shotgun on the way home.

Ten

Monday morning, I walk into the cafeteria and glance at the wall where Levi and I had our . . . moment. It's so strange how the night can make everything more intense and dreamlike. It makes Friday seem like it was a long, long time ago. Almost as if I imagined the whole thing.

I haven't spoken to anyone since the dance. Our group chat was crickets. I tried calling Mel on Saturday, but her mom answered, saying she confiscated her phone for the weekend. My heart races with anticipation as I approach our table. I hope Odelia is okay. I hope Mel didn't get in too much trouble. A selfish part of me hopes all is good because I want to tell them what happened with Levi. I think I'm finally ready to open up.

None of the girls greet me when I arrive at the table. I pull out a chair and sit, waiting for someone to say something. But no one does.

"Hey, what's going on? Everything okay?" I ask.

"Oh, the rat wants to know if everything's okay. Well, let me fill you in. After you delivered me to my father on a silver platter, I got handed the tongue-lashing of my life." Odelia leans across the table and narrows her eyes at me. "You couldn't lie and tell Mrs. Elliott you hadn't seen me? You just had to ruin my life to earn points with the Drama teacher."

What is going on? This can't be happening.

"That's not true. Your dad already knew you were there." My body trembles as shock grows into frustration. "I had to be honest."

Cat and Mel avoid eye contact with me, making it clear whose side they're on. I continue, even though my heart is beating out of my chest so fast it's hard to breathe. "This isn't my fault," I say, zeroing in on Odelia. "I'm not the one who lied to her parents about going to the dance. I'm also not the one who let her friend steal her dad's liquor and get drunk," I say, glaring at Mel. "If you're going to be mad at someone, be mad at yourselves."

I rise from my chair and storm off, fighting back tears. I count. I try to breathe. I look up. I look down. I suck in my cheeks. I have to stop the tears, at least until I make it outside.

As much as I loathe confrontation, being falsely accused of having ulterior motives is even worse. I was put in an impossible position, and instead of understanding that, they're attacking me. And why? Because I didn't know the rules or how to play along? They don't get it. They don't get *me*. I've made a terrible judgment call by allowing these girls into my life. The only person you can trust in this world is yourself.

Once outside, I push my way through a throng of potheads before running down the pond stairs. Tears flow out of me like a river as soon as I sit on the bottom step.

The mid-October morning air is crisp, but I'm so full of rage, the cool breeze makes it easier to breathe.

Quick footsteps come up behind me.

"Jessie? The bell just rang. What are you doing still out here?"

I wipe my tears away and turn to see Levi standing there. For the first time ever, I don't want to talk to him. I don't even want to see him.

"Jessie, did you hear me? The final bell rang."

"Since when did you care about being on time?" I snap.

"*I* don't care. But I know you do." Levi steps down and sits next to me. "Are you okay?"

I keep my head forward. "I'm fine."

"Then look at me."

With those four little words, I fall to pieces, struggling to catch my breath in between heaving sobs. Levi places his arm around me and, without thinking, I lean my head onto his shoulder and cry.

"What happened?"

I sit up and tuck my hair behind my ears. His shoulder is stained with my tears. "I'm sorry," I say, trying to pat it dry.

Levi waves it off and lets out a hollow laugh. "Who do I need to beat up for making you cry? And, more importantly, do you think I can take 'em?"

I snort, making myself look like an even bigger hot mess. "My friends."

"Friends?" Levi shakes his head. "Friends don't take an adorable face like yours and turn it into this."

His sweet comment manages to make me smile. I let my guard down long enough to forget I'm speaking to the guy I'm in love with. Right now I need a friend, and that's what Levi is. As I tell him what happened, he nods along, listening to every word.

"What should I do?" I ask.

"Nothing. They'll come to their senses eventually and beg for your forgiveness. In the meantime, freeze them out."

"Freeze them out?"

"Yeah. Ignore them. Wait for them to come to you. Which they will. Show them you don't need them as much as they need you." Levi stands, extending a hand. "Sitting out here won't help. Let's go in and get our late slips."

I nod and place my hand in his. *Finally. Real contact.* His skin is rough and callused. His fingers long and masculine. *He's perfect.* And the most incredible thing happens as we walk up the wooden staircase—Levi doesn't let go. We continue to walk hand in hand until we enter the building. His smile is so dreamy I almost turn into a puddle by the rusty radiator with a decades-old *Metallica Rulz* scratched into the paint.

I arrive to Art twenty minutes later with a late slip. The tears are long gone and have been replaced with a grin I can't seem to wipe off my face. Everyone is at their seats, working on the latest assignment. I grab my materials and sit at the table with Cat and Chelsie. Griffin appears to be away today.

"Where were you?" Cat whispers.

"Oh, you're talking to me now? Good to know," I say with a quick nod, playing it cool, like Levi said.

"You know how Odelia is." Cat pulls her hair into a ponytail. "So, what really happened Friday night?"

Mr. Trapp shoots our table a stern look and clears his throat.

I wait until he's on the other side of the room before answering. "Mrs. Elliott and Odelia's dad came barreling toward me, demanding to know where she was. The only reason her dad didn't burst onto the dance floor was because I promised I'd bring Odelia to him."

Chelsie looks up from her drawing. "She's right, Cat. A bunch of us saw it happen."

"Oh. Odelia didn't tell me that."

Of course she didn't. Because she didn't bother to ask me. I'll never understand why neurotypical females make things way more complicated than they need to be. It's like they thrive on drama.

Cat promises she'll explain things to Odelia over lunch. It doesn't matter. The damage has already been done. Apparently, I'm the one who has problems understanding people, but I see them for who they are.

When I get to Science, Levi is at his desk, unpacking his bag. "Feeling better?" he asks.

"Yes." I smile. "Thanks."

"Good morning, everyone. I hope you had a nice weekend because the party is over. Before we begin today's experiment, we're going to have a pop quiz." The entire room fills with groans. "Jessie." Ms. Muller's voice is hushed as her eyes land on mine. "Can we talk?"

I nod and rise from my seat, following Ms. Muller to the front of the class, to a quiet spot near the door.

"I spoke to the vice-principal, Mr. Norris, at yesterday's staff meeting. He told me about your autism diagnosis," she says.

I swallow and look around the classroom to make sure no one overheard her. "How did he know?"

"Your mother called the school. Your psychologist needed her permission to send the files to Mr. Norris, and they got to talking about IEPs and such."

"For who? Me?" I ask, leaning in.

Ms. Muller glances past my shoulder. "When students are diagnosed, they usually get an IEP, an individualized education plan, or at least some accommodations. Mr. Norris suggested I ask if you want to start writing tests in the hallway, where it's quieter."

"No." I shake my head. I don't need an IEP, or to discuss modifications. After a decade in the school system, I've adjusted to writing tests under fluorescent lights, with the noise of excessive throat-clearing and squeaky chairs. "I'm fine."

"Okay." A pitying smile stretches across her face. "You and your parents should probably speak to Mr. Norris at some point. It's likely he's told your other teachers about this as well. To be frank, I was pretty surprised when he told me. You don't seem autistic at all."

"Um. Yeah." I swallow, forcing a nod. "I will. Can I go back to my seat now?"

"Yes. Yes," she says, shooing me away before clapping to get the attention of the class again. "Split your desks apart."

I return to my seat and watch as Levi searches through his backpack. "Need a pen?" I ask, passing him one of mine. I nod to my desk, letting him know he can cheat off me. His shoulders relax and he lets out a huge breath before mouthing, "Thank you."

When class is over, I take off to try and find Cat before she heads down for lunch. I spot her by our lockers, walking toward the back staircase. As I'm about to call her name, some guy pulls her to him and they start kissing. She giggles as they disappear through the doors. Did she and Noah break up? I've been exiled from the group for only a few hours and I've missed so much already. I lean against my locker and squeeze my eyes shut.

"Forget how to use your locker again?"

I open my eyes to find Levi standing in front of me with a smirk. He needs to stop doing that. One day I am going to cease resisting and maul his face with my lips, in front of God and everyone.

"You bolted out of class so quickly you didn't get to hear Ms. Muller praise me—well, us—on the results of our experiment."

"Sorry. I was trying to catch up with someone."

He glances around. "Was it successful?"

"No."

He lets out a soft laugh. "Have lunch with me and my friends. I assume you haven't settled things with yours yet?"

"No, not yet."

"Okay, come on then."

"I can't," I answer.

"And I can't take no for an answer. Guess that means we've reached a stalemate." Levi folds his arms over his chest and taps his foot.

"You play chess?" I ask, hearing the surprise in my voice.

"With my dad sometimes, yeah. So, lunch?"

I suck my cheeks in, trying not to smile, but I'm weak. "Fine."

"Checkmate," he says with a satisfied grin.

I follow him down the stairs, still trying to process the fact that Levi Walsh has invited me to lunch. We walk into the cafeteria together and he leads me to a table full of tenth-graders.

As a show of thanks, I offer to buy him a slice of pizza. On my way to the kitchen, I glance at my regular table. Mel and Odelia are seated together but they don't appear to be speaking. *Good.* I hope they choke on their tongues.

Levi raises his head as I approach with our lunches. His eyes dart to the person next to him: the lavender-haired girl. I freeze up.

"This table is for tenth-graders," she says. Her eyes sear into mine and I quickly look away.

Levi grabs a lunch tray from me. "I invited her, Liv."

So lavender-haired girl has a name. She twists her hair and points to a seat at the other end of the table. "There's room over there."

I walk toward the empty spot and sit. It's almost impossible not to notice her giggling at everything Levi says and does.

Between Liv's tiny stature, professionally colored hair, and angular features, the two of us couldn't look more different.

"Jessie K."

I peel my eyes off Levi and Liv to find Griffin sitting across the table from me.

"Griffin? Are you friends with . . . ?"

"Levi? Yes. Olivia French? Nope." He smirks.

I shake my head, trying to put the pieces together. "Oh. I didn't know that."

"Are you friends with Levi?" he asks, pointing a finger at him. I impulsively grab his hand and slam it on the table, my eyes growing to twice their size.

"No. We're just Science partners."

"Right." He grins, looking down at my hand still on top of his. I remove it. "Science partners."

"How come you weren't in class this morning?" I ask, straightening in my seat and stealing a glance at Levi. He's busy inhaling his pizza, while Liv keeps finding reasons to touch him.

"Good news," he says. "I got into Drama. Bad news, I'll no longer be sitting across from you every morning."

"Oh." I don't know why, but hearing that makes me a little sad. Part of me was starting to look forward to seeing Griffin and his massive hair in class.

"Are you going to miss me?" he asks with a raised brow.

"No." I answer a little too defensively, but a smile slips out when my eyes meet his. "Maybe a little."

"Good answer." He looks at his phone and frowns before placing it face down on the table.

"What's wrong?" I ask.

"My, uh, girlfriend keeps texting. She flew in for the weekend. It was supposed to be a big surprise. She planned to ambush me at home, but I was at the dance with Levi and Sean. Anyway, we ended up leaving early so I could meet her."

So Griffin's the reason Levi left the dance and our almost-first-kiss was interrupted.

"Sounds like it didn't go well," I say, before taking a bite of my pizza. Griffin smiles and hands me a napkin. It's almost impossible for me to eat pizza without getting sauce on my face.

"We decided—well, I guess I decided it was time to end things. The truth is, our relationship was probably over when she moved away. We just tricked ourselves into believing we could do the long-distance thing. But—" he shrugs— "eventually I just sort of stopped missing her, you know?"

"Did you love her?" I ask.

A shy smile edges its way out of Griffin's lips.

"Sorry. I probably shouldn't have asked something so personal."

"It's okay. It's a good question." He pauses, then lets out a long breath. "No. I don't think I did."

"Still sucks to break up," I say.

"Definitely. She just wasn't the one."

"I get that." I nod. "Anyway, I'm not even sure I believe in love. Romantic love, that is."

"Go on," Griffin says, putting his sandwich down.

"Well, you can't see it. You can't hold it in your hands. It's this intangible thing that causes the entire world to lose their minds. What even is the point?" I ask, stealing another glance at Levi.

"I think the point is, when you know, you know."

"The only thing I know is that *you know* I'm right and *you* just don't want to admit it," I say with an assertive nod.

"Give it some time. You'll come around. And then you'll say, 'That Griffin. He not only has a great head of hair, he's also highly intelligent,'" he says with a grin. "So, do you live close to school?" Griffin asks as I take another bite of my pizza, wiping my face immediately.

"I live on the other side of town, in the Knob Hill subdivision," I answer, with a mouthful of food.

"You must know Ricky Matthews, then," Griffin says.

"Our brothers are best friends!" *Best friends? What am I? Five?*

We continue to chat for the rest of lunch, and it's easy. We discuss comics and music, and I don't even get embarrassed when he repeatedly points out pizza sauce on my cheeks. Okay, maybe I do a little. I recommend songs for Griffin to listen to and he downloads them on his phone. In return, he scribbles down some newer songs for me to check out.

"Are you sure you're not from the past?" he asks, squinting one eye at me.

"Why? Just because I like older music? And movies. And fashion." We laugh. "Or maybe it's 'cause I'm probably the only person in this school without a phone."

"It's not just that. You're ..."

Before Griffin can finish his thought, Levi approaches and stands behind me. "Thanks for lunch, Jessie." He places his hands on my shoulders and I turn into a pile of mush. Physical contact twice in one day. "Griffin, you ready?"

Griffin shifts his gaze to Levi, then me, then back to Levi. "Did you know Jessie and I know each other from Visual Arts?"

"Oh yeah? Well, we know each other from Science." He squeezes my shoulders, and I could die. "You coming?"

There's a beat of silence before Griffin responds. "Yeah. Give me a sec."

After the guys leave, I get up to throw my scraps in the garbage, and that Liv person shoots me a not subtle at all evil eye.

"Don't expect to sit at my table again tomorrow."

"Sorry?" I say.

"Yeah, you should be." She laughs and returns to her conversation with her friends.

By the time Phys Ed is over, I'm still shaken by my interaction with Liv at lunch. What did I do that was so wrong? She's the one who got to sit with Levi. Once again, it feels like there's a set of rules I'm expected to follow. Rules no one ever bothers to clue me in on.

I step out of the locker room to find Odelia waiting.

"Hey," she says quietly. "Can we talk?"

I don't respond, but I also don't walk away.

"I'm so sorry." Her voice trembles. "Cat explained everything to me over lunch. I'm such a jerk for blaming you."

"It's . . . ," I say. And then pause as I realize something. "Cat talked to you? I thought . . . I mean, I didn't see her at the table with you when I was in line to buy lunch."

"She showed up after her daily make-out session with Noah."

"Noah?"

"Yeah. Noah, her boyfriend," Odelia says, tilting her head. "What's going on?"

I'm confused but this doesn't seem like the right time to bring up what I saw. "Nothing, I . . . forget it. Are *you* okay?" I ask.

"Well, I probably won't be allowed to leave my house, like, ever again, but yeah, I'm okay," she says, with a smile that doesn't quite reach her eyes.

"How did your dad find out you were at the dance?" I ask as we walk down the hall.

"My little sister let it slip."

Odelia apologizes again, and I tell her it's fine, even though

I'm not sure if it is. I haven't really had time to make sense of everything. We part ways, and I race to make it to Religion on time, sliding into my seat next to Mel.

"Did Odelia talk to you?" Mel asks as I settle in.

"Yeah."

"I guess it's my turn now. I'm sorry I didn't hear you out or make Odelia listen. I get really protective over her. Always have."

"It's fine," I say, although Mel's dismissal of me at the table this morning still stings.

At this point, all I want to do is go home, close the curtains, put on my headphones, and crawl into bed. Today was a roller coaster I don't want to ride anymore. It's like there's a gray rain cloud following me around, blocking out any joy that comes my way.

The worst part of all of this is that I don't have anyone to talk to. My friends and I may have made up on the surface, but my trust in them has shattered. It's going to take time to repair the damage, and I'm not even sure if I want to.

eleven

If life were a test, if I were being graded on my problem-solving skills, if I were forced to decode the hidden meaning in people's words—I'd be screwed. I thought letting people in would open me up to new experiences, specifically good ones. But I just keep getting knocked down.

My parents always seem to be trying to protect me and my siblings from something. For Ramsey, it's failure. For Annie, it's judgment, mostly from other Arabs who believe eldest daughters should behave a certain way. And for me—it's the world. What they should have been protecting me from was myself.

I can't be the person who follows her heart anymore. It just hurts too much.

After my whirlwind of a day, I faked a sore throat in hopes I could stay home from school. I don't think Mom bought it, but she let me skip anyway. When I attempted to persuade her into letting me stay home again, she babbled on about how breaks are okay, but the longer they last, the harder it is to go back.

She wasn't kidding. Walking into the school building on this gray Wednesday morning is like walking on floors covered in honey.

Mel and Odelia are hunched over together, doodling in a notebook, when I show up at the cafeteria table. Cat's on Noah's lap and has her face buried in his sweaty neck. The frosty reception they dealt me the last time I stood here makes me want to return home to Mom and her confusing pep talks.

Odelia glances up from the table and smiles. "Hey, stranger, where were you yesterday? You didn't respond to any of our messages."

"Food poisoning," I lie. My eyes are focused on a poster for the fall dance, still hanging on the wall behind our table.

"Lucky. I can't seem to shed the three pounds I've gained since September," Cat says as she removes her face from Noah's neck. She giggles when he pinches her stomach.

"You're perfect," he coos.

The rest of us groan in response.

"Are you feeling better now?" Mel asks.

"Yeah. I haven't puked in a while," I respond, keeping the lie going. Although Noah's comment made me throw up in my mouth a little bit.

I place my backpack on the table and sit across from Odelia, who continues to watch every move I make.

"I'm sorry," she mouths.

"It's okay," I mouth back.

She reaches for my hand and squeezes it. Part of me is glad she still feels bad about what happened, while the other part says I need to let it go and accept her apology. I just wish it were that easy.

Cat giggles again after Noah whispers in her ear.

"Noah," I say, looking directly at him.

"Yes?" he responds, peeling his gaze away from Cat.

"How are you?" I don't actually care how he is, but this is how most people start conversations.

His eyebrows knit together. "I'm fine, Jessie. How are you?"

"Existing," I reply. "So, what class do you have second period?" Mel and Odelia look up from the notebook, probably trying to figure out why I'm willingly engaging in a conversation with Noah, someone I've never uttered more than two sentences to before.

He brings Cat's hand to his lips and kisses it before answering. "Math."

"Then you're typically in the upper east hall when the lunch bell rings?"

"Typically, yes."

"Which means you're on the complete opposite side of where Cat's locker is located."

"What is this about?" Cat asks. Her tone is sharp and she's giving me a cut-it-out look. My pulse quickens the longer her gaze lingers. I didn't realize how scary she could be.

I look bravely into her eyes. "I went to our lockers at lunch on Monday, and thought I saw you, but then realized it couldn't be you since the person I thought was you was with another guy."

"Well then it definitely wasn't Cat," Noah replies.

"I had lunch with Mel and Odelia on Monday," Cat says. "Right, O?"

Odelia looks up from the notebook again. "What?"

"We had lunch together on Monday. Right?"

"Yeah." She nods. "We did."

"Mystery solved. We have to go." Cat gets off Noah's lap and pulls on his arm until he's standing. "We'll see you later," she says, giving me another look before grabbing her backpack and leading Noah out of the cafeteria.

"What was that about?" Mel asks.

119

"Nothing," I say, shaking off Mel's question. "I just wanted to see if Noah was capable of having a conversation that didn't involve gushing over Cat."

"You're such a little weirdo." Odelia laughs.

I hate lying but it's not worth it for me to get into this with them. Not right now anyway. I have other things to worry about. My fight with the girls isn't the only reason I asked to stay home yesterday. After what happened with Liv at the cafeteria table, I'm almost positive she'll have said something about me to get in Levi's head. It's happened before. I make friends with a person and everything seems to be going well, until someone who doesn't like me—for whatever reason—tells my new friend something about me. Something that probably isn't even true, but it's usually enough for them to ghost me.

Cat avoids eye contact with me all through Art. When Chelsie gets up from the table to wash her paintbrushes, I turn to Cat and whisper, "I saw you."

"You saw me what?" she asks.

"I saw you by your locker on Monday, kissing another guy."

Cat glances around the room before leaning in. "Jessie, you can't tell anyone."

"Who was it?" I ask, ignoring her plea.

"No one. Just drop it."

"I will not drop it."

She exhales loudly, appearing to fight back an eye roll. "His name's Jacob. He's a friend of Noah's. We hang out sometimes."

"Why don't you just break up with Noah if you like someone else?" I ask.

She laughs. "Who said I liked him?"

"I don't understand."

"We're just having fun."

"Don't you feel bad?" I ask.

"For what?" she replies, oblivious.

"For cheating on Noah. He worships the ground you walk on."

"He does." She grins. "And it's nice. It's also kind of stifling. But you're right, I'll end things with Jacob. Thanks, Jess. You're a good friend." She offers me a tight-lipped smile before walking to the sink with her dirty paintbrushes.

Cat's going to need something a lot stronger than dish soap to wash *her* sins away.

After barely making it through homeroom, my stomach does somersaults on the way to Science. It'll be fine if we can just see each other. I always make things bigger in my head. It's probably nothing.

When I turn the corner, Levi and Liv are together, and my heart sinks all the way to my Docs. Liv looks at me and smirks. My gaze meets the floor as I continue on, walking past the two of them before entering class. The bell rings and I glance at the door, watching as Liv stands on her tippy-toes. She wraps her arms around Levi's neck and he hugs her back.

As Levi makes his way into class, I jolt up so quickly that my chair makes a loud, scratching noise. Unable to face him, I head to the back of the room and ask a random student for the notes I missed. Something has shifted between us, and I'm not ready to deal with it.

"Don't say hello or anything," Levi quips as I sit down.

"Hello," I say through gritted teeth.

"Do you need yesterday's notes?" he asks.

I stare straight ahead. "No thanks, I'm fine."

Levi leans back in his chair and folds his arms. I hate him. Except I don't. But I wish I did.

My eyes glaze over as I pretend to pay attention to Ms. Muller.

Today's lesson may as well be in German. Levi sits only a few inches away, but the distance between us feels infinite.

I spend the entire period rehearsing what I'm going to say when the bell rings. I debate telling him what Liv said. I also think about confessing my feelings. There was a moment at the dance. He had to have felt it too.

When class is dismissed, Levi gets up and stands in front of my desk. "Are you mad at me?"

"No." I avert my eyes. It hurts too much to look at him.

He continues to stand there, glaring down, like he's waiting for me to change my answer. We're the only two people left in the classroom and my chest tightens. I don't know how to do this.

"Well, nice talking with you." Levi shakes his head and turns to leave.

I summon up all my courage, bring my palms to the desk, and use them to propel me up from the chair. "What do you see in that girl?"

Levi turns back and rests his books on Muller's desk before taking a few cautious steps toward me. "Liv? I don't know. She's fun to be around."

"Do you like her? I mean, of course you do. 'Cause she's popular, she has big boobs, and, more importantly, she's not me."

"Jessie. Why would you say that?"

"Because sometimes I say things without thinking. But you already know that. It's probably why . . . never mind."

Levi's eyes move away from mine and to his feet, which he shuffles from side to side. His shoulders slump down before he manages to say quietly, "Yeah. I like her."

His answer is so simple, but it cuts like a knife to my heart.

I straighten my posture and look him in the eyes. "Well, FYI, she was extremely rude to me on Monday. All because I sat at *her* cafeteria table."

Levi shakes his head in disbelief. "No way. She's not like that."

"Are you saying I'm lying?"

"No." Levi takes another step closer, and all it does is make me angrier. "I'm saying it's possible you misread her. Liv is very dry and sarcastic."

Deciding I've heard enough, I pick up my books to leave, but Levi places his hand on my arm.

"Since I have you here alone, there is something I need to say, before you hear it from someone else."

I swallow hard. This can't be good. Levi looks like he's about to tell me he ran over my dog.

"Liv and I have known each other for a while and we've gotten closer lately." Levi tugs at his sleeve, his eyes downcast. There's a crease on his forehead I've never noticed before. It's long and goes almost the whole way across his face. "Liv is my girlfriend."

My eyes beg him to stop talking, but he keeps going.

"I can see how things maybe got a little confusing between us and I didn't want you to get the wrong idea. I just think we make better friends," he says, further twisting the knife in my heart while simultaneously delivering my mangled dog to me.

I clear my throat and try to swallow again but can't. "No . . . yeah . . . no. That's great," I say, with a forced grin on my face. "I . . . I have to go. I have to be somewhere."

I walk past Levi to exit the classroom. Our shoulders brush, making everything he said hurt so much more. I need to make it to the bathroom before falling apart. I won't let him see me cry.

The bathroom door slams shut behind me and I collapse into a ball of tears on the peach-tiled floor. How could this be happening? We were so close. We almost kissed less than a week ago. Now he's dating another girl. A girl who hates me. A girl I hate even more. I'm such a fool for thinking something would ever happen between the two of us. How could I let myself believe, even for a second, that I had a chance with someone like Levi? No one wants to date the autistic girl. Especially not Levi Walsh.

If life is a test, I've failed.

Twelve

Wake up, go to school, come home, do homework, move food around my plate, then go to bed. Rinse and repeat. Ever since Levi so graciously announced his relationship status to me two days ago, I've been sneaking my headphones to school and wearing them anytime I'm not in class. As for Levi, he doesn't ask for help with Science anymore. He clearly doesn't need me.

I'm like a disposable camera someone forgot to develop, left behind, the memories gone with them.

There's one more class to get through before I can go home and wallow in my bed for the weekend. This has seriously been the longest seven days of my life! Fiona Apple's husky voice wails into my headphones as I drag my feet to Religion. Her tortured words fill the empty parts of my soul, and I'm so lost in the lyrics, I collide with someone turning the corner.

"Sorry," I say, rubbing my forehead with my palm. When my eyes finally focus, Griffin is there. I bring my headphones down.

"Are you alright?" he asks.

"Yeah. Fine." I bend down to pick up my books and loose pages.

"What're you listening to?" Griffin matches my pose and helps me sort through our mixed-up belongings.

"Just some depressing music. Because I'm depressed."

He laughs but quickly reins it in. "What's wrong?"

"Levi is dating Liv," I blurt.

He forces a smile as we stand. "Oh. I see. Well, for some reason he seems to like her."

"The heart wants what the heart wants. Is that how the old saying goes?" I ask, rolling my eyes.

"And what does *your* heart want?" Griffin raises a brow. Before I can stammer out a response, he continues. "You don't have to tell me. I think I know. Anyway, if you ask me, he made the wrong decision."

I stare at Griffin while repeating his words in my head. Did he just imply there was a choice to be made? What if my almost-kiss with Levi hadn't been interrupted the night of the dance? Would he and I be together now?

Griffin waves his hand in front of my face to get my attention. "Hey, don't sweat it. He'll see her true colors soon enough."

"Maybe." But probably not.

"You should come to the drama club meeting after school. We're doing scenes from Shakespeare."

"I thought that meeting was members only," I say.

"It is, but I happen to know Gwen Calderon is out sick today. They'll need someone to stand in for her."

"I don't know. Feels a little morally gray to take advantage of someone's illness."

"You'd only be helping the drama club, and it would be another opportunity for Mrs. Elliott to notice your brilliance."

"Brilliance? That's a stretch. You've seen me do a few tableaux."

"You tableau very well," Griffin says, like a politician seeking a vote.

"Ah yes, it was especially challenging pretending to sit on an invisible chair while eating an invisible dinner during the *Last Supper* tableau. I almost lost my balance there for a second."

"But you didn't. You got through all of them like a pro."

"Yeah, well, it was fun but a one-time thing," I say, reminding Griffin of Mrs. Elliott's rules. "Besides, I've been kind of a downer lately."

"Perfect. *Hamlet* is depressing as hell. You'll fit right in."

"You're not going to take no for an answer, are you?" I ask, fighting back the first smile that's come to me in days.

"Why should I? I have made it my personal goal to get you into drama club."

"But . . ."

"I know, the rules. Gotta say, I'm kind of surprised you're such a stickler for them."

My cheeks burn and I look away. "I just find it helpful to have guidelines, you know? I don't always," I pause and swallow, "get people? Or how things work, like, on a social level. So I find rules kind of comforting." I need to stop talking before I confess my autism to Griffin.

"You're a type A," he says.

Something like that.

"I get it." He nods. "I am too. So, I'll meet you in the atrium after school?"

"I have to check with my parents first."

He passes me his cell. "Hurry. The bell's gonna ring."

I take Griffin's phone and call Mom. After she spends the first minute grilling me over who "G. Duffy" is, she agrees to let me stay for the meeting. I'm excited. I'm nervous, too, but excited. It's kind of nice having plans that don't revolve around me sulking over Levi Walsh, however brief the reprieve may be.

⟶

The plan was to stew in my misery all weekend, and I mostly

stuck to it. I also couldn't keep myself from grinning whenever I thought about Friday's drama club meeting. It was so fun playing different roles and participating in various scenes. It made me even more pumped for next year, but also sad I have to wait so long.

And now it's Monday again.

There used to be a time when I couldn't wait for Mondays. That was when two days away from Levi felt like an eternity. This morning, I ignore my mother's repeated attempts to wake me, turning my lights off and closing the door every time she walks away.

Mom storms into my room again after I've finally settled into a nice sleep. "Jessie. Get up. It's late. Yalla! Yalla!" She reaches over my bed and rips open the curtains. When I try to hide under my pillow, she yanks it and my warm blanket away. "Jessie, the bus comes in ten minutes. Hurry up."

She stands by the foot of my bed until I sit up. She already smells like onions and garlic.

A few minutes later, I'm in the foyer, bent over as I try to stuff everything into my backpack. A day-old croissant hangs out of my mouth.

Annie gives me a once-over and shakes her head. "You're not going to school like that, are you?"

I scowl at her. "I woke up five minutes ago." The fact is, part of me wants to look as bad as I feel. And I feel pretty bad.

On the bus, I sink into a seat and close my eyes, hoping to squeeze in a couple of extra minutes of sleep.

Walking into school, I catch a glimpse of my frightening reflection and decide to go to the bathroom to straighten myself out. Liv walks in while I'm in the middle of taming my frizzy hair with water. Her eyes travel up and down my body and she chuckles to herself before applying lip gloss in front of the mirror.

Olivia French isn't a stunner—in my totally unbiased

opinion—but her hair is always perfectly styled, and she somehow manages to make the school uniform look good. She wears the right boots, carries the coolest backpack, and knows how to work with what she has. Liv also possesses something I severely lack and am in desperate need of: confidence.

I manage to exit the bathroom without having to interact with her. On my way to meet the girls, I run into Griffin. Figures. The day when I don't want to see anyone, I see everyone.

"Jessie K., how was your weekend?" he asks in a tone that is way too cheerful for a Monday morning.

"It sucked."

Griffin holds back a laugh. "Well, I have some news that might make you happy. I just ran into Mrs. Elliott, and she told me to thank you for coming to Friday's meeting. She said you picked up on the scenes quickly, and she thinks you have real stage presence. She also said you're welcome to attend our other meetings, even if it means just observing sometimes."

"You're lying."

Griffin straightens and makes the sign of the cross. "Honest to God."

"Did she say it like that, that I had 'real stage presence'? Or just 'stage presence'?"

He clears his throat. "That Jessie Kassis," he says in a woman's voice, "can light up an entire room with her big smile and bright eyes."

"So then she didn't say I had real stage presence?"

Griffin runs a hand over his face, smothering another laugh. "You're pretty funny, you know that?"

I shrug. "I'm glad someone tolerates me."

Griffin's smile falters. He looks at me, and it's like there's a magnetic force pulling my eyes to his. "Hey. I more than tolerate you."

For a moment, I get lost in the golden flecks of his irises. I should say something back. Something to fill the silence. But I never know how to respond when someone says something nice to me. Especially boys.

The bell rings, thankfully saving me from having to say words.

"I'll see you later," Griffin says with a smile. I nod, remaining frozen in the atrium, as I watch him walk away.

I spend the next week trying my best to avoid Levi—and Liv. She's like a scab that won't heal. I walk into class as the bell rings and leave immediately once we're dismissed. I'm doing a good enough job of pretending I don't care, but the whole situation continues to eat away at me, little by little.

I love everything about Levi: the way his nose crinkles when he's confused, how his hair never stays tucked behind his ears, and especially the way he looks at me. Note: *used to* look at me.

"Halloween is on Monday and we still haven't discussed costumes." Odelia focuses her attention on me at the cafeteria table. Cat's off with Noah again. At least that's what she told the others. "I happen to know this is your favorite holiday, Jessie."

"Let's all dress up as, like, the same thing," Mel says with a twinkle in her eyes. She takes a bite of my abandoned pizza.

"People will make fun of us," I reply, sounding almost as pathetic as I look.

Odelia slides her lunch tray away and folds her arms onto the table. "Are you still pissed at me?"

"No," I answer before taking a sip of my water.

"Then why have you been so down lately?" Odelia asks.

"I haven't," I protest.

"You have, Jess. You've been quiet and kind of distant. Does this have something to do with Levi?" Mel asks, peering into my eyes. "You know you can tell us anything, right?"

A long silence descends as I have an internal debate over what to say or not to say.

"We're your friends," Mel reminds me. "Would it help if we told you a secret about ourselves?"

Odelia sits up straight. "Great idea. I'll go first." She pauses and looks around the table before leaning in. "I cut Honors English last week and made out with Evan Brown in the back of his car."

"Evan Brown? Which one is he?" I ask Mel, as if she's Odelia's spokesperson.

"He's in eleventh grade. He's got crunchy hair and plays sports," Mel answers.

"His hair is gelled, and he plays basketball and rugby," Odelia clarifies, while elbowing Mel.

"Okay, my turn," Mel says, without skipping a beat. "I've been talking to someone. He's older."

"How much older?" I ask.

She covers her face with her hands. "He's nineteen."

Eww.

"Did you know about this?" I ask Odelia.

"News to me."

"I met him at the hockey rink. He plays in a men's league on Saturdays and buys a lime Gatorade from me after every game. His name is Richard. He's got black hair and the bluest eyes I've ever seen."

She's clearly never looked into Levi's eyes.

"*Men's league,*" I repeat. "Does he know how old you are?"

Mel laughs. "Yes, Jessie."

"So, what do you call him? Richard? Rich? Dick?"

Odelia spits her water out at the last one.

"Jessie!" Mel smiles as she pinches my arm.

"I'm sorry. If you're happy, I'm happy," I say, even though I don't mean it.

"Ok, funny guy," Mel says. "It's your turn."

I try to think up an excuse to get out of telling them what happened, but when I compare my secrets to theirs, well . . . mine sound juvenile, at best. So I start from the dance and share how Levi and I almost kissed. Then I tell them how Levi comforted me at the pond that day before inviting me to lunch. I end with the news that he and Liv are dating.

"He's a fool," Odelia says.

"Agree." Mel nods. "He'll regret his decision."

"Yes." Odelia smiles. "Jessie, you need to make Levi regret choosing that purple-haired vixen over you."

"How?" I ask. "And it's less purple, more violet."

"By being a little less adorable and leaning into your sultry Middle-Eastern roots."

I bark out a laugh. "You're funny," I say to Odelia.

"Look, you have two options here: keep fighting for Levi, or move on."

Odelia's words are like a light switch, helping me see the truth of the situation. What's done is done. Levi chose Liv, and I need to accept it.

Goal #9: Get over Levi Walsh.

After some terrible suggestions from Mel, the three of us agree to go as teenage vampires from the nineties for Halloween—an idea inspired by my love of *Buffy the Vampire Slayer*.

Over the weekend, I piece together my "costume." I've chosen a maroon slip dress, black T-shirt, and dark stockings, which I'll pair with my Docs. To finish it off, I'll throw a flannel shirt on top, but this time, leave it unbuttoned. A surge of excitement races through my veins at the thought of grabbing Levi's attention.

~~Goal #9: Get over Levi Walsh.~~

I guess I still have some fight left in me.

On the bus Monday morning, I'm one of only a handful of students who dressed up. Maybe this wasn't such a good idea. Of course, I went all the way with my costume. I woke up early and put my hair into a tight bun so my neck would be exposed to showcase the vampire bite marks I drew. Then I dowsed my face with Mom's white body powder and had her line my eyes with black liquid liner.

When I arrive at school, I'm relieved to see lots of people actually in costume. Even teachers.

"You look spectacular!" Mel practically screams as I approach our table.

Mel and Odelia beg me to duplicate the bite marks on their necks. Cat stands over us with a hand on her hip, in her very original sexy cat costume. She sighs repeatedly as she watches me draw fake drops of blood on Mel and Odelia's collarbones.

After homeroom, I mentally prepare to face Levi and Liv. They've made a habit of hanging out in front of Science, which makes timing my entrance tricky. I can almost hear her cackle at the sight of my costume while simultaneously fawning over Levi.

My heart is in my throat the entire walk to class. Relief washes over me as I turn the corner to find Levi with Griffin.

"Jessie?" Levi's eyes scan my costume. "What are you supposed to be?"

Not exactly the response I had hoped for.

"I'm a vampire," I say, grateful the white powder disguises the blush I feel burning through my cheeks.

"The bite marks are a nice touch," Griffin says. "Was this inspired by *Buffy*?"

"Maybe," I reply, coyly.

Levi looks between me and Griffin. He opens his mouth to say something but Griffin's words come out faster.

"Team Angel or Team Spike? You must pick one."

"No! It's impossible," I say, trying very hard to fight the urge to explain how loaded a question that actually is.

"I'll let it slide, for now. But I'm Team Spike, all the way."

"Hmm." I nod. "That's very telling. So, what are you supposed to be: boy who forgot it was Halloween? Or do you just really love the school uniform?"

"Shut up." He laughs. "I got back from New York City late last night. My dad had a meeting on Friday and I tagged along. Totally forgot what today was."

"First you transfer out of Art, then you go to New York City—somewhere I'm dying to go. You're making it very hard for me to like you," I say.

"I guess I'll just have to try harder." Griffin smiles, and I can't help but smile back. "I see you decided not to go with fangs."

"I tried. I got some dollar-store fakies but they didn't fit right and made me drool a lot. My teeth must be too big or something."

"Nah. Your teeth are perfect," Griffin responds.

Levi clears his throat. "You should get going," he says to Griffin. "The bell is about to ring."

Griffin gives Levi a weird look. "Okay, Mr. Studious," he says with a nod before taking off.

Levi extends an arm, suggesting I walk into the classroom first. Studious and chivalrous.

"Where's your costume?" I ask him as we take our seats.

"Liv wanted us to go as a couple from the eighties, but

when I tried her dad's clothes on, I looked kind of sleazy. So we scrapped the whole idea."

Huh. Levi's been inside Liv's house. I guess that means he's met her parents. He's probably also seen her bedroom. I wonder if they've had sex. The visual alone makes me want to hurl. Even if they haven't, the fact that Liv and Levi don't have to sneak around serves as another giant reminder that Levi and I don't make sense. If we dated, we'd have to hide our relationship from my parents, and I'm not hot enough for any guy to be willing to put up with that.

When the dismissal bell rings, I take my time packing up. Maybe Levi will say something else to me. It doesn't even matter what.

"Turns out Jessie Kassis has decent legs," Jason Rivers says, standing in front of my desk. We've been in this class together for two months, and this is the moment he decides to remember who I am?

Daniel Branson, Jason's best friend since kindergarten, sidles up next to him and smirks. "Not bad. Not great, but not bad."

"I don't usually go for your kind, but maybe if you were to keep the white powder on your face, I'd be willing to make an exception," Jason says as he elbows Daniel.

"Yeah, but it still doesn't hide the weird." They both laugh like their ancestors—obnoxious, rich, white guys.

Before I can reply to the bros, Levi steps in front of me and puffs his chest toward them, in an almost primal way.

"Are guys still pulling this?" he asks.

Daniel exchanges a glance with Jason. "Pulling what?"

"The whole 'I'm gonna be a dick to this girl and then when I ask her out she'll be so flattered she'll say yes' thing."

"We didn't ask her out," Jason says.

"She wishes," Daniel mutters under his breath.

"Her name is Jessie, and *you* fucking wish."

Jason shakes his head. "We were just messing around. Jessie knows that. We went to elementary school together. Right, Jess?"

"Don't address her." Levi takes another step until his face is inches away from Jason's. "Don't try to bring her down to your level. It'll never happen. She's so much better than you'll ever be, and you know it."

Jason and Daniel freeze up at Levi's words. To be honest, so do I.

"Sorry," Jason finally says.

"Yeah, sorry." They clear their throats before making a swift exit, leaving me and Levi in the Science room alone—again.

"Thanks, but I could have handled those two. They're mostly harmless," I say, in an attempt to underplay what happened.

"I didn't like how they spoke to you."

"It's what they do." I shrug. "They comment on my looks, then circle it back to something about me being weird or Palestinian. I've gotten used to it."

"You shouldn't have to get used to that, Jessie."

I raise my eyes to find his peering into mine, and I'm suddenly overcome with the urge to tell him how much I've missed him.

"Levi." A shrill voice from the hall interrupts the first real interaction Levi and I have had in weeks. "Let's go," Liv demands.

As Levi turns to leave, he stops and faces me. "For what it's worth, I think you make a cute vampire, but I like you better without the makeup."

He smiles, then walks out the door, leaving me behind. But it doesn't matter. It doesn't even matter that he's with Liv. I know his heart belongs to me. I just need to find a way to convince him of it.

I head to the cafeteria, ready to spill the details of what

happened to the girls. When I get to our table, Cat is sobbing hysterically.

"Noah broke up with Cat," Mel whispers as I take my seat next to her.

"Why?" I ask, looking right at Cat.

Mel appears to fight back a smile as Odelia wipes Cat's tears.

"That's kind of an insensitive question, Jessie," Cat says.

"Well, there must be a reason," I respond, not backing down.

She sniffles and sits up straight in her seat. "Yeah. The reason is he left me for someone else."

"Who?" I ask, calling her bluff. My guess is he found out she was cheating and dumped her ass, but Cat would never admit to that. Otherwise, no one would feel sorry for her.

"I didn't ask," she bites back.

"Noah is a waste of space," Odelia says, removing tear-soaked strands of hair from Cat's face. "Forget about him. You'll find someone better in no time."

"Let's start now," Cat says, before wiping away her remaining tears and rising from the table.

"You girls coming?" Odelia asks.

"No," Mel and I say, as if on cue.

The two of them spend the rest of lunch walking laps around the cafeteria, searching for Cat's next victim. I decide to tell Mel about Cat cheating on Noah. Mel doesn't seem the least bit surprised. She confesses that she's not all that fond of Cat, but puts up with her because Odelia seems to really like her. Mel says it's probably better we don't tell Odelia about what we know. She says it makes things "less messy."

I don't love keeping secrets but maybe this is how things operate within a friend group. As much as I wanted this, life was a lot easier when it was just me, myself, and I.

THIRTEEN

It's been almost two weeks since Halloween, and one of us has made great strides in advancing her romantic status . . . and it isn't Cat. Not that she hasn't tried. She's been batting her lashes at every male who crosses her radar. She just hasn't managed to sucker one in yet.

"Have you two heard from Odelia?" Cat asks Mel and me during a tech club lunch meeting for the Remembrance Day assembly. I'm in charge of the projector and PowerPoint presentation, which feels like a big responsibility.

"I think she's with Evan," I say, making sure the link to the presentation is on the desktop. Cat and Mel spent the meeting setting up chairs for tomorrow. They're currently perched on a couple while they wait for me to finish.

"Again?" Cat asks. "They're not even dating. Why are they always together?"

Mel shifts to face Cat. "Do I really need to explain this to you?"

"So what? They make out once in a while. Doesn't mean they're serious," Cat replies.

"I don't know," I say. "Odelia seems to really like Evan. I haven't heard her talk about any other guy in weeks."

"You think?" Mel asks. "He's a big-time bro."

"I think he's cute," Cat says, twirling a lock of her long red hair around her finger. She watches Noah on the makeshift stage as he shows a tenth-grader how to adjust the microphone.

Mel turns her gaze to me and I half shrug in defeat.

"I'm going to find them." Cat gets up quickly and walks away.

I twist in my chair to face Mel. "So what's new with you? You haven't mentioned Dick lately."

"It's Richard." Mel laughs, kicking my foot with hers. "It's a family name."

It's an old man's name.

"And I don't talk to you about him because I know you don't approve."

"It's not that I don't approve. I was just surprised at how old he was," I say, in an attempt to cover up my real feelings.

I don't know why Mel is so hung up on Richard/Dick. There are lots of cute guys at our school. The whole situation grosses me out, but I'm trying to be supportive. Truth is, if I told her how I really felt, she'd probably unfriend me.

"There's not much to tell," she says, tucking her hands into her sleeves. "We text, and he drives me home sometimes after work. I don't know. It's like he's afraid to make a move or something."

"Maybe he doesn't know you like him back. I've heard guys can be a bit slow to catch on."

A corner of Mel's mouth lifts. "Maybe you're right."

Before I have a chance to open up to her about Levi, the bell rings.

What would I even say? Levi and I have been stuck in neutral for weeks. We're back to talking to each other in Science, but the conversations only leave me wanting more. Sometimes our legs accidentally touch under the desk and Levi leaves his pressed against mine. It's enough to keep me holding onto my frayed thread of hope, even if things like that only happen within the confines of our classroom.

⟋

Mid-November, and midterms are next week. To be honest, they're a welcome distraction from my nonexistent love life. At this point, my grades are the only thing I can control. Odelia and Mel are on a class trip today, which means I can get an extra study session in at the library. I should probably tell Cat I'm not meeting her for lunch. Or not. She'll be fine without me. She's always going on about knowing everyone. This will give her the opportunity to put that theory to the test.

After a few minutes of writing out study notes, my hand cramps up. I decide it'll be faster and way less painful if I make copies of my existing notes and highlight the important stuff. On my way to the photocopier, a familiar giggle from behind one of the bookshelves catches my attention. I spread some books apart to sneak a peek and find Annie kissing her secret boyfriend. Through some investigative work (Annie's yearbook) I found out his name is Xavier Jones. He's on the hockey, rugby, and basketball teams, sits on Student Council, and is an honor roll student. He's perfect except for one thing: he's not an Arab.

"Hey, creeper," a voice from behind whispers.

I jump and turn to see Griffin squinting at me with a smirk on his face.

"Who are we spying on?" he asks.

"No one. I dropped my money for the copier."

I pretend to pick up some change and walk over to the machine. Griffin follows close behind.

"Can I help you?" I ask, holding in a smile.

"Nope." Griffin watches as I make copies.

When I'm done, he follows me back to where I'm working and sits across from me. He rests his elbows on the table and leans in. "What are we studying for?"

"Science. Need some help?" I ask.

"Nah, got a 94 in that class. Muller loves me," Griffin says.

"I'm currently averaging a 95," I say, raising my brows obnoxiously.

"Then why don't you ask Levi if he'd like some private tutoring?"

"Your friend Levi doesn't know I exist outside of class," I say.

Griffin's smile falters. "I happen to know that's not true."

"Well, we haven't spoken much since he started dating Olivia French."

He laughs. "No one has spoken much to Levi since he started dating her."

I stare at the ceiling, then directly at Griffin, ignoring the little voice in my head telling me to keep my thoughts to myself. "How could he willingly choose to spend time with someone like her? She's not nice at all, and not even that pretty. Okay, like, maybe a little, but not enough to compensate for that personality. Any time we've interacted she's been rude and smarmy and mean."

Griffin doesn't flinch as he listens to me ramble on about the other girl in Levi's life. "Liv thinks she's the queen bee of our school. My guess is she sensed something was brewing between the two of you and didn't like it." Griffin pauses, then leans in even further. "Levi's had a thing for Liv since last year, so, like, you can't really blame him for going after his crush, you know?"

Unfortunately, I do know.

"Can I ask you a question? And this stays between the two of us." My eyes survey the library before continuing. "Did Levi ever tell you how he felt about me?" I instantly cover my face with my hands, wishing I could take back those words.

Griffin places his hands over mine and brings them down. "Do you honestly not know?"

I shake my head and run my fingers over the $N + F$ carved into the table.

"You didn't imagine it. Levi was definitely into you. Probably still is."

"But he said he just wants to be friends," I tell Griffin, in a voice that comes out much whinier than I was expecting.

"Levi needs to get Liv out of his system. When he does, he'll find his way back to you. That is," he says, a smile tugging at his lips, "unless you decide to move on, which I personally think you should do."

That's easier said than done. If I could quit my feelings for Levi, I would have done so a long time ago. It lasted as a goal in my journal for 2.5 seconds. I'd probably wait forever for him, but I can't admit that to Griffin. I have a hard enough time admitting it to myself.

I fold my arms over the table and bury my head in them. "I should have gone to an all-girls school."

"But then you would have never met me."

I look up to see Griffin with a silly grin on his face, and it makes me smile.

"I hate to see you like this," he says.

"Like what? Pathetic?"

He laughs. "No. Not pathetic. I guess I just . . ." He pauses, scratching at the back of his head.

"Just what?" I ask.

"Just want you to let yourself be happy. Outside of Levi."

"I'm trying." I swallow while straightening my study sheets.

"Good. 'Cause there are other things out there waiting for you. Just make sure you're not tying someone else's shoelace when it passes by."

"What's that supposed to mean?" I ask, suppressing a giggle.

He pinches the bridge of his nose, holding back another laugh. "I'm not sure. It sounded better in my head."

I like Griffin. He's so easy to talk to. Sometimes I think he's *too* easy to talk to. Even when I end up spilling my guts to him, he's never judgey. The thing is, he knows more about my relationship with Levi than my friends do. It probably helps that he bothers to ask how I'm doing—something the girls rarely ever do. And I kind of miss seeing him in class every morning, but it's like our dynamic has leveled up since he transferred out. Like we're almost friends or something.

Goal #9 (revised): Make Griffin Duffy my first male friend.

This seems like an easy one. I'd say we're nearly there.

FOURTEEN

It's day three of a four-day reprieve from school. Midterms are over and I'm feeling confident I've maintained my low-nineties average. Would be higher if it weren't for my B in Phys Ed dragging me down. My only goal for the rest of this weekend is to become one with the couch. I've already made my rounds in individual DMs with Odelia, Mel, and Cat and spent each of those conversations discussing their issues: Odelia's burgeoning relationship with Evan, Cat moping about Noah and confessing she has a crush on Evan, and Mel debating how to take things to the next level with Richard/Dick.

It would be nice if someone bothered to ask how I was doing before diving into their problems. Once again, a wall has formed around me, brick by brick. But this time, it's stronger.

The girls don't know that Griffin and I studied together almost every day leading up to midterms. They also don't know that he's invited me to a total of three drama club meetings, and that I've gotten to participate in all of them. And they haven't asked for updates on the Levi situation. I thought opening up about Levi would bring us closer, yet they continue to be wrapped up in their own issues. And their problems are starting to suffocate me.

Annie comes in and plops down on the other couch. "What are you watching?"

I turn back and shrug. "Nothing. Was thinking of starting a movie."

"*Empire Records* again?" she asks.

"Probably."

"Are you ever going to join the rest of us who live in this century?"

"Movies and music were better in the nineties," I say.

"You mean the good ol' days?" She laughs. "You're such a grandpa." Annie settles into the couch as the opening credits roll. "A girl from my Law class is coming by tonight. We want to get a head start on our case project. Mom and Dad are going to another one of their church parties."

I adjust the cushion on the couch before lying back down. "That's fine. I don't plan on leaving this couch."

"Well, you can join us for dinner. We're getting Chinese takeout."

"Oh, can you order me—"

"E32. Rice noodles with sliced beef and vegetables. I know, Jessie. You get the same thing every time."

"I know what I like," I say.

"That you do."

My sister sits through the whole movie with me, laughing at all the same parts I do, and it's the most time we've spent together in ages. She returns to her room once the movie is over.

When the time comes for my parents to leave, Mom gives me the same spiel she always does about not making a mess and listening to Annie, like I'm five. My mother will take any opportunity she can to dress up and go out. Dad is usually a good sport about it. While it takes Mom hours to get ready, Dad jumps in the shower twenty minutes before they leave and comes out looking just as good.

Almost as soon as my parents walk out the front door, Ramsey comes up from the basement and sits next to me on the couch.

"What are we doing tonight?" he asks with a grin.

"Right. As if you'd actually spend a Saturday night at home with the peasants."

He taps my knee with his. "Uh-oh, what's wrong?"

"What's wrong is you're taking up all the space on the couch," I snap, not sure why I'm spewing my frustrations at my brother.

"Hey, I'm Team Jessie, but when you get moody like this, you're impossible. Your autism isn't an excuse to be rude."

"Sorry," I say, rocking back and forth slightly.

Ramsey places a hand on my back and it helps calm me down. "Life treating you hard?"

"It's like, one minute I'm flying high, and the next . . . I hate everyone."

Ramsey laughs. "Relatable."

"Really?" I ask, turning to face him.

"Sure. The ups and downs are not an autism thing, Jess. It's a life thing. Is it, maybe, a boy thing?"

I squeeze my eyes shut like I did when I was in second grade and Ramsey found out I had a crush on his best friend, Charlie.

"It's totally a boy thing," he says, tickling my side. "Do I need to get my knuckles bloody? 'Cause I would, for you. But these hands are pretty much how I make a living these days."

"How's that going? Working with Dad," I ask, in an attempt to change the subject.

He shrugs. "Not bad. But he gets on my ass for any mistakes I make, even tiny ones. And every day at lunch, like clockwork, he tries to change my mind about the culinary program. At least he doesn't seem as disappointed in me anymore." Ramsey forces a smile, and there appears to be hope in his eyes—something

I haven't seen in a while. "Oh, you're slick, shifting gears like that." We both laugh.

"Is there something I can do to help?" he asks in earnest.

"I could always use more magazines," I say with wide eyes.

"You got it. Just stay the course, Jess. Things have a way of working out." He gets up and ruffles my hair before disappearing back into the dude den.

A few minutes later, I'm in the kitchen, rummaging the cupboards for snacks, when the doorbell rings. I ignore the first two rings, assuming Annie will answer it.

"Would you get that?" Annie yells from the upstairs bathroom.

I stumble over to the door with my arms so full of chip bags and boxes of cookies that I barely manage to turn the knob.

Levi's sister smiles at me from our front porch before letting herself in. "Jessie, right? I'm Lucy. We met at the party."

I stand there, speechless.

"Hey, Lucy," Annie says as she skips down the stairs. "Let's go to the kitchen."

As I'm closing the door with my back, arms still full of food, my reflection in the hallway mirror startles me. I'm dressed in old sweats and my hair is in a messy topknot. Why am I always a train wreck when I talk to that girl?

I drop the snacks by the stairs and run up to my bedroom, where I grab my journal from behind my desk. I scribble down nonsensical sentences about Levi's sister being in our house. *She remembered me. She smiled and let herself in, as if we're old-timey friends. How am I supposed to act or think with a Walsh under my roof?*

After I'm done barfing my feelings into my journal, I brush out my tangles and put on a pair of jeans and a clean sweatshirt. I spend the rest of the time holed up in the family room, pretending to watch TV while eavesdropping on Annie and Lucy's conversations. When the food arrives, I sit across from Lucy at the kitchen table, distracted by her resemblance to Levi. It's uncanny. Except his eyes are a brighter shade of blue.

"Annie, did you know your sister and my little brother are friends?" Lucy asks as she uses chopsticks to pick up a piece of sweet-and-sour pork.

Her use of the word "friends" causes me to choke on my water. "We're in the same class, that's all."

Lucy smiles so wide that all her perfect white teeth show. "Levi tells me you're helping him get through Science."

"I was," I say, stabbing a thin slice of beef with my fork. "But he doesn't need my help anymore." Even I can hear the hurt in my voice. Annie asks Lucy a question regarding their assignment and it puts an end to our conversation about Levi.

After dinner, and a movie—which I watch in a daze—I work on tidying the family room. Lucy walks in with her things and sits on top of a cushion I fluffed seconds earlier.

"Just waiting for my ride."

I paint on a smile while secretly cringing at the cushion being squished under her butt.

Lucy stares at me, her eyebrows knitted together. "My brother's miserable."

"What do you . . . Levi?"

"He's not happy with Liv," she goes on to say.

I stand there, mid-blanket-fold, frozen.

"He likes *you*," Lucy continues.

What are these words coming out of Levi's sister's mouth? He likes *me*? Barely able to stand, I put the blanket down and sit next to her on the couch. I should be thrilled. Instead, I'm one blink away from tears streaming down.

Lucy places her hand on top of mine. "You like him too, don't you?"

I nod with my eyes downcast.

"He'll come around. I'm sure of it," she says.

I wish I could believe her.

Lucy excuses herself to the powder room and I rise from the couch to finish tidying up, immediately re-fluffing the cushion she sat on. Someone knocks at the front door. Annie has disappeared upstairs, which leaves me to answer it.

I pull myself together, wiping away the few tears that managed to escape, and turn the knob.

Levi stands across from me. "Jessie?"

Oh, that Lucy's a sneaky one.

"Come in," I say, my voice cracking. "Lucy's in the bathroom."

Levi steps inside to wait. I pull at my sleeves, my knees about to buckle beneath me. Levi is a staircase away from my bedroom. The bedroom where I have spent countless hours fantasizing about him. About us.

His gaze wanders around my house. He nods repeatedly, to nothing, and places both hands in his pockets.

"Man, our sisters are nerds. Who does homework on a Saturday night?" He laughs, then shifts from one foot to the other.

Lucy steps out of the powder room, grinning.

"Luce, Dad's waiting outside. Tell him I'll be right there."

Levi waits for Lucy to leave and closes the door behind her. When he turns around, there's a familiar look in his eyes. *God, those eyes.* I'd give up music for them. He takes a step toward me and gently tugs on my sweatshirt, bringing my body closer to his. My heart is beating so fast I'm afraid it may burst out of my chest.

Levi bites down on his lip. "Hi."

I swallow before meeting his gaze. "Hi."

Just as Levi begins the descent to my lips, the sound of the garage opener jolts us apart. *Seriously?*

"That's my parents. You'd better go."

The color red creeps up Levi's cheeks. I'm not sure I've seen him blush before. Visions of locking my parents out of their own house and tackling Levi to the ground tempt me, but I force those thoughts away.

"See you Monday," Levi says.

"See you Monday," I reply, unable to contain my smile. I close the front door behind him just as Mom walks through the garage entrance.

"Whose car is that outside?" she asks, removing her coat.

"Annie's friend. She just left." My heart beats overtime while every inch of my body is on fire.

I run upstairs to catch a glimpse of Levi out the bathroom window, but his dad has already driven away. I lean up against the counter and run my fingers over my lips. That's the second time Levi has tried to kiss me. Maybe it's true what they say, and the third time will be the charm.

~

A light dusting of snow covers the ground Monday morning. Without even realizing it, I'm tracing an *L* in the white powder with my feet while I wait for the bus to arrive. I've been grinning like a fool nonstop since Saturday night. Levi and Liv must have broken up. Why else would he have almost kissed me?

On my way to meet the girls in the cafeteria, I overhear multiple conversations about our football team. Apparently, they qualified to play for the division title this Friday against our rival school. Whatever that means. I don't follow sports, and I'm not even sure what the point of football is, but I know attendance is pretty much mandatory whenever we face off against Varley High.

"Jessie," Odelia yells as I approach the three of them. "Where the hell have you been?"

"Just hanging out with my family," I say, pulling out a chair. I took yesterday off from the group chat for the sake of my mental health.

Odelia nudges Mel out of her daydream. "Do you want to fill Jessie in on your weekend festivities?"

Mel doesn't respond. Her eyes are still glazed over.

"If you're not going to say it, then I will." Odelia stares at me, eyes wide. "Mel finally sucked face with Richard!"

Mel turns her gaze back to us. "Odelia!"

"Sorry, I couldn't help myself. I'll leave you to tell Jessie all the sordid details. I'm going to find Evan. Toodles," Odelia sings as she takes off.

I tug on Mel's sleeve. "So . . . what happened?"

Cat stands and puts her backpack on. "I've already heard this story. I'll see you in homeroom."

Mel's eyes narrow as she watches Cat walk away. She turns to face me. "Well, Richard drove me home after my shift Saturday. My parents were out so he parked in the driveway and we talked for a bit. He admitted he liked me but wasn't sure if I felt the same." Mel's cheeks turn bright red. "I told him I liked him, too. Then he asked if it was okay to kiss me."

I force out a smile. "How was it?"

"I'll tell you something, Richard definitely doesn't kiss like a fifteen-year-old boy."

Yeah. 'Cause he's a man. A real, old, gross, old man.

151

In Art, Cat's already at work on our latest assignment. I take my seat next to her.

"I was thinking about our conversation over the weekend. The one about Evan," she says, glancing up from her sketchbook. "Odelia can have him. For now. We'll see how long they last."

New goal. What am I at now? Ten?

Goal #10: Keep Cat away from Evan.

"We need to find you a new love interest," I say.

"That's a great idea," Cat responds, her big, brown eyes beaming.

"There will be lots of guys at the football game Friday. We can start there. Let's all go and make it a girls' night," I say.

"Sounds fun," Cat replies.

When class is over, I pack up and head to Science. This is the moment I've waited all weekend for. Just as I'm imagining my blissful reunion with Levi, the one where he tells me things are over with Liv, the wind is taken out of my sails. With a baseball bat covered in spikes. Levi and Liv walk toward me, hand in hand. Seeing the two of them together is like watching a bad reality show. It's terrible, and yet I can't seem to look away from their interlocked fingers.

"Can we help you?" Liv sneers.

Levi drops her hand and opens his mouth, but no words come out. I shake my head, eyes downcast, before walking into class. Levi makes his way inside and I flip my textbook open, pretending to read it.

"I can explain," he says quietly as he slides into his chair.

"You don't owe me any explanations," I say, trying in vain to stop my lower lip from quivering. "We're just . . . friends."

FIFTEEN

Convincing my parents to let me attend the football game gave me an opportunity to work on *Goal #8: Get them to chill the F out about boys and everything else!!!* They didn't like that the game is in another town, or that it's in a large, outdoor football field at night. But I reminded them that Annie will be there, along with teachers from school. I also threw in a comment about *Goal #7: Convince the wardens to get me a cellphone!!!* and how, if I had one, they wouldn't have to worry so much. Once again, nada.

Ramsey does his part to reassure them over dinner. "Jessie has to be at this game. Everyone from school will be there." He points his fork at me. "Remember that time in eleventh grade, I scored the winning touchdown against Varley High?"

"No, but that's probably because I was ten," I say over my plate of warak, grape leaves stuffed with ground beef and rice. One of my favorites.

"It's almost December. Isn't it too cold to play outside?" Mom asks as she places another helping of food onto Dad's plate.

"It's the final game of the season. Cold. Rain. Snow. It's all part of the experience," Ramsey says, with a far-off look in his eyes.

"At least let me get your winter coat out of the basement." Mom puts the spatula down and turns to head downstairs.

"Mom, stop," Annie says. "There's not even any snow on the ground. Don't make Jessie walk around like the Michelin Man all night."

Ramsey, Annie, and I laugh.

"What's a Michelle man?" Dad whispers to Mom.

"The trick is layers." Annie takes her last bite of food. "I'll help her get ready."

My head jolts up. I'm shocked that Annie has volunteered to assist me, unprompted.

Ramsey wipes his face with a napkin. "I'll drop you guys off. Maybe I'll run into a few people I know."

"A night off from being Mr. Taxi Driver? I'll take it," Dad says with a mouth full of food.

Mom and Dad exchange multiple glances. There are a few head tilts and shoulder shrugs before Mom gets up and walks over to the cabinet next to the refrigerator, the one where she keeps her surplus baking ingredients and spices. She returns to the table carrying a small box.

"We were going to wait until Christmas to give this to you, but since it's only a few weeks away, and because you're going to be outside all night, we want you to have it now," Mom says.

"Is that a phone?" A large smile takes over my face and I have to stop myself from yanking the box out of my mother's hands.

"Jessie, calm down," Dad says, his lips set in a hard line. I follow his orders while Annie and Ramsey watch with matching amused expressions. "A phone is a big responsibility. The boy at the store installed Safety Search, which means you can't look at any dirty websites—"

"Dad!" I say, my eyeballs expanding to twice their size.

Ramsey struggles to hold in a laugh. Even Annie chuckles. I was sure she'd point out bitterly that I'm getting a phone before she did.

"And you can't go wild calling people all the time or sending messages or buying appetizers," Mom says.

"You mean apps. And I won't. I promise." My fingers feel twitchy, like a mom waiting to hold her new baby in her arms.

"And," Mom adds, "me and Daddy will check your phone whenever we want."

"Anything else?" I ask, clenching my jaw.

"Yes. This is mostly for emergencies. Don't become addicted like your sister. Merry Christmas." Dad smiles, and I get up and take turns hugging both my parents. I immediately message the girls, sharing my new phone number with about a million exclamation marks.

—

We stop to pick up Cat on the way to the game. She smiles as she slides into the back seat and notices my brother behind the wheel with Annie next to him on the passenger side. Mom would flip if she saw Cat's outfit. Her tight jeans are paired with a fitted white shirt and a really impractical leather jacket.

"So, I finally get to meet Ramsey. I was starting to think you didn't exist." Cat giggles. "He's cute," she whispers to me.

My eyes catch Ramsey's in the rearview mirror. He fights back a laugh. Cat pulls out her phone and uses the camera to apply makeup in the back of Ramsey's car. With my high ponytail and clear lip gloss, I look like a child seated next to her.

"How did you manage to walk out of the house dressed like that? If my mom had her way, I'd be in a snowsuit right now."

"They think I'm going to the movies with you and your sister. Do you know if Odelia will be there tonight?" Cat asks, covering her lips with dark red lipstick.

"I think so. The game is only a few minutes from her house.

She said she was going to try to convince them to let her stay until jerk-off."

"Kickoff, Jessie," Ramsey says from the front seat.

"Why even bother? I wonder if Evan will be there too." Cat puts her phone down and stares out the window.

I hope not.

Ramsey drops us off, leaving his car idling to say hi to a few people in the parking lot. Annie hightails it to the bleachers while Cat and I walk toward the action. Floodlights illuminate the football field as students from both schools begin to take their seats in the stands. It's chilly, but all the layers are keeping me warm. Annie honored her word and helped me get dressed. In return, she made me promise not to speak to her once we got to the game.

"How do I look?" Cat asks, shivering.

"Cold." When that doesn't seem to suffice, I try again. "You look pretty."

A grin forms on Cat's face, revealing lipstick on her front two teeth. I keep this to myself.

"I told Mel we'd meet her by the entrance," I remind Cat. We head back, and Mel strolls over from the concession stand with a bag of popcorn. "Where's Odelia? Was she not able to convince her parents to let her come?" After getting the words out, I take a step back and eye up Mel, who is even more dressed up than Cat. Her long, blond hair cascades down her back. Under her open coat, she's wearing a short, black dress.

"She's here with Evan." Mel brings a handful of popcorn to her mouth. "You should have seen them. They were so cute."

From the corner of my eye, I see Cat fold her arms over her chest.

"Everything okay?" Mel asks her.

"I'm just cold," Cat replies, her chin pointed down.

"So, like, did I miss the dress code for tonight or something?" I say, gesturing to their outfits.

Mel grins. "I'm not staying for the game. Richard is coming to pick me up. Promise not to tell my sister, okay?"

"Where's he taking you?" Cat asks.

"I'm not sure. Somewhere we can be alone," Mel says, her eyes sparkling.

Doesn't Mel realize what a horrible idea this is? I want to say something but need to come at it from another angle or she'll assume I'm being paranoid and overprotective.

"Why doesn't Dick stay here and watch the game with all of us? That way we'll get to know him." Maybe see what all the fuss is about.

"Don't you think Richard is a little old to be going to high school football games?" Mel asks, the irony lost on her.

She spots a few friends from the other high school and takes off to say hi to them.

I turn to Cat and grip her arms. "We can't let Mel go off with this guy."

Cat sighs and shakes her head. "Mel's a big girl. She can make her own decisions."

I pace around in short strides, trying to figure out a way to keep Mel from leaving. It all rests on my shoulders. Odelia is nowhere to be found, and Cat, as usual, is only concerned with things involving herself.

Mel skips over, her long hair bouncing behind her. "He's here. If you run into my sister and she asks where I am, tell her I'm in the bathroom or something. I'll have Richard drop me back here at eight thirty." A car horn honks, and Mel turns to signal to Richard that she'll be right there.

I glance past Mel's shoulder, trying to peer into his car. All I can see is his silhouette. God, even that has a five-o'clock shadow.

The horn blares again and Mel walks backward. "I'd introduce you guys, but we're not really at the 'meeting each other's friends' stage, you know?"

Of course not. That would make it too easy for us to identify him in a police lineup.

Once Mel is gone, I turn back to face Cat. She has both hands on her hips and she's tapping her foot. "Let's go find Odelia and Evan." She pulls my arm, but I resist.

"I think they want to be alone."

"We'll say hi, then leave."

I grudgingly agree. If I know Cat, there are ulterior motives at play, and Odelia will need me there to head off any of her moves.

As we circle the football field in search of Odelia, my mind races back to Mel. Why doesn't she see how messed up it is for a nineteen-year-old to be interested in a ninth-grader? Am I missing something? I thought I was supposed to be the one who didn't always "get" things, but in this situation, it feels like I'm the only one who sees things clearly.

Cat spots Odelia and Evan on a hill, where a decent-sized crowd has gathered to watch the game. We reach the top and I stop to take in the sights while I catch my breath. The entire football field is visible from up here, and, as an added benefit, it doesn't require sitting on cold metal bleachers.

"Hiiiiii," Cat sings as she prances over to Odelia before pulling her in for a phony hug. The fakeness radiates from her porcelain skin. Odelia raises a brow at me. I shrug my shoulders in defeat.

"Long time no see, Evan," Cat says as she playfully punches his arm. Cat flashes him a toothy grin. Evan motions with his finger that she has something on her teeth. I step away to bury a laugh.

I've situated myself far enough outside the love triangle to observe them like they're characters in one of Mom's Arabic soaps. Odelia tries to insert herself back in the exchange between Cat and Evan, but she can't seem to find a way in. And I've lost count of how many hair flips and cringeworthy giggles Cat's directed Evan's way.

What is it about this guy that has two of my friends willing to go through a passive-aggressive war over him? I guess Evan's attractive in a textbook definition kind of way, but he uses way too much gel and it makes his dark brown curls look greasy, unlike Griffin's soft curls. I suppose he does have a nice athletic body. Though I prefer long and lean. Good thing too, otherwise this love triangle would turn into a square.

"Hey, Cat," I say, squeezing my way into the group, "I'm thirsty. Let's get some drinks. My treat."

Cat turns to me and glares. "I'm fine."

"Well, I'm not. I really need to pee," I say, squirming.

"You just said you were thirsty," she replies.

My feet wriggle around. "Yeah, it came on all of a sudden. It does that. I need to talk to my doctor about it. We'll see you guys later." I grab Cat's arm and pull her all the way down the hill.

"What're you doing?" She rips her arm away from my grasp. "You completely embarrassed me. That whole act up there was so . . . immature."

"You said we were only going to say hi," I remind her.

"Oh, grow up, Jessie. You knew exactly what I was doing."

"I don't get you," I say, shaking my head. "I thought you were going to let Odelia have Evan."

Cat stands there, her eyes to the sky. "What does he even see in her?"

"You realize this is our friend you're talking about, right?"

"It started as a hookup," Cat says. "He probably never expected her to latch on for this long."

I don't even know what to say to that. Is she for real?

The football game hasn't started and I'm already mentally and physically exhausted. The fun night I envisioned in my head has officially gone down the toilet. To make matters worse, all around me are groups of friends laughing, having the time of their lives. I've spent most of the evening running interference and intercepting plays, and I'm not even on the damn football team!

The next twenty minutes or so with Cat are spent in awkward silence. I don't like how she spoke to me or what she said about Odelia, but I'm too shaken to say anything. I don't even want to see her face. My loyalty is to Odelia first. Except, I'm also kind of irritated with Odelia. I can understand why she wants to be alone with Evan, but we all agreed this would be a night for the four of us to hang out together. I'd be mad at Mel, too, if I weren't so worried about her.

Odelia and Evan come down the hill and stand just a few feet away from us, holding hands. They stop to hug goodbye. As Odelia turns to leave, Evan pulls her back in and kisses her on the lips. Cat lets out an exaggerated sigh.

Odelia walks over, her eyes twinkling and dimples on display. "Hi, guys. What's new?" she asks, barely able to keep it together. She waits for Evan to be out of sight before she grabs my arms and jumps up and down. "Evan just asked me to be his girlfriend! I'm dying. I'm actually dead."

"I'm so happy for you." *Is that what I'm supposed to say?*

"Sorry I didn't get to spend much time with you guys

tonight. I hope you understand," Odelia says, her eyes focused on me alone.

"It's okay," I lie.

Odelia's ride will be here in a few minutes so I get right to the point. "Did you know Mel took off on a date with Dick tonight? Like, in his car?"

"Yeah, she told me they had plans."

Odelia appears entirely unfazed by my question. How can I be the only one who has a problem with this? If no one else is going to waste their time flipping out over Mel's poor life choices, then neither am I.

Cat and I hug Odelia goodbye as her mom pulls into the parking lot. Once again, it's just the two of us.

"I see a friend from Varley. I'll catch up with you later," Cat says before taking off.

As much as I don't want to hang out with Cat, I want to be left alone even less. I close my eyes and try to breathe out all the stress from this "fun" night out with my "friends." After wandering around aimlessly for a while, I park myself on a grassy knoll on top of the hill. On my way up, I spied Annie with her friends and Xavier. For a second, I thought about walking over and asking if I could hang out, but I know better than that. At least from up here I can pretend to watch the game and keep an eye out for Mel.

Cuddling couples and laughing friends surround me. Cheers and boos from the crowd infuse the field with a palpable energy. There's a couple at the bottom of the hill going at it, making me feel even more pathetic.

Sitting here takes me back to all those recesses I spent alone on the small hill in the playground, while the other kids played around me. I'm right back where I started. It was naive to think I'd moved past that. No matter how much I try to be this new version of Jessie, I can't seem to escape who I was and who I really am.

I take this time to come up with a list of reasons why my friends suck. I rehearse all the things I plan to say to them on Monday. I'll tell them how disappointed I am and how they misled me about tonight. How they put their own needs above the group's. How they ditched me. How they really don't know me at all because they haven't tried to.

"Come here often?"

I release a fistful of grass and look up to see Levi laughing at his cheesy one-liner. The frown I feared was a permanent fixture on my face transforms into a smile. A relieved smile. A hopeful smile.

He sits next to me and crosses his legs. Our knees touch, and I'm overcome by the feeling of his body against mine—even in this small, seemingly insignificant way. He opens his mouth to speak, but I cut him off.

"I'm having the worst night. All my friends took off without me. I'm stuck here for another two hours. It's freezing and I don't even understand football. Why do the players keep stopping?"

Levi gets up. Great. My whining has scared him off. I fiddle with the laces on my boots to avoid having to watch him walk away. He clears his throat, and I look up to see him standing over me with his arm extended.

"Let's go for a walk. It will help warm you up, and that way, I won't have to pretend to like football either."

I take his hand as he pulls me off the cold, hard ground. He continues to hold it as we make our way down the hill.

We walk together, fingers intertwined, and I want to take back everything I said about tonight being awful. There are no classroom walls to divide us from the rest of the school or evil girlfriends in our way. I could never put a price tag on this feeling.

Once we reach the bottom of the hill, the couple I eyed earlier comes into focus.

"What's wrong?" Levi asks, as I stand frozen.

Cat has her arms wrapped around Evan's neck, while his grubby hands paw at her butt. Cat attacks Evan's mouth like he's water and she hasn't had anything to drink in days. Their kiss is messy, and their faces are mashed together. I should confront them. Catch Cat in the act. But there's one problem: I don't want to.

I'm with Levi, and I don't want anything to ruin it. I make the selfish decision and choose my own happiness. After all, isn't that what my friends have done all along?

I turn my attention back to Levi. "Let's go this way instead."

Thoughts start to swirl around my head as we walk together. *Don't do this, Jessie. Leave it be. This moment is a dream.* Except I know it's not . . . a dream. This is real. All of it. Including the fact that I'm holding hands with someone who may have a girlfriend.

"Are you here alone?"

Levi sucks in his lips. "I think what you're trying to ask me is, where's Liv? The short answer is, not here."

"And what's the long answer?"

We make our way through crowds of people smoking pot and chugging beer behind the large willow trees. We're on the outskirts of the football field and can no longer see the game.

"She's home tonight. Her ex-boyfriend is in town from college and her parents invited him to dinner. I know, it's messed up."

I yank my hand from Levi's and pause midstride. "You know what would be even more messed up? If you were using me right now to make Liv jealous."

Levi shakes his head. "That's not what this is, Jessie. I didn't plan this. I didn't know you'd be here alone. I split off from my friends when I saw you up on the hill. I wanted to spend time with you."

"And what happens on Monday? You parade around the school with Liv, while I get kicked to the curb, again."

"I didn't kick you to the curb. Is that what you think?" The crease in his forehead is back.

I remain still as Levi takes a step toward me. My eyes shift away from his. "I don't know what to think. I just know how I feel."

Levi moves closer, bridging the gap between us. "How do you feel?"

Without meaning to, I meet Levi's gaze. His blue eyes always draw me in and make me weak. "You know how I feel." I don't want to do this right now. I don't want to hear Levi tell me again how we should just be friends. I turn around and start to leave, but he follows and blocks my path.

"No. Don't walk away. Be honest with me."

Be honest? Do I tell him I think about him almost every minute of every day? That I dream about him every night? Should I tell him I try to imagine what it would feel like to kiss him? What if I told him all I want to do right now is touch him, breathe him in, and never let go?

There's no point.

It won't change anything.

"Are you still with Liv?" I ask, hopeful his answer will be different this time.

"Yes, but—"

I throw my hands up in the air. "Then that's that."

"But Liv isn't here tonight. It's you and me."

Levi gently pulls on my sweater, and before I know it, my

body is pressed up against his. He places one hand on my back while the other strokes my face. Levi's long, brown hair curls out from underneath his wool hat. His fingertips are ice-cold, but his body is warm, and I allow myself to fall into it. Levi holds on tight, probably to stop me from running away again, but I'm not going anywhere. This is the moment I've waited my whole life for, and it's perfect.

Except for one thing.

He brings his mouth to mine, but I turn away before our lips meet and twist out of his arms. "I won't kiss another girl's boyfriend."

He sighs. "This is why I didn't want to get involved with you."

"I'm sorry I have morals," I say, folding my arms in front of my chest.

"This isn't about morals. Not everything is black and white, Jessie. You're not ready for this."

"I can't believe the words coming out of your mouth. Do you realize how—?"

My phone vibrates in my sweater pocket. I pull it out to see Mel's name on the screen. "Hello?"

"Jessie," Mel says, almost breathless. "Jessie, I need your help."

My eyes meet Levi's. "What's wrong?"

"Richard deserted me at some school parking lot. I don't know where I am. It's dark and I'm scared."

"What's going on?" Levi asks.

"My friend Mel was on a date, and the creep ditched her. She doesn't know where she is."

"Do you mind?" Levi asks before taking my phone. I nod. "Hey, Mel, this is Levi. Do you know how to share your location?" He looks at me while listening to Mel. "Okay, try sharing it with Jessie's phone." Levi brings my phone down and stares at the screen. A message comes through saying Mel wants to share her location. Levi accepts it. "Right, you're not too far. Jessie and I will come get you. Just stay on the call with her while we drive."

Levi hands the phone back to me and I hold it up against my ear. He takes my other hand and guides me to the parking lot. As he opens his car door for me, I can't help but feel a little guilty. While Mel is scared out of her mind, a part of me is excited to be in Levi's car, with him, alone.

He pulls out of the lot and turns left onto the main street. We drive for a few minutes while I keep Mel occupied on the line. Levi turns down a dark road and we pull up to the abandoned school. He flashes his headlights and we spot Mel off at the corner of the building. She comes running toward us. I end the call and get out to meet her.

"Thank you," she says as she wraps her arms around me.

"What happened?"

Mel tosses Levi a polite smile, and he gets out of the car and says we can talk alone while he waits outside.

I climb into the back seat with Mel and my mind wanders again. This isn't who I saw myself sharing a back seat with if I were ever in Levi's car. *Focus, Jessie.*

"Richard brought me here to be alone. We kissed and stuff, but when he tried to pull up my dress, I told him no, and he got pissed and kicked me out of his car."

"I'm sorry."

"No. You were right about him being too old."

"I'm just glad you're okay. Are you . . . okay?"

"Yeah." Mel wraps her coat around her body. "I just want to go home."

"I'll see if Levi can take you." I get out of the car and walk over to Levi, who's standing by an old basketball net a few feet away. "Mel's fine, but she'd like to go home."

"No problem."

"Thanks."

As I'm about to walk back to the car, Levi puts his hand on my wrist. "Wait."

I turn to face him. Even in the dark, even after everything that happened tonight, even though I'm confused, one look from him is enough to erase all my doubts.

"What I said before . . . I was wrong. Mel is lucky to have you as a friend. And I'm pretty lucky to have you in my life too." He tucks a piece of hair behind my ear. "I just need some time to figure things out." He places his fingers below my chin and raises it. "In case you couldn't tell, I like you. A lot."

"I like you too." Four simple words, but they hold so much power, and saying them out loud sets me free.

After we drop Mel off at home, Levi drives us back to the football game. He parks and turns the car off, but neither of us seems to want to get out.

A corner of his lips curves up. "So, you have a phone now."

"I do," I say with a proud smile.

He nods to the phone in my hands and I pass it to him. Levi types in his number and adds his first *and* last name to my list of contacts. He passes it back to me. "Send me a message so I'll have your information on mine."

I send him a football and an eye-roll emoji. He responds with a heart-eyes emoji, and I feel myself blush for the millionth time tonight.

"Thanks for helping me out with Mel," I say.

"I'm just glad the old man let me borrow his wheels tonight so I could be of use."

"So am I." I run my hands over my face. "My parents will be here soon to pick up me and Cat. I can't wait to get in bed and numb my brain with reruns of *Friends*."

"Okay, but I have a really serious question to ask before you leave." He pauses, looking directly at me. "Are you a Joey or a Chandler?"

"Definitely Chandler," I say, matching his serious expression.

"I guess that makes me Joey."

"Was there ever any doubt?" We laugh, and it's so comfortable and natural, it makes me wonder why we're not together. How could I have ever questioned the connection between us? It's like nothing I've ever experienced. Levi is my silo. He's my person. He's everything.

SiXTeeN

The mood at our table Monday morning is like a balloon with all its air released, deflated but unable to return to its original shape. Which is also kind of like Mom's stomach, a truth I'm reminded of every time she squeezes herself into shapewear. Mel fills Cat and Odelia in on what happened to her Friday night. I didn't tell Cat anything on the drive home because, for one, my parents were there and, two, it didn't feel like it was my story to share. Now I sit by, pretending to listen; my mind is elsewhere.

I look up to see three pairs of eyes on me. "What?"

Mel smiles. "I was just saying we all owe you an apology."

"You tried to tell us you were worried about Mel. Maybe if we'd teamed up, we could have stopped this from happening," Odelia says.

Cat sits with one elbow propped and her face resting in her hand, almost as if she's forcing herself to stay awake.

"Let's just be thankful nothing worse happened," I say, brushing off their attempt to apologize. I don't know why I'm always doing that. Like I'm not worthy of an apology. "Actually, to be honest, I was pretty annoyed Friday. Not only for not listening to me about Mel, but because it was supposed to be a girls' night, and the four of us didn't spend any time together."

"You're right," Odelia says. "We've all been so wrapped up in our own guy drama, we haven't stopped to ask how things are going with you. I'm sorry, Jess."

"So am I." Mel nods.

Cat shifts in her seat and scrolls through her phone. She doesn't pipe in to apologize or admit her own shortcomings. It makes me question why I'm keeping her secret.

"It's okay," I say, my eyes focused on the other two. I don't need an apology from Cat. I already know the truth about her.

Odelia and Cat get up to use the bathroom before morning bell, and Mel comes over to my side of the table. There's a big grin on her face. "So, Levi was pretty wonderful Friday night."

I bite the inside of my cheeks to fight back my own grin. "He was, wasn't he?"

"What did he say to you in the school parking lot?" she asks.

"He admitted he liked me, and he said he needed time to figure things out."

She leans back in her seat. "That's good. It means he's planning on dumping Liv."

I shake my head. "We'll see. I'm not holding my breath."

"Jessie, you don't always have to overanalyze everything. Levi likes you. You like him. Let that be enough for now."

I want to believe Mel, but every time I get my hopes up, my heart breaks. And not just with Levi.

I make a pit stop at the lockers before homeroom. Just as I'm about to place my gym bag inside, my phone vibrates. A text message from Levi appears on the screen.

Chandler, I haven't stopped thinking about you since Friday. ♥ Joey

170

OMG. I look around, wanting to share this with anyone and everyone, but instead hold the phone to my heart, soaking his sweet words in. No one else would understand anyway. Maybe this is enough—for now.

After an awkward first period seated next to Cat, trying to pretend I didn't see what I saw at the football game, the dismissal bell is music to my ears. I make it to Science before Levi and sit at my seat, tapping my foot and glancing at the door every five seconds.

My stomach drops as Liv walks in. She stops in front of me and lays her palms down on my desk. All I can seem to focus on are her perfectly manicured lavender fingernails. "I've had three people come up to me today to say they saw you chasing Levi around the football game. One even said they saw you coming out of his car. Care to explain?"

I swallow the lump in my throat. She has every right to be angry with me. I crossed the line with her boyfriend. I'm no better than Cat. "You should probably ask Levi," I say, my words coming out squeaky.

"Coward." Liv turns to leave, and I try to steady my racing heart. Feeling all eyes on me, I want nothing more than to disappear.

Levi walks in as Liv heads to the door. He looks at her, then back at me.

Please don't follow her. Stay here.

Levi drops his books off at his desk. "I'll be right back," he says, before chasing after Liv.

As far as I'm concerned, he's made his decision.

Levi's books remain next to me, untouched, for the duration of the period. When class is over, I head to the cafeteria table where Griffin is seated.

"Here." I dump Levi's things in front of Griffin. "Tell your friend he forgot his books in class."

Just as I'm about to storm off, Griffin gets up and grabs my arm. "What's going on?"

"I don't want to talk about it." *Of course I want to talk about it.* Griffin knows it, too. He tells me to wait while he grabs his belongings, and he leads me to the library. We sit at a table near the back.

"He's never going to leave her, is he?" I ask, hope drained from my voice.

Griffin pauses before he replies. "I don't know."

I run my fingers through my hair, almost pulling it in frustration. "I don't understand. He said he likes me." I lean in and whisper. "He's even tried to kiss me twice . . . no, three times . . . no, two times. Whatever, enough times I've lost count."

Griffin shifts in his seat and leans his elbows on the table. I end up telling him about Friday night and Levi's text.

"Honestly, Jess, I don't think Levi has the guts to break up with Liv. Which isn't fair to you. So you need to ask yourself: can you keep doing this?"

"Doing what?"

"Being his second choice. Do you like him so much you're willing to stand on the sidelines waiting, all so you can be part of his life in some small way?"

My face contorts with confusion as anger rises to the surface. The words coming out of Griffin's mouth are worse than anything Levi has ever said or done. Levi never means to hurt me. It feels like Griffin is trying to.

"You don't get it. It might seem like I'm second choice from where you stand, but I know Levi cares about me. And I'm not afraid to put myself out there and take risks for the chance to experience something real."

Griffin shakes his head and starts to say something, but I push my chair back and stand. "I shouldn't have put you in the middle. Just make sure he gets his books."

I walk out of the library with my stomach tied in knots, not knowing whether I want to scream or cry. My phone buzzes. It's a text from Levi asking me to meet him at my locker. I respond with fine.

When I arrive, he's leaning against my locker, with a look of defeat on his annoyingly perfect face. "Thanks for coming."

"I gave your books to Griffin," I say, unable to meet his gaze.

"I didn't ask you to meet me because of my books. I'm sorry about Liv. I hope she wasn't too awful."

"It hurt more seeing you chase after her."

Levi runs his hands through his hair. "You're not making this easy for me. Liv is my girlfriend. What did you expect me to do?"

"Nothing," I say with a shrug. "I'm learning to keep my expectations low."

"That's a mean thing to say." Levi pauses and leans in. "You know how I feel about you. It's just not the right time for us."

I glance up at Levi, ready to give him the two cents he didn't ask for, but I freeze. His lips look so soft, and my mind drifts back to how warm his body felt pressed up against mine at the football game. A surge of something powerful flows through me and I can't think about anything except how much I want to push him up against the lockers and kiss him.

I reach behind Levi and grab my lock. My breaths are rapid as I stare straight into his eyes, our lips only inches apart.

"I need to get inside my locker," I say.

Levi cups my face with his hand. His touch wakes up parts of my body that have been asleep for fifteen years. He smiles, then releases me and steps aside. A few strands of hair rest in front of his face, his sleeves are rolled, revealing strong forearms, and the curve of his lips take my mind somewhere it's never been before.

"I hate when you're mad at me," he says, tipping his forehead into mine. "Don't be mad." He pouts slightly, then winks before turning to walk away.

And just like that, I'm sucked back into his vortex. My body's all flushed, and I can't tell if it's because I'm still angry or worked up.

Once I've cooled down and changed for Phys Ed, our teacher bombards the class with details about our football team's win Friday night. In celebration of their victory, she decides to teach us how to throw and catch a football. I consider it a success when I walk away from class without a broken nose. Unfortunately, my hands didn't fare so well. I rub my sore knuckles on my way out of the locker room. Griffin catches me off guard, leaning against the wall, his lips pressed together tightly.

"Can I walk you to class?" he asks.

I nod.

"I didn't mean to be such a jerk," he says. "I wasn't thinking."

"That's okay. I probably overthink enough for the both of us." Griffin smiles as we continue to walk. "I have this tendency to, like, dissect things to the nth degree. I'll pick at it, overanalyze, or go over something so many times that in the end it doesn't make sense anymore. It's probably just something I do to avoid the truth," I reply, saying too much again.

"Maybe it's an act of self-preservation."

"Call me pickle," I say.

"Nah. Pickles are preserved in vinegar or salty water. You're something sweeter, like apricot jelly."

"Thanks . . . I think." I bite my lip and keep my eyes down as we arrive at my class.

"So, you finally convinced your parents to get you a phone," Griffin says, seemingly out of nowhere.

"Convinced. Wore them down. What's the difference?"

"Maybe I should give you my number so you can send me angry texts the next time I piss you off."

"Sure," I say, passing him my phone. He adds his number then sends himself a text from my phone. "I'm not angry at you, Griffin. Just frustrated by how hard all this is." He hands my phone back to me and his fingers rest on mine for a few seconds. Long enough for it to make me feel something I wasn't expecting. I'm probably still recovering from that moment at the lockers with Levi. A door could brush up against my body and I'd probably want to hump it too. "The thing is, you're Levi's friend. Does he know we talk as much as we do?"

"I don't know." Griffin shrugs. "And to be honest, I don't care. Yes, I'm friends with Levi, but I also thought *we* were friends."

Hearing him call us friends warms my heart and makes me remember *Goal #9 (revised): Make Griffin Duffy my first male friend.*

"You are," I say, nodding at this bittersweet moment. "It's just, you were Levi's friend first."

Ever since learning Levi and Griffin are friends, things have been . . . confusing. There's part of me that thinks I probably shouldn't tell Griffin all these things about Levi, but the other part can't seem to stop myself. Maybe I'm doing that oversharing thing Dr. Cassidy warned me about.

Griffin's eyes shift to the side while he adjusts the straps on his backpack. "Let me worry about my friendship with Levi. Besides, we don't always talk about him. There is more to you than Levi, Jessie K. And I like that side more."

Griffin's honesty and willingness to break the rules is kind of refreshing. Even better, I don't feel like I'm trying to solve a complicated equation every time we're together. I walk into class and my phone buzzes. A text from Griffin: You may regret exchanging numbers. I'm the king of memes. Below his message is a meme of a monkey wearing a crown.

Text to Griffin: I'm new to all this but give me time. I'll catch on.

He responds with a meme of Yoda that says *Teach you I will.*

I smile as I tuck my phone away and take a seat. I'm not sure how Levi would really feel about my growing friendship with Griffin, but I don't see why I should give it up. After all, according to Levi, he and I are just friends.

After school, I bolt over to Odelia's locker to tell her about Levi. I've also decided to tell her about Cat. There's no reason for me to keep Cat's secret. I turn the corner to find her and Cat talking to some guy. My feet stay planted, waiting for the right moment to interrupt. A second later, Odelia spots me and waves.

"Hey, Jess." I head over, feeling super flustered. "This is Evan's friend, Darren."

I nod awkwardly at Darren before turning my attention back to Odelia. "Call me when you get home."

"An actual call?" Odelia asks, her brow furrowed in confusion.

"Yes. I have a lot to say."

Cat and I make eye contact briefly, and it's all I can do not to rat her out right here.

"Where were you at lunch?" Odelia asks.

"Long story. Just call me later, okay? I've got to catch my bus."

Once at home, I race upstairs. My uniform is extra-suffocating today and I can't wait to rip it off. I search through a pile of clean, folded clothes sitting on top of a neatly made bed. Mom always scrubs the house from top to bottom at the start of every week. With my personal life in shambles, her anal-retentive ways are comforting.

I undress in front of the mirror and stop to look at my body once I'm down to my bra and underwear. Turns out it wasn't the uniform that was cutting off my circulation—I appear to be spilling out of my A cups. Where did these come from? I feel like they weren't here a week ago. This is both awesome and totally weird.

I wonder if Levi has noticed. I can't help but observe all the ways his body has changed since we met. Then again, I notice everything about him. Goosebumps cover my skin whenever I think back to our physical interactions. My entire body reacts when Levi so much as glances my way. With the sparks that flew between us today, there's no denying he feels something too.

My phone rings. *Odelia*. I throw on some comfortable clothes before answering and waste no time getting to the point. "Are you going to tell me what I walked in on after school? It kind of felt like I was interrupting something."

"You were." Odelia laughs. "I was in the middle of setting Darren and Cat up."

"Oh." I plop down on my bed as relief flows through me. "That's great news."

"It is?" Odelia asks.

"Yeah, I mean, I'm getting kind of tired of listening to her complain about being single." Anything that will get Cat's claws out of Evan is a good idea in my book. "Do you think it'll work out?"

"I hope so. I can't seem to shake this gut feeling that Cat has a crush on Evan. Let's just hope Darren manages to sweep her off her feet."

My stomach twists listening to Odelia. Little does she know how spot-on her gut is. I need to tell her. I *should* tell her. Why is this so hard? Maybe it's because Odelia seems genuinely happy, and telling her about Cat and Evan would ruin all that. Mostly I think it's because I'm afraid of losing the first group of friends I've ever had. Even if Cat isn't my favorite person, she brought me to Mel and Odelia. People are always saying the world isn't black and white. Everyone makes mistakes—including me.

"Cat's just pissed you have a boyfriend and she doesn't."

"You're probably right." *I'm probably the worst friend ever.*

"So, my little puppy, is there anything you want to catch me up on . . . about you and Levi?"

"Do you have a few minutes?"

"Tell me everything," Odelia says.

We spend the next hour talking about me and Levi and everything in between. Whenever it's just me and Odelia talking, I feel safe, kind of like I'm wrapped in a warm blanket. She never makes me question my feelings or belittles my experiences. There were times I had reservations about the depth of my relationship with Mel and Odelia, but moments like this remind me that it's okay for me to put my trust in them.

I decide this is as good a time as any to come clean about who I really am. "Can we make this a three-way call with Mel? There's something I want to tell you both."

"Sure."

I add Mel to the call and take in a shaky breath.

"I've been keeping a secret from both of you," I say, diving right in. "It's not something I like to talk about, and I'm still wrapping my brain around it." I run my fingers up and down my leg and try to steady my breathing. "Before school started, I was diagnosed with ASD: Autism Spectrum Disorder."

Mel and Odelia listen as I explain my diagnosis and what it means, or at least what I think it means. I rattle off examples of certain things I struggle with, like eye contact and opening up, and then for some reason I give them examples of famous autistic people. When I've run out of things to say, silence stretches between us, making my heart race.

"I know that was hard," Mel finally says. "Thank you for trusting us enough to share that piece of you."

"Well," Odelia adds, "I knew there was something special about you the second we met. And I was right. We love you, Jessie. Autism or not. You're one of us."

I've never been "one of us" before. I've always existed outside the square. Partly because that's how I wanted it. But not anymore. At least not with Mel and Odelia. They've been by my side since day one, and this felt like the right time to let them in. Besides, they're more than just friends . . . they're my people.

Seventeen

For the next few weeks, Levi and I continue to flirt under the radar. I tried to stay mad at him, I really did, but I've come to see it's the situation, not Levi, that I'm frustrated with. However, I made a promise to myself not to kiss him until he's single. Which hasn't stopped me from doing some questionable things. He sends me a text every morning, and sometimes Levi will press his luck and wink at me when we cross paths outside of class, purposely brushing his shoulder with mine.

We secretly meet at my locker every day at the end of lunch. It's the only time we get to be alone. We don't do more than smile excessively at each other, but it's nice to pretend for a few minutes a day that he's mine. Yesterday, he said his relationship with Liv was pretty much over. He thinks it will be easier if she dumps him. That way she won't be able to blame me once we're together. But it sucks having to wait. It's even worse continuing to see the two of them together.

"What did today's text say?" Odelia asks during lunch.

I tuck my phone away and try to fight the blush burning through my cheeks, but I'm pretty sure I'm blinding the entire cafeteria. Levi's texts are usually cute and sweet, but sometimes, like today, they make my pulse race. This is definitely one I'll have to screenshot and email to myself before deleting.

(Who am I kidding? I do that with all his texts.)

"That means she got a spicy one," Odelia practically sings as she does a little clap.

"I don't understand your relationship with him," Cat interrupts. "If he likes you so much, why aren't you two together?"

It's pretty rich that Cat is judging my relationship with Levi when she's the one who cheated on Noah, and again with her best friend's boyfriend. It's times like this that make it almost impossible for me to keep what happened between Cat and Evan to myself.

Fortunately, Mel steps in. "No offense, Cat, but I don't think Jessie needs relationship advice from you."

Cat sits up straight in her chair. "What's that supposed to mean?"

Before Mel can reply, Odelia stands and pulls Cat up with her. "We said we'd meet Evan and Darren in the gym to watch their basketball practice."

Cat exhales while she gathers her belongings. She has officially coupled up with Evan's best friend, Darren. Both guys play the same sports and have the same haircut, but Darren is shorter and stockier. I wonder how long Cat will be satisfied dating Evan's sidekick.

"Ladies, I'll catch up with you later," Odelia says with raised brows as she and Cat walk away.

Once the girls leave, I scoot my chair closer to Mel. Her arms are folded over her chest and her breathing is slow and deliberate. "Remind me again why we're friends with that . . . person."

I shrug, not really knowing how to respond. Instead, I unlock my phone and open it to Levi's text before sliding it over to Mel. "Don't tell anyone."

Your lips smell like strawberries. I wish I could feel them on mine.

Mel reads the text, then slides my phone back. She turns to me and smirks. "That's hot!"

We both start giggling, and I bury my head in her shoulder.

"How did you respond?" she asks.

"I can't tell you. It's embarrassing."

"Okay, well, now I *have* to know," she demands.

"Um." I stall to make sure no one is listening. "When I got to class, I sat down and lined my lips with my strawberry ChapStick. Then I rolled it over to his desk and said . . . Oh god, I can't. It's so cringe." The whole act of flirting is cringey, but that doesn't seem to stop the human race from participating in it.

"Yes you can!" Mel says, pulling my arm.

"I said, 'Want some?'"

Mel leans back in her chair and fans herself. "Who taught you to flirt like this?"

I pull my sweater over my face to hide, positive my cheeks are as red as a strawberry.

"I know you're trying to do the right thing by keeping some distance from Levi until he's single, but at the rate the two of you are going, you'll be pushing a baby stroller in nine months."

"I wouldn't go that far," I say, removing the sweater from my face. "A kiss before Christmas would be pretty amazing, though."

Mid-December. I've been in high school nearly four months. Almost as long as I've been fifteen. I'm hitting my peak teenage years now. At least that's what those teen magazines from the nineties say. But they also use words like "easy" and "slut," so they're probably not the best resources for sound advice.

I figure this is a good time to check in with all the goals I've made and see how well I'm progressing.

Goal #1: Convince Mom to buy me a real bra!!!

Not only did I upgrade to an official bra this year, I also had to buy a whole set of new ones. I'm a solid 34B now. I love my boobs. They're definitely not of the round and luscious variety, like that salesgirl in the underwear store, but they're nice, if I do say so myself.

Goal #2: Make friends!!!

I'd say I accomplished this goal. Mel and Odelia are so much fun. They almost make hanging out with Cat tolerable.

Goal #3: Do not let anyone see me cry at school!!!

Okay, so I haven't been perfect at this one. There was the time I snotted all over Levi's shoulder on the pond steps, and a few times I ran into the bathroom to cry. Aside from that, though, I've been pretty good at managing my emotions . . . at least publicly.

Goal #4: Don't tell anyone about my autism!!!

Hmm. I think I'll adjust this goal and vow to tell only the people I trust, which so far has been Levi, Mel, and Odelia. It's still not something I want the whole school to know.

Goal #5: Convince the Drama teacher to let me in drama club. (And to perform on stage!)

Joining the technical company has been a decent way of making connections with the drama club, but I mostly have Griffin to thank for getting me in front of Mrs. Elliott. Multiple times. There have been whispers that the spring production will be *Little Shop of Horrors*. I would KILL to have a role in that musical. Maybe I can convince Mrs. Elliott to let me audition, even if it's just for a small role. Then again, no one actually auditions for the small roles. Those are just the consolation prizes.

Goal #6: GET LEVI WALSH TO BE MY FIRST KISS!!!!!

Well, wasn't I a precocious niner when I set this goal? At the time it seemed somewhere between totally plausible and completely impossible. And now? I'm not sure. There have been a few close calls, and I feel like we're headed that way, but I've also stopped it from happening. *Who am I?* I guess I'm trying really hard to take the moral high ground. It's not easy. In fact, it sucks. But I'll wait for Levi. I'll wait for us.

Goal #7: Convince the wardens to get me a cellphone!!!

Goal accomplished. Ahead of schedule.

Goal #8: Get them to chill the F out about boys and everything else!!!

Oh, silly Jessie. This is a goal that will never be fulfilled. I shouldn't have wasted the ink.

Goal #9: Get over Levi Walsh!

Another silly goal. I take it back. I never want to get over Levi Walsh. I want to get under him!

Goal #9 (revised): Make Griffin Duffy my first male friend.

I'd say this was my easiest goal to date. A quick glance at our text message history shows a meme obsession that usually results in long text conversations. We frequently meet up for study sessions in the library, and he's always there when I need someone to talk to.

Goal #10: Keep Cat away from Evan.

I hesitate to put a check mark next to this goal, even though Cat's dating Darren. I don't feel like I've earned the right to cross this one off my list.

—

"Jessie, let's go," Annie calls from the front door.

I kiss Mom goodbye and grab my things. This is the second week in a row Annie has walked with me to the bus stop, as opposed to her usual five steps ahead. She's been a lot less moody lately. One might even say she's been downright pleasant. Maybe

Xavier makes her happy. If she would ever open up to me, then I'd tell her about Levi. Perhaps she'd have some older-sister wisdom to impart.

Truthfully, my messed-up relationship with Levi has started to take a toll on me. At first the ups and downs were exciting, but something in my gut tells me it isn't right. Any of it.

Most of the time I know what I *should* do, but it's not as cut-and-dried as it used to be. There's a lot of gray. Maybe some blue, in the form of Levi Walsh's distracting eyes. More and more, other people's thoughts and opinions swim around my head, clouding my instincts. I'm failing everyone. Especially myself.

After writing in my journal last night, I thought about whether Jessie from a year ago would be disappointed in who I am today. One thing is for sure, old me would never sneak around with someone else's boyfriend, or keep secrets from one of her best friends. I used to think in absolutes, and I don't know whether it's high school or Levi or maybe even my autism diagnosis, but making the "right" decision just isn't as easy as it used to be.

Levi texted last night and asked me to meet him at my locker before morning bell. I spent a little extra time getting ready this morning, choosing my kilt instead of gray slacks and wearing my hair down—the way Levi likes it. I race up the steps, eager to see what awaits. Perhaps Levi covered in a giant bow, waiting to be unwrapped.

I've got to get my mind out of the gutter. It's been spending more and more time there lately.

I spot Levi up ahead and my heart skips a beat. No giant bow, but he definitely understood the assignment. Then again, he always does.

"Wow." His eyes travel down my body. "You look really good. Like, really, *really* good."

Levi gives a quick look around before wrapping his arms around my waist. He lifts me just enough that my feet are off the ground. I unwind my arms and place them around his neck. He smells like clean laundry. I close my eyes and breathe in, banking this moment in my brain to remember forever.

He whispers, "I can't wait to be able to do this in front of everyone else." His hands release their grip on me and he moves away as footsteps come down the hall. The more I'm around Levi, the more I find myself surprised by the things I do or think about doing. My brain says one thing, but it's fighting a losing battle with my heart and body. Constantly adjusting my crooked halo gets tiring.

The rest of the day seems to fly. I skipped my lunch tech club meeting to hang out with Levi in the stairwell. One missed meeting shouldn't matter. Cat misses them all the time, and Mr. Wolfe never says a thing.

"Jessie, hey, Jessie." Griffin reaches me as I'm about to get on the bus. He holds out a finger while he catches his breath.

"What's wrong?"

"Where were you at lunch? We're doing vignettes from *A Christmas Carol* for Thursday's assembly, and they needed someone to play the Ghost of Christmas Past."

"Oh. I must have forgotten we were meeting," I lie. Damn it. That would have been a great opportunity. "Did they give the role to someone?"

"Yeah. Your friend Mel."

"Awesome," I say, with mock cheer.

Griffin pauses the way he does before he's about to say

something important. He reaches into his backpack and passes me a crumpled brown paper bag.

"What's this?" I ask.

"Merry Christmas."

"But I didn't get you anything."

"You didn't?" Griffin grabs the bag, then laughs before handing it back to me.

I reach inside and pull out a small action figure. "No way. You got me Buffy." I told Griffin once how bummed I was about Mom throwing away my Buffy action figure during one of her purges. My older cousin, Rainy, let me have it after a visit when I was, like, six, and I refused to let go of it. "How did you find this?"

"My Aunt Maren had it lying around. No big deal. Thought you'd like to have it again."

"It's exactly like the one I had. I love it."

Griffin nods and smiles. I nod and smile back. The bus engine turns over and breaks up our nodding smiles.

"I'd better let you go," Griffin says.

I think about stretching my arms out for a hug, but I stop myself. Not sure why. I hug all my friends.

Griffin playfully punches my shoulder before walking away. Maybe he decided against a hug as well. We're both so painfully awkward, it's no wonder we found each other. I climb onto the bus and immediately send him a gif of Buffy kicking someone's butt with the message You're welcome. He replies a second later with Thank you and a gif of Spike tied to a chair with #TeamSpike.

This last week of school before Christmas holidays has pretty much been a write-off. Between the Christmas Mass, concert, and assembly—not to mention all the accompanying tech club meetings—teachers have stopped teaching new lessons and are giving us free time to get a head start on our final projects. Most people skip the last day, but I've decided to stick it out. Probably 'cause I have the fear of my parents instilled in me.

After homeroom, I see a text from Levi asking me to meet him in front of the library. When I reach the bottom of the stairs, he's leaning against a support beam with his hands in his pockets, his usual grin gone.

"Why do you look like that?"

"Like what?" he asks, shrugging off my question.

"Like something's wrong."

"Let's go somewhere we can be alone," he says.

I follow Levi into the library. Sweat starts to form on the palms of my hands, and my mouth feels as dry as the Sahara Desert. He leads me to some old couches. I sit on one side and wait for him to join. My stomach drops when he pulls up a chair and sits across from me.

He rests his elbows on his knees, tapping his foot incessantly. "I wanted to see you before we broke for Christmas."

Levi pulls at his sleeves and repeatedly tucks long strands of hair behind his ears. His eyes shift around, avoiding contact with mine.

"Liv broke up with me last night," he finally stammers out.

I feel my face scrunch up. Why isn't he happier? This is great news. We've been waiting for this for weeks. Just as I'm about to tell him as much, he goes on.

"She wants to get back together with her ex. We ended things on good terms. Mostly."

Levi pauses, but I don't speak. I know there's more. There has to be.

"She made me promise her something." He stops again and tucks his hands under his legs. "I had to promise not to date you."

Something between a laugh and an exhale comes out of my mouth. "And what did you say?"

He runs his hand through his hair, still unable to meet my eyes.

"You agreed, didn't you?" I ask, my voice cracking.

"I didn't have a choice, Jessie. She said she'd ruin you if we got together. I can't let her do that."

"Ruin me with what?"

"It only takes one whisper to make the school shout, and Liv never whispers. I won't let you get hurt because of me."

"It's too late." I sigh. "You already did."

We remain facing one another in the empty library. Levi fiddles with the laces of his worn Chucks while I try to digest this latest blow.

"Maybe we give her what she wants, for a few weeks," he says, his eyes finally on mine. "We'll keep things between us quiet until she no longer cares." Levi grabs my hands and places them on his lap.

This is all a game to Liv. She's finally getting her revenge. And it's what I deserve for crossing the line with Levi.

"I'll call and text you over the break," Levi says, probably thinking those words will comfort me. They don't. "We'll figure something out."

Merry Christmas to me.

eiGHTeeN

A dispute from the main floor wakes me. I roll onto my back and struggle to open my eyes. My lids are covered in a film of crust from crying myself to sleep. At least I waited until I was home and in the safety of my room before I allowed myself to be a blubbering mess. In a fog, I listen as Mom and Dad struggle to insert a leaf into the dining room table.

"Pull," Mom says.

"I am pulling. There must be a latch," Dad yells back.

"There's no latch. Use your muscles."

Dad grumbles something in Arabic before calling Ramsey to help. My parents are hosting Christmas Eve dinner for my amo, amto, cousins, and teta, and everything has to be perfect. Absolutely nothing about Christmas this year excites me. I want to stay holed up in my room, depressed and miserable.

I didn't tell the girls what happened with Levi yesterday. I'm not ready to talk about it. Maybe because talking about it makes it real. Besides, the last thing I want to hear is some snide remark from Cat about how if Levi really liked me he wouldn't listen to Liv. Only . . . I can't help but think the same thing.

After a big feast of every kind of meat known to man, during which my grandmother whines to my mother about how thin I've gotten, my cousins and I retreat to the basement to argue over which Christmas movie to watch. We do this every year. Sam will insist on *It's a Wonderful Life* while I'll groan about it being a black-and-white movie. Annie and Rainy will curl up on the couch and gossip while Ramsey and Sam quarrel about everything from who the best Batman was to which fast-food chain makes the crispiest fries.

I manage to sit through half an hour of the movie before sneaking off to my room. My path is intercepted by Teta, who insists on hugging me so tight I can barely breathe. She uses this opportunity to once again remind me of how skinny I am. Can't people just puberty in peace?

Once alone, I open my journal. My emotions are all over the place and I need to get them down in one spot. I write about how unfair life is and how I wish Liv would go away. Then I go into my feelings for Levi and detail all the things we've done together, and everything I want to do with him. I rant about how he acts tough but can't stand up to Liv. How everyone, including Griffin, sees what an awful person she is. Griffin always listens to me, like, really listens, and gives great advice. Even when I don't want to hear it. And he supports my dream of being on stage. He gets it. He gets me.

I put the pen down and guilt sloshes around my stomach. Shouldn't Levi be the one I want to talk to? When I think back to our conversations, most of them revolve around Science, his relationship with Liv, and how much he wants us to be together. We've only scratched the surface of what we know about one another. But there's no denying the electricity between us. It goes beyond knowing what his favorite movie is or whether or not he's broken a limb. (For the record, Griffin's favorite movie is *Rocky* and he's broken his nose twice.) It's hard to put my connection with Levi into words, but it was there the moment we met. And he's the first person I trusted enough to tell about my autism diagnosis. So what if I know more about Griffin than Levi? That's how it is with my friends, and Griffin is just that, a friend. I slam my journal shut and shove it underneath my pillow before rejoining everyone in the basement.

I come downstairs to find them watching *Die Hard*. I must have missed the uprising against *It's a Wonderful Life*. As I cozy myself onto the couch, I smile remembering something Levi told me once: *Die Hard* is his favorite Christmas movie.

The holidays go as well as can be expected. Annie and I stay up late most nights watching movies. She even convinces me to try some newer ones. I sleep in every morning, which would be blissful if it weren't for the Levi-sized pit in my stomach. I only get dressed when I have to leave the house, which isn't often, and I'm doing my best not to think about Levi all the time. I suppose listening to sad songs on repeat that remind me of him doesn't help.

Mom and Dad have agreed to let Annie throw a small New Year's Eve party. It's the first one they've allowed since Ramsey's big bash years ago. We came home to find our house trashed and a huge guy passed out in my bed. Dad and Ramsey spent the first hours of the new year in the car, trying to figure out where this guy lived. Turns out when you follow a drunk's directions, it leads you to a horse farm in the country.

The parents are headed to Niagara Falls for the night. Dad surprised Mom with a suite overlooking the Falls, but they'll probably spend most of their time playing the slots.

Over breakfast, Mom tells me to take my cereal into the

family room so she can speak to Annie alone. I sit on the armrest of the couch near the door and listen in.

"Daddy and me are trusting you to follow the rules tonight. That means all the bedroom doors stay closed. And no smoking inside the house. Or drinking. Last time Ramsey let his friends drink, there was a hole in the wall and we had to get all of our carpets cleaned."

"Mom, I'm not Ramsey. My friends are fully evolved. Don't worry."

"I'm not worried. Jessie will be here, and she will be another set of eyes and ears, so remember that," Mom warns.

Later that afternoon, Mom and Dad are upstairs packing while Annie monopolizes our bathroom prepping for her party. Ramsey's already left for Charlie's, down the street. They're hosting a poker night. A "cash game." The two of them are always coming up with different ways to make a fast buck. I can't text Mel because she's at her family's cottage up north and cell reception sucks, and Odelia has visitors from out of town. That leaves me with Cat, but I'm not that desperate.

With a blanket wrapped around my shoulders, I open the sliding door leading out from the kitchen. It's crisp outside and smells like snow. Blue jays approach the deck without hesitation to grab what's left of the peanuts that Dad scattered for them in the morning.

"Jessie, where are you? We're leaving," Mom calls.

I sigh and close the door. Mom and Dad are in the foyer, putting their coats on. A small suitcase rests at their feet. Mom stretches her arms out for a hug.

"Keep your eyes and ears open for any funny business," she whispers. "And call me if there's any trouble."

If only Mom knew what funny business I've been involved with since meeting Levi. But she has nothing to worry about anymore. I haven't heard from him in seven days. Not a call. Not a text. Nothing. I'm pretty sure whatever was happening between us is over now.

My phone has been ringing nonstop the last couple of hours, all calls from Annie's best friend, Marisa, asking me to relay another question pertaining to the party. She's somehow taken on the role of cohost, and I've become their middle-woman while Annie's in the bathroom completing her extensive pre-party beauty regimen. When my phone rings for the hundredth time, I let out an exasperated sigh and answer, "Oh my god, Marisa. Call Annie on her phone with your annoying questions about this annoying party. I quit!"

"You never told me about a party."

"Levi?"

"Why wasn't I invited to this party?" he asks, pretending to be offended.

"It's Annie's party, and I was under the impression we were to remain low-key. Except I didn't realize I'd be left wondering if you were still alive." The anger seeps through my words.

Levi clears his throat. "Lucy's going to be there tonight. Mind if I tag along?"

So he's just going to gloss over everything I said?

"Sure," I reply. "I'm stuck here anyway." I know I'm supposed to be mad—and I am—but I'd never be able to live with myself if I turned down an opportunity to spend New Year's Eve with Levi.

After hanging up, I run upstairs to shower in my parents' bathroom. Not wanting to appear as if I'm trying too hard, I throw on a pair of black leggings and an oversized sweatshirt.

I put my hair up in a ponytail and don't bother with any makeup. When I'm done, Annie asks me to come to the basement to help set up. My job is to fill bowls with chips and pretzels, while hers is to watch me.

"You know, you could have invited a friend," she says, grabbing a chip. Annie is dressed in a pink silk slip dress. Her normally straight hair has carefully crafted waves, and her makeup is flawless, as usual.

"My friends wouldn't have been able to come. Don't worry, I'll stay out of your way and won't embarrass you."

Annie lets out a small laugh. "It's been a while since you embarrassed me." She begins to walk away, then stops. "Xavier will be here tonight. It's pretty cool you haven't told Mom and Dad about him. I really like Xavier, but . . . you know how they are."

I nod while emptying a bag of chips into a large plastic bowl. "Your relationship with Xavier is your business. I doubt Mom and Dad would be happy if we brought home Mr. Arab Universe himself."

Annie's lips part as if she's going to say something, but she offers me a strained smile instead. I debate telling her about Levi, but decide to cross that bridge when I need to. *If* I need to.

The first guests to arrive are Marisa and her boyfriend, Eric. Eric volunteered to be tonight's DJ and has a crate full of vinyl and a portable DJ system. Eric likes old school music too, but mostly R&B and rap. I follow him downstairs as he sets up.

"Do you have anything good in here?" I ask, rifling through his collection of Michael Jackson and Prince albums.

"You didn't just say that! Jessie, Prince was a musical genius. Do you even understand the impact he had on the music industry?"

"I guess that's a no."

By eight thirty most of the guests have arrived, except for Lucy and Levi. He'll probably text me with some elaborate excuse as to why he couldn't come, and I'll probably buy it. I've just found a comfortable spot on the couch to settle into for the evening when the doorbell rings.

"Come in," I yell. It rings again. I rip my blanket off and storm toward the foyer. "I said, come in."

I open the door and my stomach somersaults onto itself. Levi and Lucy are standing there, with Griffin.

Lucy grins and goes straight to the basement after dumping her coat in the living room with the others.

"I hope it's okay I invited Griffin. He didn't have anything better to do," Levi says with a smirk.

Griffin glares at him before jabbing his elbow into Levi's side.

"The more the merrier," I respond.

Sub-Goal/New Year's Resolution: Stop talking like an old man.

The guys drop off their coats and return to the foyer. Levi catches me off guard and scoops me up in a tight hug. "I missed you, Chandler."

"Really? 'Cause I thought you forgot I existed," I say quietly as he puts me down.

"Never." Levi shakes his head while staring directly into my eyes.

"What's the plan?" Griffin asks.

I break away from Levi's gaze. "Um . . . we can hang out in the family room."

Griffin's eyes light up as we make our way over. "Is that a Super Nintendo?"

"Yeah, my brother bought it online. It's the real deal. Wanna play?"

"You guys go ahead," Levi says. "I suck at video games."

Griffin and I sit next to one another on the floor and play

Super Mario World. Levi is sitting on the coffee table behind us, and I lean my back against his legs. He plays with my ponytail, pretending he's braiding it. It's very distracting, and also sensory overload. We continue to play for a while and I kick Griffin's butt. He throws down his controller in mock anger as we argue back and forth. He says I have an unfair advantage and even accuses me of cheating.

Levi stands and holds out his hand to help me off the ground. "Where can I light up?"

"Out on my deck."

"Cool. We'll be right back," he says to Griffin. Levi grabs his coat from the living room while I get mine from the closet. It takes a minute for Levi to find his shoes in the pile left by the front door. As we pass the family room on our way to the kitchen, Griffin winks at me. I'd send him an "OMG" text if I could, but I don't want to jinx anything.

We ended up with a light dusting of snow, and Levi and I are the first to make footprints on the deck. The night sky is clear, the moon a thin crescent above us. There's an icy chill in the air, and I breathe it in.

A Prince song reverberates from the party. The music grows clearer every time someone opens the basement door below us. We can hear them, but they don't know we're up here. Tires hitting the wet ground sound in the distance, along with the occasional car horn.

Levi and I stand across from one another. He rubs my arms to warm me up. The speed at which my heart races does a good job of that on its own.

Whenever anyone else's eyes are on mine, I look away, but not Levi's. I find safety in them. Snowflakes start to fall slowly. A single flake lands on the tip of his long, perfect nose. His lips are irresistible, and I bite down on my own in an attempt to show some restraint. But there is none. That's long gone.

Levi studies me as if I'm the most important person in the world, and right now, I feel like I am. "I've lost count," he says with a smile. "How many times have we tried to do this?"

My heart throbs out of my chest as Levi brings his head down to reach my quivering lips. This time, I don't turn away. It takes forever for his mouth to reach mine and, for a second, we pause. But there's no turning back.

Levi presses his warm lips up against mine. They're even softer than I imagined. I'm not sure which way to tilt my head or where to put my hands so I follow Levi's lead. He cups my face with his right hand and places his left against the small of my back, gently bringing me closer to him.

Our first kiss starts off like a slow heartbeat, but then all caution is thrown to the wind. I run my fingers through his hair, something I've been dying to do since the first time I saw him tuck a piece of it behind his ear, and he pulls me in even closer.

We take a second to catch our breath, our bodies still entangled. He looks at me and, I swear to god, the ground could give out below us and I wouldn't even notice. Our lips meet again and it's slow and sweet. Then background noises return to the forefront and the song from the basement comes in loud and clear.

I reluctantly remove my lips from Levi's. For a moment, we were able to escape into a world of our own. I want to go back there. I want to pitch a tent and live there forever.

"I remember reading once how a first kiss after five months means more than a first kiss after five minutes," I say with an uncontrollable grin.

Levi blushes. "I guess what you're saying is, it was worth the wait?"

We both smile and look down at our feet. It's like we're two little kids with crushes. Levi takes my hands and holds them in his. His trademark smirk is replaced with a look that is more pensive.

"Have I ever told you how beautiful you are?" He runs his hand over some strands of hair that have come loose from my ponytail. "You're so confident. You don't need to try as hard as everyone else. It makes me want to hold on tight and never let go."

Levi's words, as sweet as they are, make me feel like a phony. I'm always trying. I never stop trying.

"You're overthinking what I've said, aren't you?" Levi asks with a laugh. "Accept the compliment, Jess."

Levi strokes my face and I lean into his hand. It's hard to put into words what his touch does to me. It's like there's an electrical current pulsing through my body that is both intoxicating and addictive. Whenever we're apart, something is missing, and I count down until the next time I can get another fix.

"I like that song."

"Which one?" I ask, in a lovestruck daze.

"The one that was playing when we . . ." he trails off and smiles. "It's an old one, right? Is it one of your favorites?"

"'Purple Rain'? Yeah, I love it. Prince was a musical genius." According to Eric, anyway. But it's fair to say Prince's music has definitely made an impact on me.

Goal #6: CHECK! CHECK! CHECK! CHECK! CHECK! CHECK! CHECK! CHECK!

NiNeTeeN

I take a step back, releasing myself from Levi's embrace. "Griffin."

Levi searches through his pockets before he brings a joint to his lips. "What about him?"

"He's all alone inside."

"Griffin's fine." Levi's hand hovers over the joint and a flame briefly lights up his face.

A sharp gust of wind blows through us and I shiver, wrapping my coat around me. "It's pretty frigid out here. I think I'll head back in."

"I can warm you up again." Levi winks as a puff of smoke exits his mouth.

"Maybe later." I smile. Clearly, I'm getting better at flirting.

Levi stays on the deck to finish his joint while I walk inside and stomp the snow off my boots before removing them. My body practically floats all the way back to the family room.

"Someone finally got lucky tonight," Griffin teases after he catches a glimpse of me in the doorway. He's on the couch, watching TV. The TV that sits in front of the big window facing the backyard. "Before you ask, yes, I saw everything, and I mean *everything*." He lets out a laugh that sounds kind of forced.

I grab a cushion and whip it at his head. "You perv!"

"Yeah, yeah. So, how was it?" he asks.

I slip off my coat and prance over to the couch, sitting beside him. "Perfection."

A corner of Griffin's mouth lifts. "You might want to put some ice on those lips. They're looking pretty puffy."

I try to whack him with a cushion again, but he ducks and covers his head. Levi walks into the room and drops his coat on the opposite couch.

"Anyone want to check out the party?" he asks, rubbing his hands together. How is it possible I already want to kiss him again?

"Not really," Griffin replies.

"I kind of promised Annie I'd stay out of her way."

"Mind if I go down for a few minutes? Just to grab a drink?" Levi looks at me like a kid waiting for permission to go to the candy store.

My eyes dart to Griffin and then back to Levi. "Sure, go ahead."

"You're the best." Levi plants a kiss on my forehead before heading to the basement. I almost have to pinch my skin to remind myself I'm not actually dreaming.

"You know he's not coming back up for at least an hour, right?" Leave it to Griffin to ruin my high. "He can't help himself. The guy's a social butterfly. He ditches me every time we go to a party."

"Then why'd you come?" I ask, kind of offended.

"It was this or the tenth-grade party. Here I knew there'd be at least two people I like." Griffin raises his face to reveal a half smile and it softens me. "Are you going to join him?"

"I'd rather not. But you should," I suggest.

Griffin wiggles in his seat. "I'm fine here. Do you mind that I tagged along tonight?"

"Even if I did, it's too late now."

"Oh, nice. Kick a guy when he's down."

"That's right. I did already destroy you in *Super Mario World*."

"That's 'cause I was sitting to your left and your giant elbow kept nudging me."

"Sounds like someone wants to have a rematch," I challenge.

"You're on."

Griffin and I sit next to one another on the rug and battle it out. Without Levi here, we manage to catch up on everything. He tells me Mrs. Elliott didn't seem impressed by Mel's portrayal of the Ghost of Christmas Past. Normally I'd think Griffin was just trying to make me feel better about missing out, but truthfully, I cringed through Mel's performance at the holiday assembly. She is definitely much better suited behind the scenes.

After a silent debate with myself, I decide to tell Griffin about Liv's ultimatum. He pauses the game and turns to face me.

"Did Levi really tell you that?"

"Yes."

Griffin furrows his brow. "Liv probably wants to keep Levi waiting in the wings, in case things don't work out with the other guy." He takes a breath, then continues. "Maybe if you give it some time, it'll fizzle out."

"That's what Levi said." I shake my head and Griffin unpauses the game. Even if Liv does want to keep Levi in her back pocket, I can't help but wonder if he wants to be there. I drop the controller and watch as my little Mario on the screen falls into the mouth of the Piranha Plant.

"I'm hungry," I say. "Let's get a snack." I stand and reach out to Griffin. He grabs my hand, pulling too hard as he gets up, and almost knocks us both over. He recovers and catches me before I fall. For a moment his arms remain wrapped around my body and our eyes meet. I quickly move my gaze to a tiny group of freckles on his cheek that's shaped like a heart.

"You okay?" he asks, holding me so tightly I can feel his heart beating against mine.

"Y-yeah, fine. Good catch," I say, before he lets go.

While I scan my fridge for food, Griffin walks over to the kitchen table and chuckles.

"Let me guess, this gigantic puzzle monopolizing the table is yours?" Griffin lifts up the front half of the puzzle box. "Fifteen hundred pieces! Is this some evil plan you've orchestrated to starve your family? Where have you guys been eating?"

"It's simple, really. I lay a thick tablecloth on top of the puzzle when we have to eat." I try to hold in my laughter, but it comes out like a big puff. "The plan was for everyone to help, but they say it's too hard." I glance down at the picture on the box showing three hot-air balloons floating in a large, blue sky.

Griffin raises his eyebrow. "You think?"

As I put together our snack plate of cheese and crackers, Griffin grabs a couple of Cokes out of the fridge. "Hey, what's this?" He nods to a platter next to the stove.

"Baklawa. It's a Lebanese dessert," I say.

"Can I have some?"

I don't know why, but Griffin's willingness to try Arab cuisine makes me smile.

"Sure. It's pretty sweet," I warn as he inhales an entire piece in one bite.

"It's delicious is what it is," he says, bringing two more servings to the table. "Okay, let's do this Amazonian-sized puzzle." He licks his fingers, then points to a stack of pieces. I slide them over and watch as he struggles to fit any together. He rakes his hands through his curls in frustration, and I laugh. "Jesus

Christ, Jessie, you couldn't have picked a more difficult puzzle if you'd tried. Your family is never eating another meal here ever again."

"It relaxes me," I say, grabbing a handful of pieces to sort through.

"Yes, I can see that." Griffin grins.

"Aren't you even a little bit curious to see what's going on down there?" I ask, releasing Griffin from his babysitting duties.

"Nah, I'm good," he says, eyes focused on the puzzle. "Would you look at that? I made a match!" Griffin raises his hand for a high five before he inserts his pieces into the puzzle. Aside from the music vibrating below our feet, we sit in silence searching for more matches.

The quiet doesn't bother me. It's comfortable, and a stark contrast to Levi, whose mere presence distracts me nonstop. One touch from him gives my heart palpitations. His words make me dizzy when I try to interpret a simple line fifty different ways. But Griffin's easy. There's none of that weird sexual tension between us.

"Hey, guys." Levi walks into the kitchen with a beer in hand. His eyes are half open and the smell of pot trails behind him as he hovers over the table. "Jessie, I met your brother."

"Ramsey's here?"

"Yeah, he's hosting a cash game with Ricky's brother and charging a ten percent rake. He said their party was a bust, but he's making bank here."

"I don't know what that means," I say. Levi opens his mouth, presumably to explain, but I cut in before he gets a chance. "Wait. Who did you say you were?"

"Levi." He smiles as he pokes my cheek with his finger. "You sure you don't want to come down?" he asks, his lips in a pout.

"Yeah, we'll join you in a few. Just want to finish this section," I say.

Levi and his heavy eyelids glance down at the puzzle and he stifles a laugh. "Okay, I'll be waiting."

Griffin takes a swig of his pop as he watches Levi walk away. He puts his drink down and his eyes zero in on mine. "Tell me something you've never told anyone before."

I laugh nervously.

"It doesn't have to be anything scandalous. I'll go first." He straightens. "I was the star of the choir in elementary school."

I raise a brow at his not-so-big reveal.

"Hold on, I'm not done yet. What I haven't told anyone is, I really miss singing and performing. It's why I wanted to start a band and why I'm in the drama club. Most of my friends wouldn't get it. Plus, you've seen the guys that are in choir at our school." Griffin winces. "The reason I didn't get into Drama right away is because I was too afraid to put it down as an elective last year. I guess I was still worried about what other people thought. But I decided on the first day to walk into guidance and ask to be transferred to Drama. Luckily, it took a few weeks, otherwise I wouldn't have met you."

"Sing something now."

Griffin shakes his head. "It doesn't work like that. I need an actual audience, otherwise I'm serenading you and, well, that's just weird."

"True." I laugh.

Goal #11: Get Griffin to sing on stage!

"Sometimes I daydream about getting on stage and singing in front of the whole school. It kind of goes hand in hand with Goal

#5, joining the drama club." *Oh no, I didn't!* The word *goal* hangs in the air. I reach for a pile of puzzle pieces, nervously sorting them, unable to look Griffin in the eye.

"Tell me more about these goals of yours," he says. I watch as his fingers tap a steady rhythm on the table.

"It's like New Year's resolutions." I shrug. "But ongoing. They keep me focused."

"Let me guess: you were able to check off one of your goals tonight?"

I suck in my lips and stare at the ceiling, trying very hard to fight back my smile, but nothing will stop the blush burning through my damn chubby cheeks. "Yes. I checked off one of my goals tonight."

Griffin lets out a soft chuckle and leans back. "As for your drama club goal, I think you're well on your way."

I shake my head. "I messed up my chance to be part of the Christmas vignettes."

"There will be more opportunities. Actually, I'm not supposed to tell anyone this yet since it hasn't been announced, but *Little Shop of Horrors* is a go."

"Ugh. You guys are so lucky. I love that movie!"

"Really?"

"Yes! Why are you surprised?"

"'Cause the movie didn't come out in the nineties," he says with a grin.

"Okay, fair enough. But how can you not love a musical horror comedy about a pathetic and infatuated floral shop worker who raises a plant that feasts on human blood and flesh? It's relatable content!"

"Totally." He smiles.

"Plus, the soundtrack is amazing. Too bad I'll get stuck

pointing the spotlight or something equally boring."

"Um, excuse me? Did you forget that I, too, Griffin Duffy, have goals? I'll get you in the musical. I haven't failed you yet, have I?"

"No, but all those other times were about being in the right place at the right time. Mrs. Elliott isn't going to let me take a spot from someone who's actually in drama club. It wouldn't be fair to the others."

"Stop being such a martyr. Sure, there was some luck involved, but if you'd sucked the first time, like your friend Mel—sorry, it's true—Mrs. Elliott wouldn't have invited you back."

"You're pretty cutthroat," I say, trying to hide another smile.

"You have to be when you really want something. You can't let fears or doubts stand in the way. Or rules."

"And why's this goal so important to you?" I ask.

"'Cause you're important to me," he says without hesitation. "It comes with being my friend."

"Actually..." I stall, deciding whether I should admit the next thing. "You're my first male friend and . . . you're also Goal #9."

"Go on," he says, his words sounding like a song.

"Goal #9: Make Griffin Duffy my first male friend."

Griffin shakes his head, then smiles. "Jessie, I'm honored, I really am, but I don't need to be on your list. Our friendship was a done deal the first time you said 'You're welcome.'"

My chest expands as I take in his words. He's so good with them. He always knows exactly what to say. And how to say it.

"I guess I can successfully check it off, then," I reply, passing Griffin a stack of puzzle pieces to sift through.

"Guess so." I feel his gaze linger as I make unsuccessful matches. "Your turn," he says. "Something you've never told anyone else."

"But I just told you about the drama club goal."

"That's not a secret. I already knew that you want to be in the drama club."

My eyes look past Griffin's shoulder to the window behind him, thinking really hard about something safe I can share. "Okay. You know how I'm really into alternative music from the nineties?"

"Yeah."

"Well, I secretly also really love nineties love songs. The kind people make babies to. Don't tell anyone," I say, pointing my finger at him.

"So, Jessie K. is a cornball. Can't say I'm surprised. Which one's your favorite?"

"My favorite?" I scrunch up my nose. My phone is in the other room and I can only think of one off the top of my head. "It's so cheesy," I say, wanting to bury my face in my hands. "'(Everything I Do) I Do It For You,' by Bryan Adams."

Griffin laughs. "My mom loves him *and* that song. Okay, that was a good warm-up secret. Now tell me the real one."

I swallow the lump that keeps trying to creep up my throat. By the end of the night, Griffin is going to know more about me than my own journal does.

"There's something else. I can feel it," he says, his green eyes searing into mine.

I move some puzzle pieces around as I try to figure out how to tell Griffin my not-so-secret secret. "Okay, fine. There is something else. And it's not that I haven't told anyone else this. I just haven't told many people." He's quiet, seemingly waiting for the big reveal. I sit up straight and take a deep breath, and then another. "I'm autistic."

"Yeah, right. Try again."

"No, really. I was diagnosed over the summer."

"Jessie, my youngest brother is autistic. He's nonverbal. *You are not autistic.*"

"Then you should know that autism is a spectrum, and it usually presents differently in females. I wouldn't lie about this," I say, tucking my hands under my thighs.

A crease settles over Griffin's forehead. "I'm sorry. I just . . . never would have guessed."

"That's because I try really hard to blend in with everyone else."

"But you're not like everyone else. You're better." Griffin smiles. It's a different kind of smile. It's soft and genuine and it makes my entire face light up.

Not wanting Griffin to see me blush again, I turn to the kitchen clock. "It's already eleven thirty. Think we'll see Levi before midnight?"

"We did say we'd go down. Besides, my eyes are starting to glaze over. Even you are starting to look like a tiny, blue puzzle piece."

We get up and head toward the basement stairs. My pulse quickens at the thought of walking into a room with Levi and my siblings. I'm not sure how I feel about those two worlds colliding.

We make it to the basement and it's littered with empty beer cans and red Solo cups. *The Dark Knight* is on TV, but it's hard to see through the cloud of smoke or hear over the music. Annie's going to have a hard time explaining away the skunky stench of pot to our parents. Marisa has her arms folded over her chest while Eric takes his role of party DJ a little too seriously. Annie and Xavier are cuddled up together on a couch. Around the corner, Ramsey and Charlie are busy scamming Annie's friends out of money at the poker table. Griffin and I settle on watching the poker game for a few minutes. Across from us, Lucy and Levi are having what appears to be an intense discussion. Levi spots me and Griffin and joins us at the table, placing an arm around my shoulders. Ramsey looks up from his cards and raises an eyebrow just as Levi nuzzles my neck.

"Let's go upstairs," Levi shouts over the music. He grabs my hand, and Griffin trails behind us.

Ramsey bolts up from the poker table and races over, almost falling. "Where do you think you're going?" He blocks our path and zeroes in on my hand in Levi's.

"We're going to the family room."

"To do what?"

I roll my eyes. "I thought I'd try my first ménage à trois."

"Jessie!" Levi, Ramsey, and Griffin respond, with varying degrees of shock.

"I'm obviously kidding. We're just going to watch a movie or something. Relax."

"Fine, but I'll be up to check on you," Ramsey says, pointing his finger to my nose. By the size of his pupils, I take his threat as an empty one and continue up the stairs.

"God, older siblings are such a pain in the ass, am I right?" Levi asks, his pupils also the size of black marbles. "Got any snacks?"

While Levi proceeds to raid my kitchen cupboards, Griffin comes up behind me. "Don't worry, he'll probably take two bites before he passes out."

Griffin's right, as soon as Levi's head hits the cushion, he's lights-out. His left hand hangs off the couch, inside a bag of chips. Quite a different sight from earlier this evening.

"I bet you never guessed you'd be ringing in the new year like this," I say.

Griffin hunches his shoulders. "It could be worse."

I bring Levi's hands to rest on his stomach and flick on the TV before heading to the other couch with Griffin. *Dick Clark's*

New Year's Rockin' Eve with Ryan Seacrest is on, and the clock on the screen reads 11:58 p.m.

Ryan Seacrest spouts off facts about the giant ball, how it's made, and the wet weather in New York City. *"You can see it, you can feel it, you can see the ball lowering . . ."*

Griffin and I sit next to one another as the ball drops. With Levi asleep and the countdown beginning, my chances for a midnight kiss are toast.

". . . 5 . . . 4 . . . 3 . . . 2 . . . 1 . . . Happy New Year!"

A loud burst of noise comes from the basement as the party-goers below us cheer and blow on their horns. "Auld Lang Syne" plays on the television, and for the first time in the history of our friendship, Griffin and I sit in awkward silence. We turn to face each other, then laugh when Levi's snore breaks the tension.

"Want to watch a movie?" I ask.

"Sure. *Little Shop of Horrors*?"

I grin as I make my way through the streaming service, landing on the movie. I hit play and fluff up the cushion before lying down and tucking my knees to my chest.

"It's okay," Griffin says, "you can stretch out." He moves to the other side of the couch, resting his arm over my legs.

During the movie, I weave in and out of sleep. Too tired to grab a blanket, I rub my feet together. I've recently learned this is a form of stimming. It's something I've always done to warm up and help soothe myself. With my eyes closed, I feel Griffin place a blanket on top of me and move a strand of hair off my face.

Eventually, I doze off. When I wake up, the movie credits are rolling. Griffin is seated on the floor, his back against the couch. I have this strange urge to run my fingers through his curls, but I sit up and tap him on the shoulder instead.

He turns around and smirks. "Enjoy the movie?"

"Audrey II's voice must have lulled me to sleep," I say before patting the seat next to me, inviting him to join.

Griffin sits and runs his hands over his thighs. His pinky finger is outstretched on his right hand, and it grazes my leg, almost as if on purpose. I turn my head to his and our eyes lock with sudden intensity. He smells nice. It's subtle, like lavender or musk. I can't tell which. His freckles are so adorable up close, and his lips have this cute little dip in the middle.

"I missed everything, didn't I?" Levi sits up and rubs his eyes. He staggers over and wedges himself between me and Griffin. Placing his arm around my shoulders, he whispers, "Happy New Year, Jess," before leaving a soft, gentle kiss on my cheek. A familiar tingle races through my body. "This year is going to be great."

Griffin gets up and sinks down on the other couch, pressing play on a new movie. Levi's buzz seems to be wearing off, and we spend the remainder of the evening cuddling together and stealing kisses back and forth.

"Time to go, boys," Lucy says from the top of the basement staircase. She smiles and winks when she spots me and Levi on the couch together. These Walshes love a good wink.

Levi and Griffin get their coats and I walk them to the door. Griffin and I nod at one another on his way out. Levi stays behind and pulls me in for one last kiss. It makes me all weak-kneed. I almost collapse in the foyer as the door closes behind him. Instead, I twirl around and dance like the happy fool I am.

This entire evening has been the most monumental night of my life—so far, anyway.

New year, new goals!

TWENTY

Instead of rushing up to my bedroom to recount every detail of New Year's Eve in my journal like I wanted to, I was forced to help Annie and Ramsey clean. We teamed up and scrubbed the house until almost dawn. When we were done, Ramsey made us sleep with all the windows open to air out the smell of pot and bad decisions. We must have done a good job because when I woke up that afternoon, Mom and Dad were home and their only complaint was that the house was cold.

More challenging than cleaning after staying up all night was keeping the events of New Year's Eve to myself. But I'd decided news this big needed to be shared in person.

The four of us meet at a coffee shop near Odelia's house the Saturday before school starts again to catch up. We huddle together, cupping our steaming hot chocolates, while I wait for the right moment to speak.

"I have to tell you something!" I finally blurt.

With all eyes on me, I begin to detail the events of the evening leading up to my first kiss. Cat, Mel, and Odelia lean in, big grins plastered on their faces. Sure, typing it out once and sharing it in our group chat would have been easier, but seeing their real-time reactions is pretty priceless.

"Finally," Cat responds.

"Welcome to the club," Mel says, beaming.

"You little vixen!" Odelia grins.

I've officially earned my spot at the table, no longer the friend who's never been kissed. We may not all be on the same base, but at least I've stepped up to the plate. And I happen to think I scored myself the hottest ~~player~~ teammate.

We spend a good chunk of time discussing and dissecting the kiss, which is fun, but then they all seem to want to know what's next for me and Levi. I fiddle with my sleeves, unable to think of the right thing to say.

My dream came true when I kissed Levi's lips, and I guess I'm still in the afterglow of that moment. What if thinking about what's next takes away from what is and what was? One thing I know for sure is I'm not going to tell them Levi and I haven't spoken since it happened. Not even a text. I've drafted many to send him, but I always chicken out. Truthfully, I don't know where things stand between us, and I was kind of hoping he'd be the one to reach out first.

I always do this. Every time there's quiet on Levi's end, I assume the worst. These long bouts of silence do nothing to stop the insecurities from forming. Plus, the whole Liv thing is still a cloud over our heads.

"We're seeing what happens," I respond. It's not a complete lie. "Okay," I say, placing my palms on the table, "enough about me. I want to hear about your Christmases. Two weeks apart felt like months."

The first day back at school is bittersweet. Even though I'm on pins and needles waiting to see Levi, it was nice to get a break from real life. As I'm heading to my locker, I glance back, unable to shake the feeling that someone is watching, and meet a pair of green eyes from across the atrium. Griffin. I pause for a moment, debating whether or not I should stop and say hi.

It's kind of weird how we spent most of New Year's Eve together and haven't spoken since. Before that night, we texted or sent one another gifs and memes multiple times a day. There was a moment there, on the couch, when Griffin looked at me and I looked at him and things between us got a little intense. Almost as if the lines of our friendship were starting to blur. I don't know. I'm probably imagining it. Griffin's my friend. I need to stop confusing kindness for romantic interest.

I wave to Griffin quickly before heading upstairs.

Just as I thought—Levi isn't at my locker waiting for me. What did I expect? This is our pattern: Levi and I get close ... and he takes five steps back. *New year, same old story.*

The hallways fill up and happy couples surround me. Everyone else's relationships seem so easy and effortless. Why do I think it's normal for things to be complicated with Levi? Is it because it's always been that way? Is it too much for me to expect to have a normal relationship when I'm not ... normal?

In Art, Mr. Trapp spouts off the details of our final assignment, but I can't focus on anything he says for more than five seconds at a time. Aside from my pitiful non-relationship with Levi, I'm unable to get Griffin out of my head. My phone buzzes in my bag and I glance down to see a text from Griffin: Everything okay?

No, Griffin. Everything is *not* okay! I'm confused and anxious and sad and I'm not sure why.

My eyes burn and I try my best to hold back tears. My stomach is all twisty and I'm starting to come undone. I bolt up and leave class without asking to be excused.

In the bathroom, I splash cold water on my face and stare at my reflection. I thought things would be different, *better*, but I'm just the same old Jessie. The one thing that's kept me going since September was the thought of kissing Levi. Once that happened, everything else was supposed to fall into place. The lies we tell ourselves.

When I return to class, Mr. Trapp has finished teaching the assignment. The room is eerily quiet as people set up their supplies. I'm clearly not the only one suffering from a holiday hangover. January's the worst: it's cold, dark, and there's nothing left to look forward to.

After Art, I take my time walking to Science, not sure which version of Levi I'll get today. I untuck my school shirt and undo a button. My uniform feels three sizes too small. Another annoying thing about January: your decisions come back to haunt you. Like those Christmas cookies inhaled by the pound. Thanks, Teta.

Levi is already in class, sitting at his desk. I take a deep breath and walk in. He's fiddling with a folded piece of paper and slides it over to me as soon as I'm seated. I pick it up, but hesitate before opening it. Whatever it says is bound to impact not only my entire day, but my life. My hands shake as I unfold his note:

Jess,
I'm sorry I didn't reach out after new year's. I'm
embarrassed about the way I acted at the party, getting
drunk and high and ditching you with Griffin. Our first
kiss was amazing (and all the ones after, too).
Love, Levi

Love, Levi. My shoulders drop as I let out a breath. I fold his note up and place it in my binder. Levi appears to be giving me space, but it's the last thing I want. I scoot my chair closer and grab his hand under the table. Our fingers intertwine as they rest on his thigh.

All I want to do is kiss him again. The hairs on the back of my neck rise each time his thumb strokes my hand. Levi seems even more restless than I feel. He releases me and raises his hand to ask to use the bathroom. Before he exits, he turns back and cocks his head to me so I'll follow. I wait until Ms. Muller is done with her lesson before I ask to be excused, fighting to hide my smile the entire time.

"Jessie," Levi calls from down the hall. I pick up my pace to meet him and the two of us scurry off down a flight of stairs and sneak out of view underneath the staircase. We're finally alone. Levi places his fingers on the inside of my waistband and pulls me to him. We're chest to chest, this time without bulky winter coats in the way. Our lips meet without hesitation, and I wrap my arms around him. His fingers race up and down my spine before he takes his mouth off mine.

"I've been waiting nine days to do that," he says.

"I wasn't finished." I yank Levi's tie, inviting him in for another kiss. Blood rushes through my body at infinite speed. Every touch is more thrilling than the last. Levi places his hands on my arms and gently pushes me off.

His chest rises and falls as he runs a hand through his hair. "We need to stop."

"Oh. OH," I say, my face flaming hot. "I'll go back to class first."

Levi nods, his cheeks bright red. He pulls me in for one last, quick kiss before I make my way up the stairs.

⟋

The next couple of weeks are spent trying to find creative ways to make more moments like the one underneath the staircase happen. Levi and I secretly meet up and make out before class, during lunch, and everywhere in between.

The invisible wall that existed between us when we were just friends is gone. I no longer have to stop myself from running my fingers through his hair or resting my hand on him when I want to. The barriers have been removed (well, some of them). It's so exciting and fun and I never want it to end.

Kissing Levi has become all I can think about. And it's starting to interfere with other parts of my life.

I've missed the last two tech club meetings, I'm repeatedly late to class, and my head has been in the clouds more than usual, but I can't seem to help myself. Levi is like an addiction I can't quit. And as with other addictions, I'm starting to feel bad about it and myself.

On the last day of classes before exams, I wait for Levi in our usual spot at the back of the library. I suggested we meet in the atrium or have lunch together in the caf, but Levi insisted on the Medieval section. Again. Up until recently, kissing Levi in private was enough, but I can't shake this feeling that something is off. I don't remember ever agreeing to keep a low profile. All it seems to be doing is protecting Liv's feelings, and why should we? We don't owe her anything!

Somewhere along the way I lost myself in Levi, and my obsession with him started to take over my common sense. It needs to be more than this. More than just the kissing and the high of sneaking around. I need to know he cares about me as much as I care about him.

Levi walks toward me, tucking a loose strand of hair behind his ear. He leans in for a kiss, and I take a step back.

"How much longer do we have to keep doing this?"

Levi shakes his head, the smile gone. "No one is forcing you to kiss me."

"Sorry, that came out wrong. I'm just tired of all the sneaking around. Why exactly are we hiding from everyone?"

"You know why." Levi takes another step and grabs my hand.

"You're letting her control your life. It's not fair to you, or me."
I tilt my head to the side and look into Levi's eyes. "What if we
both talked to Liv, like the mature almost-adults we are? I'm sure
we could reason with her."

"No. Definitely not."

"Why?"

Levi sighs, dropping my hand. "I don't want to deal with
it . . . with her."

"You're not giving me enough credit. I can handle Liv," I say,
my voice rising.

Levi tips his head down to mine and speaks in a quiet but
stern tone. "I don't think you can."

We stand face-to-face, both of us with our arms crossed over
our chests. I wait for him to apologize or say something to make it
all better. He doesn't. Then it comes to me. The reason for all of this.

"This is about my autism, isn't it?"

"What? No." Levi shakes his head, but I can see in his eyes
I'm right.

"You're embarrassed to be seen with me, and you've been
using Liv as an excuse this whole time."

He frowns and his forehead fills up with creases. "It's not like
that. You don't understand."

"Then help me understand," I say.

"I'm just not ready to go public. I don't want other people's
opinions of us to get in the way of what we have."

"I didn't realize you cared so much about what other people
think."

Levi rakes his hands through his hair. "It's not myself I'm
worried about."

"What are you worried about? That their opinions will change
how you feel about me? What ever happened to free will?"

"Not everyone sees the world the way you do, Jess. A lot of us have to play along to keep things . . . I don't know, status quo?"

"You don't think I understand what it means to 'play along'? I can't believe this." Levi's words come at me like a tennis ball machine on speed. "Leaving aside your reasoning for all this, what I can't get past is that you used my paranoia with Liv against me. You made it all up." I walk into the main part of the library, toward the windows that look out onto the atrium, and Levi follows me. People go on about their days without a care in the world, while my heart breaks into a million pieces.

"I should have listened to Griffin."

"Griffin? What does he have to do with any of this?"

"Nothing. Forget it."

Levi places his hands on my arms and gently persuades me to turn and face him. "Nothing's changed, Jess. I'm still the same Levi. Everything I feel for you is real."

"No." I shake my head. "Everything *I feel* is real, and I know that because I would never do this to you." His fingers are still wrapped around my arms, but he softens his grip before releasing me. The impression he's left on my skin fades slowly. "You know what hurts the most? I've been made to feel less than adequate my whole life. I turn left when everyone else goes right. But I'm okay with that. I'm learning to be okay with that, and I thought you were, too. Once again, joke's on me."

Levi doesn't try to defend himself. There's nothing he can say or do to fix things. This entire time I thought Liv was the one keeping us apart, but as it turns out, Levi was manipulating the entire situation. My stomach knots as nausea swirls. A mix of grief and anger rages inside me. Without saying another word, I push past Levi and storm out of the library, my faith in him completely shattered.

TWENTY-one

My polka-dot journal, full of all my hopes and dreams for ninth grade, sits open on my lap. I'm crouched inside my bedroom closet, hiding from everyone. Eleven goals, at varying degrees of completion. No one ever told me checking items off my list would produce only a temporary high. My time with Levi, however short-lived, was just me being in a state of euphoria, not fully understanding what we were to each other. We didn't put a label on what we had. Levi was never my boyfriend. Does that mean a relationship never existed between us?

All of this couldn't be happening at a worse time. With end-of-semester exams a few days away, I need to reserve my functioning brain cells for studying and not use them up on my pathetic excuse for a love life. The fact is, Levi strung me along and led me to believe I was special. Special enough to keep someone like him interested. Then he pulled the rug out from under me.

I texted Mel and Odelia and told them things didn't go well with Levi but chose not to expand beyond that. I'm not ready to tell them what happened yet, and they seem to be okay with waiting. They're learning I need time to process things, and I'm learning they'll be there for me when I'm ready. Until then, I'll do what I always do: hibernate with my books.

The worst part is, I actually feel bad for Levi. Even though he doesn't rely on my help the way he used to, he still needs me to get through this Science final. It's an exercise in self-restraint not to reach out, until I remember how crappy he made me feel. I don't want to be with someone who's embarrassed by my autism. Maybe he didn't say it in those words, but the message was loud and clear.

I spent the weekend trying to take my mind off things by preparing for exams, but there were too many distractions at home.

On Monday I take public transit to school, figuring I'll have better luck studying in the library. It should be fairly quiet there. Most people only come in to write an exam, and they don't stick around after. And since my Science final isn't until Thursday, I have plenty of time to prepare.

As predicted, the library is almost vacant. I sit at Griffin's favorite table and lay all my notes across the surface, hoping the information will somehow find its way inside my brain. The beige walls and the smell of musty books is exactly the kind of non-stimulating background I need. Every now and then I glance over at the Medieval section where Levi and I had our big . . . fight? Breakup? Whatever it was, it ruined me.

This is silly. I shouldn't let someone else have so much power over how I feel. I'm my own person. I lived fifteen years without Levi Walsh, and I can live the rest of my years without him, too.

Goal #12: Come up with new goals that don't involve Levi Walsh.

Goal #13: Make good with the tech club by volunteering to do the menial tasks no one else wants to do. And stop missing meetings!

My stomach-rumbles grow more aggressive as time continues to tick away. I rifle through my backpack for something to stave off the hunger until I'm done with this chapter. A piece of watermelon bubble gum will have to do.

"Good god, could you smack your lips any louder?" Griffin pulls out a chair and sits, uninvited. He squints at me and leans in. "Is there a reason you've been avoiding me? 'Cause I have to say, it's starting to hurt my feelings."

I sit up straight. "I'm not avoiding you. I've been busy."

"Too busy to answer my texts?" Griffin's eyes move to my phone, resting on the table. "I sent some quality gifs that went unanswered."

"I'm sorry. I didn't mean to leave you on read. I've just been dealing with a lot."

"Like hooking up with Levi all over school?" I can tell by his gritted-teeth smile he regrets his words. "Levi didn't brag or anything, I just . . . sorry."

I want to be angry, because I am, but instead a flood of tears comes. Griffin gets up and sits in the chair next to me, wrapping his arm around my shoulders. He pulls me to him, and I cry all over his forest green shirt. So much for Goal #3 . . . again.

I wipe my face dry and sit up. "I'm so bad at all of this. I don't know what to do. Shouldn't it be easier? You like someone. They like you back. End of story. But that's not enough. Apparently, I'm not enough for him."

The corners of Griffin's lips curve up. "There's no way you're not enough for anyone. Levi just isn't equipped to handle all your awesomeness."

"Right. That's why he wanted to keep us a secret," I say, with a very attractive sniffle.

"Hey, Jessie," Griffin says, forcing eye contact with me, "you know you don't have to put up with this, right? You have a say here. Maybe it's time you walk away."

"I did. Right out those doors, actually." I nod in the direction of the library entrance.

Griffin manages a half smile before he stands. "Let's get some lunch." He places his hands on my notebook. "Leave your stuff here. No one is going to steal your precious study notes."

His words manage to make me laugh. I'm not sure why I've pushed him away all this time. Talking to him always makes me feel better. "Do you have an exam today?" I ask on our way out of the library.

"No. I came here to study. All of my brothers have the stomach flu."

"Gross."

He nods and smirks. "Very."

After grabbing a bite to eat at the sandwich shop across from school, we spend the rest of the afternoon studying together. Griffin and I make plans to meet again the next day, and the day after. Our study sessions are productive and quiet, with talking only during lunch breaks—which Griffin insists upon—and neither of us utters Levi's name.

On Wednesday, I break away from Griffin long enough to send Levi a text. It's been over five days since we spoke. I write that I'm at the school library if he needs help. I let him know it's important to me that he does well on his exam. He replies immediately and says he's on his way. My heart betrays me by speeding up.

A few minutes later, Griffin's head jolts up toward the library doors. He stares across the table at me and sighs. Levi seems even more surprised to see Griffin. They greet one another with a nod and grunt of acknowledgment before Levi slides in next to me. He hands over his study notes, which are pathetically sparse. I ask him for change to make copies of mine.

Within a few seconds of starting the copier, Levi sulks over, hands in his pockets. *Stay strong.*

"Thanks so much for doing this. Especially after . . . everything. I feel awful. I haven't slept in days. I've barely eaten anything. Jessie, would you look at me?"

My eyes remain fixed on the photocopier. I know the second I look into his blue eyes I'll be sucked back into the disaster that is us. When the copies are done, I shuffle the papers.

"Ouch." I put the stack of notes down and shake my hand. "Papercut."

Levi takes my hand and inspects the cut. "It's funny how such a tiny cut can hurt so much." He places his lips up against my finger. The warmth of his mouth eases the pain, but only temporarily.

"It's not always about the size of the cut, but the location." I pull away and nod to the notes. "Read those until it all makes sense. It's everything you need to know."

I can't be here. Back at the table, a story about getting picked up early flies out of my mouth. I rush out of the library and walk to a bus stop two streets over, hiding out until the bus arrives.

Thursday morning, the day of the Science exam, I choose a seat near the exit. The plan is to sneak out as soon as it's over, avoiding any more awkward encounters with Levi. Mom is coming to pick me up. I have two finals tomorrow I still need to study for. That will give me the weekend to recuperate at home and gear up for second semester. God knows, if it's anything like the first one, I'm going to need all the help I can get.

⁓

January sucked. Between final assignments, exams, and everything with Levi blowing up in my face, I welcome the change a new month and a new semester bring. My heart feels heavy, as though it's weighted down by something . . . or everything.

I've barely seen Levi since that day in the library. When our paths do cross, we both pretend not to see each other, yet we always manage somehow to make eye contact. None of this makes sense. I miss his texts, and the excitement that came with knowing I'd see him every day. Isn't time supposed to heal all wounds? Why do I feel worse with each passing day?

I couldn't think clearly when I was with Levi, and now I can't think clearly without him.

I'm failing at Goal #12. Miserably.

"Sometimes things don't work out." That was my canned response to the girls when they asked what happened. I said it with a casual, cool shrug. I didn't want to expose how dead inside I really was. *Am.* Anyway, with Math, English, and French all in the same semester, my new course load is keeping me busy. The only easy class I have is Intro to Coding. But I'd be better off taking Intro to Human Beings.

On my way to tech club, where I'm following through on my goal to make amends for missing so many meetings by offering to do undesirable tasks, my path is intercepted by Griffin. We haven't spoken since exams, aside from a just checking in to see how you're doing text, to which I replied I'm okay. He then replied I'm here if you want to talk, and I guess I didn't, want to talk, because I never responded. I shouldn't be pushing him away again. Griffin is my friend. He's also Levi's friend, and now that Levi and I are done, it's probably weird for him. But standing here with Griffin makes me realize I miss him. I miss them both.

Griffin places his hand on my elbow. "Can I talk to you for a minute?"

"I promised Mr. Wolfe I'd straighten out the tech storage closet," I respond.

"I won't be long," he says, guiding me to a quiet spot in the atrium. "Levi wants to see you." Griffin sighs before continuing. "I told him I didn't want to get involved, but he practically begged me to come speak to you."

"Why didn't he just text?" I ask. Levi's made no effort to contact me since that day at the library with Griffin over a week ago. I assumed he was over it and our story was finished.

"I don't know. He probably thought you blocked his number. He's waiting at your locker."

"He's there now?"

"It's your choice," Griffin says, reassuring me.

"I guess it can't hurt to hear him out."

I leave Griffin in the atrium and make my way up the stairs. My heart beats faster with every step I take. Levi is seated on the floor, his knees bent up to his chest. He raises his head as I slide down next to him.

"Griffin said you want to talk."

"I passed Science. Finished with a 79. Couldn't have done it without you." Levi fiddles with the button on his cuff. His eyes meet mine for a moment.

I ended with a 97.

"That's great."

He reaches into his backpack, pulls out a magazine, and passes it to me. "I got you this, to thank you for everything."

It's an issue of SPIN magazine from 1994. A tribute to Kurt Cobain. "Where did you find this?"

Levi shrugs. "Online. I was worried you already had it."

"No." I run my hands over the cover, almost wanting to bring the magazine to my face to inhale the scent. "Ramsey keeps checking for it when he goes to that vintage record store downtown, but this one is hard to come by. Was it expensive?"

Levi laughs. "Don't worry about it."

"Thank you."

"So you like it?"

"I *love* it."

"Good." He smiles and tucks a piece of hair behind his ear.

We flip through the magazine, and I have to stop myself from going into detailed explanations of the meaning behind certain photos and quotes. Levi tells me his new schedule, and we joke about missing Ms. Muller's egg salad sandwich episodes. I find myself staring at his hands, wanting to hold them. He wouldn't mind if I did. Knowing that makes it harder. I yearn to nuzzle my head into the space between his shoulder and neck, breathing him in.

He turns to face me. "I miss you."

My tough exterior softens and my mask starts to slip, but his words are not enough. Neither is this magazine, regardless of how sweet or thoughtful the gesture is.

"Does that mean you're ready to go public?" The silence is deafening as Levi continues to fiddle with his sleeve. "I'm going to take that as a no."

His apathy burns through me like an out-of-control grease fire. As I'm about to stand, Levi places his hand on my arm, and that damn crease on his forehead is back. "I just need more time." He tries to use his sad eyes to convince me, but I need more than that.

"I've given you time. I've given you more of myself than I've ever given anyone, and now, I don't have anything left to give. Face it: I'm never going to be enough for you."

"That's not true. You are enough."

"Then give me one good reason why you can't be with me right now."

Levi opens his mouth but words don't come out. He probably thought I'd cave. In the past I would have, but I'm not the girl he met five months ago. Kissing Levi Walsh is not the end goal anymore. My happiness is.

"I have to go," I say, standing. "I made a commitment to Mr. Wolfe and I intend to honor it."

Back at home, I try to concentrate on my math homework, but I keep coming up with the same wrong answer.

I pick up my phone to see a text from Griffin: Did you organize the tech closet?

Me: Is that your way of asking how things went with Levi?

Griffin: Maybe. So, how'd it go?

I glance at the issue of *SPIN* on my desk and sigh.

Me: Messy, as usual. He doesn't seem to get it. Thankfully, I've started to see things more clearly. Can you promise me something?

Griffin: Anything.

Me: Don't let me miss any more tech club meetings, okay? Organizing the tech closet today was oddly satisfying. Especially seeing Mr. Wolfe's reaction. It reminded me of how important being part of that club really is.

Griffin: I'll make it my personal mission. I'll even force you to tag along to more of mine. And for what it's worth, I'm glad to see you held strong with Levi.

Me: I don't feel strong.

Griffin sends me a gif of an ant carrying a potato chip. He's such a dork. But I like him. Blurry lines and all.

I decide to call Odelia to help take my mind off things. She picks up on the first ring.

"Hello?"

"Hey, it's me," I say. She doesn't respond. "What's wrong?"

"I think Evan is cheating on me," she says in a calm but icy tone.

"What?" I ask, the lump in my throat making it hard to speak.

"We were hanging out in his car and he got a text. He picked up his phone, smiled, then tucked it away, completely out of my reach. That's weird, right?"

"Possibly."

"Well, I called him on it and asked him who texted and he said no one, so I asked him to show me his phone and he flat-out refused." Odelia speaks quickly, her voice rising with each sentence.

Could Cat and Evan still be messing around? I knew I should have said something months ago.

"If you don't trust Evan, you should break up with him."

"Oh, I'm going to, don't you worry. First, though, I need to catch him in the act."

Odelia is not one to back down or sweep things under the rug. There's no telling what she is capable of. When she finds out Evan has cheated on her with Cat, the walls of our school will come crashing down. Odelia Rossi prays at the altar of revenge. I need to brace myself for the gigantic wave headed our way. I just hope the tide doesn't sweep me under.

TWENTY-TWO

Judging by the number of construction paper hearts and all the cheap dollar-store decorations littering the school walls this Thursday morning, it appears Valentine's Day will be rearing its ugly head soon. And I will once again be spending it alone. It's true what they say: the more things change, the more they stay the damn same.

Our school's answer to Valentine's Day is not to bury it in the ground, where it belongs, but to celebrate it with a Karaoke-a-thon. Truthfully, if I weren't so depressed about the state of my "love life," I'd probably be looking forward to this event.

Odelia removes a poster for the Karaoke-a-thon, with Cupid holding a microphone, from the atrium wall. "Any of you planning on participating?"

"Oh god," Cat replies. "You couldn't pay me enough to get on stage and sing in front of the whole school."

"It sounds okay," Mel says. "They're doing it to raise money for the Heart & Stroke Foundation. Tech club is helping organize it."

Odelia examines the poster more closely. "Who should we nominate?"

"Nominate?" Cat asks.

"Yeah, it says you can enter a secret ballot nominating someone to perform. You write down what you're willing to pay to hear them, and if they refuse to sing, they have to pay that amount. Either way, a donation is made." Odelia narrows her eyes at Cat. "Aren't you in tech club?"

"I haven't been to a meeting since before Christmas," Cat says.

"If you haven't been going to all the meetings with Jessie and Mel, then where have you been spending those lunches?" Odelia asks, studying Cat.

"Jessie hasn't been to *all* the meetings," Mel teases.

Cat shrugs. "I've been around."

I swallow as my gaze moves between Odelia and Cat. I decide to cut the tension by asking a question. "What if you want to sing at the Karaoke-a-thon? Do you have to be appointed by someone else or whatever?" I probably should have paid more attention at our last tech club meeting, but my mind, as usual, was elsewhere.

Odelia smiles widely. "Jessie, is there something you're not telling us?"

I shake my head. "Just want to understand how it works." I don't plan on performing, but I'm pretty set on someone else getting up there.

Goal #11 (revised): Get Griffin to sing on stage <u>at the Karaoke-a-thon!</u>

Griffin keeps telling me how much he loves to sing, and yet I haven't heard him. If I submit Griffin's name secretly, and save my lunch money for a few days, there's no way he'll be able to refuse.

"If you want to sing, you can, as long as you make your own donation," Mel says, as someone who was clearly paying attention at our last meeting.

"Interesting," Odelia replies, with a twinkle in her eye.

Annie and I are coming home from school and we're about to set foot on the driveway when we hear yelling from inside our house. We shoot each other a knowing look. We're about to walk into a war zone. It's been months since the last blowup between Ramsey and our parents. Between continuing to work with our dad and starting college in January with a double major, things have been going pretty smoothly for my brother. The fact is, he's been too busy to get himself into any trouble.

We sneak inside and run upstairs to my bedroom. Annie leaves the door open a smidge and sets her backpack on my desk. I plop onto the bed and unclasp my suffocating bra. At the rate my boobs are growing, I'll be up another size by Easter. That hot underwear salesgirl was right, these things are more trouble than they're worth.

"Here we go again," she says, eavesdropping.

"What are they fighting about?"

Annie shushes me and angles her ear into the crack of the door. "Ramsey wants to move out. Says he can't continue to go to school full-time, work with Dad on weekends, *and* live at home. He needs space. Privacy."

It's no great surprise that a twenty-one-year-old would want to live on their own, but Ramsey seems to be forgetting something: he has no money.

Annie eventually returns to her room, saying she's bored of listening to Ramsey and our parents arguing in circles. An hour or so later, the front door slams so hard it causes my bedroom door to close with a loud click. I run to the bathroom and watch through the window as Ramsey takes off in his car, tires screeching. The car my parents paid for.

After a very quiet and uncomfortable dinner, Annie invites me to watch TV in her room. I sit on the foot of her bed with my back pushed up against the wall.

"You're different," she says during a commercial break.

"Yes. I know," I say, glaring at Annie sideways.

"No, I mean, you seem to have come into your own this year. You're more confident," she says. "You have friends. You're not this recluse with your headphones, off in the corner. Mom and Dad used to get so mad at you when you wouldn't look their guests in the eye. Now I see you smile and nod at people when you pass them, like it's almost natural."

I'm surprised Annie has noticed. She seems to like pretending we're strangers when we see each other at school.

"Do you think having the diagnosis helped?"

I shrug. I don't feel all the things Annie is saying about me. Maybe I do carry myself differently, but it likely means I'm masking. "I don't know. I'm still coming to terms with it. I guess learning there was a reason why I've always felt like the odd one out was a little comforting."

"It makes me feel kind of bad." Annie fiddles with the hem of her shirt before looking up at me. "Something was going on with you, and instead of seeing that you were struggling, I made it about me. I just thought you were an annoying, weird little sister."

"I am." I smile.

We sit in silence watching some brain-dead reality show. When another commercial comes on, she lowers the volume. "So, who were those guys that came over on New Year's?"

"Just friends. Levi is Lucy's brother, and Griffin is Levi's friend," I say, sticking to the facts.

"Yeah, right . . . friends. Which one do you like?" Before

I have a chance to respond, she goes on. "My guess is the one with the long hair. Levi." Annie's eyes pierce mine and I can't help but smile. "I know you so well."

"It's not a sin to like someone, is it?" I ask, crossing my arms over my chest.

Annie ignores my question. "He came to the party for you, right?"

I nod.

"Then he likes you too?"

"Yes, but not enough to be my boyfriend."

"Mom and Dad won't let you have a boyfriend yet anyway," she says.

"And did that ever stop you?"

Annie focuses her attention back on the TV. Her eyes are glossy and red. "Xavier and I broke up. There's no point dating someone Mom and Dad will never accept. I regret getting involved with him in the first place," she says, running a finger under her eye. "Trust me, it's not worth it."

"It is worth it when the person is important to you."

"I don't get it," Annie says, shaking her head. "You're so rigid and focused on right versus wrong on so many things . . . except guys."

"What do you mean?" I feel like I need to defend myself, but I'm not sure why.

"I see you around cute boys, Jessie. You turn into this lovestruck version of yourself. In elementary school, you'd get these crushes on older guys and follow them around."

"We all get crushes."

"Do we all become the 'ball girl' and chase after out-of-bounds balls during the eighth-graders' basketball games when we're in fourth grade?"

"I was just being helpful," I say, before chewing on a jagged fingernail.

"So it had nothing to do with your very obvious crush on Robbie Stuart?"

"How did you know I liked him?"

"Jessie, everyone knew. That's my point. You get tunnel vision."

"Well, I was a child then." I turn my attention away from my sister's intense glare and study the hole forming at the knee of my favorite gray sweatpants.

"You say Levi doesn't want to be your boyfriend. Did you ask him why?"

I clear my throat, then swallow. If I were to tell Annie the real reason behind why Levi and I are not together, she'd tell me to cut him out of my life. It's what any good friend or sister would say. It's probably why I haven't told anyone the truth. But it's not that simple. "It's not the right time," I say instead. "And I don't push it because, as you noted earlier, I'm not even allowed to have a boyfriend."

There's a pause in our conversation, but I feel Annie's eyes linger, like she's trying to see inside my brain. "This Levi guy fits your whole nineties aesthetic, and he's shown interest in you. But can you see past the Kurt Cobain hair and overall grunge-lord look?"

"It's more than that. We have a connection."

Annie rolls her eyes. "Spare me the gross details. Just don't let him become an obsession that takes over your life. Too much of anything isn't good."

"You act as if I'm the only girl who's ever liked a boy before." Blood boils beneath my skin. This speech is so hypocritical. I thought Annie was starting to understand me, but instead I'm being judged and ridiculed for opening up to her.

"I'm not saying Levi is a bad guy with bad intentions. I don't even know him." She leans forward, trying to make me meet her gaze. "I'm just saying you need to learn how to separate your heart from your brain. Question the things that don't feel right in your gut. Demand respect. Make sure it goes beyond the attraction."

"It does," I say, grabbing the remote and raising the volume. Levi's the first guy I've ever liked who's liked me back, and I'm sure there's some sort of chemical that goes off in your brain when that happens, but it's more than that. We're more than that. There's an unexplainable chemistry. It's always exciting with him. It's . . . magic. I've never felt like I've belonged, but with one touch from Levi, I do. He's my escape from all the things in my life I can't control. When it gets too hard to breathe, I close my eyes, see Levi, and everything is okay.

At least it used to be.

"This guy is a real person, you realize that, right? Like, you didn't invent him."

"What are you even saying?" I ask.

"I'm saying don't put him on a pedestal. It's not fair to either of you." She leans back against her propped-up pillows. "This is why people date. You test the waters. If one boat makes you seasick, you hop on another."

Another boat? I get that Annie's trying to look out for me, but she couldn't possibly understand how Levi makes me feel. She may believe that breaking things off with Xavier was the right thing to do, but I don't fold that easily. I'm not like Annie, Odelia, or Cat. I can't just move from one guy to the next. Besides, Levi isn't just any old boat. He's a mega-yacht in a sea of busted canoes.

The next morning, Mel and I head to Math. Evan nods as he passes us in the hall, and Mel pulls me into the bathroom. "I think Cat is the one who's been sending texts to Evan."

"What? Why?" My heart leaps into my throat at Mel's words.

"I saw something sus on her phone yesterday when I was coming back from the kitchen with my lunch. Before you and Odelia got there." Mel leans in and says quietly, "I could have sworn there was a shirtless selfie of Evan on her screen followed by two heart-eye emojis. And then, when I made my presence known, Cat basically catapulted out of her seat and slammed her phone facedown on the table."

"Did you confront her about it?"

"No, because I wasn't sure. But I wouldn't put it past her. You said yourself you saw Cat cheat on Noah. So it's not a complete stretch that she'd cheat again."

I swallow, and keep my eyes fixed on Mel. "Are you going to tell Odelia?"

"Not yet. I need to gather more evidence first."

If only I could share what I know, but I'm afraid I've passed the statute of limitations on that one. Not to mention, I'd be incriminating myself.

On my way to last period, I run into Griffin.

He smiles. "You didn't hear it from me, but Mrs. Elliott is going to announce auditions for *Little Shop* after Valentine's Day."

"So jealous! You're going for Seymour, right?"

"Yeah. Me and every other guy in drama club."

"I guess I'll finally get to hear you sing. Maybe even before then." A grin slips out, which I try to conceal, but it's too late, he's noticed.

"Why are you looking at me like that?"

I shake my head and bite down on my lip. There's a poster for the Karaoke-a-thon behind him that I can't stop staring at. He follows my gaze.

"Jessie K., please tell me you're not planning on nominating me."

"I have no idea what you're talking about," I say, grinning again. I try to sneak into Coding before he asks more questions, but he playfully grabs my bag and pulls me back into the hall. He tickles my sides, trying to force out a confession, but all I can do is laugh.

"What the hell, man?" Levi appears. His eyes laser-focus on Griffin.

The two of us straighten ourselves out. "We're just messing around," Griffin says.

Levi moves slowly and deliberately toward Griffin, while staring him down. Griffin takes a step forward, his shoulders back and chest puffed out. They stand nose to nose, eyes locked on one another, as a small crowd begins to form around them.

"Find someone else to mess around with." Levi brings his hands to Griffin's chest and pushes him away.

Griffin shakes it off and remains calm. "You don't want to do that, Levi. I'm not your enemy."

"No? Is that why you're feeding Jessie lies about me?"

"I don't lie to Jessie. I respect her too much to do that."

The air is rife with tension, and I feel like an unwilling participant in a production of *West Side Story*. I'm afraid if I leave the two of them, they'll duke it out like Neanderthals. My eyes meet Griffin's and I incline my head slightly, suggesting he exit stage left. Griffin exhales before he turns and walks away. The crowd thins out once they realize they're not getting the big fight they expected.

"Griffin didn't do anything wrong. You have no reason to be mad at him," I say.

"Why is it every time I look over at you, Griffin is somewhere nearby?"

"Because we're friends."

Levi shakes his head. "You're so naive, Jessie."

Who does he think he is, speaking to me this way? He is not entitled to have a say in who I choose to be friends with. He forfeited any right to having an opinion on my life when he decided I wasn't good enough to be part of his. At least Griffin has no problem being seen with me in public. He accepts me for who I am.

"Screw you, Levi," I say before storming into class.

TWENTY-THREE

Things at home are not any better than they are at school. Annie doesn't seem to be dealing with her split from Xavier as well as she initially let on. But, by some odd twist of fate, her melancholy has made her a nicer sister. She's stayed in the last two nights, and she invited me to watch TV in her room again yesterday. We barely spoke. I think she just wanted company.

My parents are still mulling over Ramsey's request to move out. Neither of them will admit that agreeing to this idea means they'll be footing the bill for his rent, and everything else. Dad will probably end up giving my brother a raise at work so he can "pay" his own way. Nothing would make my father happier than Ramsey taking over his business one day, which means he'll do anything he can to make it happen.

My sister's right. Ramsey always gets what he wants.

Annie leans against my doorway as I run a brush through my wet hair. "Here, let me." She stands behind me and works through my many tangles. "What do you do to your hair to get it like this?" she asks as my head is yanked back with each pass of the brush. "You need to start putting product in it after washing. We'll go to the drugstore after school Monday."

She puts the brush down once she's done and I tie up my hair with a scrunchie before getting into bed.

"You'll never believe what Mom and Dad did," she says, sitting on the edge of my bed, a smile dancing on her lips. "They told me I could go on the senior trip to Paris for spring break. Can you believe it?"

Actually, it doesn't surprise me at all. Our parents have been desperate to cheer Annie up. When they came to me the other day with questions about why she was so depressed, I pretended not to know anything. They can't expect me to be their little informant forever.

Sunday morning, Dad takes Annie out for a driving lesson. She's finally decided to take another stab at it. The last time Dad attempted to teach Annie the rules of the road, the two of them didn't speak for days. But that was last year. Maybe Annie has developed her own secret list of goals since then.

Inspired by Annie's change of mood, I get dressed and head to the kitchen to study. Or listen to the *Little Shop of Horrors* soundtrack. One can do both, presumably. I can only rehash my fight with Levi so many times. He just makes me so . . . I mean, *who is he*? What right does he have to . . . ugh! Mom calls from the foyer as I'm about to put on my headphones.

I head to the front door and stop short seeing Mom standing there, next to Levi. Her hands are on her hips and both brows are raised. She mutters something to me in Arabic about keeping it short since Dad will be home soon. Mom makes her way to the laundry room while I slip on some shoes and practically push Levi out the door.

"What are you doing here?"

"I need to talk to you."

I feel my eyes grow wide. "Did you lose my number?"

"I wanted to see you." He cocks his head to the side and exhales.

"My very large and short-tempered father will be home any minute."

Levi laughs and it makes me smile. *Damn it.*

"I can't stand that you hate me."

"I don't hate you." My eyes dart over Levi's shoulder, on the lookout for Dad's car.

"Jessie." Levi takes a cautious step toward me. "I miss you. You're all I think about. Can't we be together until the time is right? I'm willing to do things for you, like put up with your parents' rules. Why can't you do the same for me?"

"When will the time be right, Levi? How much longer can we keep doing this? I'm not going to continue to wait around for you until you decide I'm good enough."

"I don't know why you think that. I've never said it."

"You didn't have to!" I snap back. "And while we're at it, I'd appreciate you keeping your opinions on who I hang out with to yourself." My teeth chatter, and I don't know if it's from the nerves or the below-freezing temperature. "Could you please leave?"

Levi heaves a sigh. I fold my arms over my chest, undeterred. He turns to leave but stops and heads back. "Can we talk more tomorrow?"

His nose and cheeks are red. His eyes are icy blue. I don't want to be mad at him anymore. I want to invite him in for hot chocolate. I want to feed him tiny marshmallows one at a time. I want to lock Mom in the laundry room and cover his face with kisses. "Fine. Meet me at my locker in the morning." A pleased smile grows on his face, and it has a mirroring effect on mine. He strides with confidence down the driveway. Once his car pulls away I breathe a sigh of relief, and then take another deep breath at the front door.

I remove my snow-covered shoes and stand in our eerily quiet foyer. From the corner of my eye, I see Mom in the living room, sitting on one of the pristine couches reserved for guests. She pats the seat next to her.

I try to think of a lie on the spot to explain Levi's visit, but my heart beats too fast for my brain to compute.

"Who was that, Jessie?" Mom's voice is calm. This isn't good. I can't assess her mood this way.

"A boy from school." I sit next to her, facing the doorway and planning my exit.

"Why did this boy from school come to our house? How does he know where we live?"

I clear my throat. "Because Annie is friends with his older sister. And his sister has been here before," I say, nodding along to my own story. "He's just a friend."

Mom lets out an exaggerated sigh. "You know, Daddy wouldn't like it if he knew a boy came to our house asking for you. You're only fifteen, Jessie. What would people think?"

"He didn't come to see me." The lie flies out of my mouth. "He came to visit Charlie's brother, but Ricky's not home so he wanted to borrow my phone because he forgot his, but while we were out there, we saw Ricky pull into his driveway and so he didn't need to use my phone after all." I don't recognize the sound of my own high-pitched voice as this elaborate story weaves its way out.

Mom purses her lips together then clicks her tongue. "He's a nice-looking boy. He'd be better looking if he cut his hair. Have you noticed he's handsome?"

Unable to tell whether this is a trick question, I stay neutral. "He's okay." That's probably the biggest lie I've told Mom today. Levi is gorgeous. And he likes *me*. Why am I not with him? I must be out of my mind.

Mom stands and straightens her apron. "Well, remember, you're not allowed to date until you're nineteen, and then it has to be someone we approve of. Make sure Mr. Blue Eyes knows that."

"Okay. I get it," I say, feeling my jaw tighten. Nineteen! When all my prime dating years are behind me.

Goal #14: Revisit Goal #8 (Get them to chill the F out about boys and everything else!!!)

The next morning, I spend a few extra minutes in front of the mirror. Levi showing up at my door was pretty gutsy (and foolish—it was lucky for both of us that Dad wasn't home). It definitely took more effort than calling or texting. He seems really upset about where things stand between us. Maybe me holding firm is what it took for him to fully grasp that I won't wait around forever. I deserve a gold star for my acting skills. Not that I didn't mean it. I am genuinely annoyed with Levi and his indecisiveness. I've probably given him more chances than I would anyone. And the sad truth is, he probably has a couple more left.

After getting off the bus, I walk with quick feet all the way to my locker, thinking about how idyllic it would be to make our debut as a couple the day before Valentine's.

As a bused student, I tend to arrive at school earlier than Levi, who walks, so I don't panic when he's not waiting for me at my locker. Instead, I send him a text: Hi, I'm here. ☺ When five minutes pass and he still hasn't answered, I send him another text, and then another, until finally: I'm leaving. As I turn the corner on my way to the stairs, I see Levi walking with Liv. His eyes widen as he spots me. I pause for a moment, unsure of what to do. My breaths grow short and rapid. The tirade of words I want to spew is lodged in my throat . . . until it's not.

"You suck!" I blurt, before continuing on alone.

Goal #15: Cut Levi out of my life! FOR GOOD!!!

I race down the steps and hurl myself toward the cafeteria. Griffin appears.

"So, how was your weekend?" he asks with a smirk.

"Great. Amazing," I say with a fake smile. I try to walk on, but Griffin steps in front of me.

"Okay, clearly you're in a bad mood, and we'll get to that. First, let me buy you a gigantic chocolate chip cookie from the caf."

"Griffin, I'm not three."

"You're not?" he asks in mock surprise. "But seriously, I can see something's bothering you. We'll share a cookie and you can tell me all about it. We've got," he checks his phone, "fifteen minutes until the bell."

Griffin's offer is pretty hard to resist. The truth is, I need someone to vent to, and he knows more about what's been going on with Levi than my other friends do. We escape to a quiet hallway and sit side by side, splitting a cookie. He gives me the bigger half.

"And then there he was, with Liv. Like, seriously?" I ask, after catching him up and licking melted chocolate off my finger.

"Levi clearly doesn't know what he wants. Do you?"

"At this point, I just want to stop loving him."

"Love?"

I shrug. "Maybe."

"Shouldn't love make you feel, I don't know, good?"

I shift to face him. "What would you call it?"

"Infatuation."

"No." I shake my head. "It's got to be more than that. I've been infatuated with other guys before. This is different." A group of girls walk by. They glance at me and Griffin sitting on the floor and smile. "What about you?"

"What about me?" he asks, looking into my eyes.

"Have you ever been in love before?"

Griffin dusts the cookie crumbs off his school pants and stands. He reaches out and helps me up. He doesn't let go. We stand so close I can see those golden flecks again. "Yeah. I have."

"Then what makes love different from infatuation?"

"Being around the person you love should make you happy. Like nothing else in the world matters."

"All the time?" Being around Levi usually makes me feel those things. Maybe not as much lately.

Griffin brings his other hand up and sweeps away a strand of hair from my face. "Yeah. All the time." He looks at me the same way he did on the couch at New Year's, and I finally get it.

"You don't see me the way other people do. I mean, most people don't see me at all. But you," I pause and swallow before continuing. "You see the real me."

"All those people are missing out on an incredible person. Selfishly, this way, I don't have to share you with them."

A nervous laugh escapes me just as the bell rings. Griffin releases my hand and we both take a step back. He bends down to pick up his backpack and throws it over his shoulder.

"Thanks for the cookie, and for the talk," I say.

"Of course. And, Jess, you deserve to be with someone who loves you back. Maybe someone who even loves you a little more than you love him."

Griffin's words echo in my ears as we walk to first period.

Since day one, it's been clear my feelings for Levi have always been two steps ahead of his. Possibly more.

TWENTY-FOUR

I wake up feeling thoroughly exhausted. I guess that's what happens when your brain can't shut off and you don't fall asleep until three in the morning. To make matters worse, it's Valentine's Day. The day when obnoxious couples become even more intolerable as they parade around their love and rub the noses of those less fortunate in it.

It's a wear-whatever-you-want-to-school day. I debate all black, as a statement against this pointless holiday. Instead I throw on my light-blue jeans with worn-out holes in the knees, a baggy Nirvana shirt I usually reserve for sleeping, and a fuzzy yellow cardigan I picked up at a thrift store. If I'm going to make it through this day, I can at least be comfortable. Even Annie, who's been in a much better mood since the Paris trip announcement, can't hide her irritation. She snapped when Mom made a comment about her shirt being too tight and rolled her eyes when she saw me come down the stairs in my bright sweater.

On the bus ride to school, I replay Levi's surprise visit from the weekend. Why would he go through all that trouble only to ignore me the next day? And what's he doing hanging around Liv? Maybe Griffin's right. Maybe I'm just infatuated with Levi and it's time to move on.

How do you even break up with someone if you were never

actually with them? I lean my head against the cold bus window. The chill of the winter air seeps through the cheap glass. I sink further into my seat and exhale, watching as my breath fogs up the windowpane.

I brace myself as I enter the building. The smell of roses and cheap cologne permeates the halls. To my left, a group of girls squeal in excitement over the pink carnations one of them received. Funeral flowers. How romantic. The school speakers play cheesy love songs while announcing today's dessert special: chocolate-covered strawberries.

I drag my feet over to our cafeteria table. No one is here yet. I toss my backpack on the table, pull out a chair, and drop my face onto my bag. Maybe it will hurt less if I can make it all disappear, myself included.

After a few minutes of brooding, I peek out to see if any of the girls are headed this way but am instead greeted by a green eyeball.

"Jesus!" I yell, jumping in my seat.

"Good morning to you, too." Griffin laughs before pulling out the chair next to mine. "I'm here to kindly ask you to change your mind about your plan for later today. You know, the one that involves me singing on stage and humiliating myself in front of the whole school."

"I don't know what you're talking about," I say, unable to stop my lips from curving upward.

"Uh-huh." He nods, clearly unconvinced. Odelia, Mel, and Cat arrive at the table and Griffin bolts up. "I'll catch you later."

"Do we offend?" Odelia asks as Griffin walks away. "What's up with that guy?"

"He's shy," I answer.

"I think he's cute," Mel says, as they all sit.

This again?

"Good luck," Cat scoffs. "I tried. I bet he's gay."

"He's definitely not gay," I reply. Mel and Odelia raise their eyebrows at me and I look away. Maybe I should have kept that to myself.

Odelia and Cat each have half a dozen red roses in their hands. Looks like their boys decided to save money by getting together and splitting their gift in two. Odelia's nose is buried in her flowers. She breathes them in and smiles. I slump further in my chair, surrounded by the three of them in their curve-hugging clothes, while I channel Big Bird.

The Karaoke-a-thon begins at lunch, and tech club members are excused from second period to help set up. For some reason, Mel is nowhere to be found, and she's not answering my texts. It's not like Mel to shrug off her responsibilities.

I tuck my phone away and help Cat's ex, Noah, carry the microphone and speakers to the stage.

"I get what you were trying to do," he says to me as he puts down a speaker.

"What do you mean?" I ask.

"That day you asked me about my schedule and where I was at lunch. You knew, didn't you?"

I swallow as I pass him the mic. "Yeah. I knew. I'm sorry—"

"No." He shakes his head. "I was so obsessed with Cat at that time, I wouldn't have believed you if you'd said something. It took Jacob showing me multiple texts between them for me to finally open my eyes."

"I'm glad you did," I say.

"You live and you learn." He offers me a tight-lipped smile as he adjusts the mic stand. Mr. Wolfe calls Noah over to help with the karaoke machine, leaving me to figure out the wiring for the speakers. I have no idea what I'm doing. This is Mel's area of expertise. I text her again and still no response. I continue to fiddle around with the cables, annoyed at Mr. Wolfe for calling Noah away, Mel for not being here, and life in general.

The lunch bell rings and students trickle into the cafeteria. Noah rushes over and finishes the job I was unable to do. I probably could have figured it out if I'd tried harder, but my focus today is nonexistent. A nervous flutter develops in my stomach as the room fills up. What was I thinking nominating Griffin? What if he's awful and everyone laughs? Just because he likes singing doesn't mean he's any good at it.

The event begins and I join the rest of the school in the cafeteria, watching the onstage performances. The brave souls who have performed so far have ranged from hilarious to cringeworthy. The girls are AWOL, and I've chewed my nails down to the stubs waiting for Griffin's name to be called. I haven't seen him since this morning.

Someone else seems to be missing from the festivities. The day is half over and I still haven't seen Levi. There were no gifts or cards waiting for me at my locker. No stolen kisses. Nothing. That last bit of hope I'd been holding on to has been dashed.

"If you're looking for Levi, he's not here today. At least I haven't seen him," Griffin says, sneaking up on me again.

"Actually, I was just about to text you." I smile before shoving him with my shoulder and tucking my phone away.

Griffin's eyes squint in my direction. "Jessie, why are you so happy to see me?"

"Shh." I point to the stage and the three girls butchering "Bohemian Rhapsody."

"Wow," the emcee says after the applause dies down. "I will never listen to that song the same way again." She dips her hand into the nominee box and her eyes expand as she reads the pink slip. "I hope this next nominee has deep pockets or else he'll be forced to follow that last performance. Our secret pledger has donated sixty dollars for Griffin Duffy to sing. Oh Griffin, where art thou?"

Griffin turns to me, and I slowly meet his gaze. His eyes light up and he shoots me a big, toothy grin. "Let's do this!" he says, pulling me to the front of the crowd. He releases my hand and makes his way up onto the stage.

Griffin sifts through the catalogue of music while I try to find something to do with my fidgety hands. Mel sidles up to me as I stand front and center.

"Where have you been?" I ask.

She starts to say, "I have to tell you someth—"

"After." I point to the stage, then lock my arm with hers.

Griffin walks to the microphone with his head down. He fiddles around with it, adjusting the height until it's right. The first few chords of a familiar song plays. "(Everything I Do) I Do It For You." *He remembered.* My heart races, wondering if he'll be able to pull it off. And then something magical happens: the most beautiful, soulful voice comes out over the speakers.

My mouth drops open as Griffin sings this song he most likely chose because of me. His voice is dreamy and swoony and I can't help but fall under his spell. And it's not just me. The whole school has come to a halt, eyes glued to the stage. *Look up, Griffin. You're missing it.*

His fingers release the thin metal pole and he raises his eyes. They meet mine as he sings the chorus. The audience cheers and Griffin's shoulders relax. His gaze remains locked on me, and I can't look away.

"Did you know he could sing like this?" Mel asks.

I shake my head and smile.

The instrumental solo plays and Mel tells me to turn around. The entire audience is swaying back and forth. When I turn back to face the stage, Griffin is no longer there. He's standing in front of me.

"Come on," he says, pulling my arms. "You said this was your dream, too."

I plant my feet on the ground, mouthing, "No."

"Jessie, I'm not getting back up there without you."

I turn to Mel for help, but she pushes me toward Griffin. I reluctantly follow him up the stairs and somehow find myself center stage, standing behind a microphone. Griffin nods as the solo comes to an end. He steps to the side, leaving me hanging. I contemplate storming off, but the crowd's cheers cause a rush of endorphins to wash over me.

Goal #16: Sing a nineties love song on stage in front of the entire school?!?!?!?!? CHECK!

The lyrics fly out of my mouth. I stare at Griffin, then the audience, then back at Griffin again. He rejoins me at the mic after I sing the first half of the chorus. We duet on the next part. Our voices blend together perfectly, and, judging by the loud hollers, everyone agrees.

Griffin removes the microphone from the stand and grabs my hand. He stares directly into my eyes, and I forget we're on stage as he sings the last line of the song to me.

I don't know if it's the adrenaline or the song itself, but the Griffin standing in front of me is not the Griffin I goof around with. He's so passionate and focused. It's almost as if he's playing a role. Maybe he is. Maybe this is his slick way of auditioning for *Little Shop.* He definitely has me convinced of his leading man potential.

The audience's applause is so loud, I can't think. Griffin sucks in his lips, his hand still holding mine. He opens his mouth to say something . . . but Levi appears and snatches the microphone from him.

Griffin takes a step back, letting go of my hand. The entire school is silent as Levi brings the mic to his mouth. *What is happening?*

"This girl is amazing and has been since the second I met her. Jessie," Levi turns to face me, "I'm sorry I hurt you. I want everyone here to know that I love you, and I don't care what anyone has to say about it." He puts the mic back on the stand and cups my face with both his hands, kissing me in front of everyone.

I feel like I'm in a car spinning on ice. And the chorus of "*Aww!*" floating through the cafeteria suggests that the crowd approves of Levi's very public display of affection. But all I want to do is sink through the floor and disappear.

As Levi pulls away, my eyes search for Griffin. He's gone.

The emcee scrambles to get the event back on track, turning off the music and uttering a lot of "um"s and "ah"s. Levi grabs my hand and leads me backstage. He kisses me again, and this time I kiss him back. How could I not? He has declared his love for me, in front of the whole school. But I can't stop thinking about Griffin, even with Levi's lips on mine.

After a few minutes of kissing (I guess I didn't realize how much I missed kissing him) we exit and make our way to the less crowded atrium.

"What was that all about?" I ask Levi.

He laughs. "I just saw you up there, and suddenly everything I had been making such a big deal about in my head didn't matter anymore. It finally clicked." He takes my hands in his and faces me. "There you were, on the stage, so confident and adorable, and I thought, *I love her. I love Jessie.* And I had to tell you right then and there."

Levi's words melt me, and once again I surrender to his spell. "But what about Griffin?"

"That's what you have to say? After I just . . ." Levi runs a hand through his hair and exhales. "What *about* Griffin?"

"Well, we kind of interrupted his big moment."

"Don't worry about him. There's probably a horde of girls surrounding him right now. Girls love a guy who can sing."

Levi's right. Girls who never noticed Griffin before could be chasing him down this very second.

"Jessie," Odelia calls from across the atrium. Cat and Mel trail behind her. Odelia's eyes travel down to Levi's hand in mine and then back up to my face. "Okay, hi, that was sensational. Do you realize every girl in this entire school is dying to be you right now?" I shake my head, eyes downcast, not wanting any more attention.

Mel squeezes my arm and gives me a reassuring smile. "That was amazing."

"Yeah, it was pretty cool," Cat replies.

At this point, I can't be sure if their accolades are directed to *my* performance or *Levi's*. Levi whispers he's going to get us drinks.

Odelia grins as he walks away. "Well, ladies, I've decided to follow in Jessie's footsteps and sing a song as well. You won't want to miss this performance," she says with a wink. Odelia heads back into the cafeteria and Cat follows.

Mel stays behind and waits until they're both out of sight. She leans in, her eyes wide. "Odelia knows. About Cat and Evan."

"Wait, what?"

"I saw them kissing underneath the north staircase this morning. I told Odelia before second period." Mel glances at the stage, then turns back to me. "I'm worried, Jess. She didn't bat an eye.

Not even when Cat showed up. Just kept acting like everything was normal." Mel and I stare at one another. We both know there will be nothing normal about how Odelia deals with this.

The emcee clears her throat, and it directs everyone's attention back to the stage. "Our next performance is a self-nominated act. Odelia Rossi, the floor is yours."

Levi returns with our bottles of water. I grip the cold bottle in one hand while Levi holds my other hand. Mel winces as the three of us walk into the cafeteria. Levi gulps down half his drink, blissfully unaware that all hell is about to break loose.

Odelia saunters up to the microphone. Her long, lithe frame and broad shoulders instantly command attention. After tucking a strand of hair behind one ear, she reaches in her pocket and pulls out a piece of paper. As she slowly unfolds it, the music starts up. Odelia is good at a lot of things, but singing is not one of them. My doubt elevates as "Runaround Sue" begins.

Listen to my story,
Pathetic but true,
About a friend
I thought I knew.
She took my trust
And screwed around
With my boyfriend
Evan Brown.

The upbeat tempo of the song kicks in and the entire cafeteria claps along. They're likely clueless about the fact that Odelia changed the lyrics to this golden oldie. A quick glance at Cat and Evan tells me all I need to know. The two of them edge toward the back doors, but their plan is foiled by Darren and Mel, who have teamed up to block their escape. Not wanting to get involved in the whole fiasco, I stay rooted where I am, next to Levi.

Knew I should have listened to my gut and heart.
This girl would use my friendship like a dart.
She flapped her eyelashes like a bat
And Evan fell for it just like that.

I might miss her friendship and her pretty face
Her too-short kilt and makeup by the case.
So if you don't like the sight of a rat,
Keep away from Runaround Cat.

Gasps echo through the crowd as Odelia points to Cat and Evan in the audience. I'm jolted from behind as Mrs. Elliott and Mr. Trapp make their way to the stage.

She likes to open her legs, oh,
She'll bang you and she'll even go down.
Now girls you must be aware
That Cat lives—off your boyfriend's stares.

Here's the lesson of this story from the girl who knows.
I had a friend and that friend is a ho.
My other pals are pussycats.
Keep your man away from Runaround Cat.

The music continues to play as Odelia runs behind the curtains. Both teachers make it up to the stage. Mr. Trapp follows Odelia, while Mrs. Elliott tries to defuse the situation by finishing up "Runaround Sue" with the proper lyrics.

As the crowd cheers and captures the scene with their phones, Mr. Trapp escorts Odelia down the steps from the stage. She escapes his clutches and hightails it to Cat and Evan.

Cat clasps Evan's arm, and he practically shoves her away as Odelia approaches.

"Did you enjoy my little performance?" Odelia shouts over the music. "It was inspired by the two of you. Congratulations. You tie for being the people I hate most in this world."

Evan shakes his head and tries to reason with Odelia, but she's having none of it.

"Odelia," Mr. Trapp calls from behind.

"I'm coming," she snaps. Mel follows Odelia and they both leave the cafeteria with Mr. Trapp.

I grab Levi's hand and lead him back to the atrium.

He gives me a funny look. "Is there somewhere else you need to be?"

I stare into his blue eyes and sigh. "No."

"Want to go somewhere and . . . talk?" he asks with a smile.

"Yeah." I smile back. "We have lots we need to . . . talk about."

When the bus arrives at our stop, I rush to the front and race home, too embarrassed to face anyone after what happened. I can't handle any more "Congratulations!" from people I don't know. Honestly, what am I even supposed to say to that? And also, what are they congratulating me for? Singing with Griffin? Or Levi telling the whole school he loves me?

Levi loves me.

He told the entire school, and I never said it back.

I close the bedroom door before sitting on the edge of my bed, where I stare straight ahead. A gentle knock startles me.

"Can I come in?" Annie asks.

"Yes," I say, my pulse thumping. She opens the door.

"I guess congratulations are in order," she says, failing to hold in her smile. "It was pretty cute how Levi rushed up to the stage to declare his love for you. Maybe I was wrong about him."

I let out a humorless laugh.

"The other guy, the one who serenaded you, he came to the New Year's party with Levi?"

"Yeah. But he wasn't serenading me. It was a duet."

"His name's Griffin, right?" she asks, ignoring my previous correction.

"Yeah. Why?"

"He's cute!" Annie turns to leave but stops and smirks. "Who would have thought you'd be such a heartbreaker?"

Heartbreaker? Now there's a word I'd never use to describe myself.

After dinner, I FaceTime with Mel. She fills me in on how Odelia managed to finagle her way out of after-school detention. "All she has to do is tutor during lunch for the rest of the month. I thought the school would expel her for sure."

"What about Cat?" I ask.

"Odelia insisted on confronting her at her locker at the end of the day. I think part of her was hoping Cat would apologize or at least explain herself."

"Did she?" Not sure why I'm asking. I'm pretty sure I already know the answer.

"No. She actually went off on Odelia for embarrassing her in front of the whole school. That girl always knows how to make things about herself. Classic narcissist."

"So, now what?"

"According to Odelia, Cat is 'dead to us.'"

I'm not surprised. I'm also not as relieved as I thought I'd be. In fact, I'm disappointed in myself for keeping what I knew about the situation under wraps. Mel told Odelia as soon as she found out. She's a way better friend than I am. I let Mel do the dirty work, and that's not fair.

"Mel, I have to tell you something."

She smiles. "Is it about Levi? Did you let him feel you up?"

"What?" A flaming blush takes over my face. "No. Not about Levi. I did something kind of terrible, or I should say, *didn't* do something." I lean back in my bed and draw my knees up to my chest before taking a deep breath. "Can we do this without the camera?"

"Jessie, you're making me worry."

"Please?"

"Sure."

We switch to a voice call and I let out a nervous yawn before continuing. "I knew. About Cat and Evan. I saw them making out at the football game."

"The football game?"

"Yeah. I was going to say something, but then Cat started dating Darren."

"Okay." Mel's voice is steady, and I can't tell if she's angry or surprised or anything.

"When Odelia told me about her suspicions, I knew it meant they were still messing around. I should have said something then, but . . ." I stall, not knowing what the right words are.

"You didn't want to be the bad guy," Mel says, as if she's reading my thoughts.

"Odelia seemed so happy. I also felt like I owed Cat my secrecy. The only reason I know you and Odelia is because she introduced you both to me."

As I give Mel time to process the information I've dropped into her lap, sporadic tears stream down my face. I'm surprised I've managed to keep the flood at bay, but I need to be strong and face my mistakes. I'm not the victim here.

"I get it," Mel finally says.

"You do?"

"The only reason why I told Odelia is because I can. We've known each other a long time. I'm not scared or intimidated by her. And I knew, coming from me, she could take it. I don't think you were in the wrong here, Jessie. It's not like you're the one who cheated."

"Then you think we should tell Odelia?"

"I didn't say that. Telling Odelia won't help or change anything. Cat's gone. The truth is out. Everyone knows." Before I can protest, Mel goes on. "Do you feel better now that you've told me the truth?"

"Yes, but . . ."

"Good. Now it's my secret, too. Let it go, Jessie. There's no reason to get Odelia even more upset."

"I don't understand."

"I have something at stake here as well. You. If Odelia made me choose between you and her, I'd have to choose her, and I really don't want to lose you. Please, Jessie, keep this one between us."

"Okay," I say, feeling a strange sense of calm. "If there's anything I can do for you, just ask. Anything at all."

"Actually," Mel says, "there is." Her voice rises an octave and I'm ready to offer her whatever she wants. "Could you talk me up to Griffin, maybe set something up? He was so hot on stage today. My crush has been reignited. And you guys seem pretty tight. I figured you might be able to work some magic."

Griffin and Mel? I don't see it, but there's no way I could say no, especially after Mel promised to keep my secret.

"Of course." I clear my throat. The words struggle to come out. "I'll see what I can do."

After we say goodbye, I check to see if Griffin texted. He didn't. There is a text from Levi asking to FaceTime, and just as I'm about to press the call button, I clear the screen and dial Griffin's number instead.

"Hello?" Griffin answers, and my pulse quickens.

"Hey...it's me." Silence greets me on the other end. "Where did you disappear to today?"

"I came home," Griffin says. His chilly tone rattles me. "Guess I didn't want to be part of the Jessie and Levi show."

"I'm sorry. I didn't know he was going to do that. It was so embarrassing," I say, trying to downplay what happened.

"Well, the whole school seemed to love it."

"Wrong. The whole school loved your performance. You blew everyone away. I may even be willing to forgive you for dragging me up there."

Griffin lets out a small laugh. "I guess this means you finally got what you wanted?"

I sigh. "Yeah." Except, I never made it a goal in my journal for Levi to be my boyfriend. And now that I think about it, it's kind of weird I didn't.

"So, is there a reason you called?"

"Yes," I answer, my voice shaky. "You know my friend Melissa? She wanted me to find out if you'd be interested in going out with her sometime."

"Maybe," Griffin replies.

"Great," I manage to squeak out.

Not sure why I'm so in my feelings about this. Griffin and Mel are my friends and I should want to see them happy. But Griffin was my friend first, and if he discovers how amazing Mel is, the two of them will probably end up falling in love and ditching me. Just like all my other friends have.

And there it is. The fear.

I can do and say all the right things. I can be the best listener, friend, and girlfriend. I could even be perfect. And it will never be enough. Because it's never *been* enough. No matter how far I've come and no matter how hard I try, beneath the mask will always be a girl who's afraid of being left behind.

TWENTY-FIVE

Turns out when a crack forms in the foundation of your friend group, having a boyfriend comes in handy. Being with Levi gives me the perfect excuse to duck out of tension-filled lunches, where Odelia alternates between sad and angry, Mel pouts because she doesn't know how to fix it, and I stew in my guilt. It's a time.

It's kind of sad how quickly someone who was part of your everyday life can just disappear and you're expected to go on like nothing happened. Cat was wrong, and it's not like she was my favorite person, but there's still a void left behind by her absence. I think we all feel it, and we're grieving in our own, unique ways.

The last few weeks have been such a blur, it barely registers that February has come and gone and we're already a few days into March. Levi's lips attached to mine daily have not only been a distraction but also a huge adjustment.

It took me a few days to get used to public displays of affection. It's funny, I wanted so badly to be out with Levi, but when we officially became a couple, it was me who struggled with holding hands and kissing in front of other people. I thought I'd want to stroll through the halls announcing to everyone who passed us that Levi is *my* boyfriend and I'm *his* girlfriend. But it's not like that. For me at least. Levi has done a complete one-eighty. He even requests that I wear my kilt more often to show off my upturned pin. It makes me feel like some sort of prize cow.

When I do manage to spend time with Mel and Odelia, it's not the same. The dynamics have shifted slightly. Now I'm the one with a boyfriend, Mel's the one with a crush, and Odelia, well, she has a new pastime. Her recent extracurricular activities involve skipping class and hooking up with randoms.

"Who's Odelia off with today?" I ask Mel over lunch.

"Oh god, I don't know," Mel says. "I'm trying to be the supportive friend by not telling her what to do. It's how she deals. But she doesn't seem to be 'dealing' all that well." She shrugs. "You should have seen her this morning. She broke into Evan's locker and threw all his things in the trash."

"Why?"

"You haven't heard?"

"Heard what?" I ask, glancing at my phone.

"Cat and Evan are officially a thing now. I guess when he realized Odelia wouldn't take him back, he settled for runner-up."

I roll my eyes. "Are we supposed to be surprised by this?"

Mel grabs a fry off my plate. "Nope. Why do you keep looking at your phone?"

"Levi texted. He wants to see me," I say, scrunching my face up.

"Then go." Mel nods to the exit as she steals another fry.

We have a tech club meeting in a few minutes. The drama club will be there, too. It's the first official rehearsal for *Little Shop of Horrors*. Auditions were held the week after Valentine's Day and, as I predicted, Griffin landed the lead role of Seymour Krelborn. Rosalind Chen scored the role of Audrey (I)—Griffin's love interest. Rosalind's nice. Everyone in the drama club is nice. Including Mrs. Elliott, though Griffin couldn't get her to budge on her no-ninth-graders rule. But it was sweet that he tried.

"I'll just tell Levi we have a meeting."

"Tell him in person." Mel winks. "Seriously, can you tell him in person? Griffin texted too. He's on his way so we can walk to the meeting together." Her eyes sparkle like a kid on Christmas morning. The girl is smitten.

As a good friend, I should nudge Griffin along, but every time I think of the two of them together my stomach does this weird churny thing.

A couple of days after our awkward phone call, Griffin sent me a goofy meme. I responded with an equally goofy meme. He asked if I'd watch his audition for *Little Shop* and I agreed. We didn't bring up Levi, Mel, or what happened at the Karaoke-a-thon. Still haven't.

Griffin, Mel, and I have become somewhat of an odd threesome, attending all the tech/drama club meetings together. At our first combined meeting after auditions, Mrs. Elliott said I "shone like a diamond" at the Karaoke-a-thon with Griffin. It was pretty impossible to hide my grin, especially since the validation was nice. When my eyes met Griffin's, he smiled too, and it made me feel some kind of way.

A way a girl with a boyfriend isn't supposed to feel about her friend who's a boy.

Even though I know Mel and Griffin are "talking"—whatever that means—Griffin and I usually end up sitting next to each other at the meetings, placing bets on how late Mikey Pez will be. Mikey landed the role of Audrey II, the man-eating plant from space, and he never shows up on time. I find this super annoying since I'd kill for a role as small as "drunk passed out on the street." And yet Mikey, who scored the coolest role in the entire musical, can't even be bothered to grace us with his presence. If you ask me, he's not even all that good, just loud, plus he has a sizable social media following for his mocktails account.

"I'll take notes at the meeting if you somehow find yourself distracted," Mel says.

"I'm not going to let Levi talk me into missing another meeting. Especially this one." Mr. Wolfe is finally assigning roles to the tech club members, and I want to get there early enough to make sure I don't get stuck pointing the spotlight.

I grab my things and walk to the atrium, where Levi's waiting.

"Hey. I have a tech meeting in five minutes so I can't be long."

"Again? I was kind of hoping we could go somewhere and be alone." Levi pulls me in closer, bridging the gap between us.

"Levi. People are looking," I say, leaning away slightly.

"So let them." He wraps his arms around me and smiles that irresistible smile. "I've been waiting all day to be with you." He gives me his best puppy dog eyes, and I cave. Levi takes my hand and leads me to the Medieval section of the library, where we kiss. Well, more like make out.

Lately, Levi's hands have had a mind of their own. My body is uncharted territory, and Levi's the handsome Irish settler seeking permanent residence. Right before he's about to touch me where only Sydney, the busty underwear salesgirl, ever has, he stares at me with such intensity, it's hard to tell him to stop. It's not that I don't want him to, especially when we're in the moment, it's just that I tend to feel a little guilty afterward. I want to be all sex-positive, but it's hard when one look from your parents can make you feel like the sticky residue on the floor of a public restroom. After spicy make-out sessions, I promise myself not to let things go that far again, but one look into his eyes makes me forget about those fake-ass delusions. Factually speaking, it feels good. *Really good*. SO GOOD! Instead, I've set boundaries for Levi—and myself. He knows not to go under my clothes. I'm not ready for that yet. But damned if Mr. Blue Eyes ain't persistent.

"Stop." I swat his fingers away before they make it under my kilt.

"Sorry." Levi holds his hands up and backs away. His hair is a mess and his lips are puffed out from kissing me so hard. *God, he's so perfect.*

Unable to resist my Irish settler, I stick a finger in between the buttons of his shirt and pull him toward me. He presses his mouth up against mine.

"What's wrong with this?" I ask, mid-kiss.

"Absolutely nothing." He licks his lips. Within seconds we're right back at it. He tugs at the hem of my shirt, walking his fingers up my bare stomach, while his tongue explores places only my dentist has seen.

I pull away as he tries to sneak his fingers beneath my bra. "Not under the clothes."

He stops and sighs.

"Can't we just kiss?" I ask. My first kiss was only three months ago. Why do things have to move so quickly? If kissing and holding hands satisfies me, then why isn't it enough for him? Unless he's used to doing more. Maybe his relationship with Liv set a standard I'm supposed to meet. Once again, I'm in completely over my head.

"Sure." Levi tips his forehead to mine. "You know I love you, right?"

I meet his gaze and nod. "I know."

A slightly deflated smile appears on his face before he tucks a piece of hair behind my ear. "I'll walk you to your meeting. Is it okay if I wait outside for you to be done?"

"That would be nice," I say, before interlocking my fingers with his.

I show up to the meeting late and Mr. Wolfe assigns me spotlight operator alongside Julia Han.

Because of course.

It's the Friday before spring break, and Mel and I are sitting at our regular table at the back of the cafeteria having lunch. Odelia pulls up a chair across from me.

"Hey, Mel," I say, leaning in and supressing a grin, "remember that girl we used to be friends with? You know, the tall one with shoulder-length dark hair and thick bangs? She gets two dimples in her cheeks when she smiles real hard?"

"Cordelia?" Mel smirks. "Yeah, what about her?"

"Well, don't be alarmed, but I think she's sitting next to you, eyeing your fries."

"Ha ha, very funny, guys," Odelia says. "Yes, I know I've been a bit AWOL, but it's for a good reason."

"Which is?" I ask. "And speak fast. There's only a few minutes until the bell."

She steals a few of Mel's fries and dips them into the ketchup playfully. "I'm seeing someone new."

Mel and I look at one another, then back at Odelia.

"It's Darren." She hides her face in her hands, then peeks out between her fingers. "I know what you're thinking: Cat's leftovers? But he's really great. He reached out to me, and as soon as we started talking, we clicked. Like, really, really well. Like, in *all* areas," she adds with a wink.

"That's so cool," I say, meaning it. "Darren has always seemed decent."

"If you're happy, we're happy," Mel says. "And I have some news of my own to share. Griffin finally asked me out. We're going to see a movie over the break. Isn't that exciting?" She squeals while grabbing my arm.

"Took him long enough," I respond, in mock annoyance.

"Jessie." I turn and see that it's Annie calling to me. This never happens. "Jess, we have to go. Get your things." Annie's skin is pale, her eyes bloodshot.

"What's wrong?" I ask.

"Teta had a heart attack. She's in the hospital. Mom is on her way to pick us up."

"Mel, um, can you tell Levi I had to leave? My phone's dead." I try to pack up, but my shaky hands make it almost impossible. Odelia and Mel help and walk with me to the front doors with Annie. They each give me a hug before I get into the back seat of Mom's car. Mom doesn't say anything, she just stares ahead, seemingly waiting for me to put on my seat belt.

There's a chill in the air, but the sun shines bright on my face. No one speaks the entire drive to the hospital. I start to think back to the last time I saw my teta. It was over the Christmas holidays. She seemed healthy, strong even. What could have happened between then and now?

Tears roll down my face as guilt sets in. I've been so wrapped up in my own life, Teta has barely registered as a flicker in my mind since December. I took her presence for granted. Why am I such an awful, selfish person? I don't consider myself to be super religious, but I spend the rest of the drive praying over and over to God to fix my grandma. She's going to be fine. She has to be.

We arrive at the cold and stark-white hospital. Dad is on his phone, still in dirty work clothes. Mom races over and he places one arm around her while the other grips his cell. He ends the call and rests his forehead against the wall. Mom wraps her arms around him, and for the first time in my life, I witness tears come out of my father's eyes.

Dad wipes his face and speaks to Mom in a hushed tone. They both nod before heading to Annie and me.

"Teta had a stroke, not a heart attack. It was a bad one. They've had to put her in a coma. The doctors don't think she will come out of it." Dad pauses and looks away. He clears his throat and faces us again. "You need to come to the room and say goodbye to her."

The elevator doors open and Ramsey walks out with our amto, amo, and cousins. We all wait for our turn to be called in, not saying a word. My cousin Rainy locks her arm through mine. It's the only thing keeping me upright.

I've never had to do this before. I don't want to. I want to get on that elevator and leave this sterile place full of sick people and go back to school with my friends.

One by one, we take turns saying our goodbyes. My cousins and siblings go in before me, only to come out moments later with flushed cheeks and red-stained eyes. Mom comes to get me and I follow her into the room, gripping her hand. Dad sits next to Teta, his mother, one hand holding hers, the other stroking her black-and-gray hair.

I move stiffly toward the bed. I can't stop swallowing. Teta looks peaceful, like she's asleep, except with a bunch of wires attached to her. There's a constant beep in the background. I don't want to cry in front of Dad—he needs me to be strong— so I swallow to hold back tears. This is the last time I will see my grandmother alive, and all I can think about is how much I want to get it over with. I don't like seeing her this way. It hurts too much. I bend down, placing a kiss on her cheek. It's warm and feels hollow.

I bring my mouth to her ear and whisper, "I love you, Teta, and I promise to eat more." I swallow again, studying her wrinkled hand in my father's. It looks so tiny. "I'm really going to miss your hugs."

I leave the room and walk past my family members. I don't want anyone to try to comfort me. I just want to be alone.

After traveling down the echoey halls of the hospital for a while, I come to a waiting area filled with empty seats. I sit on a beige, cushioned chair facing the window, pull my knees up to my chest, and rock back and forth, allowing the tears to finally come out.

⟋

The next week is both excruciatingly slow and goes by in a flash. There are multiple visits to the funeral home, church services, the actual funeral, and what feels like a revolving door of visitors to our house.

There's finally a reprieve from everything the Friday before spring break ends. The five of us are home, all in our separate corners. I'm in my room trying to read but can't seem to get past the first page. Annie wasn't able to go on her trip to Paris. She sold her seat to someone on the waiting list. Mom and Dad let her keep the money. For the time being, Ramsey has stopped pestering our parents about moving out.

Losing my grandmother so suddenly rocked me. If anything, it forced me to see life outside the bubble I've built for myself. It's been all about me coping with my autism, friends, and Levi. I need to make more room for other things. Other people.

Goal #17: Spend more time with family. Show them you love them.

I haven't spoken to anyone in a week and I decide to start

with Levi. After several texts go unanswered, I call him. Lucy answers his phone and gives me her condolences. She says he's not home and must have forgotten his cell. Convenient. But for some reason, I'm relieved.

As soon as I end the call with Lucy, my phone rings.

"Hello?"

"Jessie? Hi, it's Griffin. How are you? Mel told me what happened. I'm really sorry. I've been thinking about you all week. I mean, I've been thinking about reaching out all week but I didn't want to overstep."

Even though Griffin's rambling, I'm really happy to hear his voice.

"I'm doing okay."

"I have some news that might cheer you up," he says.

Oh no. Is this about his date with Mel? Did they hit it off? Are they officially a couple now? "What is it?" I ask.

"You didn't hear it from me, but Mrs. Elliott is completely over Mikey Pez and his late arrivals. Which means there might be an opening in the musical soon."

"Who's his understudy?"

"He doesn't have one. Elliott is paranoid about assigning understudies. Says it brings bad karma to the set."

"So, you think she'll find someone from within to replace him? Or she'll hold new auditions?"

Silence greets me on the other end of the line. Just as I'm about to say something, the beginning of "Feed Me" plays.

"This is the song," Griffin says. "This is the song you need to learn to wow Mrs. Elliott. And I'll help."

"Wait . . . what?"

"I overheard Mrs. Elliott tell Mikey if he's late for rehearsal once more, he's out. And I think we both know how that's going to end. Once Mikey's cut, Elliott will need someone great to replace him. Someone with the vocal range to pull off Audrey II's solos. *Someone* who has the stage presence to play a loud, obnoxious character."

"Thank you?"

"Thank me after you get the role."

"Griffin, I really appreciate your faith in me, but there's no way Mrs. Elliott is going to give me the role of Audrey II."

"Why not?"

"Why not?"

"Yeah, why not?" he presses.

"Well, for one, Audrey II is typically played by a male actor."

"Weak. Next?"

"Okay," I say, burying a laugh. "How about the fact that Mrs. Elliott wouldn't even let me audition for a minor role? Audrey II is like . . . second from the top."

"With desperation there's always a way. When Mikey leaves Mrs. Elliott stranded and she's at her lowest low, you and I will swoop in and amaze her with our performance of 'Feed Me.'"

"You really think this will work?" I ask, finding myself starting to fall for this scheme he's hatched.

"I know it will. Practice the song. And when we're back at school, we'll rehearse it together. At least half of luck is being prepared."

"Okay," I say, "I'll try. But I'm not sure I can hit the notes."

"You can. I believe in you."

"I'm glad someone does. This could all blow up in my face. And yours."

"I wouldn't let that happen, you know that."

"Yeah, I do."

We listen to the song a few times, and each time I get more

excited. More than anything, I'm impressed that Griffin cares enough to try. He's putting himself on the line here too. After the fourth listen, I muster up the guts to ask him something I've been dying to know. "How was your date with Mel?"

"It was fine." Griffin pauses. "Mel's nice and I like hanging out with her, but there's no real spark, you know?"

The smile on my face betrays my supportive-friend pose; it's probably a good thing he can't see it. *What kind of friend am I? Why do I care so much anyway? I have a boyfriend. Somewhere out there.*

Griffin and I continue to talk on the phone for the next hour. He asks me to share my favorite memory of my grandma and tells me about losing his grandfather last year. Then the conversation switches back to the play, ranking our favorite numbers, and daydreaming about what it might be like to work together.

Every time one of us is about to end the call, the other says "One more thing" or "I forgot to tell you . . ." It's as if we're trying to cram a month of conversations into this one. When we do eventually get off the phone, I lie in bed and close my eyes.

The strange thing is, I see Griffin's face.

TWENTY-SIX

Spring break has come and gone and it's definitely one I will never forget, even though I'd like to. The mood at home has been understandably bleak, which makes school a slightly more attractive option. When I step off the bus, Mel and Odelia are there waiting for me. They wrap me up in their arms for a group hug.

Odelia places a lock of hair behind my ear when we pull apart. I kind of like it when she dotes on me. She and Mel link their arms through mine as we walk to the atrium, amid the Monday morning rush.

"Have you spoken to Levi yet?" Mel asks as we pause by the stairs.

"Nope." I fold my arms over my chest. "He never reached out. Nice boyfriend, eh?"

"Men are rage-inducing," Odelia says. "And on that note, I'm meeting mine before the bell. Catch up with you ladies at lunch." Odelia plants a kiss on my cheek before skipping off to see Darren.

I turn to Mel and sigh. "I left in such a hurry before the break, half my things are still upstairs in my locker. Walk with me?"

She nods.

"So, how was your movie date with Griffin?" I ask, curious to hear her side of things.

"Uneventful," she says, with a half-hearted smile. "He didn't try to hold my hand or kiss me. He seemed reluctant to even split fries at the food court after the movie. He made it pretty clear, in a nice way, that he's not interested."

"Oh. How do you feel about that?"

"Okay." She shrugs. "At least we gave it a try. It's not like I was ever in love with him or anything. I just thought he was cute. Still do."

"Well, like Annie says, if one boat makes you seasick, you hop on another."

"What are you talking about?" Mel asks, appearing to fight back a laugh.

"I actually don't know," I say, shaking my head.

On our way to my locker, we pass Liv, who practically cackles in my presence.

"What?" I snap back, not in any mood to deal with her mind games.

Liv's mouth curves into a wide grin. "How many hours of community service does Levi get for dating you?"

"What're you talking about?"

She sizes me up. "I mean, you almost look normal. I might not have known if Levi hadn't said anything." Liv smirks, then walks between me and Mel before disappearing down the hall.

I feel my brow furrow in confusion. "What do you think she meant by that?"

Mel studies her shoes before bringing her eyes up to mine. "I think you need to talk to Levi."

The morning goes by at a snail's pace. It's excruciating trying to listen to my Math teacher explain equations when my whole world feels like it's about to come crashing down. Levi and I haven't spoken in over a week, but clearly he's been running his mouth with Liv. The closer I get to seeing him, the angrier and more anxious I become.

We have a standing date to meet at my locker after second period. My heart races as I walk out of English class. The stack of books in my arms is like dead weight. I turn the corner expecting to see Levi. He isn't there. I'm now a ball of fury waiting to be unleashed. As the crowd thins out, Levi appears in the distance, and he's headed my way.

I breathe deeply and follow that with a slow exhale. I shut my locker and force myself to look at him. His hands are in his pockets, his shoulders slumped. It appears he wants to be anywhere in the world but here.

"Can we talk?" he asks, unable to make eye contact with me.

In spite of myself, I nod.

He cranks his neck in circles. "I'm sorry about your grandma."

"What did you tell Liv?" I grip the straps of my backpack as if they're the only things keeping me vertical.

Levi's eyes grow wide, and in that instant I know.

"It was a mistake. Kind of like how you left without saying goodbye."

"What? My grandmother *died*!"

"And I had to hear about it from Griffin. *Always* Griffin."

"I asked Mel to tell you. And then I texted. You never texted back." I close my eyes and try to steady my breathing. "What did you tell her, Levi?"

"We were at a party and I was wasted. Liv wouldn't let up about you. I wasn't thinking clearly. I should have told her to leave."

I edge closer to him, forcing eye contact. "Stop avoiding my question. Tell me what you said."

Levi runs his hand over his mouth and pulls on his chin.

"She just kept ragging on you. At first I ignored it, but then she started saying mean things."

"What kind of mean things?"

His eyes dart around the empty hallway. "About you being weird. That you won't look her in the eye when she talks. Said stuff about you being an Arab. I couldn't listen to it anymore."

"Then why didn't you walk away?"

"I was just trying to defend you."

"What did you tell her?" My heart pounds against my chest in slow, heavy beats.

"I just told her what you told me, about how your brain works differently, 'cause of the autism."

My mouth drops open. "Levi, I told you that in complete confidence. Now the whole school is going to know."

"I made her promise not to say anything."

"Some promise," I say, laughing to myself. "She couldn't wait to tell me about how you opened up to her. Why did you do it?"

"I was drunk."

"That's not an excuse and you know it. Is this because I won't . . . ?"

"No. It's not. I swear. I screwed up." He takes a step toward me. "I can fix it." There's a glimmer of hope in his eyes, but I don't need to look in a mirror to know there's none left in mine.

"You can't fix this. It's already out there. And even if by some miracle Liv doesn't say anything, it doesn't matter." I need to get out of here. I can't look at him for another second.

"No." Levi blocks my path. "Please." His eyes search for mine. "I'll do whatever it takes to show you how sorry I am. I'll talk to her. I'll do anything." Levi grabs my wrists. "Jessie, I love you."

I twist out of Levi's grasp and shake my head. "You don't get it. I can't trust you anymore." I place my hands in front of me like a shield. "Maybe if this were the first time you let me down, but it's not. You know that. I know that. I need to be with someone who loves me as much as I love them."

"But you've never told me you love me," Levi says, his voice raw with emotion.

"No." I meet his eyes. "I haven't."

Levi exhales. A bathroom door shuts with a loud click down the hall. Someone coughs in the stairwell behind us. Every sound plays like a drumbeat in my head. We stand for a few minutes not saying anything. I look at him once more before walking away. This time, he doesn't try to stop me.

Once at home, I rip open my journal and draw a giant *X* over every goal that has to do with Levi Walsh. Why did I let myself get so wrapped up in another person? I did what Ramsey told me to do. I let my guard down. I let people in. But all that ever does is screw me over. Seven months into school and I'm down one friend and one boyfriend. At this rate, I'll end the year alone. I'd probably be better off, too. You can't fight destiny.

There should be a handbook on how to deal with breakups. Like, how to *really* deal with them. Every chapter would tackle a different situation, because no heartache is one size fits all. And most importantly, the following words would never appear: *time heals all wounds*. Because right now, I can't see past my own callused hand in front of my face.

The last place I want to be today is in the same building as Levi Walsh, but the drama and tech clubs are meeting after school. Volunteers are already at work building sets, and the senior Art class has been tasked with creating all four Audrey IIs, from hand puppet to gigantic, hollowed out stage prop.

Things are well underway and I just feel kind of . . . stalled.

"Jessie K.," Griffin calls from outside the caf. "Where have you been? I texted you, like, twenty times today to see if you want to go over 'Feed Me.'"

"Oh." I check my phone as he approaches. "Sorry. I've been kind of out of it."

Griffin takes my hand and guides me to a quiet spot in the atrium. "What's going on?"

"I guess Levi didn't tell you?"

Griffin's eyes shift down. "We don't really talk much these days."

"Room for one more in that club?" I ask. The tears are fighting to come out but I just keep shaking my head, hoping it'll stop me from crying. If I look at Griffin and see his pitying eyes looking back at me, I'll lose it completely.

"Did you break up?"

I nod and swallow. Griffin pulls me in for a hug, his big arms tight around me. I finally lose it, and Griffin pulls away slightly, removing the strands of hair covering my face and wiping away my tears.

"Your first breakup is the worst," he says with a smile that spreads a bit of comfort through me. "You know what'll make you feel better?"

"A lobotomy?"

Griffin's laughter fills up the atrium and makes me laugh. "No. Blowing Mrs. Elliott's mind with your Audrey II audition."

"About that," I say. "I don't know if it's such a good idea." The stage is filled with people working on sets. The cast is roaming around, running lines from the script they received weeks ago.

And my spotlight partner, Julia, is waiting on the scaffold for me to join her so we can take turns pointing the gigantic spotlight when needed.

"Look around," Griffin says, turning my body so I'm facing the stage. "Do you see Mikey Pez?"

"No."

"What else do you see?"

"Actors who have been in their roles for weeks. Who already know their lines."

"Besides that," he says.

My eyes search the stage until I spot Mrs. Elliott, checking her phone as her eyes dart around the caf.

"A pissed-off Mrs. Elliott."

"Exactly." Griffin gets in front of me. "This is our moment to swoop in. Everyone is busy. We'll pull her aside and pitch the idea to her."

"We haven't even gotten together to practice it yet," I remind him.

"So, we'll wing it!"

"I can't. I just . . ." I sigh. "I don't have it in me."

"Fine. Then I'll talk to her."

Griffin takes off toward the stage before I can stop him. He climbs up the steps until he's standing across from Mrs. Elliott. I stay where I am and watch it all unfold before me. Mrs. Elliott's eyes land on mine, then shift back to Griffin. She's hesitating, but Griffin isn't backing down. She crosses her arms over her chest, crushing the script she's holding, as her eyes land on mine again. Griffin turns back and shoots me a wink and a smile that lights up the whole room.

A minute later he's coming down the steps again, practically running toward me. "Let's go," he says, taking my hand.

"Where? What did she say? Griffin, slow down."

He pauses, takes in a breath, and releases it. "Sorry. I spoke to Mrs. Elliott. She was a bit reluctant at first, but she agreed to watch us perform 'Feed Me.' And then she'll decide."

"I'm not auditioning in front of all these people."

"I know. I knew you wouldn't feel comfortable doing that, so she's meeting us in the Drama room. It'll just be you, me, her, and Antonia, playing the piano."

"I don't know. I'm just . . . I'm not really feeling up to it."

"Channel that grief. That anger. Gather it up inside you and spit it out while you sing. It's what you do, Jess. You're a performer."

More than he realizes.

"Okay, fine. Just know, I'm only doing this for you."

"I'm good with that. Come on. Elliott's giving us twenty minutes with Antonia to rehearse before she comes to watch. Yalla," he says, and I almost have to lift my jaw off the floor.

With Antonia at the piano, Griffin and I manage to run through the song three times before Mrs. Elliott strolls in, her layers of necklaces and bracelets chiming as she walks. She pulls up a chair and sits, crossing her legs.

"What have you got for me?" she asks.

I exchange glances with Griffin and a sliver of a smile sneaks its way out. He mirrors my smile before mouthing, "You got this."

Griffin nods for Antonia to begin. As soon as the first chord is played, I'm transformed into Audrey II, putting on the most outlandish voice I can think of for a gigantic alien plant who feasts on human flesh. My jaw stretches as I sing, and seeing Mrs. Elliott's grin gives me permission to play it even more over the top.

Griffin watches the theatrical insanity happening in front of him, holding back laughter as he slips into the role of Seymour. Soon we're duetting, and everything that's been weighing me down falls off my shoulders. Griffin and I stand face-to-face, our noses almost touching, as we sing the last few lines together. When we're done, he scoops me off the ground in another hug. This time, there are no tears.

Mrs. Elliott rises from her seat and claps enthusiastically.

"You two are *perfection* together! Jessie, I am going to get into hot water for allowing a ninth-grader to play a lead role, but, as Audrey II would say, 'Tough titty.' As far as I'm concerned, the role is yours."

I cover my mouth with my hand in shock. "Really?"

"Really."

Griffin, standing behind me, places both hands on my shoulders. "I know Jessie's a little behind, but I'll see to it that she gets caught up."

Mrs. Elliott's eyes shift from Griffin's to mine before she smiles widely. "I'm sure you will. Come see me backstage for an actor's script, and then I'll get your measurements for the costume. Come on, kids, we have a show to put on."

Antonia follows Mrs. Elliott out. The door closes behind them, leaving Griffin and me alone in the room.

"I guess Julia's going to have to learn how to operate the spotlight herself," I say, knowing full well she'll be thrilled to not have to work with me and my pouty ass anymore.

"These people won't know what hit them when they see you as Audrey II."

"Thank you. For pushing me to do this. And for letting me cry all over your shoulder about Levi."

Griffin clears his throat. "Let's make a deal, shall we?"

"I don't agree to anything until I know all the terms and conditions."

He smiles, and it makes me smile back. Again. "From here on out, this," he says, waving a finger between us, "is a Levi-free zone. We have a lot of work to do together, and I think it's important we focus on the show and not on the person whose name shall not be uttered."

"I think I can agree to that."

He offers his hand to seal the deal. I place my hand in his and we shake on it with our eyes locked. Just as I'm about to look away, he grasps my hand tighter and steps up to me so our faces are only inches apart.

"I guess I get to give myself a check mark in my metaphorical journal tonight."

"Same," I say. "Except . . . whatever the opposite of metaphorical is."

He doesn't smile or laugh. He just looks at me, his gaze unwavering. "I'd like to discuss the possibility of revising Goal #9. I'm thinking an upgrade from first male friend."

"Definitely," I respond. Griffin isn't only my first male friend, he's the friend I've spent my whole life searching for. He just came in a different package than I expected. "Maybe this sounds kind of juvenile," I say, while continuing to shake Griffin's hand slowly, "but I think you might be my *best* friend."

"Best friend?" Griffin blinks then looks away. He swallows as he brings his eyes back to mine. "I guess I can deal with that." We release our extended handshake and step away slightly from one another.

"Come on, best friend," he says, picking up his script. "We have work to do."

TWENTY-SEVEN

Rehearsals for *Little Shop* have taken over my life, and the lines between reality and my role as Audrey II are starting to blur. Well, maybe not so much my role as Audrey II, more like my role as an actor.

We spend so much of our lives hearing how we should "be ourselves," as if that's something you can order online and have delivered at your door the next day. It's probably the kind of ableist advice that only works for neurotypicals.

I've tried on so many masks and have absorbed so many different personalities over the years that it's hard for me to strip them away and find the girl who lies beneath. But every now and then I get a quick glimpse of what I assume is the real me, and I like her. What's confusing is, sometimes I saw that person when I was with Levi.

I miss Levi. I think about him all the time, and I hate myself for it. When our paths cross and he smiles at me, it's so sweet and endearing, it almost makes me want to forgive him. I've been trying to keep him at arm's length, and so far it's been working, but it's hard. How do you treat someone like a stranger when he knows a side of you no one else does? I can't pretend he doesn't matter when, at one point, he was everything to me.

"I think that's good enough for today," Mrs. Elliott says. She called a cast-only table read in the Drama room over lunch to go over a few changes she made to the script. "Griffin, Rosalind, can you two stick around to go over blocking for the kiss?"

My eyes meet Griffin's across the table. His face is bright red. Audrey and Seymour are supposed to share a kiss after "Suddenly, Seymour," and up until now, Griffin and Rosalind have only rehearsed the vocals. It seems like every time the subject comes up, Griffin's entire face turns a shade of crimson. At first I thought it was because he had a crush on Rosalind. Then I met Rosalind's girlfriend and figured it likely wasn't that. I was oddly relieved to learn that Rosalind was already spoken for. At some point, I am going to need to stop being so possessive about Griffin. One of these days he'll fall in love with a girl and I'll just have to suck it up.

"Hey, Jess," Griffin calls out as I leave the room. I turn to face him and his cheeks are still cherry-red. "I want to ask you something."

"Okay," I say, nodding. "What is it?"

He laughs and runs a hand through his curls. "Are you going to the spring formal?"

"Ugh," I reply, rolling my eyes. "Yes. I got roped into it by Mel and Odelia. I can't tell you how much I'm looking forward to being the fifth wheel."

"Mel has a date?" he asks.

"Yeah. She's going with Dylan Whitworth from tech club. Why? Did you want to go with her?"

"No. No. I just..." He pauses and runs a hand through his hair again before looking back at the class. "Each table seats eight, right?"

"I think so." I shrug.

"So, who's sitting in the other three spots?"

"Another couple. Friends of Darren's. Hey, maybe if I bring

my brother's suit jacket and drape it over the eighth chair, I could score extra dessert."

"You could do that, or . . ." he says, rocking back and forth on his heels, "I could buy the last seat at the table and go with you."

"You'd do that for me?"

"*For* you?"

"Well, yeah, 'cause otherwise it's just me at a table with three other couples. I don't really need the visual reminder of how pathetically single I am."

Griffin lets out a hollow laugh and nods. "Yeah. I'd do that for you. Hey, it might even be fun."

"It usually is when we're together," I reply.

He opens his mouth to say something else but Mrs. Elliott walks through the door and gives him an expectant look.

"I'll text you later and we can go over details," he says before heading back in.

Details? What details? I wonder if Griffin thinks he has to, like, come to my door or something. I'll let him know he's off the hook and we can just meet at the school. There's no way my parents would be cool with me going to the formal with a guy, even if he is just a friend.

I make my way to the cafeteria to meet Odelia and Mel. With rehearsals amping up and the show date quickly approaching, the three of us don't get to hang out as much as we used to.

"How was it?" Mel asks as I slide into my seat.

"Good. Elliott let us out early so she could go over the kiss with Griffin and Rosalind."

"And how do you feel about that?" Odelia asks, her brown eyes narrowing in my direction.

"Fine. It's just acting."

Mel raises a brow. "And if it wasn't?"

"This feels like an inquisition or something," I say.

"Pretend it is," Odelia replies, sliding her lunch tray away and leaning her elbows on the table. "How would you feel about Griffin dating another girl?"

"Griffin can date whoever he wants." I sit up straight in my seat, looking between them.

"Jessie," Mel says.

"What?"

"She doesn't know, does she?" Odelia says to Mel.

"Know what?" I ask.

"Oh my god, she doesn't." Odelia tilts her head and looks at me like I'm a kid who can't stand up straight in her skates. "Jessie, Griffin is in love with you."

"What?" I practically shout. "No way."

Mel nods. "Yes, way."

"Nuh-uh. He's never said anything," I respond, indignant.

"He doesn't have to," Odelia says, clearly holding back a laugh. "It's written all over his face."

"How do you feel about him?" Mel asks.

"He's my friend," I reply.

"Maybe you should consider moving him out of the friend zone. I mean, you and Levi are over, and there *is* an extra seat at the table for spring formal."

My mouth falls open and I look away.

"Wait, did he ask you to go with him?" Mel laughs and looks at Odelia, who has a wide grin splashed across her face.

"He did, but just as friends."

"Did *he* say you'd be going just as friends?" Mel asks.

"No, but it's what he meant."

"Sure, Jess. Just keep telling yourself that," Odelia says, before opening her bottle of water and taking a big gulp.

"I need some air," I say, standing. "I'll catch up with you guys later."

I grab my things and head toward the pond. Mel and Odelia don't know what they're talking about. Griffin and I are friends. It is possible for a guy and a girl to be platonic. This formal thing is just him doing me a favor. Besides, even if I did like Griffin in that way, I wouldn't want to do anything to jeopardize our friendship. It's too important to me. And as much as I'd like to believe I'm over Levi, I'm really not. That relationship left me devastated, and I'm still trying to pick up the pieces—even though it's been forty-two days. (But who's counting?)

It's a perfect May day. A mix of warm and breezy. I've been spending so much time inside at rehearsals that I haven't noticed how blue the sky is or how full the trees are. I find a partially shaded patch of grass to sit on and pull out my new earbuds. They're more discreet than my big headphones and easier to sneak to school.

"What're you listening to?"

I tilt my head up. The sun is blinding but I still recognize the silhouette in front of me.

Levi sits and boldly takes one of my earbuds. The scent of Tide and freshly cut grass fills the air between us. Sunlight highlights his already twinkling blue eyes, making it almost impossible for me not to run my hands through his shaggy hair.

"I like this song. Who's it by?" He cocks his head to the side and a strand of hair falls in front of his eye. Without thinking, I brush it aside, then quickly look away.

"'Fade into You,' by Mazzy Star."

Levi grabs my hand, interlacing his fingers with mine. His thumb strokes my skin as the slow melody plays. God, I've missed his touch. There's nothing like it. I should pull away. Show him he means nothing to me anymore. Instead, I lean back onto the grass, and Levi follows. We lie side by side, the sunrays on our faces. The captivating voice of the singer brings us to a simpler time. When mistakes hadn't yet been made. When it was just the two of us. When it was easier.

But things were never really easy with Levi.

I sit up and stop the music. "My battery's low. Need to reserve it for the ride home."

Levi returns the earbud to me. I stuff them into their small case and toss it into my backpack, trying to steady my breathing.

"I didn't get it before," Levi says, his eyes on me as I sit with bent knees on the grass. "Everything is meaningful to you." He shifts to face me. "I was reading about autism and girls. I mean, autistic girls."

"Why?"

He runs a hand through his hair and exhales. "Because I want to understand you better. It made me see that you don't make decisions impulsively. If you say something, you mean it, and it makes sense that you expect the same from others."

I swallow, and my eyes remain on Levi's. "I make impulsive decisions sometimes."

"Even then, there's probably a reason behind them." He smiles. "The rest of us, we don't always think things through on the same level. I'm nowhere near as thoughtful as you are. Or kind. I really respect that about you. And I should have respected your secret."

I raise my shoulders. "What's done is done. Besides, Liv hasn't said anything."

"Yeah, well, that wasn't out of the kindness of her heart. I had a talk with her. She won't be saying anything to anyone." Levi rips grass from the ground and glances up at me.

"Do I want to know?"

"Just know I got through to her. The Liv chapter is fully closed."

"So I guess I can check that worry off my list." I pull myself off the ground, and Levi stands too.

"Are you going to spring formal?" he asks.

I immediately look away. His question feels like a test with only one right answer.

When I don't respond, Levi continues. "I'm not asking you to go with me. Don't get me wrong, I'd love to be your date, but after everything that's happened I know it's not a possibility. But maybe, if I'm there and you're there, we could dance? We didn't get a chance to at the fall dance. I was too nervous."

"Nervous? When has Levi Walsh ever been nervous?"

"You're right. I don't get nervous a lot. It only seems to happen around you." He twists his heel into the grass and looks up at me. "I thought you'd say no. I was kind of afraid of you then. I never knew what to expect. It's funny, all the things that scared me about you at first are the things I love the most."

His words radiate warmth, melting the cold layers around my heart. But I can't give in. I'm still angry. Somewhere, deep inside. "I wouldn't have said no."

Levi looks at me with an adorable smirk and I feel my entire face light up.

"Griffin," I say aloud, as if my brain has finally shifted out of neutral. "I told Griffin I'd go to the formal with him. As friends."

"Well, if you're only going as friends, then he shouldn't mind if we dance," Levi replies, cool as always.

"I don't see why not," I say, focusing on Levi's blue eyes staring back at me.

TWENTY-EIGHT

"You don't have a say in the matter. You are coming with us this summer, end of story." Dad's fist hits the kitchen table so hard, dishes rattle.

Our parents break it to us over dinner that they've planned a trip to Palestine this July. Neither I nor my siblings are happy about it.

"I'm twenty-two. You can't expect me to keep going on family vacations. I have a life," Ramsey says. He's here for his weekly meal. One family dinner a week is what he agreed to when my parents finally caved and gave him their blessing to move out in April. He's renting a ratty old bungalow with Charlie, but Mom still does his laundry. Ramsey completed his first term of college last week and is back to working with Dad full-time. To my father's absolute delight (and surprise) he's planning on returning to college in the fall, but this time with only one major—Machining.

"Yes, we can. Want to know why? Because we pay for that life of yours," Dad says, reminding my brother where his rent checks come from. "Listen." Dad puts down his fork and sighs. "Your teta was always getting on me about working too hard, saying I need to enjoy life more. I haven't been back since moving to Canada. I want you all to see the home country. For Teta."

"But why do we have to go for an entire month?" I whine. Four weeks away from Mel, Odelia, Griffin . . . Levi?

Mom places her hand on top of Dad's. "There are a lot of people to see while we're there. We need time."

Annie rolls her eyes. "Great. We're going to the most historical place on earth and we'll be stuck inside, visiting people."

"We'll see family. We'll see Bethlehem. We'll go to Petra, in Jordan. We'll even go to the Dead Sea. And we'll do it all—together." With one last stern look from Dad, the conversation ends. We all have our reasons for not wanting to go, but there's no point fighting it. The tickets have already been purchased. Besides, this trip is over a month away. I have enough worries to keep me busy until then.

The next morning, over chocolate chip muffins, I break the news to Odelia and Mel.

"Palestine? Like, near Bethlehem, where Jesus himself was born? Wow! The most exotic place my family ever goes is up north to the Mennonite furniture store," Odelia jokes.

Mel tilts her head and smiles. "It'll be amazing, Jess. You'll see."

"Just don't go and replace me with Cat while I'm gone, okay?"

Odelia's expression instantly hardens. "Over my dead body."

"Over your dead body what?" Griffin asks, sliding into the seat across from me.

Mel rises, pulling Odelia up with her. "We have to go. We have a . . . thing."

"No we don't," Odelia says, resisting.

Mel's eyes grow to twice their size. These two are about as subtle as Ms. Muller's accent.

"Oh!" Odelia nods. "We have a thing. We'll see you later." She holds in a giggle as she follows Mel out the back doors.

"What's with them?" Griffin asks.

"They're just digesting my latest news," I answer, trying to come up with something to say besides, *Oh, they think you're in love with me.*

"What news?" Griffin sits up in his seat.

"My dad announced last night that we're going to Palestine this summer, the whole family."

"I see." Griffin nods. "For how long?"

"One month. We'll be back the fourth of August. Just in time for my sixteenth birthday."

Griffin's eyes light up. "Well, then we are going to have to make up for lost time by having the biggest sweet-sixteen party ever!"

"Um, hi, do you know me?" I say, furrowing my brow at him.

"You're right. We'll binge nineties movies and split a pizza. That's if you can manage to eat it without getting sauce all over your face," he teases.

"They put too much sauce on the pizza!"

"*All* the pizzas?" Griffin smiles.

"Yes. *All* the pizzas!"

"I'll be sure to pack extra napkins."

"If I were perfect, life would be boring," I say, taking a bite of my muffin.

He brings his thumb and index finger together. "But you're so close." His smile fades slightly. "I will miss you, though."

"Yeah. It'll be hard being away from everyone for so long."

"I'm sure it'll be great. For you, I mean!"

"And a complete culture shock, especially for someone who doesn't like change. Anyway, it's a while off. We have other things to get through first. The formal is this weekend. Then opening night a month after that. Feeling ready?"

"For what? The formal or the play?"

"Both?"

"I was born ready, baby," he says, stealing my muffin and taking a big bite out of it.

"Ah, to have the confidence of a neurotypical white male." I laugh, and Griffin picks off a piece of my muffin and tosses it at me. It lands in my hair. I rip a chunk of muffin off and throw it at him, aiming for his curls. Somehow I miss.

"Come on," he says, standing and plucking a chocolate chip out of my ponytail. "Let me walk you to class. I need to squeeze in as much Jessie K. time as I can before you ditch me."

I rise and shoulder my backpack, then grab my table scraps. "I would never willingly ditch you. I'm being forced against my will."

Griffin drapes his arm over my shoulders as we walk. "Excellent answer."

―

Mel and Odelia made a plan to come over to my place before the formal. They said it would be fun to get ready together. I didn't see how getting dressed in front of each other and jabbing our eyes with mascara wands could be fun, but I decided to play along, because that's what I do.

Odelia's parents agreed to let her attend as long as she did well on her midterms, which seemed like an odd condition given that Odelia could ace all her exams blindfolded. She also had to promise—on her life and the lives of her siblings—that there would be no drinking. Mel and I made her promise us this as well.

Mom was thrilled when I told her I was going to the formal. She forced me to get my hair done at the salon and seemed thoroughly disappointed when I came out sporting a "boring" bun. She wanted me to wear my hair down with big, bouncy waves. And now that there are a multitude of bobby pins poking my brain,

I can see maybe she was right. But I'd never admit that to her.

While Mel and Odelia dance around my room, I'm perched on the edge of my bed, biting my nails. Griffin and I never really got around to discussing the expectations for tonight. Maybe he'll want to talk to other girls. And what if Levi actually shows up and wants to dance? What if I want to dance with him? Or Griffin?

"Jessie, are you going to get dressed, or what?" Odelia asks.

"Right." I get up and open the closet, pulling out my outfit: a black, long-sleeved, crushed velvet bohemian dress, cut above my knee. It's so nineties. Mom wasn't impressed when I picked it out, but she agreed to buy it as long as I wore "nice shoes."

With the girls distracted, I sneak off to my parents' room to change in private. Mom comes in to help zip me up.

She smiles, then proceeds to adjust and smooth out my dress as if I'm her little doll. "Now Jessie, if a boy wants to dance with you tonight, you can say yes . . . even to Mr. Blue Eyes. Just make sure he watches where he puts his hands."

If she only knew where Mr. Blue Eyes' hands have been. "I'm only going because my friends are making me. There won't be any dancing."

"Well, don't be an old lady," she chides. "You're only young once."

When I return to my room, Mel is on my bed flipping through an old magazine, and Odelia is seated in front of the mirror trying out different hairstyles. She runs a brush through her thick, black hair and tries to style it into an updo. When that doesn't work, she slams the brush down on my dresser.

"The more I try to tame my hair, the frizzier it gets." She swivels the chair around and sizes me up. "You look like you just stepped off the runway."

As Odelia sits there in her frumpy, outdated dress, an idea comes to me.

"Hold on a sec." I pop into Annie's room. "Odelia's having trouble with her hair. Can you help?"

Annie tells Odelia to follow her to the bathroom.

Mel and I search through my closet for a dress. She pulls out a red halter dress Mom bought me last summer, brand new with tags. I'd never wear this thing in a million years. It's way too flashy, and there are no sleeves. But if anyone can pull it off, it's Odelia.

Annie works her magic on Odelia's hair, giving her a sleek bob. I avert my eyes as Odelia slips the red dress on in front of us. It fits like a glove. As we head downstairs to take pictures, Odelia pulls me aside.

"You're really lucky, Jessie. You live in this great house, and I know you think your parents are uptight but they're so sweet. Even Annie is a dream compared to my family."

She wraps her arms around me in a hug. A part of me debates telling her the truth about Cat and Evan, but all that would do is destroy this friendship, which has become so important to both of us. Maybe there *are* shades of gray. And maybe it's okay to exist within them sometimes.

Annie agreed to drive us to the school tonight in her brand-new car: a consolation prize for having to miss out on her trip to Paris. She finally got her license last month, and it only took three tries. As soon as I climb into Annie's front seat, I swap my "nice shoes" for my worn-in Docs.

"Why aren't you coming tonight?" Odelia asks Annie.

"Senior prom is next month."

"Are you going with anyone?" Mel inquires.

Annie smiles as she reverses out of the driveway.

I turn to her. "Who?"

"Xavier."

"You're back together?"

"Not officially. Any other questions?" Annie asks, giving me side-eye.

"Yes. What about Mom and Dad?"

"I decided it was worth it," she says, stealing a glance at me as she drives.

Good for Annie. I hope it works out for her. And, thinking selfishly for a second, every battle she fights with the family knocks down a wall and makes things just a little easier for me. Perhaps there's a reason why middle children have a bit of an edge to them. It's a survival tactic.

We arrive at school. A fleet of buses wait to take us downtown to the lakeshore, to the boat where the dance is being held.

I take pictures of the girls with their dates while we wait to board. The buses start their engines and there's still no sign of Griffin, or Levi. I've bitten down on my lips so often, I'm pretty sure all the lip gloss is gone.

"Griffin's not answering my texts," I say to the girls. "Do you think he changed his mind? Or maybe he forgot?"

Odelia and Mel look past me and giggle. I turn around to find Griffin bent double, panting.

"Sorry I'm late." He huffs. "Parents took the car. Had to run here."

Once he's vertical, I whack his arm. "I thought you ghosted me. Why didn't you respond to any of my messages?"

"First of all, I'd never ghost you. That's a promise. Second, I was too focused on getting here in time." Griffin grabs my hand and pulls me out of the bus line. "Here." From his front pocket he takes out a corsage made with a single white rose. "I heard corsages were big in the nineties." His fingers tremble as he slips it over my wrist. "Sorry, it's a little crumpled."

"I love it." A tingle surges from my chest and spreads through me as I examine the corsage and my date. "You look hot."

"Thanks," he says, blushing. "You're, I mean, you look beautiful. I especially love the boots." He pulls up his pant legs to reveal a matching set.

We rejoin the line to board the bus, which seems to be moving incredibly slowly. Griffin keeps smiling and tugging at his sleeves every time our eyes meet. I guess it's strange for him to see me all dressed up. At least when guys put on a suit, they still look like themselves. Being in a dress with fancy hair and makeup, I feel like I'm playing a role, which isn't an uncommon feeling, but it kind of is around Griffin.

As we wait to board, I keep checking my phone to see if there's any message from Levi. When I think I've spotted him in the bus line ahead of us, I arch my neck, but it's just a guy with a similar hairstyle.

Once we're in our seats, Griffin turns his face to the window. I stare right at him, hoping he'll notice and say something, but he remains quiet for the duration of the bus ride. Did I miss something? He went from smiling incessantly to completely ignoring me.

Griffin's lips stay sealed as we exit the bus and make our way down the dock and aboard the boat. Inside, it's adorned with hundreds of twinkle lights, giving it a warm glow. There's a sizeable dance floor surrounded by tables. The large windows look out onto Lake Ontario, which would be much nicer if this docked boat was actually going anywhere. I walk through the doors that lead to the deck alone, and gaze up at the stars in the evening sky. It's such a romantic setting. I find this both hilarious and pathetic, since my "date" isn't speaking to me and Levi is MIA.

Back inside, Griffin is seated at our table. I pull out my chair and sit next to him. "Okay, what did you do to the real Griffin?" I ask, fed up with the silent treatment.

Griffin sighs loudly. "Is everything a joke with you?"

My eyes widen at his tone. Everyone else at the table seems too lost in their own happiness to notice the tension arising between Griffin and me.

"You shouldn't have come tonight," I say. "It's pretty obvious you don't want to be here."

Griffin shakes his head. "I can't believe how dense you can be sometimes."

"If you have a problem, just say what it is."

He remains silent. Unable to sit next to him for another second, I push my chair out and get up. As I'm about to storm out the deck doors, someone grabs my arm.

"Hi, gorgeous." Levi stands before me, wearing a suit and a smile.

"You're here."

He laughs. "Almost didn't make it. Missed the bus and had to take an Uber down. But I couldn't miss out on a chance to dance with you tonight."

Any willpower I have left to push Levi away is officially gone. I take his hand and guide him outside. Around the corner, away from everyone else, the warm breeze and fresh air make me forget about Griffin's strange mood.

"Does Griffin know you're out here with me?"

I reach out and grip the railing. "No. I'm sure if he saw you he would have warned me that you probably have a plan in your back pocket to sway me."

"Oh."

"Sorry. That came out wrong," I say, letting go of the railing. "He was just . . . there for me, after everything that happened, so he's kind of protective."

"*I* should have been there for you," he says, his eyes lifting to meet mine. When I don't respond, he steps back slightly and takes me in. "I like your hair, but there's one problem. It's very distracting. All I can think about is how much I want to kiss this spot right here." I quiver as he strokes my neck and shoulder, placing a gentle kiss there before cupping my face in his hand. "I miss this face. And this mouth. And those eyes."

Levi's words are like hot water rising up my body; I drown in them quickly. The rest of the world disappears as he wraps his arms around me. I can't help but do the same. Even though his touch is familiar, it always feels like the first time.

"I wanted to come here tonight so I could apologize, really apologize, for everything I did. I even prepared a speech," he says.

"A speech? That's so . . . me." I laugh, and it makes Levi blush. "Well, let me hear it."

"Okay." He clears his throat and looks down at me, his arms still wrapped around my body. "I'm sorry for everything. For stringing you along. For trying to keep our relationship a secret. For making you doubt yourself. Liv. All of it." Levi scratches his forehead. "This is cheesy, right?"

"Is there more?" I ask.

"A bit."

"Then sway me," I say.

He nods and holds me even tighter. "I wanted to tell you all the things I love about you. Like how you overthink every-thing. The way you look at me with those big, brown eyes. How smart and funny you are. Your big heart. The way you make me feel when we're together, like I can do anything." A meaningful silence settles between us as I try to process his speech. "That's pretty much it. Not everything can be explained with words," he says, leaning in and virtually eliminating any gap left between us.

I wonder if he can feel my heart thumping inside my chest.

"You have a new freckle," I say, meeting his gaze. I bring my hand up and run a finger along his face.

"I miss you so much, Jess." He tips his forehead to mine and sighs. His warm breath sends a shiver through me. Levi's lips are so close. He's saying all the right words. Would it be so terrible to give him another chance?

My brain is telling me to step away from Levi and go back inside. Griffin is probably wondering where I am. At least I hope he is. It just gets so tiring. Trying to do the right thing, never knowing what the right thing is. Standing here with Levi, I feel like the Jessie I was when we first met, infatuated and distracted by everything he did. I can't hide how I feel when I'm around him. Maybe that's why I like him so much, because I don't have to pretend. It's like I can finally take the mask off.

Then again, that's how I feel with Griffin, but without the heartache. Levi knows a side of me no one else does. So does Griffin. The question is, which Jessie is the real Jessie?

It would be so easy to stay out here with Levi, dancing, kissing, talking, but he's not the one I came to the formal with.

"I have to go," I say, staring directly into Levi's blue eyes. "Thank you for saying all that."

"Don't go. Stay here with me."

"I can't." I sigh. "I need to do something."

Levi frowns as I twist out of his embrace.

"What?"

"Something I should have done a long time ago."

Without looking back, I make my way inside the boat.

The dance floor is full but it doesn't take long for me to spot Mel and Odelia with their dates. I head back to the table, determined to get Griffin to tell me what's wrong. But when I find him sitting alone, all the angry feelings I had dissolve. I take a deep breath and approach him.

"Do you . . ." I pause and clear my throat to get his attention. "Do you want to dance?"

To my surprise, Griffin pushes out his chair and stands. He holds my hand and leads me to the dance floor. I stand in front of him like a statue as a slow song begins.

"I don't know how to . . ." I stall, while pulling at my sleeves. "The thing is, I've never . . ."

Griffin's serious expression softens, and the corners of his lips turn up slightly. He takes my left hand and places it on his shoulder. He puts his right hand around my waist and holds my other hand in his. We look at one another and smile, silently agreeing to put an end to whatever it is we're fighting about.

He tries to twirl me a couple of times, but I end up bumping into other couples. We laugh, and as I'm about to make a joke, I stop. Griffin's looking at me like he did on the couch at New Year's. And in the hall when he was comforting me over Levi and Liv. He's got that same intense stare he had onstage at the Karaoke-a-thon when he sang the last line of the song to me. Except it's different, because this time, my knees feel like they might give out.

He guides my hands around his neck and places his on my waist, pulling me in closer. The magnitude of his gaze gives my entire body goosebumps. Griffin's hands rest intimately on my lower back, and I move my fingers around the nape of his neck. The distance between us diminishes. I don't know what's happening, but it feels like something more than just friends dancing.

When the song ends, he takes my hand and leads me back

to the edge of the dance floor. Levi cuts us off on our way to the table. *Levi!*

No words are exchanged as Griffin and Levi lock eyes. They stand chest to chest, undeterred by one another's presence.

My eyes meet Levi's as he steps to the side and reaches out to me.

"Not this time." Griffin places his body between me and Levi. "She came with me; she's leaving with me. You had your chance. Lots of them."

"Why don't we ask Jessie what she wants to do?"

They both turn their attention to me, and I freeze.

"I don't know . . . I don't want . . . I'm sorry." I shake my head before running off to the bathroom. The tears fly out this time before I make it. This entire evening has been an epic disaster— of my own making.

I spend the rest of the night hiding out in the bathroom, ignoring the girls' pleas to return to the formal. When the DJ announces the last song, I grab my things and head to the waiting bus. Griffin is already there. I debate turning around, but I can't keep running away. I walk up the aisle and sit next to him.

"I think we should talk," Griffin says.

"Okay. Why don't you start by telling me why you were so rude earlier?"

Griffin turns to face me. "You really don't know?"

"No, and don't call me dense again."

He gives me a weak smile. When I don't return it, he continues. "I shouldn't have said that. I'm sorry. It's just, I was really excited about tonight. Bought a new suit and everything. But within seconds, you were on the lookout for *him*. How do you think that made me feel?"

Oh my god. I *am* dense.

"I'm sorry. Levi's like this bad habit I can't seem to kick. And I've been kind of confused about my feelings for him lately."

Griffin shakes his head and leans backward. Almost immediately, he snaps his attention back to me. "Don't do that."

"Do what?"

"Don't talk to me about him. I'm not one of your girlfriends." He sighs, his mouth tight with emotion. "Ever since we were kids, Levi has been the one people gravitate to. When I saw how much you liked him, I stepped back, even though it was killing me inside. He's good at convincing people to give him another chance. I don't blame you. But he never deserved you in the first place." Griffin shifts in his seat, his eyes forward. "I don't want to wait on the sidelines in hopes that this might be the moment you finally realize . . ." His voice trails off. Quietly, he finishes. "I can't be your friend anymore."

"No. Wait." I run my hands down my face; my entire body is shaking. "Why didn't you say something sooner?"

"Jessie, I could have held out a sign that said I was hopelessly in love with you, and you would have brushed it off as a typo."

"Love?" My question comes out like a whisper.

Griffin stares at the floor, letting out a long breath. "Just forget it."

Desperate to find something to do or say to keep him from slipping away, I grab his arms. "I didn't want to lose you. I *don't* want to lose you. It's why I wouldn't let myself think about you in that way. Our friendship is the most important thing in the world to me. And now you're sitting there telling me you can't be my friend anymore."

"Is that really the one thing stopping you from being with me? Or is it that you're not ready to cut ties with Levi? You just said a minute ago that you're still confused about your feelings for him."

My hands release Griffin's arms. "You're right. I am confused about him. And about you. I need time."

"You need time, and I need space. So, while you're taking time, this," he motions between us, "is done. That means no more study sessions or one-on-one rehearsals. We don't eat lunch together or talk at night. No memes. Nothing." The silence between us is loud. Deafening. I can't think. I can't speak. I can barely move. "I'm not Levi," Griffin says, his voice low and brittle. "I know what I want. I have from day one. And I can't be just your friend anymore."

As the bus starts to fill up, I cover my face in an attempt to hide my tears. Griffin guides my head onto his shoulder and opens his hand out in front of me as one last act of friendship. I grab it in mine and keep it there the whole way back to school. I have to keep Griffin in my life, but I don't know what my heart wants.

TWENTY-NINE

It's been three weeks since the disastrous spring formal, and instead of facing the mess I created head-on, I've been avoiding making any decision at all. With opening night five days away, it's been kind of easy to let my personal life take a back seat.

That doesn't mean it's taken a back seat in my head.

It's June and we're in the final stretch of school. Once I'm done with the musical, it'll be exams, and after that, Palestine. I can't go anywhere without hearing people talk about their summer plans, excited for what's to come. Odelia landed a job as a camp counselor, working alongside Darren, and Mel will be at her family's cottage most of the summer.

I'm not sure if I want these next couple of weeks to fly by so I can put it all behind me, or slow to a crawl, in hopes that the "right thing to do" will pop into my muddled brain.

I'm in my room going over my lines when there's a knock at the door.

"Come in," I say, putting my script down. Dad walks in and sits across from me on my bed. "I thought you were at work."

"I came home early. Ramsey's coming over for Sunday dinner."

"Again? That's three times this week."

"I give it two months before he moves back," Dad says with

a knowing grin. He nods to the script by my feet. "Mommy says you're playing a flower in the school play."

I laugh. "Not a flower. A plant from outer space that eats humans and has a diabolical plan to take over the world."

He chuckles to himself. "It's this week, yes?"

"Yeah. We're doing a dress rehearsal in front of the school on Thursday and our first show is on Friday night. That's the one you're coming to."

Dad smiles but it doesn't quite reach his eyes. He looks away, and when he faces me again, his eyes are tinged with red. "Me and Mommy are so proud, Jessie. You didn't let this thing stop you."

My shoulders drop at my father's "pep talk." He still has a hard time saying the *A*-word.

"Dad, it's not a thing. It's autism. It's okay to say it. It's part of who I am. I've accepted it. Mom has mostly accepted it. I think it's time you do, too."

"You know," he says, clearing his throat, "human beings, we fear the unknown. At first, I worried how this . . . autism would make your life harder. The main reason we came to Canada was to give our children a life easier than the one we had."

"It's okay to want to protect us. But you also have to give us a little space to experience things on our own." I've been through so much since high school started. Even before. Living in a world surrounded by neurotypicals and trying to figure out where I belong has been hard. It was hard when I was four and it's still hard at fifteen.

"You're right." Dad nods. "It's not always easy letting go."

"Was it difficult deciding to come to Canada?" I ask.

Dad swallows as he runs his hand over my comforter. "Palestine was my first love, and you never forget your first love. To be honest, I didn't like Canada very much when we moved here.

It's cold. We didn't know anyone. I failed many times before I found my way." His eyes meet mine, and it hits me how much my father has sacrificed for us. "Eventually, I saw beauty in the freedom and endless opportunities. I learned to appreciate all the different seasons. It was like falling in love again, for the first time. But better."

"Still," I say, "it must have been hard walking away from the only life you'd ever known. The only *home* you'd ever known."

"Sure. It's never easy leaving behind something or someone that's important to you. But I believe with all my heart that coming to Canada was the right decision for us. All life experiences, good or bad, hard or easy, have led me to who I am today. *Where* I am today."

"I find it impossible to ever know if I'm making the right decision." Especially when I'm choosing between two people I care deeply for. "It just feels so final. Like locking a door and throwing away the key."

"Sometimes you have to take the leap."

"And what if you're not sure?" I ask. "Or what if you want the option of going back?"

"Life doesn't always work that way. I know you don't like change, but change is growth. Change is necessary. And in my humble opinion, you'll never be able to move forward if the door isn't fully closed."

He makes it sound so easy. Dad doesn't know the full story. He doesn't know doors have been opened and closed and opened and closed . . . but maybe never at the right time. Maybe never long enough for me to really let love in.

Dad squeezes my knee before getting up.

"Habibi, some decisions are harder to make and don't come with a yes or no answer, but there's always an answer. Sometimes there's more than one answer, and that's when you have to listen to this," he says, pointing to his heart. He starts to walk away, then pauses in my doorway and turns. "If someone asked me to choose which country I loved more, you know what I would say?"

I shrug, because I have no idea what his answer would be. Dad is proud to be a Canadian citizen. He's also proud to be Palestinian.

"I'd answer, 'Wherever my family is, because they're my heart.' What's that English saying? Home is where the heart is?"

"Yeah. You got it right," I say.

"I know I did." Dad winks before walking out my door.

—

Rehearsals are bizarre. It's like everyone's been let out of their cages after a day of being chained to their desks and we're all frolicking around in character.

Mrs. Elliott is on edge. Tomorrow afternoon is our dress rehearsal in front of the entire school, and Rosalind is currently at the orthodontist getting her braces off. I'd be freaking out too if the star of the show was absent for the last rehearsal—our first with the band. Not to mention that Griffin and Rosalind still haven't managed to get the blocking for "Suddenly, Seymour" right.

Griffin.

The only time we've spoken to each other the last few weeks is when we've been in character. I want to tell him I miss him and that I think we should give it a try. But then I psych myself out with excuses, like the fact that I'll be leaving for a month and how the timing is off. Then there's Levi. I'm still not one hundred percent sure I'm over him. We haven't communicated since I sent him a text after the formal saying I needed time to think—alone.

"Jessie," Mrs. Elliott calls. "We need you." She snaps her fingers from the stage. She's standing with Griffin, who avoids eye contact as I come up next to them.

"What is it?"

"We need you to stand in for Rosalind. Just for this one song. We have to finalize the blocking and the lighting. You're probably the only one here who can hit those notes, and I already know you and Griffin share a sizzling onstage chemistry."

"There's got to be someone else," I say, shaking my head.

"Who?" Mrs. Elliott's arms fly up in frustration. "Most of the actors have gone home for the day. Do I have to remind you how I broke my own rule by allowing you to participate in this musical?"

"No. You don't. I'll do it," I answer grudgingly.

Mrs. Elliott clasps her hands together like a giddy child.

"Give me five minutes and then we'll go over the blocking," she says before zooming past me and Griffin.

"Do you know the words?" he asks, his tone devoid of emotion.

"Yeah. Of course I do."

"Think you can pretend to be in love with me for three minutes in order to give a convincing performance?"

"Griffin."

He laughs to himself. "It doesn't really matter though, does it? You're just filling in for someone else."

"Can we talk?" I ask. "After rehearsal?"

"I really need to focus on the show right now."

"I understand." It's as if my heart has just been smashed in two. "If Mrs. Elliott asks where I am, could you tell her I'll be right back?"

"Sure," he says. He draws his mouth in a tight line as he sits on a prop bench.

I swallow to fight back tears and race down the stage steps, through the back doors of the cafeteria. Once the door closes, I turn and bang my forehead against it.

"Careful. You might put a dent in it." Levi approaches with his hands in both pockets. "Why aren't you in there rehearsing?" he asks as I peel myself off the door.

"I just needed a quiet place to think."

"Funny. You texted something similar to me after the formal."

He leans up against the lockers. His uniform is a mess, as usual, and even I can admit he needs a haircut. He also seems older. I guess we've both grown up. Levi smiles, and he's even more handsome than the day we met. The day I fell in love with him.

Or so I thought.

In some ways it feels like no time has passed, especially when he gazes at me with those blue eyes, but something is different now. I'm different.

"I guess I thought, with time and distance, I'd figure out what I want."

"Did it help?" he asks.

I clear my throat, then swallow. "When we were together, it bothered you that I was never able to say I loved you back, and it's not because I didn't love you. I think on some level I did. But now I can see love isn't just one thing. There's no equation. Or formula. Love is sneaky. Most times you never see it coming." Levi stands up straight and walks toward me. "What I'm trying to say is, I couldn't fully give you my heart because I'm in love with someone else."

A sad smile edges its way out of Levi's lips. "I wish I could go back and do it all differently."

"I think things work out the way they're supposed to. We were meant to meet and get wrapped up in each other's lives. We made the mistakes we did so we could learn from them." I pause, letting the words sink in. "I don't regret choosing you. You're the first boy I ever liked who liked me back. Maybe this is selfish of me or naive, but I still want you to be part of my life. And I want to be part of yours. As friends."

"You're not selfish or naive. And I'd like that." He nods. "For the record, I don't regret choosing you, either. You have definitely made my life more colorful." He lets out a soft laugh.

"Same," I say, allowing myself to smile in this really difficult moment. A moment I hadn't prepared for. One I never could have predicted ten months ago. Maybe even ten days ago.

"I've watched a few of your rehearsals," he says. "You're such a natural on stage."

"Thanks. It's a fun character to play."

"Nah." He shuffles his feet. "I mean when you're not in character. When you're goofing around in between scenes. When you're yourself. That's when you really glow."

Levi cups my face with his hand and I lean into it, closing my eyes to take in one last breath of his scent and touch before he releases me. He brings his lips to my forehead and plants a soft kiss on it. "Break a leg, Jess. I'll be there tomorrow, cheering you on."

His fingers graze my hand before he turns to walk down the hall. My heart is heavy. Seeing him just now feels kind of like it does when you drive by the house you used to live in. It looks the same on the outside, but it's not yours anymore.

"Where's Jessie?" I hear Mrs. Elliott call from behind the doors. I exhale and wipe my eyes before returning to the stage.

We spend the next half hour going over blocking. Most of the cast has left for the afternoon and it's just me, Griffin, and the three female backup singers along with the crew and band.

"Okay, the clock is ticking. You two ready?" she asks, her eyes shifting between mine and Griffin's.

We nod.

Mrs. Elliott heads down the stage steps and takes a seat up front. I sit on the bench and wait for the music to begin. Here I am, about to sing a love song to a boy I love who once loved me. How do I get myself into these situations?

"Put yourself in Audrey's shoes," Mrs. Elliott says from her seat. "Try to imagine what it is she's feeling. How it must be for her when she suddenly realizes the person she loves has been standing in front of her all along. It's in there, Jessie. You just need to channel it."

"Got it," I reply. *All too well.*

The music for "Suddenly, Seymour" begins and I take a deep breath. The spotlight shines on me and I try to steady my racing heart. This is only a rehearsal. I'm standing in for someone else. It doesn't matter if I hit the notes. I just need to get the blocking right.

Griffin's singing pulls me out of my thoughts and into the scene. I love his voice. I love how he looks at me. I've missed it. I've missed him. He reaches out his hands and I accept, standing so close our noses touch.

It's my cue, and despite this being a rehearsal I can't help but give it my all. As I sing the heartbreaking and sweet lyrics, the last year with Griffin flashes through my mind. Hanging out in the library. Texting each other at all hours. New Year's Eve. Rehearsing during lunch. Goofing off in the hall during Art. The moment we met. Tears stream down my face as I sing the last line, struggling to keep it together.

Griffin holds my hands in his, his grip tightening. He has to feel it too. Can he forgive me for taking so long to realize he was there, waiting for me to open my eyes? Does he see a future with me despite everything that's happened?

The last chord plays. This is the part where Seymour and Audrey are supposed to kiss for the first time. I lift my eyes to meet Griffin's, willing him to kiss me, to show me he still cares. Instead, he shakes his head slightly before releasing my hands. Griffin walks off stage, leaving me behind.

"Brava! Brava, Jessie!" Mrs. Elliott stands, clapping as if her life depended on it. "You know," she says, nodding, "Griffin was right. You would have made an excellent Audrey."

My throat constricts. The bright lights are blinding. My breaths are short and growing faster by the second. I run backstage and crumple into a ball on the floor. It's over. I messed it all up. My lifelong insecurities, compounded by my autism diagnosis, led to these self-destructive behaviors. I was so hyper-fixated on all the wrong things that I couldn't see the one right thing standing in front of me. The one constant. Griffin.

So much of this last year was spent trying to change my outside appearance and learning to "play along" with others, all while trying to hide who I really was. I didn't realize the biggest change was happening inside me, and there was nothing I could do to stop it.

Goal #18: Let go of the girl I used to be. Learn to embrace whatever the hell this is. The ups and the downs. The mistakes. The in-between. And the future. Because I deserve it.

I rise from the backstage floor and wipe away my remaining tears.

The show must go on.

And so must I.

THIRTY

It's all come down to this. Hours of rehearsals. Dusty knees. Sore throats. Awkward interactions with Griffin. Trying to be a present friend and good daughter. Learning that perfection, in everything, is not only impossible but impossibly overrated.

"I need everyone to gather." Mrs. Elliott's voice is calm, cool, and even as she waves the cast and crew to the stage. In a few minutes, the entire school will come to the cafeteria to watch the dress rehearsal for *Little Shop of Horrors.* "Each and every one of you is essential to this production. Whether it's remembering your lines or when to flick a switch, you all play an important role. So let's put on the show of a lifetime! Everyone take your mark."

We all clap, and some of us holler. Hollering was never my thing.

"You ready?" Mel asks as she adjusts my mic pack.

"I'm ready to get it over with," I say.

Mel grabs my shoulders and shakes me. "Jessie, look how far you've come. You're the only ninth-grader who gets to perform on stage today. That's pretty effing awesome. Celebrate it."

"I'll be sure to give myself a nice check mark in my journal tonight."

"Well, that's better than nothing." She pulls me in for a bear hug. "Break a leg."

Mel takes off to the wings and I head backstage. I have to wear a suffocating unitard under my Audrey II costume. Since I don't have to put the plant part of the costume on until halfway through the musical, I had Mom buy me matching boxer shorts to cover up. I feel less exposed now, but it still looks like I'm wearing a green-tinted sausage casing. Anyway, it doesn't really matter since I'll either be out of sight or disguised as an evil plant.

It was comforting at first to know I could hide from everyone, but after singing with Griffin on stage yesterday and being able to look into his eyes, I kind of wish I didn't have to spend half the musical tucked away.

The murmur of voices grows louder as the cafeteria fills up. I settle into my chair backstage. It'll be a while before I'm needed.

The noise from the crowd simmers. Mrs. Elliott walks to the center of the stage and pulls the curtains apart. She thanks everyone for coming and goes into a long spiel about the history of the musical, making sure to tell everyone how hard we've all worked.

The audience applauds as Mrs. Elliott returns behind the curtains. The lights go off and I allow myself a second to soak in the fact that I'm here. I have a lead role in the school musical. I defied the odds *and* the rules to get here.

All is silent for a brief moment before "Prologue (Little Shop of Horrors)" begins. My skin fills with goosebumps as the drumroll starts. I glance over at Griffin and offer him a smile but he looks away. I wish he'd stop being so mad at me, but I don't blame him. I waited too long.

The opening act goes off without a hitch. The crowd's applause grows louder with the ending of each number. Everything is going perfectly. Onstage. I just hope I don't screw it all up.

The time has come for me to bring Audrey II to life. Mel helps me get into my costume and I take many deep breaths to prepare for my big number alongside Griffin.

After I deliver my first line, the audience roars with laughter. The encouragement helps me fully transform into Audrey II and I give the biggest, most obnoxious rendition of "Feed Me" I can. The crowd eats it up. Griffin and I make an awesome team. We always have.

The rest of the show goes off flawlessly. In the scene before the finale, Audrey II eats Seymour, which means Griffin has to enter the plant's final form, a gigantic, hollow prop I'm also hiding inside of. It's tight quarters and more than a little awkward as he maneuvers past me and slips backstage.

I've accomplished so much just to get to this point, but my heart literally aches being this close to Griffin and not being able to share in the excitement of it all. I wouldn't even be here if it weren't for his insistence and belief in me.

And that is bigger and greater than any role in the school play. Griffin has changed my life, and he might be mad and he might never want to speak to me again, but I refuse to let him slip away like all the others. This is a friendship worth fighting for.

We have five shows to do after today's dress rehearsal and I'm not getting back on stage until Griffin knows exactly how I feel. It has to be big and it has to be now.

Curtain call. A million nerves pulse through my body as I wage a silent battle within, deciding whether or not to go through with my plan, which at this point is nothing more than an idea. An impulsive one at that.

Still inside the gigantic prop, I feel the spotlight shine on Audrey II. Griffin and Rosalind open its mouth and I step out, standing on the taped X marking center stage.

I take my bow, and when I look up, Levi is on his feet giving me an enthusiastic (and slightly embarrassing) standing ovation. Odelia follows, then Annie. Soon the entire student body has risen, cheering us on and celebrating our first show.

I stand in between Griffin and Rosalind, holding both their hands as we take our final bow together as a cast. As everyone else salutes the crew and Mrs. Elliott, I turn to Griffin, hoping one more look might convince him to give me another chance and save me from possible public humiliation. Instead, he slips his hand from mine and takes a step back.

All of this, everything I've done, my goals, it means nothing if I don't have Griffin in my life.

It's now or never.

Before I lose my nerve, I grab the microphone out of Mrs. Elliott's delicate hands.

"I'm sorry, Mrs. Elliott. There's something I have to do," I say over the clapping, which has begun to die down.

Griffin and the rest of the cast step off to the wings. I wait for the band to finish their number and for the audience to take their seats. "Hi," I say, in a voice that comes out much quieter than I was expecting. When the chatter doesn't cease, I clear my throat to get everyone's attention.

"I have something I want to say, and I'm afraid if I don't say it now, I might never find the courage again." I swallow hard and pause. It's mostly silent now aside from a few whispers, but I've gotten used to those. "Do you ever stop to ask yourself, 'How did I get here?' I've asked myself that a lot this year. In fact, I'm asking myself that right now as I stand in front of the entire school in a green unitard." The audience laughs, breaking the tension in the room.

"Performing on this stage was one of the goals I made for myself this year. When I set that goal back in September, it felt like the biggest, scariest thing I could think of. But it wasn't scary. It was fun. Exhilarating even. I'm not afraid to get on stage and pretend to be someone else. And that's probably because I do it every day." I close my eyes and will myself to keep going. "My stage is the hallway when you see me smile at you, or the classroom when I try to ignore all the background noises so I can write a test with everyone else." I suck in my lips before letting out another shaky breath. "Looking back, I should have added another goal to my list. But I guess it's not too late. *Goal #19: Take off the mask I wear every day and learn to accept myself.* I don't want to be afraid of people finding out my 'secret' and weaponizing it against me. And for that to happen, I need to stop being ashamed of what this is and who I am."

I bring a hand to my heart and nod. "This is me: Jessie Kassis. No mask. No fake personas. Just an autistic girl who, like you, is trying to figure out who she is." Hope sparks in my chest, giving me the courage to keep going. "I've made a lot of mistakes this year. But that's all part of growing up, right? It's hard and messy and scary. It's also amazing and fun and incredible."

I keep my stance forward, too afraid to look to my right where Griffin stands. "By far, the scariest thing I've had to face this year is losing someone who means everything to me. I will forever be sorry for the actions, or lack of actions, that led to hurting this person. My best friend." Tears start to escape and I squeeze my eyes shut, letting a few fall before wiping them away. "My whole life, friends have come and gone. Most of the time they go without me knowing why, but Griffin, you promised you'd never ghost me. And a promise is a promise."

I turn to look at Griffin in the wings, hoping my words are enough, but he's no longer there.

"I swear I won't do this tomorrow night," I whisper into the mic before passing it back to Mrs. Elliott and running offstage. I run past the atrium, through the back doors, and keep running until I'm at the pond.

I wanted closure. I wanted a happy ending. I guess you can't always have both at the same time.

But hope is what got me here. And it'll be what keeps me going.

I sit on the warm grass, looking over the glistening water in front of me. Ninth grade is over. It's done. And what a ride it's been.

I found my people: Mel and Odelia. They took me under their wings and accepted me for who I was and who I turned out to be.

And I did get that perfect first kiss with Levi.

Then there's Griffin. A happy accident that fell into my lap. Even if he hates me now, at least I got to experience for a while what it was like to have a best friend.

"What does it feel like knowing you not only dominated the school play but won over the heart of every single person in that building with your speech?"

I look up to find Griffin, still in his Seymour costume.

"I only really cared about winning over the heart of one person, and he wasn't there to accept my apology," I say as I stand to meet him.

"I heard it."

"But you weren't there."

Griffin moves a step closer and takes my hands in his. "Jessie, I've always been there."

"I thought you hated me."

He shakes his head. "No. I could never hate you. I just needed time to process things, and I needed to do it alone."

"Are you done processing?" I ask, studying Griffin's hands holding mine.

"Yeah. Turns out I'm pretty damn miserable without you." He smiles, and it makes my entire body flutter. It's like I'm onstage again, but better. "I guess it didn't make sense to me."

"What didn't?"

"How I could have such strong feelings for you, and you were still so unsure. Then it hit me. You didn't have all the facts. And Jessie K. needs facts. You've only ever seen me as your friend Griffin."

"*Best* friend," I correct him.

"Best friend," he repeats. "I guess I expected you to be on the same page as me when I told you how I felt. I hit you with my feelings like a ton of bricks and buried you in them. I should have understood you needed time to make an informed decision. So . . . I'll wait until you're ready."

"I'm ready," I blurt. "That whole speech in there, yeah, part of it was for me, but it was also for you. I don't want to pretend anymore. Pretend I don't like how it feels when you look at me. Pretend my body doesn't react every time you touch me. Pretend I'm not completely, one hundred percent head over heels in love with you."

Griffin grins, a smile that stretches across his entire face. "Look at your phone."

I reach down and grab my phone from inside my Docs. There's a gif of Spike from *Buffy the Vampire Slayer* telling Buffy he loves her.

"Check the time stamp," he says. "I sent it during your speech. I was waiting for you backstage but you ran off instead."

"Hashtag Team Spike," I say, breathing out a sigh of relief.

"You were wrong about love being intangible." He swallows and takes a step forward, running a hand down my cheek. "'Cause I'm touching you now, and it feels like love."

My entire body lights up at his words. "That Griffin," I say, fighting back a smile. "He not only has a great head of hair, he's also highly intelligent."

He blushes and looks down before his eyes meet mine again. "You're good."

"I have a knack for recalling certain events. There's one more thing I need to do," I say, typing quickly into my phone. A few seconds after I hit send, Griffin pulls his phone out of his back pocket and laughs. "Read it out loud."

"Goal #20: Kiss Griffin Duffy!"

We tuck our phones away, biting back smiles. My heart beats out of my chest like a drum as I wipe my sweaty palms on my green boxers. Griffin takes my shaky hands in his. He's steady as a rock.

The earth spins around us, but we stand still. Griffin smiles as he tilts my chin up. "A promise is a promise." We stare at one another. Then, like two magnets, our lips meet, and everything else disappears. I wrap my arms around his neck as I lean into him. We kiss under the hot sun, crossing the bridge from friends to something more.

When we pull apart, Griffin has a gleam in his eye I've never seen before.

"Check," I say, a little too enthusiastically.

"You're welcome," Griffin says, matching my tone.

I adjust his bow tie. "In the history of *Little Shop of Horrors*, do you think any of the actors who played Seymour and Audrey II fell in love?"

"I think," Griffin says, lacing his fingers with mine as we head back to the building, "that is highly improbable. Leave it to us to break the mold."

"Stick with me and you'll get used to living outside the lines," I say. "It's actually kind of fun."

"I wouldn't have it any other way."

Griffin kisses me once more before we walk through the doors of the school, hand in hand.

Sometimes it feels like we're in this alone, and the only way to survive is to be someone we're not, someone we think other people will like.

But all that does is make us prisoners of our own hate.

And no one should hate who they are.

I've spent so much of my life in my head, practising, daydreaming, and rehearsing. It felt good stepping outside my comfort zone this year. It forced me to take off my mask. And I didn't do it for anyone else. I did it for myself.

For so long, I didn't know who the real Jessie was. I expected her to fit inside a box and stay there. I didn't realize it was okay to grow, change, and evolve.

The real crime in all of this would have been keeping the mask on, and cheating people out of getting to know the person behind it.

And that's not just an autism thing. It's a human thing.

People are weird and complicated and not always easy to understand, especially if you're me. But when you really stop to think about it, our weaknesses and quirks, the things we spend so much time trying to hide from others, these are the things that make us beautiful.

Even me.

I know there will be times where I'll have to readjust my mask to get through certain moments, but then there will be other moments, like right now, when being myself is enough.

THE END

JESSIE'S PLAYLIST

1. About a Girl (Live)—Nirvana
2. Fifteen (Taylor's Version)—Taylor Swift
3. Sittin' Up In My Room—Brandy
4. Today—The Smashing Pumpkins
5. Jessie's Girl—Rick Springfield
6. Linger—The Cranberries
7. Pale September—Fiona Apple
8. Found Out About You—Gin Blossoms
9. All I Want—Toad the Wet Sprocket
10. Purple Rain—Prince & The Revolution
11. Without Me—Halsey
12. (Everything I Do) I Do It For You—Bryan Adams
13. Runaround Sue—Dion
14. High and Dry—Radiohead
15. Feed Me (Git It)—Levi Stubbs, Rick Moranis, Michelle Weeks, Tichina Arnold & Tisha Campbell
16. Fade Into You—Mazzy Star
17. A Groovy Kind of Love—Phil Collins
18. You All Over Me (Taylor's Version)—Taylor Swift
19. Suddenly, Seymour—Rick Moranis, Ellen Greene, Michelle Weeks, Tichina Arnold & Tisha Campbell
20. The Whole of the Moon—The Waterboys
21. Dreams—The Cranberries

ACKNOWLEDGMENTS

Writing may be a solitary act, but it takes many, many people to publish a novel.

To my editor, Lynne Missen, and the entire team at Tundra/Penguin Random House Canada—I will be forever grateful that you helped bring my beloved Jessie Kassis to life. I love what we've managed to do together! Thanks also to Catherine Marjoribanks, Bharti Bedi, Evan Munday, and Mindy Fichter.

Thank-you to Peijin Yang, the artist responsible for the beautiful cover! I absolutely love it!

To my literary agent, Valerie Noble—you took a chance on both me and my stories. You're both my biggest cheerleader and the one to calm my stormy waters. You never let me apologize for going after what I want, and I can't wait to publish more books with you. Thanks also to Stacey Donaghy and Donaghy Literary Group for having my back.

Peter Knapp—your thoughtful words and feedback helped resurrect a story I was seconds away from shelving. Your kindness and generosity literally changed my life.

Maren Soderbeck, my writing twin flame. There would be no *Something More* without you. You taught me so much, helped me through countless revisions, and read every single version of this story.

To my beta readers and writing besties, whose feedback and support helped strengthen my craft and my story: Julia Foster (I am in awe of your talent), Liz Kessick (you have an amazing editorial eye), Elise Kuder (your positivity is contagious!), Sky Regina (somewhere, Jessie and Lo are hanging out and talking boys and music).

Sher Lee, Lindsay Maple, Joanne Machin, Esme Symes-Smith, my SP writing group—you keep me sane! And I love you all.

Thank-you to the following fabulous authors who took time from their very busy schedules to read and provide blurbs for *Something More*. I am so honored and grateful. Olivia Abtahi, Aaron H. Aceves, Farah Heron, Chloe Liese, and Lynn Painter.

To Sherri Rossi-Chou, my very best friend of twenty-nine years and counting. Thank you for always supporting me and seeing me through my many passions and obsessions.

To the original Khalilieh five and the best, maybe most reluctant muses ever. To my parents, Nicola and Firouz, who may not have always understood their "weird" daughter but loved me unconditionally—thank you for giving me your blessing to use Ramzi's name and helping me keep his memory alive.

To my brother, Mahfuz, for providing so much material. Dude, you should write your own book. I'll ghostwrite.

To my sister, Nancy—I apologize for annoying and embarrassing you growing up (and probably last week), but the truth is, I just wanted to spend time with you.

To my nieces, Kiara and Mia—I'm jealous that you're both so much cooler than me and would never start high school with a unibrow. To my nephews, Nicolas and Joey, who redefined (for me) what it means to be an Arab male teen today. You both inspired me to write my first Arab male love interest. (Stay tuned!) I love you, dummies.

My thanks to my extended family, Ruba Khalilieh, Frank Mueller, Reefa Khalilieh, Mahfuz (Meezo) Khalilieh. And to my Amo Sami and Auntie Nany, who I wish were here to read this story.

Thanks to my in-laws, Michael and Susan Stuparyk, who I think were more excited about this book deal than I was.

To my non-blood-related muses—Jane M. Brennan, Glenn Calderon, Liam Devlin, Dori Elliott, Melanie Hollands, Marisa Chong-Fabroa, Eric Fabroa, and Michael "Pez" Pesnyak—thank you for not (completely) freaking out when I told you, out of nowhere, I'd written characters inspired by you.

And to the most supportive (and patient) husband in the world, Rob Stuparyk, and my two dreams come true, Elsie and Emma—I love us (and our Samoyeds).

I'd also like to thank, in no particular order, Diet Coke and Taylor Swift, for getting me through revisions and inspiring me daily.

While writing *Something More*, I had my own coming-of-age experience. Or, more correctly, experiences.

I'm Palestinian and autistic, and while I cannot speak for all Palestinians or all autistic females, I *can* speak for myself and what these identities have come to mean to me.

To my fellow Palestinians, I'm sorry it took me so long to get here. There were times I tried to hide where I came from. My parents are proud Palestinians but, sadly, as a first-generation child growing up in the nineties, I was heavily influenced by North American media, which spun a tired narrative making us out to be the "bad guys." As much as I wanted to tell people they had the wrong idea about us, I was always too afraid to speak up. It wasn't until the last few years, through writing, that I took real pride in my roots. Jessie Kassis is my first—not last—Palestinian main character. There are more. There *will* be more. It's not our job to change people's perceptions of who we are, but I do feel a responsibility for creating realistic and positive representation. The kind I never had. The kind I want for my daughters and for generations to follow. I'm never going to be the Palestinian who knows all the facts and is able to speak up and debate off the cuff (Hi, Reefa)—what I can do is create stories that celebrate our culture, our families, our big personalities, and our passion.

Allistic (non-autistic) readers may find, to their surprise, how much they relate to Jessie. Her relatability, however, may lead some to downplay her autism. Although many of us may appear "just like everyone else" on the outside, it often means we're just very good at masking. I was well into adulthood before I learned how to "properly" respond to social norms, such as answering the everyday question of, "How are you?" My husband likes to tease me for the "mental gymnastics" my mind will go through to reason something away. I spent much of my life being told that I have interpreted certain situations or people incorrectly (often in less nice terms) and because of that it's not as easy as 1+1=2 for me. Unless you are autistic yourself, you could not begin to fully understand what it is like for us. You may try and you may believe that you get it, or get us, but there is so much more to how our brains work than meets the eye. More than I can properly convey in a book. Our brains are beautiful, complicated, hilarious, and frustrating. We often come off as type A's, know-it-alls, rude, and also, sweet, innocent, pushy, quiet—sometimes all of the above in one single interaction. But it's not about trying to understand us, it's about accepting us for who we are.

One last thing to anyone still reading: Don't shrink who you are to make others feel comfortable. You deserve to take up all the space you need.